TOOTH AND CLAW

THE CHRONICLES OF BREED: BOOK TWO

K.T. DAVIES

SCIMITAR MEDIA

Text copyright © 2018 K.T. Davies

Published by Scimitar Media

www.scimitar-media.co.uk

ISBN-13: 978-1999747411

Cover design by Scimitar Media

Original cover art by Michael Gauss

To Raven and Gabe,

the best rum crew a cove could wish for

TOOTH AND CLAW

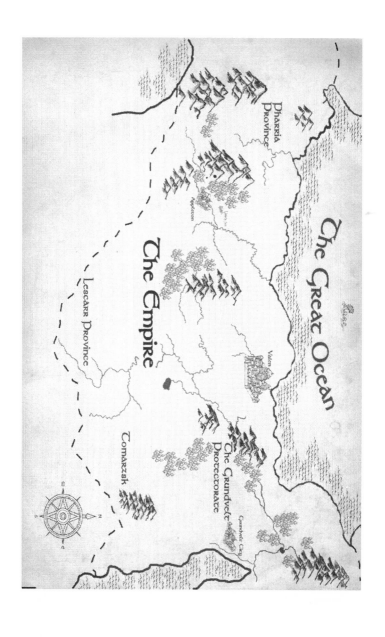

Chapter One

Dragged from the blood-black deeps, the song of the sea erupted joyfully on the waves and kissed the hem of the sky with sparkling, silvered lips…

And then everything turned to shit.

The sky darkened to a mournful shade of grim and the song of the sea drowned in the tears of a mud-skied morning. The joyful pipes were no longer raised in praise of the day but in gurgling mockery of this stranger on the waves, as I puked my guts down the curvaceous flank of the *Widow of Ching*.

To be clear, I was not mistreating some poor dame with my vomitus effusions. The *Widow* in question was a ship. More precisely, she was an independent, Shen trading vessel which, as all know is a polite way of saying 'pirate'. Wide-bellied and under full sail the *Widow* bullied her way through the waves. Captain Shih had proudly told me that her vessel's reputation was so fearsome that the very sight of her four masts on the horizon was enough to drive the most stout-hearted crew to the longboats before a shot was fired. I could well believe it and had chosen the ship because she was well accoutered for sharp work. Such insurance was needed as I had powerful enemies and a knack for catching trouble. It, therefore, came as a great surprise and crushing disappointment both to the redoubtable Captain Shih and me when we discovered that the *Widow* was no match *whatsoever* for a fighting shoal of brachuri and their kraken.

But I'm getting ahead of myself.

Thirteen days ago I was an ordinary Guild Blade, albeit one possessed of the lightest of fingers, and above average skill with the sharp and pointies. I was a bene cove, a member of the Midnight Court in good standing, but no one special and happy about it.

Then I met the demon Shallunsard, and that ill-starred encounter turned my world into a steaming vat of arsepickle. For those of a delicate constitution, I'll not recapitulate the grim details here. Suffice it to say, I had been roughly swived by Fate and ill-used by its scab-hearted minions. There was some minor compensation for my trouble. I had in my possession a powerful artifact— namely, the hammer of the Hammer of the North. The long dead hero had lain undisturbed in a frozen pocket of existence which had been hived off from the world for over 700 hundred years until I found him and robbed him. I felt no guilt over this intrusion. He didn't need the hammer, and I did. After this little adventure, the balance of my life's account had left me with a deficit of friends and a surplus of enemies. It was time to make myself scarce.

And so, leaving chaos in my wake, I hied to the coast where a fistful of gold bought the discretion of Captain Shih and passage to Shen on her vessel. We set sail that very night, laden with contraband, my fugitive self, and with an ill-wind roaring up a storm behind us.

Driven by the gale, the *Widow* knifed through the oily black as sweet as a blade through a kidney. I sat in the stern and supped one of the many bottles of Grundvelt Blast Whiskey I had procured for the journey. With every pull of the five hundred oars, the Empire and all my many troubles receded like a bad dream on waking.

I quaffed the whiskey and drank in the taste of the land-born breeze that waved us a brusk farewell. It was tainted with the faint aroma of smoke and fire— not uncommon, but there was also blood in the breeze, underlying the smell of destruction. I didn't know for sure, but I guessed that the demon I'd accidentally loosed upon the world was making good his promise to destroy everything, starting with the Empire. I decided that in the circumstances the best thing I could do was get drunk and forget about demons, the destruction of my country, and the troubling details about whose fault it was.

We had been at sea four days by which time I was foxed to the gills on Grundvelt's most exceptional brew. I'm half thoasa, warspawn, bred for battle. My body did not take well to intoxication and decided against my wishes to purge itself most violently of the expensive poison I had diligently guzzled. Much like a passenger in my own body, I observed my booze-sodden meat sack lurch to the ship's rail. What amusement I might have derived from this drink induced tomfoolery was cut short when my guts began pumping like hell's bellows.

I lost track of how long I spent anchored to the ship's rail like a dying limpet. All I knew was that I had never been this sick in my life. I lamented my plight between bouts of puking. My kind had been bred to fight on the sorcery-blighted battlefields of the Schism War. It had therefore taken a crate of the strongest drink in the Empire to drown what sense I possessed, and if I hadn't been throwing up and praying for death, I would have been proud of that achievement. As it was, I couldn't even remember my name, let alone celebrate much of anything aside of breathing.

On the upside, I had managed to get so outrageously cup-shot that I completely forgot my troubles. Alas, trouble rarely forgets me. I yawned another gutful of bile into the abyss and much to my drink-fuddled surprise, saw the moon shining up at me through the murky depths.

"That isn't right." I looked up. The suns were shining. "Why is there a big shiny *thing* in the sea?" I asked as I tried to focus on the silver disc. The crew ignored me, an act that my booze-stewed brain considered a mortal slight. "Bastards." I unhooked the Hammer's hammer from my belt. I was going to teach these curs a lesson. How dare they run around shouting, and hauling on ropes when I, the heroic savior of something I couldn't remember, was speaking to them? "Captain." I waved the hammer to get her attention. "Captain Shih. Your crew are ignoramuses. The fucking moon has fallen into the sea, and nobody cares. You should have them flogged." I swung the hammer emphatically in the direction of the silvery disc and almost fell overboard.

"Idiot," Shih hissed before bellowing a string of orders at her crew. I had a slender grasp of Shenish but couldn't make out what she was saying due to my head being full of drunk. I could tell she was angry because she'd drawn a pair of handcannons from her sash and was jabbing them at rigging, crew, and deck guns like the two-fisted conductor of an unconventional orchestra. The intoxicating brew that I'd chosen to pickle my brain with also fueled my irrational ire. I decided that, like her crew, Shih had slighted me and that I was going to teach them all a lesson in manners.

I tried to summon a spell to mind but stumbled against the rail. The incantation fluttered from my mind like a butterfly. A tiny part of my brain which wasn't entirely pickled noted that it was the ship and not me which was lurching drunkenly. I glanced over the listing rail and saw that the silver disc was still floating just beneath the skin of the sea and then it and the world began to tilt. Given that I was as soused as it was possible to be, this shift in axis didn't alarm me as much as it probably should have. The suns' light peeked through the clouds and sparked off the bright disc which blinked against the glare.

It was then that I realized my error. It wasn't the moon. It was the biggest eye I'd ever seen. Thus enlightened, I turned to the nearest sea dog to share my insight. "You're right, Captain. I am an idiot. It's not the moon, it's a big fucking eye. Can you believe it?"

Angry shouts and bellowed curses erupted all around me. The sea roared, the ship growled and bucked in the foaming brine. The eye blinked again and the sea thinned across a rocky, mottled green island that was rising through the waves. The mighty *Widow* rolled over like a whipped cur. In a breath, I went from standing by the rail to hanging from it. Shouts turned to screams. Sails cracked, ropes snapped, and the masts groaned like the restless dead.

Splintered oars speared past my head as the ship settled awkwardly on the unnatural reef. By some magic I did not know, we had been beached. The *Widow of Ching*, the scourge of the Great Ocean, had been bested by a more dreaded leviathan than herself.

Beyond the prow a dozen, massive tentacles broke the surface and thrashed the brine into suds. As the lumpen head of the kraken rose, I saw that the baleful oculus was one of a dozen arrayed about its head. At the stern of the ship, the sea was churned to a frenzy as a horde of brachuri burst from the water and swarmed over the hull. They charged across the planks, plucked hapless oarsmen from portholes like whelks from their shells.

It was fair revenge. In the Empire brachuri fry were eaten as a delicacy — a Gods' Day treat for those wealthy enough to afford them. The story of how this grisly occurrence came to pass was that some hundred years ago, Emperor Drusus the XI, also known as Drusus the Insatiable, developed a taste for brachuri. To avoid having to point out that eating fellow sentients was a touch on the sinful side, and thereby sign his death warrant, the Eklesiasti of the day declared that brachuri were mindless animals and not, in fact, an aquatic race of sentient beings. Something that I imagine came as quite a shock to the brachuri traders who were living and working in the Empire at the time.

I'd never eaten brachuri myself. I couldn't afford it even if I'd wanted to, which I didn't. Alive or dead, they smelled like fish which fed exclusively on a diet of well-rotted rat although I've been assured that they taste like chicken. As I pondered the irony of being eaten by a vittle I had always eschewed, another human oarsman was dragged from a porthole some mere feet away from where I was dangling. He screamed and squirmed before the brachuri snipped him to ribbons with its massive claws.

Those crew members who'd survived the initial onslaught and still had their wits about them began to rally. With firelances, blades, and belaying pins the pirates mounted a spirited, if ultimately futile defense. While the bulk of her crew were fighting the brachuri, Shih and a fistful of her most favored officers had cut loose a lifeboat and were quietly rowing away from the carnage. I had to admire her quick wits even if the salty cow hadn't taken me with her.

Trapped amid the screaming and the killing, I began to sober up. I decided that waiting to be eaten was not in my best interests and that I should perhaps swim after the good captain and demand passage to Shen for which I had paid her handsomely. Unfortunately, my wits returned faster than my reflexes, and I fell the second I tried to climb over the rail onto the uppermost bow. By luck rather than judgment I landed flat on the spongy back of the kraken. A wave of bloodstained brine slapped me in the face, finishing the job of sobering me up.

Fighting raged all around. Fire broke out on board the stricken vessel as pirates fought desperately against the cold savagery of the brachuri. A shell festooned warrior charged towards me, in as much as something without legs can charge. It undulated on the coils of its body, foreclaws clacking, all six eye-stalks fully extended as focused and rigid as cocks in a brothel. I leaped to my feet and pointed the hammer at it, felt power gather and run through me as I discharged a blast of sorcerous fire from the artifact. The kraken stirred and shuddered beneath me as the smoldering remains splattered the deck of the *Widow*.

To my right, a section of what looked like a rocky outcrop flipped open like a trapdoor and propelled by its tail, a small brachuri sprang out. I was supremely confident that nothing, including the kraken itself, was a match for me and the relic I wielded and so took a leisurely aim at the ambusher. The Kraken raised its head, swiveled a cluster of eyes in my direction, the *Widow* slid along its massive back, towards the tail. I flung out my arms, tried to halt my slide towards the arse end of the beast and whatever horrors lurked beneath the waves. The brachuri had no such misgivings and lunged towards me, claws snapping. By some fluke it caught hold of the hammer shaft. I remained unconcerned. It might have been strong enough to wrench the weapon from my grasp, but I was going to melt its face off before it got the chance. That was the plan. With a loud snap, it cut through the shaft.

Just like that.

Without fuss or flourish, the hammer of the Hammer of the North, holy relic and one of the most powerful weapons of the age, became a stick. Horrified, I watched the severed head of the hammer roll across the kraken's knobbly back and tumble into the ocean with an unceremonious *plop*. The brachuri seemed almost as surprised as I was and gazed admiringly at its claw until it remembered me and lunged at my head, the offending appendage click-clacking viciously. Never one to dwell on misfortune I smashed the fucker between the eyestalks with the shaft of the hammer. Stunned, it blasted snotty salt water from its neck gills and collapsed unconscious into a heap of coils. I kicked it in what might have been its cods, but my victory was short lived as more of the brachuri turned their snippy snappy attention to me. Despite my devastating loss, I wasn't going to go down without a fight and lay about me with sorcery, the Stick of the North, and my trusty blade. Magic came easily to me these days, and I gave a respectable account of myself, but Shih's crew were no match for the swarm. After a brutal fight, I stood alone. The brachuri closed in. The *Widow* was burning, and the kraken was slowly submerging.

I was sure I must have been in worse situations, I just couldn't think of when or where. Lightheaded from casting spells, and with nothing to hand except for a broken sword and a legendary *stick*, the jeering brachuri backed me towards the flames that were greedily devouring the *Widow*. The heat was blistering, the oily smoke choking and blinding.

It wasn't dying that I minded so much, it was how that mattered, so I took a moment to consider whether being dismembered was a better way to get snuffed than burning to death. From what I'd seen of the way the crabby folk went about their bloody-clawed work, it was messier but quicker than frying. Aside from the onerous task of choosing the least worst death, the thing that vexed me most was that, in the last couple of days while getting soused aboard the *Widow*, I'd begun to hope for something more than a rough life and a violent end. I should have known better— shouldn't have taunted Fate with my desire not to be nose-to-nose with death for once in my life, but then as Mother always said, *hope was for fools*.

The brachuri didn't have the wherewithal to shout. Their pudendal mouth parts rendered growls and battle cries flatulently comical. Not that any of the unlucky survivors crawling through the brine were laughing as they were dispatched without discernible mercy. Body parts and cargo bobbed amid the reef-like growths on the behemoth's back and cheerful pink suds sloshed against my legs, quite at odds with the stinking viscera that floated amongst them. I braced myself, hammer shaft in one hand, broken sword in the other, ready for the final charge. The raiders waved their bloody pincers but seemed content to watch me slowly choke to death on smoke rather than finish me off themselves. I wondered if smoked thoasa was a delicacy among their kind.

As I pondered my imminent demise, the baying mob parted and an old brachuri half hopped, half slithered forwards. This fellow had either been in some titanic scrapes or was accident prone. One of its claws was missing leaving it with three large, barnacle-encrusted pincers. Its weathered hide was as grey as death and crisscrossed by a web of fading scars and its tail had been severed two feet from its body, which explained its halting gait. The thick plates of its headshell swept over its shoulders. A dozen chain links pierced the pie crust edge of the shell, from which dangled bent mirror frames, lockets, rusted keys, and other random objects. Patinated by sea and salt, the mostly valueless gewgaws shone like bright emeralds and burnished gold.

Grey Hide leaned on a staff made from an old harpoon. The verdigris blade was festooned with ribbons of seaweed, slices of carved shell, and small wire cages looped around the rust-pocked shaft. Trapped in the cages were fat snails with iridescent shells that cast an unearthly and brilliant luminance. The brachuri's four eyestalks bent towards me. It hammered the staff against the kraken's back. I felt the magic, felt the slick, oily touch of sorcery thrum through me. The beast surfaced, water drained off its back, and the ship's overtaxed keel groaned and cracked.

"Youm be the savior." Grey Hide struggled to fit the words into a mouth ill-suited to the common tongue. "Youm want live, skin bag?" It shrugged. "Or die?" There was no threat implied. It asked in much the same way a bartender might enquire if you wanted ale or water.

"Live, most assuredly. I'm all for living," I said with conviction.

The old brachuri made a grunting, bubbling noise that might have been laughter.

Chapter Two

"It live," Grey Hide announced and tapped the heel of its staff against a huge knobbly growth on the kraken's back. To my disgust, a scab of stone-hard skin was peeled back to reveal a raw, fleshy cavity, gummed at the edges with a sticky, white pus-like substance. Nestled within the deep wound was a thin, bluish-grey creature with tiny eyes and a mouth like a lamprey. It was naked, and I noticed the gills on its head and neck had been sliced off leaving open vents that puffed and wheezed and oozed watery blood. I knew very little about the aquatic races, but I doubted that the mutilation was self-inflicted.

The lamprey creature had arms, legs, and fins. As I got a better look at it, I noted that its right pectoral fin had also been crudely severed. After Grey Hide's pronouncement, the brachuri swarm lost interest in me and set about putting out the fires on the *Widow* before getting down to the serious business of looting the ship. The old brachuri said something to the lamprey creature. It shuffled over to me and nervously divested me of my weapons, including the shaft of the Hammer's hammer. I suddenly felt vulnerable, acutely aware that my only defense against the demon Shallunsard was gone.

Grey Hide leaned on its staff. Its eyestalks swayed thoughtfully. "Follow, skin bag," it said to me and undulated towards the head of the kraken. Given that I had nowhere else to go, I followed. Seabirds gathered overhead, wove the sky between the silver needles of their wings as they sang in joyful anticipation of the feast to come.

"Not that I'm complaining, but why did you call me 'savior'?" I asked.

It shrugged its blubbery shoulders. "Youm saved fry. In the lands of ash and death, youm saved 'em. When youm go to strange waters, youm save others."

"I did not," I said out of habit but instantly recanted. "I mean, yes, yes I did." It took a moment to recall the heroic deed, I'd done so much in the last few weeks it was hard for my noodle to keep track, but then it came to me. "The market in Valen?"

Grey Hide nodded.

It was less a rescue than a happy accident. I'd been staggering through a fish market, wounded, and pursued, when I fell into a stall selling brachuri and managed to tip a basket of the wriggling fry over me who then escaped into the sewers.

It nodded. "Not many land lice would save fry. Youm *dark waters*."

I didn't question the epithet, I presumed it was a compliment and besides which, I'd been called much worse. "It was only, what, a week ago? How did you find out about the er, *rescue,* all the way out here?" I waved at the vast expanse of nothing surrounding the ship.

"Youm all the way 'out here,' ain't youm?" The brachuri turned three eye stems towards the *Widow's* fire-blackened hull and watched its kin swarm over the hulk. The remaining eyestalk it turned towards me. "Out here ain't far from anywhere. Out here is the heart of the world. From the heart flow the veins, through the veins, all life flows."

"Ah, I see." I didn't, but I let it go. They weren't cutting me into fish food, which was all that mattered. For the next hour or so the swarm tore the ship apart, discarding bolts of silk and barrels of spices in favor of rope, wood, and metal. I scanned the horizon in the vain hope I'd see sails or the shadowy outline of coast, but other than this fleshy island the ocean was empty. 'Out here' felt like the exact middle of nowhere. Once, when the sea rolled high, and the horizon seemed to sink below us, I thought that I caught a glimpse of Captain Shih's small craft heading north to Shen. The sea rolled again and wild, crashing waves hid the vessel from sight, or it might have been nothing more than a trick played by eyes starved of variety and bored of looking at waves tumbling over waves in an endless, monotonous procession. I also needed to head north, at the very least I needed to get off this floating graveyard before they changed their minds and slotted me. Shen couldn't be that far surely?

I coughed to get Grey Hide's attention. "It's been a delight and a pleasure t' meet you, but I need to be off now."

Grey Hide cut off further explanation with a slobbering guffaw. "Youm won't make it, skin sack. Not alone."

"Well, I wasn't planning on swimming," I lied. "I was rather hoping you'd give me passage on your... er...   kraken." Grey Hide nodded. "Yes. Good. The waters of my fief run deep and wild. Youm no tail, youm drown if you tried to swim." It waved two eyestalks quizzically in my direction. "What happened to youm's tail? Youm lose it in battle? I lost mine tail in battle." It raised itself up on the stump of the aforesaid tail, slapped its bony chest plates with its staff. "Great fight against the Shushan, deep, deep down. Water turned thick with blood and ink. Good days," it sighed wetly.

"That sounds marvelous, it really does. Alas, time is pressing and I really must be elsewhere." *Before a demon finds me and kills me,* was the part I left unsaid.

The brachuri shrugged. "Youm savior. Youm do People a service. We honor you. We'em take you to the death lands."

I didn't like the sound of that. "Death lands?"

"Death land, dry land, *land.*" It shrugged. "All same."

"Ah. In that case." I inclined my head. I was so relieved, I could have kissed him. "Thank ye kindly."

He nodded and tapped the ridge of bone that protected the kraken's head. It was then that I noticed a chain as thick as my wrist, attached at one end to a row of flattened anchors which were stitched through the gill holes in the kraken's neck. The other end of the chain disappeared into the folds of flesh at its throat. It looked like a crude bridle that could either open or close the gills which must have been how they controlled the beast.

"How in the name of the Holy Eye did you manage to capture a kraken?" I asked, curiosity momentarily distracting me from my woes.

"Capture?" Grey Hide shook its head. Its crown of chains and flotsam jangled. "No one captures a kraken. We'em bred him from a hatchling."

Thoasa are a pragmatic race. My irrational, emotional side was a backhanded gift from my human mother— one that I most often ignored. But it still took a mental, sideways leap to wrap my noodle around how wildly different this aquatic world was from the dry one I knew. Strangeness aside, I was mightily jealous that they had such a beast under their control. Why with such a pet no bullion ship on the Great Ocean would be safe from me.

The old brachuri gave orders to the swarm and cooed at the kraken. More of the lamprey creatures emerged from the scabs on the beast's back. Like the one I'd seen earlier, they all had cut fins and slashed gills. Cringing and subservient, they set about cleaning the blood off the shells of the brachuri and performing tasks where hands were more useful than claws. Although the brachuri had human torsos the rest of their physiognomy was decidedly crustacean; more a mix of lobster and crab. I had no idea what the lamprey creatures were called but counted them desperately unlucky to have been captured by the brachuri. It was ironic that I had pitied the brachuri when it turned out that they were as cruel as those who enjoyed eating their young deep-fried in garlic butter.

Grey Hide lowered its body until it was almost horizontal, fixed its soft lips on the kraken's back and began to croon. It was a disturbing sound that seemed to resonate deep within the beast. Though it was most likely too big in the body and small in the brain to understand that the creatures living on its back were anything more than ticks, the kraken was aware of the old brachuri. Its long, serpentine tentacles riffled the waves in time to the haunting murmurings. I watched the touching exchange, all the while standing ankle deep in sea scum and blood. The song went on for the best part of an hour. When it had finished, the old brachuri levered itself upright.

"Come, we'em go." It lumbered over to a giant cluster of barnacles which, on closer inspection, I saw were huge mounds of scar tissue; a result no doubt of ramming ships and heaving them out of the water. Grey Hide stood before the largest growth situated just behind the kraken's head and hammered on the mound with his staff. A moment later a flap of blubbery skin peeled back. I watched fascinated and revolted in equal measure, as another of the lamprey creatures folded the heavy curtain of skin aside, leaving a skein of sticky pus glittering like loom weft across the gaping wound.

The brachuri swept his staff through the muculent strands and bade me enter. The prospect didn't thrill me, but neither did drowning, so I acquiesced without complaint. Not many days ago, I'd spent a few hours I'd never forget hiding in a gong pot. A giant scab on a sea monster's back was a step up from that. Once inside it was evident that the kraken was a remarkably tolerant creature. It looked like the razor-mouthed lampreys had excavated the wound because the fatty walls and floor had been gnawed and scarred by circular rows of tiny teeth. A rough scaffold of wooden beams kept the injury from healing. This, I hesitate to call it, 'room', this *space*, was where the chains attached to the anchors in the beast's gills were joined. The brachuri thrust his staff through the central link and wedged it into a bony vee in the skull of the kraken. This ghastly chamber was a wheelhouse.

"We'em shall not go deep, for youm's head might burst, but we'em shall go fast," Grey Hide said. The lamprey drew the flap of skin back over the hole and when it was in place, licked the edges of the wound. An overpoweringly strong smell of ammonia cut through that of fat and fish. My feet began to tingle and went numb.

"What's that smell?" I asked through the tears.

A single eyestalk swiveled in my direction. "Shushun spit," Grey Hide said as he picked up the chain. "It keeps things clean, stops pain." The brachuri heaved on the chain. A shudder ran through everything, and the cold, spongy floor rippled. "Now we go fast, so youm sit."

The lamprey knew the drill and nestled itself between two upright beams. I was too broad to do likewise and unsure as to what to hold that wouldn't flinch. Even though I doubted that the kraken would be able to feel my tiny claws hooked into its flesh, it didn't feel right latching on to it like a tick. Beggars, however, cannot be choosers. The beast lurched forwards. The beams groaned as the flesh contracted around them. My stomach rolled and my ears popped as we dived beneath the waves.

I cast courtesy aside and dug my toes into the floor and both hands into the wall as I was forced against the fleshy bulkhead by the sudden speed of our descent. I felt sick and dizzy and was grateful when the brachuri turned its staff in the chain and the kraken leveled out. It did not alleviate the pressure in my skull, but rather than actually exploding, my head merely felt on the verge of doing so.

As I sat there, bathed in the baleful luminescence of Grey Hide's staff snails, it struck me that if I hadn't got soused, I wouldn't be in this uniquely unpleasant situation. Sober, I'd have escaped with Shih or, even better, taken the damn boat myself and left the fish-fucking bitch to face the swarm. Of course, if I hadn't been trying to blot out the memories of my recent misadventures, I wouldn't have felt the need to drink myself into a stupor.

And on ran my thoughts, following the thread of regret back to the day the demon Shallunsard duped me. The recollections of my woeful inadvertences came thick and fast, not one of which cast me in a positive light. The awkward remembrance absorbed me entirely, so much so that it took a nudge from the brachuri to rouse me to the fact that we'd stopped.

I relaxed my white-knuckled grip on the kraken's flesh. Like my feet, my hands were pleasantly numb thanks to the Shushan spit which coated every surface. I flexed my fingers to work feeling back into them and noticed several matching pinpricks in the kraken's hide that were oozing watery blood where my claws had dug in. The accidental damage did not go unnoticed. The lamprey narrowed its tiny eyes at me before crawling over to lick the unintentional injury. The acid perfume of its sputum made me gag and burned my nostrils.

"Shushun not happy with youm, skin sack." Grey Hide heaved a gravelly laugh from the depth of its barrel chest. "Good thing youm leaving."

Although the feeling was entirely mutual, I thought it best to keep my opinion to myself. As the kraken drifted to the surface, my ears popped again. I felt lightheaded, euphoric. Grey Hide relaxed its grip on the chain.

I stood up. "That was a most singular experience," I said and aligned myself with the 'doorway' in the hope that my host would take the hint and let me out. Quite remarkably, it appeared that not a single drop of water had penetrated the gummy seal of lamprey snot at the edges of the wound. Grey Hide stretched its neck and flexed its shoulders. It swiveled its drooping eyestalks towards me. The old crab looked tired, drained by the effort of piloting the living vessel. There was magic at work here, I could taste its oily tang, but like everything else related to this watery underworld, it was unlike any sorcery I'd seen before.

"Youm the only land flea ever ride with us. Now the eyes of the ocean see youm, skin bag."

"But I'm still the savior, right?" I thought I'd better check because I didn't want it to forget I was a friend and turn me into fleshy confetti. It nodded and mouth-farted something at the lamprey who immediately began to unseal the skin flap doorway.

Grey Hide leaned on his staff. "Youm savior, yes. But what *are* youm?"

I shrugged. "Just an ordinary cove, living in interesting times."

It grunted. "No matter. Just remember that we'em helped youm too." It turned its bulk towards me. "Remember that we'em want to live."

As though to add emphasis, a shudder ran through the kraken. I hadn't the faintest idea what the oldling was talking about and cared even less. I just wanted to get out and get gone. "Yes, of course, I'll remember," I said and edged towards the widening wedge of daylight. A light breeze bathed my face in briny freshness. As soon as the lamprey creature was out of the way, I climbed from the scab. Much to my delight, the horizon was crowned by a dark mantle of coastline that had to be Shen. The lamprey flopped the skin back in place behind me, closing the scab. It struck me that the coast was a little further than I'd like it to be.

"Wait." I hammered on the mound. "Can't we get any closer?" No one answered. The 'door' was sealed as though it had never been, leaving me stranded. Water began to wash around my ankles and I realized that if the beast dived as quickly as it had last time, I'd be sucked down to my death. Calf-deep in ocean, I ran along the kraken's back. Its rear end was frilled by gently rippling tail fins which looked stout enough to support my weight. I bounded across them, dived into the water and swam like fury away from the beast. Grey Hide must have known that its rescue would have been for nothing had they set off straight away, and I was allowed 300 foot's grace before the gentle oscillation turned into powerful sweeping strokes. I felt the dark water pull, felt the huge weight of the ocean shift as the water was tugged out of shape by the living island's descent.

When the last ripple of the kraken died, I stopped swimming and paddled a while, uncomfortably aware that I was nothing more than a speck, alone upon the vast unknowable. It struck me that if something as huge and terrifying as the kraken lived in the Great Ocean, other fell giants must also haunt the deeps, silently hunting prey as big as Shen war galleons or indeed, as small as a half human, half thoasa. That I was in every way out of my depth in this place, lent strength to my limbs and I struck out with vigor for the distant rind of coastline.

Chapter Three

S hen crowned the curve of the northern horizon, craggy and welcoming, but after hours of swimming seemed to grow no closer. The frozen deeps drove the heat from my limbs and made me work for every leaden stroke. I lamented (as is my wont in times of strife) that if I'd been a full-bred thoasa equipped with a powerful tail, I'd have made short work of this paddle in the briny. Of course, if capricious Nature had rolled another dice, I might have been born entirely human and would have perished long ago given the life I'd led. There is something to be said for being neither one thing nor the other. Not all of it good, but it gives one a unique perspective on life and its little quirks.

Thus occupied in contemplating the nature of my nature, the suns sank like stones and night filled the void. I swam on, half asleep, hypnotized by the rhythm of my breathing until I plowed into something with spidery tentacles. I screamed like a bairn and attempted to kick and gouge whatever it was which was when I realized my attacker was a harmless drift of seagrass. Thankful that no one had seen my battle with the weed, I once again struck out for the coast.

With only the distant stars for company, I tried not to think too hard about what might lurk beneath the glittering waves. Weaponless and out of my element, I thought small, insignificant thoughts and kept my eyes fixed on the starry path leading me to land. I wondered if I should perhaps shape a spell to transform me into a fish or fashion a boat, but I did neither. My gut told me that I had a better chance of passing unnoticed (and most importantly, uneaten) if I made as few waves as possible, both actual and metaphysical.

I swam on, half convinced that the hand of Fate was, if not quite resting protectively on my shoulder, at least swatting some of the flies from the mountain of turd it had recently deposited on my life. Grateful though I was for this perceived benevolence, I'd had enough of gods and demons. I decided to return to the simple life of an independent cove with no one to please but my sweet self.

Eventually, the phosphorescent waves painted the rough outline of black rocks against the shadowed sky. I increased my pace and let my mind wander while my body got on with saving me. I wondered how the priest, Tobias had fared when he'd returned to Valen. It was odd, but in some small way I missed the soapy cull. His sanctimony rarely failed to amuse, and his naivety was always hilarious. Like a splinter caught under a claw, he was irritating beyond his importance. And yet, there was a priest shaped hole in my life. I hoped the Imperial Senate and Synod had treated him fairly because without the hammer of the Hammer there was no way in hell I could back up the threats I'd made if they didn't.

***

It would have been nice to come ashore on a gently shelving beach, dusted with silver sand and fringed by gently wafting witchbeard trees. Instead, I fetched up before a dark cliff face, caught in an angry swell that tried to smash me to pieces against mollusk encrusted rocks. Granite cliffs rose above the swirling fury and presented an implacable face to the Great Ocean. I wasn't overly perturbed for even in the darkness I could see chinks in its armor where a nimble cove could latch on as tight as a louse on an urux nut sack. A heavy scent, redolent of old shoes marinated in lemon juice rolled off the land and infused the spray with a musky aroma before being whipped out to sea. Above me, leafy fronds waved seductively from the clifftop, beckoning me onwards. I paused for breath and then began the climb.

An irate bird with plumage as gray as the cliff took offense at me coming within arm's reach of its nest and tried to swat me from the rock, but other than that the climb was uneventful. When I reached the top, I looked out beyond the jagged rocks at the glowing sets rolling in at angles to each other, weaving ribbons of the ocean into a shimmering whole. I stared into the paling darkness, searching for any sign of the kraken. I didn't see anything that might have marked its position, though I knew it was out there, lurking somewhere under the waves. Tired, I nestled in the grass that was laced with downy strands of cobweb and fell into a well-deserved sleep.

I woke some time later to find the salty breath of the ocean had quietly fogged the land. Drifting waves of mist rolled over the cliffs and across clumpy, dew-soaked hummocks in a ghostly echo of the sea. I lay a while in the damp grass beneath the fur-edged blanket of sea fog and might have drifted off again had not a sudden, frightful thought occurred to me. I checked my deepest poacher's pocket and was reassured to find my pouch was still there. The coins were Imperial, but I was sure gold was just as shiny in every land, irrespective of whose ugly, inbred mug was stamped upon it.

***

As I had nowhere particular to go, I lay in my clifftop nest until the suns rose and burned the mist from the land. The sight that greeted me when the gauzy curtain vanished was less than inspiring. Beyond the tufty fringe of grass where I'd slept was more grass, unremarkable save for the thousands of strands of cobweb that clung to it. The cotton coated scrub rolled up to a broken granite crag, beyond which I could see only sky. A middling crosswind had sculpted a fringe of small trees into bent-backed crones and carried the strong smell of arrachid over the toothy break in the land. I let the air roll over the buds of my not-quite-split tongue as I tasted for other scents. I caught a faint trace of woodsmoke and shit, indicating that I wasn't far from a settlement.

I got up and loped over to the windswept outcrop, from where I was rewarded with my first sight of a Shen town. It was a close-run thing if I was more puzzled than underwhelmed by what I saw. The settlement was scattered across a broad sweep of land and similar in size to an Imperial town, but that was where the similarity ended. The first thing that struck me was that there weren't any city walls. The perimeter was defined by blocky, cube-shaped buildings stacked side by side and one, two, three, sometimes, four upon another in what appeared to be random clusters. The stone was the local granite. The roofs were flat, the windows facing the sea little more than slits. The buildings were linked by swaying wooden walkways, the lowest of which hung about eight feet off the ground. Everything was bound in a thick mesh of web. West of the town with their narrow ends facing me, were four rows of single-story sheds, the presence of which explained why the land was covered in downy strands of silk.

It was an ugly place, not unlike my hometown of Appleton but instead of calthracite mines the industry here was silk production. While I watched, two carts dragged by rib-thin urux drew up outside the sheds. A swarm of young arrachids loaded them with bales of raw silk, impatiently urged on by the human cart drivers who were most likely getting paid by the load. Whips cracked, and the carts trundled back towards the town, watched by the hollow-eyed children. It was some time past noon, the suns were high and cast stark angles of light and shade across the gray, boxy dwellings. Even in a clean noon light, it was a grim picture.

I made for the spinning sheds from where I'd follow the road into town. I had no idea how friendly the locals were, so I made a point of striding openly and confidently across the heath. As I drew level with one of the windowless sheds, I saw that the road led to an undistinguished gap in the jigsaw of buildings. The doors of the shed were open. As I passed, I was hit by a wash of hot air that was spiced with the eye-watering smell of vinegar and sour milk. Lying on their backs, two to a stall, with their whatnots swinging in the breeze were dozens of arrachids. Both male and female were extruding glistening fibers from their swollen nethers. The long sticky strands were looped over hooks hanging from the roof. When they were dry enough, youngsters coiled the strands into large gunny sacks positioned at the end of the stalls. When a strand broke, or the arrachid stopped extruding to take a piss or a swig of water, the children would nimbly grab the strands from the hind legs of the spinner and loop them back over the hooks, quicker than you could say, 'what a miserable way to spend your life'.

Sacks were emptied by the children as soon as they were filled. The youngsters deftly baled the silk with their hindmost pair of legs, foreshadowing the graft that awaited them when and if they attained maturity. The whole shed was a nest of industry, the workers were pale and thin but possessed of the wiry strength born of hard physical labor, a lack of food, and hopeless desperation. As I watched them toil, it was hard not to feel a shade of sympathy for the poor culls. It also confirmed to me that I'd rather live free in the shadow of the noose than spend my life engaged in such drudgery. I headed into the town, shedding the faint idea of starting my new life as an upstanding citizen like a carapace that no longer fit. Not that it ever had, but at least I'd entertained the idea of going straight.

On the edge of town, I saw a legless old ogren giving me the squint-eye. I couldn't swerve down a side street without looking shady, so I marched on, hoping to pass by unquestioned. As I drew nearer the ogren wheeled her lacquered carriage across my path. She was wearing a gray smock with the seal of Shen embroidered in black on the right breast. The elbows of the smock were patched and had faded in places to silver, leaving dark creases in the rumpled folds where the fabric pooled around her foreshortened trunk.

"Papers?" she enquired after a litany of what I suspect was the same request made in several languages before she finally landed on Imperial.

"I'm afraid I don't have any papers." The comment was met with open-mouthed disbelief. "I've been in a shipwreck," I added and waved my hands in a, 'look at me' gesture, wafting the smell of brine in her direction.

"No papers? Not at all?"

I shook my head. I'd anticipated many and varied problems that might arise from my unconventional arrival, but I confess, a lack of documentation was not amongst them. Frowning and muttering, she rummaged through a battered satchel tucked down the side of her chariot and produced a notebook with the seal of Shen emblazoned across the front. The gold dragon and scarlet turtle looked exotic to my eyes and beautifully out of place in the squalid surroundings. "That's a problem. I take it you're here to claim citizenship?" She looked up at me, her rheumy eyes bleeding weariness. "What's your name, stranger?"

"Amberly. Chas Amberly, at your service." I performed something halfway between a bow and a wave, unsure of what the custom was hereabouts.

"No need for abasement, we're all equal here," she said with a sanctimonious lilt that belied her words. She drew one of several pencils from behind her ear and wrote my name on a fresh page in the ledger before resolutely snapping it closed. "Come, I'll take you to the Magistrate's office and see if we can get you processed today."

Imagine if you would, a town built by some cove with no imagination or love for their fellow sentients. Now imagine something much worse and you'd be close to picturing the poetically named Town 272 South. Every building was constructed along the same lines. Each consisted of square blocks, roughly ten feet by ten feet, stacked at angles, one atop the other in groups of two, three, and four. The ugly gray stacks were bound like joyless gifts in ribbons of tattered silk that linked the grim-rendered clusters to each other. There weren't any gardens to brighten the dreary, crushed cinder plots between buildings, no flourishes of decoration anywhere, just rain barrels and the necessities of life stacked against the implacable, uniformly gray walls. The word 'utilitarian' sprang to mind, swiftly followed by 'miserable' and 'soul-destroying.' Whichever way you looked, it seemed like the town had turned its back on the world and was sulking like a petulant child.

The magistrates' office was a stack of four blocks, facing a windswept, cinder quadrangle. The ogren, Citizen Officer Lunn, didn't seem to notice the oppressive drabness. She wheeled inside the blank-faced block and chirpily bade me follow. What hopes I had that the soul-grinding bleakness might be alleviated by a cheery interior died at first sight.

Like the outside, the inside was unembellished and gray. A rudimentary staircase of peg steps led up to the first floor on the right-hand wall. A circular counter dominated the center of the room. Hanging above it, suspended by a straining web of silk beneath a hole in the ceiling, was the fattest arrachid I'd ever seen.

She was attired in a smart, black smock with crisp pleats gathered with inch-perfect precision over her bulging thorax. Her eight clawed feet poked from beneath the voluminous garment, embroidered over the right breast pocket with the Shen dragon and turtle. The tips of five identical quills peeked out of the pocket like soldiers on parade. The bespectacled magistrate deftly hooked a sheaf of papers from a tray on the counter at the same time as reaching up for a scroll tube that another arrachid was passing through the hole in the ceiling. As she reached up, I caught a glimpse of her mottled undercarriage which was hanging at my eye-height.

Officer Lunn chinned for me to approach the desk. I did so cautiously. Even though all her limbs were engaged in busy work, I had a healthy respect for the dagger-like appendages that I knew were drawn up just behind the neat pleats of her uniform. Lunn said something to her in Shennish, too fast for me to catch.

The magistrate sighed, as though listening was a chore and peered at me over the rims of both pairs of spectacles. "Name and purpose?" she enquired in accented Imperial. Her amber eyes were puffy and tired, shot through with watery, pink veins, no doubt from long hours spent staring at indecipherable scrawl. Reading was a bad habit that most often ruined the eyesight of every cove given to that pernicious addiction.

I cleared my throat, fluffed my stiff, lace cuffs and inclined my head like a proper toff. "Amberly, ma'am. Chas Amberly. I'm here to seek citizenship. I was shipwrecked, some miles off the coast and lost my papers."

The angle of the magistrate's head shifted abruptly. She licked her lips, stared at me like I was a bug, before turning her gaze to Lunn. "Well, Lunn it looks like we've got our hands full for the day. Please inform Citizen Partner Luyz that I won't be home for dinner."

Three hours later, I knew, without a fraction of a shadow of a doubt, that it was easier to escape from an angry dragon than it was to become a citizen of Shen. There were no bars to citizenship, they'd take anyone, even me. You just needed stamina, patience, and deep pockets. There was a bewildering number of forms to fill out, which was bad enough for a book-shy cove like me. On top of this cruelty everything had to be paid for. From processing to accreditation, to witnessing right down to the cost of ink and sealing wax, everything was accounted for and duly charged at criminally inflated rates.

I had enough coin to cover all costs with plenty to spare but was informed that if I hadn't, the enlightened nation of Shen provided a loan scheme. Out of curiosity, I enquired what the interest was on said loans and almost fainted when she told me. I was further informed that, if I couldn't pay it back, I could work off the debt in service to the great nation of Shen. It was a sweet little scam. Shen welcomed everyone. It graciously opened its arms to all stripe of refugee, irrespective of race or station. The thing was if you didn't arrive with a purse full of coin, you were as fucked as a virgin in a brothel. No wonder Shen was one of the wealthiest countries in the Ring of the Great Ocean. This government-sanctioned game made Mother's rackets seem like those of a fledgling chancer. You want to see real larceny at work? Look in gilded council chambers and palaces, not bawdy holes, and gutters.

The sun was well set by the time the seal was applied to the document which granted me the right to live in Shen. By now, I'd grown uncommonly fond of Magistrate Luyz. She was a sway-bellied goddess of bureaucracy, gifting me the right to breathe the sacred air of Shen. Wearied, nay— bludgeoned to idiocy by the weight of legislation, I was as grateful as the most pious supplicant when she talked me through my oath of allegiance and addressed me as 'citizen' for the first time. I was so relieved that my ordeal was over that I would have shed a tear had I been able. I settled for offering my profuse thanks and left the Magistrate's

Office with a fistful of over-priced documents tucked under my arm.

Chapter Four

A short while later the euphoria of being scammed into citizenship wore off. I squeezed my coin pouch, felt the lack, and cursed the poor exchange I'd made of coin for paper. Although it had to be said, the old cunning shaver had wielded her seals as adroitly as a highway robber wielded a blade as she parted me from my gilt. She'd managed this feat without putting herself in the slightest danger and while maintaining her position on the right side of the law It was a sweet trick that many a sharper would be proud of.

"I'm in the wrong business," I observed as I set out to find State Registered Brothel 4473A. On a whim, but with more than a little cajolement from the Goddess of Bureaucracy, I'd purchased an 'all night' chit for said establishment. It was apparently a good deal as the whores were guaranteed by the state to be free of disease and vermin. Overcome by the romance of it all and with a desire to put my head down anywhere after such a trying day, I'd paid the three silver tals from my purse of newly (and extortionately) converted Shen coinage.

The brothel looked the same as every other building in the gloomy crap hole, but it was comforting to know that even here, in this silk-swathed world of wisp-shrouded ghosts and scuttling shadows, a whorehouse still stank like a whorehouse. I followed my nose to a stack of blocks on the opposite side of town to the Magistrate's Office. It was a direct, but discrete route between the two, almost as if it had been planned that way.

I knocked on block number 84. A yawning, dull-eyed ogren answered and asked for my papers and chit. I'm embarrassed to say I produced both with a measure of pride, but damn it, I'd done honest graft to get them. He grunted and invited me into the threadbare pleasure palace. Inside an ancient human with a face like a wizened nutsack gave me a tour of the establishment which as Luyz had promised, was superficially clean. The mattresses scattered around the place were hidden behind woven screens. They were stuffed with doffers which were the tight knotty ends of extruded silk that weren't worth unpicking. They made for a lumpy bed that was too soft for my taste and so, during my first tumble, I took the chubby human I'd booked on the floor. 'Lovely Bull' or so he called himself, didn't seem to mind and we fucked with gusto.

After this energetic encounter, I headed off in search of my next, pre-booked assignation. From what I could tell, customers and whores came in every stripe, although, given the local industry it was no surprise that there were more arrachids than any other species.

I'm not entirely cold-blooded, but like my thoasan kin, I'm infrequently taken with the desire to rut. When the urge does come upon me, I like to make a good go of it. So, by the time I'd finished with the fourth doxy's room, I was ready for a kip in the communal flop, which was included in the price.

***

I woke early the next morning in the sleeping room in a brighter mood than I'd been in since the encounter with the Kraken. I reasoned in a contented, post-screw doze that Shallunsard would be too busy destroying the Empire to concern himself with hunting me down. Buoyed by this entirely unfounded optimism, I employed what little charm I possessed and bartered my imperial duds with the walnut-faced brothel keeper. I got a pair of used but clean, gray hakama and a matching haori which suited me well enough. He got the better end of the deal, for even though the coat was stiff with brine, the brocade was stitched with silver thread.

Clad in my, new-to-me native garb, I set out on the road to the capital, Kandandooran. I was informed by a tusker herder I met on the way that it was the greatest, most famous city in the Ring Kingdoms. How such a grubby scarecrow of a fellow knew what was great or famous was a mystery to me, but I let his loyal boast pass. Using facts to gainsay pride never earned anyone a 'thank you'.

"'Course, the Citizen Conclave don't…" He groped for the right words in trade tongue. "Er, meet there."

"No?"

He laughed heartily at my incomer ignorance. "Of course not, the Turtle Queen lives there, don't she? It'd be disrespectful to sully the very air she breathes with low government business, wouldn't it?"

"Of course. Silly me."

"Not your fault, friend. Now, just you wait until you see the palace." He grinned and his eyes misted with pride. "The walls are covered in gold and studded with rubies."

The thief in me perked at that, so I wanted this tale to be true even though the pragmatist in me doubted it. "Have you seen the palace?"

"No, friend, never. I've not ever left the district, but that's what they say. Oh, the Turtle Queen ain't really a turtle, in case you was wondering." He spat out the pulp of a chu-chu berry. Years of chewing the intoxicating fruit had stained his beard and the whites of his eyes a vibrant shade of pink. He glanced nervously over his shoulder before speaking again, even though we were alone as far as the eye could see. "She's not the ruler of Shen either, save in name. We honor her, but the Conclave rules now, everyone knows it." He tapped his nose.

I smiled. "Good to know. Thanks, friend." Ruby-studded palaces and Turtle Queens aside, I was most keen to know who ran the Midnight Court in Kandandooran and whose palms I'd have to grease to get by, but that wasn't something a berry-chewing swineherd would be able to tell me.

"'Course, some of us liked how it used to be before the Conclave took over." He grimaced. "Did you know, 272 used to be called 'Dove Cloud'? Never knew why, because it's always been a shithole, but the name made it seem nicer somehow. I miss it." His fearful glances along the road and whispered words told me that he wasn't supposed to.

I'd seen worse places than 272. In fact, other than the stifling bureaucracy which governed every aspect of life from fucking to dying, the only other difference I'd noted between Shen and the Empire was favorable, to me at least. No one seemed to give a shit that I was warspawn. No one had sneered, spat, or cursed at me and I hadn't been swived any worse than any other cull by the beak who sorted out my papers. It was unsettling. After I politely declined his offer of a place to stay for the night, the herder and I made our farewells as the pallid sunslight sank into the violet gloom of evening.

"Suit yourself. Shen is the safest country in the whole world," he assured me. "But there's a lot of incomers, no offense. You seem all right, but some are *troche*."

My expression must have told him I didn't understand the word. He pondered a moment. "Uncivilized?" He shrugged, spat out another mouthful of berry juice. "Something like that. Anyway, they don't know how to behave like decent citizens. Some turn to banditry and stake out the road to Kandandooran. You'd best watch yourself."

"Thanks for the warning. I'll keep my eyes out."

He wiped his mouth with the back of his hand and nodded sagely. "Just doing my duty, citizen."

I waved as he headed off along a woodland track, muttering and clucking at the snuffling tuskers like a parent talking to his children. I continued on my way, as at home as a shadow in the moonless dark, confident that the most dangerous cove on the road was me.

For the next five miles or so the journey was uneventful. Aside from a couple of urux snoring in a field, my only other encounter was with a laughing lizard. When our paths crossed, the damn thing didn't laugh. It spat luminous venom at me which missed, due in no small part to the fat rat clamped in its lower pair of jaws. We stared at each other for a long moment, before it got bored and slunk into the undergrowth with its prize, hissing and chittering its annoyance at my presence in its domain. I began to relax on what was turning out to be the least eventful journey I'd taken in a long while when I caught the distinct smell of death in the air. Mingled with it was the unmistakable odor of thoasa.

I drew a breath, let the rank stench of putrefaction roll over my tongue. Whatever had met its end hadn't done so recently. Fresh corpse had a meaty punch, this was more the sickly-sweet aroma of full, fly-blown decomposition. I couldn't be bothered taking a detour across a land I didn't know so I kept going, secure in the knowledge that no matter what lay ahead, I could handle it, with or without the hammer. Half a mile or so further on, the smell of rot was stronger, and when the wind shifted, I heard a snatch of conversation followed by laughter.

The road climbed here, and on the brow of the ridge, the grim silhouette of a gallows was outlined by firelight. The leafless tree bore a brace of miscreants, bloated by death's unkind embrace. At odds with the bodies swaying in the breeze, another peel of laughter floated over the hill.

I gave the gallows a wide birth. I wasn't superstitious or squeamish, it was just that as I got closer, I could see that the gallows fruit was ripe enough to burst. Beyond the gallows further down the hill was a signpost, beyond the signpost a group of thoasa were sitting by a campfire. Being in the business of highway robbery from time to time, I can spot a bunch of cutthroats when I see them. These coves were tooled up, but they didn't look like brigands. Trusting my judgment, I walked over to the signpost and had a shufty. I recognized the sign for Kandandooran but everything else was a mystery. I could speak a little Shennish but had never learned to read much beyond what was written on the consignments of pel that Mother smuggled into the Empire. Nevertheless, I lingered as though I could read what was written on the sign. I wanted to look like a native going about my lawful business rather than a foreigner ripe for fleecing.

A green-scaled cove with short head spikes shouted something at me in Shennish that I didn't understand. I ignored her, but she shouted again. *Just one day without a fight. Is that too much to ask?* I must either reveal myself to be an outsider or look like I was ignoring them which would undoubtedly lead to *awkwardness.* "I don't speak Shennish," I said slowly and loudly.

She said something else and the whole crew burst out laughing. Sensing a slight, I reached for the hammer of the Hammer of the North. An image of the brachuri snipping the weapon in twain flashed into my mind. There would be no smiting here today.

After a quick discussion, Green Scales smiled at me and said in accented Imperial, "Hello, little one."

"*Little one*? I preferred it when I didn't know what you were saying."

She frowned before again speaking to her comrades in Shennish. I caught the odd word but frustratingly not the meaning. Whatever she said, sparked a heated debate, or perhaps they commonly spoke to each other as though they were on the point of fighting. *Time to go*. I'd never felt comfortable around full-blood thoasa, they either ignored me or treated me like I was a freak, like now. I'd get going while they argued rather than loiter and spoil a perfectly decent day by beating the damnation out of the merry-begotten princocks. I made to brisk past, but Green Scales saw and nudged one of her comrades who jumped up and planted himself in the middle of the road. Of all of them, this fellow could rightfully call me 'little one'. He was so tall that the colorful plumes bound to his hair spines must have brushed the joists of the heavens. The great dollop was too big to slip past without looking like a barley-backed cur. I was many things, including cowardly when the need arose, but that wasn't often, and it wasn't now.

"Shamak, shamak." The female snarled at the giant and chinned in my direction. I brought a spell to mind, took a step back. The giant flexed his head plates, gave a low, guttural growl, and spat in the dirt.

Chapter Five

I expected him to attack not to clear his throat and stammer in halting Imperial, "Are you a child?"

The question took me back a bit. I looked over my shoulder, just to be sure that the flat-faced cretin was talking to me and not some other cull. Aside from the corpses, there was nothing behind me save the night and the empty road. "Do I look like a fucking child?"

Seemingly undeterred by my warning tone, he gave a little nod and cast a questioning, sidelong glance at the green. She nodded encouragingly and urged him on with an impatient wave. "Were you born near Schism site, or did you lose you tail in accident?" the giant asked, again in terrible Imperial.

"No, I didn't lose my tail in an accident, neither was I born near a Schism site. My mother is human. Now, if you wouldn't mind, I have to be elsewhere."

The giant's slit pupils widened, the line of his ridged brow arched in surprise. I made to walk past him, but he held up a massive hand to stay me while he yammered at his crew. Whatever he said was greeted with knowing smiles and grunts of acknowledgment. Green Scales looked particularly smug and wrapped her arms around her tail in a way that said, 'I told you so'.

I sidestepped the lump in the road, waved to the gallery. "There you have it, gentles. Bene darkmans to you all." My gut brain was quicker on the uptake than the one in my skull. And so, when the fellow slung his arm around my shoulders, a part of me realized it was a friendly, rather than aggressive gesture and I didn't blow his head off his shoulders with the spell I had primed.

He guided me to a spot by the fire where I was invited to sit by Green Scales. Some of the others nodded a welcome before continuing their whip quick conversation which I guessed was about me. From what I could tell, this lot weren't a blood family group. They were all shapes and sizes and colors. There was Green Scales, a black, a white and gray, a turquoise banded with scarlet, and my new best friend the giant was brown with a sprinkling of scales that shone bronze in the firelight. He had wide, flat head plates that covered his skull and neck and bony head spines decorated with gaudy feathers. Natural armor and adornments aside, he was also wearing steel greaves and an old-fashioned breastplate. The longsword at his hip showed signs of wear but had been sharpened and oiled, denoting an empty purse rather than a carelessness nature.

Green Scales was similarly tooled-up, with the addition of a pair of throwing spears strapped to her back. The only one of them who didn't look like she could wage a one thoasa war on the world was the white and gray. She was short and stubby limbed, and her scales stood out like rivets on a head that was as wide as it was long— not a pretty picture by any spawn's standard. Across her lap lay a white wood staff that terminated in a neatly severed root ganglion. Tied to the root were all manner of trinkets that jangled as she moved.

This one didn't talk as much as the others, but she was taking a keen interest in me. I had a sly taste of the air. The thread of her scent was distinct from her comrades. It was cool and mossy like the ice-fringed shore of a mountain lake. She had to be a bone thrower of some kind. In their wisdom, the Mage Lords didn't make warspawn capable of using sorcery so reading signs and portents was the closest thing to real magic warspawn came. As far as I knew, their 'magic' was utter bullshit but just to be polite, I dropped her a nod of recognition, one sorcerer to another. She returned the gesture, although her storm grey eyes showed not a flicker of friendliness. Perhaps she was prescient enough to see in me what I didn't see in her.

"Eat, eat," the green ordered. Before I could decline, someone handed me a flatbread the size of a buckler and a handful of dark red fruit that I didn't recognize. I watched the others smush their portion of fruit into the dough and did likewise. The combination of bread and fruit released a mouth-watering, spiced butter smell and tasted like a slice of heaven.

The group talked as they ate, animated and fluid in speech and motion, they banished the darkness with the warmth of their friendship. I allowed myself a moment to relax, to bask in the stolen glow of their camaraderie. They weren't my crew, I'd left them in the Empire, but I could pretend, if only for a moment.

"What's your name?" Green Scales asked between mouthfuls of bread and fruit. "What do you do?"

"Amber... Breed. My name's Breed Blake." She nodded and wiped juice from her chin spikes with the back of her hand.

"Huska." She prodded herself in the chest and added a blast of musk from one of the glands beneath her ear pits. I had more developed ears than the thoasa, but no musk glands so I couldn't add a scent signature to my word name. No one mentioned it.

The one with black scales was called something like Rumbudandrev. His scent was like marmalade and hot iron. The turquoise was Terinta. A soft frill of scales around his or her neck pulsed with blood and swished like sailfish fins when fully erect. Terinta was an archer and carried a bow thicker than my wrist. He or she gave me the come-hither eyes and a blast of ripe melon and *sex* which was so strong it almost knocked me off my seat. I might have been flattered if I wasn't so surprised. Terinta fluttered its frills coquettishly but otherwise didn't speak, leaving me to stew in the musty aroma of his or her juices. I'm no prude, and in truth, it wasn't an unpleasant scent, but there was a time and a place for such things and here in the shadow of the gibbet while amongst company wasn't one of them.

"Terinta's from Ulyanova," said the giant, as though that would explain the archer's goatish antics. "Ghant Renku." He touched his chest, added a blast of fresh ginger and river cobbles.

All eyes turned to the grey and white who had until now had stayed silent. "Skink." She didn't add a scent signature. An awkward silence fell over the company.

"Pleased t'meet you," I said to the group without acknowledging the slight. Skink was obviously a surly cur and probably gifted enough at bone-throwing to know that I could use magic, while all she could do was shake a bag of horse teeth and spout shit. "Where are you headed?" I asked Huska.

"Kandandooran," she said. "What do you do and where are you headed, Bread?"

"It's Breed, and I'm a locksmith. I tapped the wallet of papers where my official trade had been noted in the solid hand of Magistrate Luyz. I'm also heading to Kandandooran. What do you do?" I fanned a hand to include all of them.

"We're dancers."

"Oh." I hadn't expected that.

"Something wrong?" Ghant asked, having noted my surprise.

"No, nothing. Only, you don't look, I mean, what with those weapons and all. They look awfully real."

Huska bristled. "Why wouldn't they be real. What are you implying?"

Skink chuckled, rolled her staff across her knees. "The word for 'dancer' and the word for 'warrior' are very similar in Ti'en."

Huska and I shared a look of dawning comprehension and our laughter sealed a lifelong friendship. I scratched the marks made by the demon and the elderling, enjoyed the relief of my nails digging into my suddenly itchy skin.

"Perhaps we could travel together?" I asked casually. There was a swift exchange of glances and pheromones before Huska grinned.

"Yes," she said. "That would be good. I've never met…" She tilted her head. "Your Mother must be an extraordinary human to mate with a thoasa."

"I think in this case, the extraordinary partner was probably my sire, but I'll grant you it was an unusual coupling."

They nodded. Ghant grinned. "I wouldn't want to..." He made a jiggling motion. "A human. You're rare, Bread Blake."

"Well, I wouldn't say that." My palm burned, but I shoved the warning to the back of my mind. I liked this crew and equally as strange, they seemed to like me. "What are you going to do in Kandandooran?"

"We're Rangers with the Queen's Highlanders," Terinta grinned and stroked the lower limb of his or her bow suggestively. "We're going to rejoin our regiment and school the Balmarn insurrectionists."

"I thought they hid out in the Shattered Plateaus?"

"They do." Huska grinned and wormed a pip from between her fangs with the tip of a claw. "We have balloons."

"That sounds interesting."

"It is." Rumbudandrev beamed. "You should sign up, come with us."

Huska chuckled. "Slow down, Drev. Not everyone wants to live by the minute."

"Why not? What are they saving themselves for?" Drev spat into the fire. "We're warspawn, doomed to short lives. I won't see another ten summers if I sit by the hearth or if I go fight in a balloon." He turned to me. "You should see my zanth cannon, Breed." He mimed pulling an enormous trigger. "Five times the size of a handcannon, mounted on the air galleons, it's a magnificent weapon." He grinned suggestively.

"I'm just a locksmith." I smiled apologetically. I preferred robbing foppish nobles, not dying for them.

Drev shrugged. "You don't know what you're missing."

"No. probably not."

"Breeeed…" Silence fell like an ax. As one, my new friends and I craned to look at the gibbet. "Did you think you could hide from meeeee?" The two corpses rasped in unison.

"Run," I heard myself say. "Sweet Salvation, run for your lives."

The thoasa either didn't hear me or just didn't heed my warning. What had I expected? They were warspawn, it wasn't in them to run. They drew blades, strung bows, and knocked arrows. "For fuck's sake, go." I scrambled away from the fire. The corpses melted through the bars of the cages like hot wax.

Huska spun towards me. "What is that?" Her crew fell into a defensive formation, not that it would do them any good. Skink hadn't moved from the fire. "It's our doom, sister," Skink said and huddled deeper into her robe, her cold gaze fell upon me. "I told you we should have killed this fucking abomination and left its body for the crows. Did I not tell you yesterday that our death would walk down that road? Didn't I fucking tell you?"

There followed an angry flurry of Shennish which was cut short when a clawed hand punched out of the unctuous pancake of corpse fat that had pooled beneath the gallows. I watched, paralyzed by dread, as the hand was followed by an arm and then a neck and another arm. Black wings sprouted from the emergent shoulders and snapped open. Sweeping ebony horns snaked from a glittering, slime-skinned skull. I watched, transfixed by the gruesome birth of my old friend Shallunsard the demon, come to collect his dues.

I've made many mistakes in my life and what I did next counts high amongst them. I should have apported as far away from here as I could, but I didn't. I threw my arms wide enough to gather the vault of heaven, let my anger shape the most powerful spell I'd ever cast, and threw a storm of lightning at the big, ugly bastard as he stepped from the filth of his birthing pool.

The fury of my fire burned the shadows to silver and for a brief, dazzling moment, turned night into day. I wreathed the demon in coruscating lightning. The gibbet exploded, the cages melted. If I say so myself, it was impressive.

It was not enough.

When the smoke cleared, Shallunsard was standing on the glassed earth, entirely unharmed. Without the blessed touch of the Hammer's hammer, I might as well have blown him a kiss. I swayed, drained to my roots by the effort. The thoasa stood staring, uncomprehending. "Sorry," I said, then ran down the road like a demon was after me.

I didn't look back when I heard the thoasas' battle cries. Neither did I steal a glance over my shoulder when I heard Shallunsard laugh in response. I did stumble when the ground shook and the sky was lit by the scarlet afterglow of flames, but I kept fucking running. When the wash of heat hit my back and the thoasas' screams died in the roar of fire, I ran harder and faster than I had ever run in my life.

It wasn't fast enough.

Pain isn't the first thing you feel when you're punched or stabbed. It isn't even the first thing you feel when you've been hurled into the middle of next week by a blast of sorcerous fire. The first thing you feel is numb, while at the same time, a tiny voice whispers in your brain that what just happened is going to really, *really* hurt. I hit the ground about thirty feet further from where I left it. The first thing I felt was my shoulder break. The second was my face bones shatter as I slid along the road and caught in a rut, which flipped me end over end and broke my back. At least all the rolling put out the flames by the time I came to a grinding halt at the head of a furrow that I'd plowed with my face.

This was the point where, if I were a real hero, I would have rallied. I would have dug deep and summoned my inner reserve of strength, whereupon I would have escaped with a wave and a wink or avenged my thoasan friends and slain the demon.

Alas, I'm not a real hero.

All I could do was lay there in a broken heap and watch the demon stomp towards me, branding the ground with every fiery step. Had Fate been kind, I would have bled out before he reached me, but Fate is ever the bastard. The demon picked me up and brought me to his eye level.

"I thought I'd lost you," I said through gritted teeth as pain ripped through my broken body.

He laughed, which I hoped was a good sign. "Why to lose you, Breed, would be like losing a piece of myself. I've always known where you were." He tightened his grip. His black eyes shone with malice. "I've just been too busy to come and claim that which is mine. Speaking of which, I see by its absence you've done for another artifact. Quite the habit you have there. I predict that it will be something you'll live to regret."

I couldn't reply because he was squeezing my throat. All I could do was hang there and choke as he strode through the fire, crushing the charred bones of the thoasa underfoot. The blistering heat burned the breath from my lungs. I felt myself slipping into blessed unconsciousness just as we apported. In the space between two ragged heartbeats, the demon dragged us back to the Empire and Valen, the greatest capital city in the Ring.

He hoisted me aloft. "Behold my work and despair." The booming echo of his words skittered across the rubble where the city had stood. Burning remnants of blind-eyed towers thrust through mounds of debris and reached plaintively for the black and boiling sky. Smoke blanketed the corpse-strewn ruins where herds of bloated spew maggots gorged, and flocks of carrion birds darkened the sky.

"It's not my fault," I said, to the dead. They didn't answer.

"Not your fault?" The demon cast me aside like a rag, spun a suit of bright mail from the air, and clothed himself in shining, silver armor. "Who freed me?"

I tried to get up, but I couldn't. It didn't matter, standing or lying down I wasn't taking the blame for this. "Oh, no. This was you, not me. And you tricked me into freeing you. If I'd known I'd have... I'd..." I tried again to sit up but failed again.

The demon smiled. "Yes, Breed, squirm beneath the weight of your guilty conscience. If you had known what I was, you would still have freed me."

"It's not my fault."

"Whose fault is it then, mine?" His jaw tightened and for a fleeting moment he looked almost pained. "Like you, warspawn, I am what I was made to be." The ground shook as he strode towards me and picked me up by my hair spines. We apported to what was left of the golden palace of the Empirifex which was now surrounded by a forest of spears and a sky black with carrion birds. Impaled on the spears were thousands of severed heads.

"Tell the brave defenders of Valen it's not your fault. Tell your friends."

I closed my eyes.

"Look at them," he demanded. I didn't. He shook me until my teeth rattled. "Look at them, or I will feed them to you." I opened my eyes. There, front and foremost were Tobias, Clary, and Leo. "They fought so very bravely, Breed," Shallunsard crooned. "It was as though they thought they could win, can you imagine that?" He leaned close. I could feel his fetid breath on my neck. "They died hard for their arrogance. Now tell them, Breed. Tell them whose fault it is that they are dead."

The words caught in my throat. "It's not my fault," I rasped.

The demon's blaring laughter felled swathes of the spears, but not those of my friends. They remained resolutely, accusingly in place.

"Do you believe in the gods, Breed? Take it from one who knows, they are fools. Blind and deaf to the suffering of their creations."

I'd heard and seen enough. I squirmed in his grasp, twisted around to face him. "You self-pitying shit biscuit." I drew a ragged breath. "Frankly, I'm disappointed. I expected more from you than, 'wah, wah, the gods don't love me.'" I knew I was talking myself into the grave. The inability to keep my tongue behind my teeth had been a lifelong affliction, except this time I wanted to die.

His lightless eyes widened in disbelief. I screwed mine shut and made peace with eternity. Nothing happened. I stole a peek and saw the demon's face split in a wide grin.

"You think to escape me by dying?"

"I was rather hoping."

"There's no escape for you, maggot. I've prepared a place, a special little corner of hell, just for you, *betrayer*. And I promise you will not die until I have turned this world and everything in it to ash."

With those terrible words ringing in my ears, I was taken on swift wings to my own private hell.

Chapter Six

I will not document how I was tormented. That I was in hell and the prisoner of a vengeful demon and his vile minions should be sufficient information for any but the most prurient. If you crave details, I suggest you annoy a demon.

Chapter Seven

It's hard to hear when you don't have ears. Without those fleshy, little shells to funnel noise, even the tortured screams of the damned are tempered. Of course, when you're the one doing the screaming, the sound is inside your braincase and there's no getting away from that horror, ears or not.

Some weeks, or perhaps months after my imprisonment, during a brief respite from torment, I dreamed that I could hear talking. It wasn't the usual, infernal screeching and cackling, it was a real voice, speaking good old Imperial.

"Dear gods. Rowan, over here," the someone said. The words were muted, diffuse, and most likely imagined, but even thinking that I'd heard them brightened an otherwise grotesquely dull day. Hard to believe I know, but torture can be tedious, especially when one's body doesn't have the decency to die. The illusory voice was accompanied by an olfactory hallucination. I thought I smelled frost, a hint of moss, and ice-rimed rosehips. It was a magical treat, given that I no longer possessed the equipment with which to smell anything. The only sense that had been left intact was my ability to feel.

The dream stranger spoke again. "Is this...?"

"Yes," another, tantalizingly familiar voice answered.

"Surely, there's nothing. I mean, is it still alive?"

"Oh, yes," Rowan answered. "You're still alive, aren't you, Breed?"

I hoped she didn't think I was being rude, but given that I lacked a tongue, I simply couldn't answer.

***

I don't recall much about my rescue. I drifted in a semi-conscious, blood-soaked haze where reality and hallucination merged in an unending succession of the fantastic followed by the horrific. Eventually, I woke from the pain-forged nightmare to find that I'd been dumped in a shed. It took a moment for the change of location from hell to shed to sink in, not least because there were so many other differences vying for my attention. I wasn't in pain and much to my joy and astonishment, I had a full complement of limbs. Unfortunately, they weren't mine. Shivering, I sat up. I was colder than I'd ever felt in my life and to add to my joy, dumped beside me was a bloodstained sack that undoubtedly contained a body. I've never been overly curious to examine bodies in sacks. I've put a few in sacks but that had always been the extent of my interest under normal circumstances, but here and now, everything was very fucking far from normal. With a trembling, humanish hand, I opened the sack and had a look.

The ravaged remains of a face I knew only too well stared up at me or would have done if it had eyes. It was me and yet here I was, very much alive, wearing a stranger's skin.

"Who the hell are you?" Someone demanded. I looked around to see a greasy looking, tiny-eyed human standing in the doorway. I'd been so engrossed gawping at my mangled corpse that I hadn't heard or smelled him approach, which was understandable considering the unique circumstances. He looked almost as surprised to see me as I was to be here. "What the hell are you doing here?" Fear manifested in the sharp tone of his voice.

I laughed.

"What are you laughing at?"

"You, being all shouty when you look like you're about to bolt or shit yourself, possibly both. It's funny." I stood up. "This floor is fucking freezing. Where am I?"

Without saying a word he stepped back into a raging blizzard. I swayed unsteadily on my narrow, borrowed pins. "Oi! Wait. Who are you and what in the name of all the angels' holy arseholes did you do to me?" The voice coming out of my mouth wasn't anything like mine. It was wheezy and light, not unlike the human retreating into the storm.

"Me?" Snow flurried around him. "I didn't do anything to you. Who the hell are you?"

I took a step towards him, stumbled. I pointed at my old bone bag. "That's me. There, in the sack. Who the—"

The human ran for it. I let him go. I was bereft. What joy I might have felt at being rescued had been obliterated by the fact that I was literally no longer myself. My body, so reliable, so swift and agile, had been destroyed, and I'd been imprisoned in a soft-shelled human carcass which was freezing to death. I looked around, found a sack that didn't have a body in it and wrapped it around my frosty nethers. If I stayed here I was going to die. A thought confirmed moments later when the massive shadow of some flying beast passed over the shed. I tried to get a look at whatever it was through a hole in the roof, but my poor, human eyesight couldn't penetrate the falling snow. I crept over to the door and stole a peek in time to see a pale, dragonish tail vanish into the storm, turning spirals of snow in its wake. If the weather didn't get me, the wildlife would.

As much fun as it was freezing to death in a borrowed body, I thought it prudent to try and find out just what the hell had happened to me after my supposed rescue. I set off in search of shelter and answers. My numb, clawless feet skidded on the icy path. I stopped a few feet from the shed where a cliff edge dropped into the yawning gullet of a rugged, mountain valley. A strong gust of wind swept the snow from a cobbled path that climbed the shoulder of the mountain. I tasted the air but couldn't discern anything other than the sting of frost, however, I could see the human's footprints in the freshly falling snow. Head bowed against the icy blast, I followed them up the path. With every step, the savage wind tried to pluck me from the mountain and hurl me into the valley and just to add to my joy, something roared loud enough to shake snow from the mountain. *At least if a dragon eats me, I'll be warm.* True though it might be, I didn't want to test the theory. Skidding, slipping, and cursing, I quickened my pace and soon caught sight of the human.

"Oi, wait up," I shouted over the gale.

"Go away."

"Where? You thick prick. Should I stay in the shed and freeze? Or mayhap I should skip down the mountain and make a new life among the fucking goats?"

"Just g… go away and leave me alone," he stammered, fell face first in the snow, scrambled up, and started to run.

"Wait for me."

"No."

"Prick," I shouted. "When I catch you, I'm going to gut you and climb inside." It was safe to say that the time spent being tortured by demons had done nothing to improve my temper.

There followed the slowest, most ridiculous chase in the history of pursuits, as we both stumbled up the trail. It became apparent that the human was headed towards what I took to be a cave entrance which he reached before me. As I got closer, I saw that it wasn't a cave, it was a tunnel that had been cut into the mountain. I staggered inside, stiff-limbed from the cold and just in time to see the human scamper around a bend, shortly after which I heard the resounding clang of a door being slammed. "Damn it." I'd been outpaced by a human. I staggered around the corner and tried the door. It was locked. I kicked it, put my shoulder to it, but this carcass was so pathetically weak that I only succeeded in hurting myself. It struck me then what a fucking miracle it was that humans managed to flourish when they were so shabbily put together. The key to their survival had to be their vicious and duplicitous nature because it certainly wasn't their physical prowess.

I pondered my predicament. I had to do something sharpish or I was going to freeze to death. I knocked on the door and shouted. "Hey, you, let me in. I'm going to freeze to death or get winkled out of this hole by a dragon and fucking eaten. Come on, just let me in, will you? I promise, I won't hurt you." I waited for a reply sure that whoever he was must be on the other side, listening. If he was, he didn't answer. "Right. Have it your way." I stepped back, aimed at the door, and let loose a blast of lightning.

I put it down to my naturally optimistic and sunny disposition that I am still surprised when my plans go awry, although I should probably know better by now. The blast rebounded from the warded door and hurled me against the wall of the tunnel and into the dark embrace of unconsciousness.

***

I have no idea how much time passed before I came to. All I know is that I opened my eyes to find that I was lying on a polished, marble floor in a vaulted hall. A cold blue fire burned in the hearth casting an eldritch glow upon the chamber. The bare mantle was supported by granite giants who gazed with sightless eyes at their twins who likewise flanked a fireplace on the opposite side of the hall. I propped myself up on my elbow. The tiny-eyed cock goblin who'd left me was shuffling nervously by a snow-blasted window. Beside him was Rowan, the glass-haired Annurashi who'd saved my life in Valen. She looked angry, not raging angry, more coldly furious. As she was giving me daggers, I had to assume that anger was directed at me. I smiled.

"Who are you?" she demanded imperiously. Her words accompanied by a spell of compulsion.

"It's me, Breed."

She tilted her head from side to side, much like a raptor trying to decide how best to devour its dinner. "What did you say?"

"It's. Me. Breed."

There was a long pause. "Sweet Salvation." A half smile played on her lips. She peered at me more closely.

The human aped the Annurashi's expression. "That's impossible... isn't it?" He coughed and behind his lank fringe, sweat sheened his brow, as though he was in the grip of a fever.

Rowan sketched the outline of my body with an elegant wave. "This is a fine trick, Breed. How did you do it?"

"Me? I thought you did it." I stood up and fashioned my sackcloth kirtle into a more formal tunic now that I was in company.

She snorted. "I'm not so perverse as to ask who the fuck you are if I already knew. I have better things on which to waste my time."

"Sorry I asked." I went over to the fire and tried to thaw out my frozen arse. The flames were spectral and offered no warmth.

She rounded on me. "I watched you die. I thought that was an end of it. Sit down." She gestured impatiently to a bench next to a granite slab of a table.

I did as she ordered. The bench, like my behind, was freezing. There was nothing comfortable in this chamber. Everything was cold and much like myself, just about functional. "I don't remember dying. Are you sure?"

"Of course, I'm sure." The immortal wasn't used to being questioned and knifed me with the narrow edge of her eye. "Jeo, fetch Breed something to wear." Jeo shuffled out. The Annurashi laced her spidery fingers behind her back and paced, coat tails flapping in time to the clip of her boot heels. Presently, Jeo returned carrying a bundle of clothes which he threw at me.

The shirt and breaches stank of sweat, but they were at least warmer than the sack. "Any chance of some grub?" My new voice echoed through the hall. "My stomach feels like my throat's been cut, which reminds me of a not so funny story."

"Jeo." The Annurashi chinned at a doorway. Her lackey shot me a filthy look before sloping off again.

I thumbed in his direction. "Why's he giving me the pig eye? I'm the one who's been swived out of their bone bag." Rowan replied with stony silence. *Well, fuck you too.* I finished dressing, caught the blurred reflection of a stranger's face in the polished table top. It was disturbing, knowing that the 'stranger' was me. I took a closer look, kidded myself that I could see something of the real me in the sardonic half-smile, perhaps a sliver of humor in the corner of the cove's tiny eye.

Bullshit, and you know it. I was as unlike myself as it was possible to be. I didn't move the same or look the same. The eyes were small, muddy, and dull. The greasy black hair was lank and irritating and the body soft and weak. I might have been born a hybrid of human and warspawn— a monster feared and hated in equal measure, but I damn well looked the part. This nithing of a shell was an insult and now that I thought about it, looked very much like Jeo. "That's horrible." I peered again at my reflection.

"What is?" Rowan asked, sharp as a scalpel.

"I was just thinking about my time in Shallunsard's lair. It was horrible." Experience lent the lie credence and she let off questioning me further.

With nothing better to do than consider my miserable fate, I made a casual appraisal of the items I might lift if I'd broken into this crib. For the home of a god, pickings were surprisingly slim. Amongst the notables were a set of twelve, silver candlesticks that ran the length of the table. The blue flames at the tip of the stylized antler branches burned without wax or wick a neat trick that would fetch a good price on the dark market. The walls and ceiling weren't adorned with paintings or tapestries. They were a uniform black, no doubt to better display a collection of skulls and bones. Suspended from the ceiling, either by sorcery or wires was the skeleton of a dragon. I hated dragons. Even dead ones looked like they wanted to eat you.

Opposite the door, a vast window offered an uninterrupted view of sawtooth mountain peaks or would have done had the storm not laminated the glass with powdery snow. Jeo returned a short while later with a bowl of thin soup, a goblet, and a bottle of red wine tucked under his arm. He set them down on the table without fuss or flourish and sketched a mocking bow. I ignored him, drank the soup, and followed it up with the bottle of wine. A warm glow spread through my borrowed limbs. I sat back, my stomach stretched as tight as a full wineskin. Jeo sulked off to sit by the fire. He made sure I was watching before, with a wave of his hand, he turned the flames from cold blue to warm red. The Annurashi either didn't care or didn't notice as she continued to wear a furrow in the floor.

***

"So, how did you do it?" she asked some hours later.

I'd been dozing and jolted awake with a start when she spoke. "Do what?" I looked round. Jeo was asleep by the fire.

"Come back from the dead. How the fuck did you do it? How did you create a new body?"

"I've told you. I don't know. I don't know if this body is new or borrowed. I just don't know."

Her gaze slid away, and she returned to her brooding and pacing. Unlike the immortal, I was not a patient cove, happy to wait hours between questions. As she'd woken me from my fitful slumber I thought it time to ask a few of my own and not let up until I had some answers. "What happened after you rescued me?"

"You died. That you survived as long as you did in the state you were in was remarkable." She gave me a questioning look.

"I can't take the credit for my survival. The demon Shallunsard cursed me to endure long after the point at which most creatures have the good fortune to die."

She slowed a step when I mentioned his name. "What do you recall about the demon?"

"He's a gilt-edged cunt with horns and fangs, bad breath, and a terrible sense of humor. I recall he told me that he was going to torture me for eternity and then his minions got busy making good on his promise."

She ran a hand through her glass-pale hair. "Do you remember anything from after we found you?"

"I heard you talking, but I thought I was dreaming. I think I remember being moved." I didn't mention that I also recalled the terrible, unendurable agony and that I lacked the means with which to cry out, or even whimper, let alone beg for death and an end to pain. It didn't matter. The past was gone, and the future didn't exist. I was alive and warm and pleasantly drunk. All that mattered was the here and now. That's what I told myself as I clasped my hands to stop them shaking. "That's about it until I woke up in this body, cold as a brachuri's pizzle with only my ragged-arse corpse for company. I've no idea how humans cope." I kneaded my jellied gut. "I feel like I'm part human, part milk pudding and I smell worse, at least I think I do. This face and its organs are mostly decorative."

"Enough prattle. How did you affect the reincarnation?"

"I prayed really, really hard."

She fixed me with a murderous cold stare. "*You* prayed?"

"No, of course not. Fuck's sake. I told you, I don't know how I came back from the dead. I'm a thief, not a necromancer. I'm disappointed that you can't tell me. I thought you were supposed to know everything."

She didn't rise to my provocation. She turned her back and stared into the fire. "I have a theory."

"I need a piss. Where's your closet?"

"You can wait. Show me your hand."

I sighed, stood up, and held out my right hand for her to see.

"The other one."

I held out the left. "Would you look at those," I said. Twinned with the silvery mark of the Annurashi was the mark of Shallunsard the demon, as plain in my new palm as it had been in the old one.

Without so much as a by-your-leave, she grabbed my hand, and turned it this way and that as she peered intently at the marks before nodding to herself. "It is possible that my blessing and Shallunsard's curse have somehow combined, which has enabled you to reincarnate."

"But why as human? Why not like my old self?"

She let go of my hand. "Jeo was probably the nearest living sentient to you when you reincarnated. Perhaps he acted as a pattern, a living template."

I'd expected something more specific, but this was just conjecture. "That's fascinating."

She gave a wry smile. "Oh, is it? You know, your new face is easier to read than the old one."

I was eye-to-eye with her, and although I could no longer smell the ice in her blood, I knew it was there, could almost see her calculating mind at work behind those strange, multihued eyes.

"Not that I wish to sound ungrateful, but why did you rescue me? And, if you knew where I was, why didn't you come sooner, before all the gouging and the ripping and the burning?"

She pinned me with her unwavering gaze. "What did you do with the Hammer's hammer?"

Two can play this game. "Was Appleton destroyed?"

She gave me a hard look. "How is it that you keep surviving when greater souls have perished?"

I narrowed *my* eyes. It was much easier mimicking expressions with such a pliant mug. "Where am I, and how the fuck do I get out?"

She folded her arms. "Answer my questions and I'll tell you."

"I lost the fucking hammer, all right?"

She gave me the fish eye which for the second time today was entirely uncalled for. "It's true," I protested. "I was caught up in a disagreement between an independent, Shen trading vessel and a shoal of Brachuri which wasn't of my making I hasten to add, and the hammer ended up at the bottom of the Great

Ocean, in a couple of pieces. Now, what happened to Appleton?"

Her jaw tightened.

"Come on, immortal, play fair."

"The demon hoard reduced it to a pile of rubble."

"Every cloud, eh?" I beamed.

The Elderling looked appalled. "That was your home."

"Have you ever been to Appleton? It was a proper shithole."

She shook her head in disbelief. "Half the Empire lies in ruins. Thousands are dead, and many more thousands have been displaced."

"Half the Empire you say?"

"Aye."

"In that case, could you drop me in Shen?"

She laughed. It wasn't a pleasant sound. "Just when I think I have seen all there is to see of this world, something, *someone* comes along and surprises me. You are unbelievable, Breed."

"Believe me, please. I've seen enough of Shallunsard and his demons to last a dozen lifetimes. I want to be as far away from him as I can get and would appreciate it if you could drop me in Shen, soon as you like."

"Why don't I just drop you here?"

"Eh?" I was confused for about half a second due in no small part to being drunk and off my guard. But, credit where it's due, the merry-begotten, arse-scrape was good and quick and stabbed me in the gut without so much as a twitch.

Time slowed as she withdrew the slender blade. I gasped and sank to my knees. Jeo woke from his fitful slumber and squealed. The sound stretched across minutes, was drawn thin as a sustained note on a viol. I looked down, saw a bead of blood drip from my gut and hit the floor as hard as a hammer blow. The Annurashi glided behind me. I looked up, saw horror in Jeo's flame-sheened eyes as, with a single, bold stroke, Rowan cut my throat.

Chapter Eight

I've never *lost* consciousness. I've never carelessly mislaid it. I've had it punched, kicked, and stabbed from my possession more times than I care to, or indeed am able, to recall. I've never lamented the loss of the waking world. Its absence has often been a relief from discomfort. Alas, Consciousness is a jealous and capricious cove. The moment it thinks you've grown used to its absence— the *instant* it's sure that you've forgotten it ever existed, it drags you from the delights of sleep or, as in my case, the peaceful oblivion of death. It is for this perverse and mean-spirited trick that I have come to regard Consciousness as quite the cunt because when I was dead, I didn't miss being alive.

I opened my eyes and the world rushed in. Once again I found myself lying on the floor, this time I was in an antechamber with two sets of doors set opposite each other. I put my hands to my neck, expecting to feel clotted blood or a gaping wound. The skin was smooth, unblemished. The mange-hearted sack of worm spew that had cut it was standing over me. Next to her was a cove who looked so much like the witch that they must have been close kin. Slumped beside me were the bloody remains of my previous body.

"Ah. You're back," Rowan said, as though I'd just returned from a morning constitutional. Her companion had close-cropped hair and a beard, but despite these superficial differences he and Rowan shared an uncanny likeness.

"Fascinating," he muttered like I was something that had washed up on a beach.

"You murderous canker," I snarled at the wench, or rather I tried to. My voice lacked substance, being as it was little more than an echoic whisper, ethereal and melodious, and entirely ill-suited to snarling. The Annurashi siblings exchanged knowing smiles. I lay there, beside my corpse and tried to fathom what manner of being I'd become this time.

"If I hadn't seen it with my own eyes," said the fellow.

"I told you," Rowan offered me her hand. I took it because I was keen to bring her face close to my fist. The moment our long, four-jointed fingers touched, I saw that my hands were like hers. I examined them more closely. There was a faint tracery of scales beneath the translucent skin that had nothing to do with their lineage. I stood up. This bone bag was lithe and stronger than it looked, far removed from the fleshy sack cooling on the floor.

"Interesting." The bearded cove reached out to touch me. "Do you see ho—?"

I slapped his hand away and turned to Rowan. "Why the fuck did you kill me?"

"To test a theory," she answered bluntly. "Now stop sulking, we need to talk. Jeo stop lurking and get in here."

A door opened, there was a blast of frosty air, and Jeo stumbled into the room. He was clutching another turnip sack. Snow clung to his shoulders, and his nose was as red as a firefly's arse. "Is this the last body?" He flicked a glance in my direction. "Only, I'd like to know how deep the hole needs to be."

"That will depend on Breed."

Muttering something under his breath about not being a servant, Jeo bagged my corpse. I felt no sorrow at its loss or his plight. He was a prick, and the body was an ugly and ungainly skin bag, no use for anything save blending into a crowd of other unremarkable humans. Even though I could happily swing for the ruthless fuck, Rowan might have done me a favor by killing me. When Jeo finished sewing up the sack, he apported away with the body, leaving me alone in the bloodstained room. The sound of laughter and conversation blew in from the hall. I followed the Annurashi twins inside, where more of their kin were sitting down to a feast.

The Elderlings weren't eating typical banquet fare. There was no roast urux stuffed with eels or chun-chun hearts drizzled with fire beetle butter. There weren't even any bread rolls. The Annurashi were eating off golden platters that were piled with granite boulders, glittering sandstone pebbles, flakes of limestone, and other rocky delicacies. Tiered silver salvers were laden with cubes of marble and copper bowls were filled to overflowing with wafer-thin basalt chips and sparkling pyrite clusters.

The magical candlelight was suffused with sparkling stone dust and cast an eerie blue glow over the peculiar scene. I could hardly believe what I was seeing, it was like a dream, so at odds with my recent experience in Shallunsard's hellish lair. The fabled Annurashi were sitting down to dinner in all their gem-encrusted splendor, making polite conversation as they crunched through rock and delicately nibbled on chips of slate. It was the most singular banquet I'd ever witnessed. Stranger still was that my new stomach was growling at the sight of it.

Rowan took a seat at the table. "What are you staring at?"

"You lot. You look like you've been cast from the same mold."

I would say she gave me a funny look, but it was hard to tell with those eyes. She picked up a fat, grey pebble. "We're family."

They weren't identical, but aside from the color of their hair and style of clothing, the differences between them were minor. And, if the reflection in the window of a naked, red-haired, yellow-eyed creature was anything to go by, I was now one of them, in body if not in spirit. I was over six feet tall, spindle-limbed and pale as milk, save for a mane of spun sugar, red hair. The color reminded me of who I was inside, who I had been. It was an echo, a memory of me pushing through death's interdiction. Not that I was complaining overmuch about having the body of a godlike being. Why, just thinking about the scams I could pull guised in the flesh of an Elderling made me giddy with excitement. Of course, there might not be anyone left to scam if Shallunsard had his way. Having said that, the world was a big place. It was bound to take him a while to destroy the whole of it, by which time these wise and ancient coves would have come up with a scheme to defeat him.

And then I remembered. Valen, Tobias, Clary, Leo. Something cold coiled itself around my gut, tightened, bit down hard enough to make me gasp. I tasted ashes, smelled death.

"Have you worked it out yet, Breed?" Rowan's voice dragged me back from the edge of a dark well of bad memories.

"Worked what out?" I snapped. I could still see their heads on spikes, could see their mouths working but I couldn't hear what they were saying. "What are you saying?"

"That you reincarnate in approximation of the nearest, living sentient."

"Yeah. Sure," I answered absently, caught between two places. My friends were dead because of me. "Me."

Some of the Annurashi sniggered, proving that even the gods can be pricks. A coldness flooded through me, and I had an almost overwhelming urge to unleash hell upon them, wipe the smug grins off their faces permanently and destroy everything. *No. It's not their fault. It's mine.*

"Does it think it has become an Eternal?" one of them asked its fellows while watching me, trying to gauge my reaction. He had golden hair and eyes like chips of polished silver. He was garbed in armor wrought from plates of some lucent, glass-like substance and looked every inch the god, save for the grit in his beard.

I took a breath. *Play the game, Blake, play the game.* "No squire, I don't." I pointed to his chin. "You've got crumbs." Those who were paying attention to our exchange laughed at their brother's expense. He smirked, brushed his beard, and carried on feasting. No one invited me to join the party, but then why would they? I wasn't a nib, raised to eat with gilded prongs. Not that this divine crew was any more refined than your average yokel lordlings. They belched and farted and dribbled just like any mortal only instead of holding their revels in some glorified cattle shed, they had an inhospitable castle on a mountain, in the arse end of nowhere. *And people worship these culls.* Some half-remembered scripture concerning false idols came to mind as I watched them gorge. Disappointingly undignified though they were, I intended to spend a good while in this bone bag, so I kept my tongue behind my teeth and merely wished that they would choke on their rocky feast rather than saying so. I went over to Rowan. "Did you learn anything else from killing me?"

Cool as water, she wiped her mouth with the back of her hand and offered me a platter of flint chips, like she hadn't recently cut my throat. "Weren't you listening? You've gained the ability to reincarnate, perhaps infinitely."

I selected a small piece of stone, sniffed it. "Yes, but let's pretend I'm not a wise and ancient godling, versed in all matters metaphysical." Although my thoasan teeth were capable of cracking bone, I'd never tried to eat rock. I was pleasantly surprised when I bit into the flake and it broke as easily as a piece of stale bread that it tasted zesty and gray was unexpected.

Rowan took a bite from an apple-sized pebble. "You're a lucky cove, Breed." She took another bite. "More than lucky."

Anger spiked as I recalled the time I'd spent at the mercy of Shallunsard's demons. "You think so?"

She snorted. "Yes. I do. You're as close to immortal as any being has ever been, in spirit if not in flesh. I'd say that makes you lucky."

I glanced around the table. "You lot are immortal. D'you consider yourselves 'lucky' or do you think you're here because you deserve it? Or is it that, like me, it's probably just a random quirk of Fate?"

The gorging slowed, chatter abated, and heads turned in my direction. The red smell of anger bloomed in the room. "We live long lives but pass through death's door eventually and only once." Rowan raised a glass to her brothers and sisters. A Shennish looking annurashi with hair like an anchor rope wrapped around her head glared at Rowan. An image flashed into my mind of formless creatures writhing in darkness, of desolation that smelled of ink and tasted of Tuesday. Rowan grunted dismissively.

Compared to the rest of the eidolons she seemed most like a mortal, probably because she spent her time meddling in their affairs. She picked up another pebble, brandished it at rope hair as though about to give her a proper basting for whatever affront her disturbing thought pictures had caused. But before she had chance to engage, the doors behind me were thrown open, stilling all conversation. An ancient crone sitting on a floating throne drifted into the hall. She headed directly for the table, forcing me to leap aside or be struck by the levitating chair.

The Annurashi rose as one and bowed in deference to what had to be the oldest of the Elderlings. She grunted her acknowledgment and set herself down beside Rowan, demonstrating a measure of favoritism that didn't go unnoticed.

"Dearest child." The elderling gently brushed an errant wisp of hair from Rowan's face. "You look tired. Have they been misbehaving again?"

"No. We have a guest." She glanced at me. A handful of tiny, winged lizards flew out of the tangled nest of the crone's hair as she gestured impatiently at a plate of flints. It was quickly passed along the table and the crone idly picked at them, sniffed, and discarded several pieces until she found one that pleased her all the while keeping her eye on me. "Pray, remind me, who is this naked gawker?"

"They call me, Breed," I said.

She frowned as though she didn't understand and turned to Rowan. "What did it say?"

More images tumbled through my mind that, by some sense innate to this form I knew came from Rowan. Iridescent scales flew apart and become birds' wings, which became burning petals and then wisps of smoke. By reincarnating in this bone bag I'd gained access to a mode of communication unique to the Annurashi. Such a pity then that I didn't understand it. The images faded like dreams upon waking.

The crone nodded. "Breed, eh? I didn't recognize you." She grabbed a handful of grit and stuffed it in her mouth.

"I hardly recognize myself," I said and tried some of the grit. It tasted of purple and velvet, with just a hint of melancholy, estuary mud, and grape— a combination that was quite delicious.

After the Annurashi had eaten their fill, human servants began clearing away the platters. Unlike their masters, the mortals were a sickly-looking crew. It wasn't that they looked starving or beaten— traits common amongst serfs and slaves. Like Jeo, they appeared to be in the grip of a fever. In contrast, the Annurashi looked much as you'd expect gods to look; perfect and healthy to the point of glowing. While the humans went about their work, the eternals chatted amongst themselves. More than once I heard them mention Shallunsard and saw images of fire and blood.

The Eldest withdrew and floated over to the window, accompanied by her flock of miniature dragons. There she stayed, gazing resolutely into the storm as though divining the future written in the sastruga ridges that patterned the mountains, her eyes filled with the reflection of dancing snow.

Jeo entered the chamber and bowed to Rowan before handing me a robe. He coughed, wiped blood-flecked spittle from his lips. "What ails you, man?" I asked as I put on the fine garment.

He cast a nervous glance over his shoulder and lowered his voice. "The air up here is thin and doesn't sit well with mortals."

His hand brushed against mine. I saw an image of sulfur burning with sickly, yellow flames. "I hope they pay you well for working here," I said.

"They're teaching us the secrets of their art. What more could they give?" He sounded offended.

"Oh, I don't know— gold, silver, gems perhaps?"

He tried to stifle another cough. "Even now, after everything you've seen, everything you've done, you still value such things?"

"Er, yes and so do most coves."

He glanced at me like I was a freshly laid turd before storming off, evidently displeased. I didn't care what he thought of me, despite the violent inception of this body I was growing to like my new senses. I could hear how the robe felt against my cold skin and taste the color of what I ate. The new sensations were enthralling, the smallest, most insignificant things enchanting, like the tiny piece of grit that had caught between my teeth that tasted like Thursday, gentle laughter, and winter sunshine.

"Breed?" Rowan was standing in front of me, clicking her fingers. Time had passed unnoticed while I'd been listening to the texture of my hair and enjoying the taste of candlelight. The table had been moved and replaced by sofas and couches on which the Annurashi languished in postprandial, silent conversation. The fire burned bright and warmly golden. The Eldest was still staring out of the window.

"What?" I said to Rowan.

"We've decided that we want you to help us save the world." My first reaction was to laugh in her face. But as I was tired of dying I waited for her to continue. "We want you to face Shallunsard. Take him down, as you might say." While she talked, the other Annurashi pretended they weren't listening. They obviously didn't know that I was privy to their collective thought images, which were flitting around the room like razor-winged moths, mauve, and glistening.

"Please, go on," I said to Rowan. I was only half listening but I tried to appear attentive.

"We will arm you with the mightiest weapons," she smiled patronizingly, as though me being a lowly street tough I'd be impressed, as though I'd forgotten what it was like to fight the demon.

A blue-haired fellow in matching leather armor strode over and clamped his hand on my shoulder like we were old friends. "We will gird you with the strongest wards, the oldest, most powerful magics. You will be invincible." He smiled. His rock breaking teeth shone like pearls.

"That is really very, very kind of you, and I don't mean to sound ungrateful, but if you can muster such a mighty arsenal and such powerful sorcery, why don't *you* fight him? Surely, you could defeat him more easily than a mere mortal?"

Worried glances flew between them and thought images skittered around the room like bats scared from their roost. Rowan spoke up. "We can't."

"Ah. I suppose that answers that then," I said.

Rowan raised an eyebrow, but my cynicism was entirely lost on the blue-hued creature.

"We're too closely matched," Rowan explained.

"That's why we created the Mage Lords," Blue Hair added. "And they did a fine job, until, well." He sighed like I should know what the fuck he was talking about.

Rowan sent an image of blades and serpents and the taste of rust to her brother. He took my hand and gazed into my eyes like a lover. "You smell like a poem that I wrote in Old Khaskarak before the blood tide rose and drowned the city."

"Er, thanks." I nodded and smiled at the loon and pretended that I hadn't heard Rowan's warning thought image.

He stroked my hair. His touch smelled of worm casts and sand. "So like us, but not one of us."

"There's also only one of me. How am I going to get near Shallunsard? He commands an army of demonspawn."

"Leave his army to us," Rowan said as she steered the blue loon back to the sofa.

I forged a look of sincere and thoughtful contemplation, as befitted a hero about to embark on a daring quest, a task made easier by my new minted angelic countenance. I hadn't the slightest intention of going against the demon. I'd played that game before and lost, spectacularly. I didn't intend to be on the same landmass as Shallunsard, let alone go toe-to-toe with him ever again.

As I saw it, the only reason these rum culls didn't want to fight him was that they feared him. He'd trimmed their numbers during the Schism War, so they'd taught the Mage Lords, who in turn made the warspawn after they'd also taken a beating. As with mortals, so it was with gods when it came to passing the shit spoon down the line. I wanted none of it. I was alive and would soon be free and far from here, which was how I intended to stay. I gave Rowan my best, fake sincere smile. "A friend once told me there comes a time in a person's life when they have to make a choice." I didn't mention that the soft-hearted idealist had ended up with his head stuck on a spike, proving what little he knew. I squared up and unflinching, looked her straight in the eye. "I will help. I will fight Shallunsard."

Chapter Nine

After I had agreed to go against Shallunsard the Annurashi lost interest in me, which suited me well enough. I slipped out of the hall, Jeo and a handful of his fellow flunkies were playing cards in the antechamber. They stopped when they saw me, conversation died.

I nodded and made to leave, but Jeo stood up and interposed himself between me and the exit. I pushed images of scarlet and iron to the forefront of my mind, but then I remembered that they couldn't see, feel, or taste my thoughts. "What do you want?" I asked.

A little pebble of a woman shoved past him. "We don't want anything from you, Breed." Like Jeo's, the dumpling's wide gray eyes shone with fever. She folded her arms, drew her bloodless lips down in a tight, horseshoe of disapproval. "You're a curse, a demon-touched blight."

"Oh, my," I exclaimed in mock horror. "It seems not even the gods can get good help these days."

A disgruntled mutter ran through the gathering. "You think we're servants?" The woman drew herself up to an unimpressive height. "We are sorcerers of renown."

I smiled. "Only in your head, pudding."

Jeo put his hand on the woman's arm. "We can't trust you, Breed." Jeo sounded less vehement than his comrade. Others in the group mumbled their agreement.

"And? Did I ask you to trust me?" I pinched his cheek. "I've not offered to do anything for you. We don't have to trust each other. Move on with your lives, be happy."

He pulled away. "I k... know your type," Jeo stammered. "I grew up around strutting coves like you, full of shit and bravado, too stupid to see further than the end of a rope. But you should know better now. You *know* what's at stake." The soft cull looked like he was on the verge of tears. He coughed.

"Oh, I know, all right. Tell me, Jeo, as one rum cove to another, where do your precious masters keep their sparklies? Only, if I'm going to save the world, I'll be needing to purchase a few odds and ends." I patted myself down. "And I seem to have left my purse with another body." It was a cruel taunt, but I wasn't feeling kindly disposed to Jeo and his friends, people who in other circumstances wouldn't piss on me if I was on fire.

"Gods' sake. You will never change, will you? The world is burning." He found a measure of bravery and squared up to me. I could smell the sickness on his breath, taste the cancer feasting on his flesh. "You're a selfish, small-m... minded bastard." His stammer grew worse the more agitated he became. "You'd b... burn if someone threw a diamond into a fire."

I laughed, I'd meant to mock but it sounded like gentle rain. "What's that, pukepail? I pray you speak plainly. Your mumbler's tongue is ill-suited to clever words and earnest speechifying."

He bristled, which was all to the good, as I intended to offend him. His comrades took hold of him, held him back. The air thickened with the acid petrichor that heralded the impending use of magic. I stared him down. They might very well be renowned sorcerers, but they were no match for me and they knew it. He lowered his gaze. The air cleared. His comrades began to draw him away with soft words and solicitous hugs, but he pulled away, spun, and had the audacity to grab my robe. "The fate of the world and everyone in it might rest in your hands; gods help us. Do not betray humanity, Breed. For once in your life, put others before yourself."

I unpeeled his hands from the robe. "Humanity, eh? And what about the rest of us? What about the warspawn and the schism touched?"

His cheeks flushed. He let go, looked anywhere but at me. "You know what I mean."

"Yes. I do." Before things got all unnecessary, the door swung open and the crone floated in on her throne. She dropped her beady gaze upon me. Not for the first time, I saw in the Annurashi something of the hawk eyeing up its prey. Cowed by the Elderling's presence, Jeo and his fellow obsequiates shuffled aside.

She sniffed at the errant wisps of emotion hanging in the air. Her curiosity uncoiling like a cat's tail. "What's this?"

"Just a little chin wag, dame." I shot her what I considered to be a charming smile. "A bout of friendly badinage."

She wrinkled her nose, unimpressed by my attempt to dissemble. "Come with me, Breed," she said and floated out of the room. In preference to staying and beating the shit out of the hired help, I followed. Jeo watched me with a bladed glare which I acknowledged with a wink. The cull was right, I didn't give two fucks for the fate of humanity, or any race come to that. I was entirely concerned with the continued existence and wellbeing of me and no one else.

***

I'd never given much thought to what the home of the godlike Annurashi might look like, which was just as well. No fantasy I could have conjured, no matter how modest, could have matched the dreary reality. The walls, floor, and ceilings beyond the hall and antechamber were carved from the same characterless, gray stone of indeterminate origin. The walls were bare and although the keep was built on a grand scale, the whole of it was drab and dusty, decorated with an abundance of cobwebs and little else.

The Eldest steered her throne towards a passageway that wound its way up and around a nameless tower. Her lizards fluttered around her head, fought each other and squabbled as they jostled for prime position. Some nestled in her hair, one sat on the back of her throne and squawked at me. Bronze and green and russet, the miniature dragons looked like carvings come to life. "Where are we going?" I asked. My voice echoed in the empty hallway.

"Away from the chatter."

"I see."

"You see nothing, fustilugs. That's your problem and your blessing."

I laughed. "You've a rum flaptrap on you for a godling."

"Godling?" She gave a rattling laugh. "I wouldn't weigh what you know of 'gods' against that which you don't if I were you. The scales will not balance in your favor."

We continued in silence. I say silence, but a steady stream of images leaked from the Eldest. The psychic incontinence spoke of loss, sorrow, frustration, and her desire to take a nap. It was a complex mix of the mundane and fantastical all bundled together, and beyond my ability to unpick or desire to interpret. I ignored the mental flux and directed my attention to working out where in the world I might be. Although extensive, the view through the slit windows offered few clues. All I could see as we climbed the circular tower were white-capped peaks and snow-filled valleys that stretched into the distance. It seemed I'd landed in the dreariest castle, in the dullest corner of a doomed world. After about a hundred turns around the tower, we arrived at a door. It was unexpectedly grand— wildly opulent compared to anything else I'd seen in the keep. Eight feet wide and ten feet high, it was cut from a slab of opaque crystal and bound in silver filigree that had been crafted to look like twisting vines.

The Eldest hovered before the door and stroked the vitreous surface. "It's been... some time since I came here." Her words birthed a vision of darkness of a moss-smothered dell, of slow rot, things crawling through fecund undergrowth, and muffled screams.

None of which filled me with confidence. Instinct told me that I was on dangerous ground.

"I don't know how much time has passed, but some certainly." She waved her hand. The vines curled back on themselves, and the door swung open. The dragonets flitted inside ahead of the crone. I resolved that, as soon as the old loon had shown me whatever she wanted to show me, I would excuse myself and quietly abscond from the keep.

"I'm no architect, but this is bigger than the tower, surely?" My words echoed through the vast expanse and were lost in the shaded depths of the cavernous room.

The old dame shrugged. "It's just a matter of perspective."

Bollocks is it. The corridor had tapered as we'd climbed the tower and should have led to a modest turret room no more than twenty feet across. This was a cavern, which alone would have been astounding but what was within the improbable space reduced its unnatural proportions to a merely interesting side note. Suspended on a web of chains or supported on slender columns was a fractured mosaic of iron platforms. They were all shapes and sizes, set high and low in the vast emptiness, they stretched into the shadows. Again, this strange wonder paled in comparison to what was on the rusting platforms.

"There must be hundreds of them." I wandered into the chamber, my gaze darting from one angle gate to the next. Woken by our presence, glow stones in the walls came to life and cast a lambent radiance across the cavern. Some of the stones were little more than piles of rubble but many appeared to be intact and looked like they'd been lifted whole from wherever they had been erected. The Eldest threw her arms wide. Her lizards flickered up, flew a ragged halo around her before scattering amongst the stones. "Behold," she intoned. "The heart of everything."

"Why are they here?" I asked. From somewhere in the chamber I could hear the faint hum of a mosquito, which was one of my least favorite insects.

"Why shouldn't they be here?" A spark of anger lit in the Eldest's glassy eyes. Her grip tightened on the arms of her throne. "I brought them here, after the Schism War."

"Why?"

"Because nothing good came of using them," she said without meeting my gaze.

The dragonets screeched and darted acrobatically, tumbling as they dived and swooped between the stones. Like other angle gates that I'd seen these stones were set in rings. Most were a single band, others two or three deep. Some were large enough for a company of knights to stand inside, but at least one was so small that I almost crushed it underfoot as I explored. The construction also varied. Many were rough-hewn from unexceptional span stone, while others had been painstakingly carved from precious hoblite or legendary gemlyne.

I climbed onto another platform. Chains rang like bells in the frosty air. "Do they still work?"

"No. They're dead." The image she bled was of a crashing wave, and the smell was akin to burning sulfur.

"What killed 'em?"

"That which kills everything; a lack of purpose."

"I've no particular purpose and I'm still alive."

"For every rule, there is an exception."

There seemed little point in arguing with a mad godling and I conceded with a curt nod. Her gaze shifted to the nearest ring of stones. She floated over and gently caressed one of them. "You know what these are?"

"Angle gates, cruelly murdered by lack of use."

She gave a theatrical sigh. "Not one for listening are you, Breed? I said, lack of purpose. They are indeed angle gates. I hear you have a knack for them."

"I got lucky finding the Hammer of the North, but other than that I can't say I've had many dealings. Tobias…" For a moment I forgot that my friend was dead, for a moment the image I conjured in my mind was of him throwing his notebook across a room when he was struggling to align a gate. And then I remembered. "I knew people who had more skill with them than I."

If she noticed the stumble, she didn't comment. She floated off the platform and drifted amongst the gates, shadowed by her dragons. After a couple of minutes, she stopped and swiped her hand through a cobweb sheet revealing a ring of rough-hewn, black monoliths. "These were old when I was a girl." She drifted into the ring. "You can't beat him, you know."

"If you mean Shallunsard, I'm acutely aware of that. I beat him once when I had the hammer, then tried it without and he basted me."

"He was supposed to be the best of them. In him, I thought I had created something magnificent, something perfect."

"We all make mistakes."

"I made two. I made him, and I let the others teach mortals the art of sorcery. It was less than successful. Shallunsard became obsessed with starting again, with wiping the slate clean. And they quite rightly opposed him." She sighed.

"Oh, dear." I stifled a yawn.

She slowly revolved to face me. "Is that the extent of your concern, your interest in the matter?"

I thought it only polite to give it a second thought before reaching my conclusion. "Yeah, pretty much."

"Really?"

"Aye. Is this a test?" I was confused. "You've told me what happened, and I believe you. He wants to destroy the world and start again, nobody else does, and I can't beat him. I get it, I understand. Can I go now?"

"Astounding."

"Thank you?" I still wasn't sure if this was a test.

She chuckled. "We created the Paradox of Power, you know? As a compromise, but mortals are clever, they found ways around it."

"I know." I'd done so myself. "Anyway, I don't understand why you bothered; sorcery's overrated."

She laughed. "Perhaps. Of course, it's nothing compared to what it was when the Mage Lords were around. Ah. They were so talented but so frivolous. They used magic for everything. Fighting, healing, building, changing the way the clouds moved across the sky, the color of a peacock's eye. So very wasteful." Waves of sorrow and anger rolled off her like furnace heat. The dragonets felt it too and shrieking, took to the air. At a glance from the Eldest, they turned into a flurry of autumn leaves that spun and twisted themselves into a copper scaled serpent. The creature regarded me with diamond eyes before it slithered through the air and around the Eldest's thin shoulders. It coiled around her neck and sucked the tip of its tail into its mouth. "Between them, they've worn me thin, Breed. You have no idea how close they've come to destroying everything."

"By using magic?"

"Sorcery eats the substance of a place, spits out poison, warps the fabric of the world."

"So, your boy was right, in a way."

She shook her head. "No. He's just as bad. He wants to take magic from mortals but would still use it himself. Arrogance."

"Kids, eh?" As usual, I was the hostage of Fate, forced to bide my time until an opportunity to abscond presented itself. Since the crone and her brood had, in different ways, pegged me as an idiot, I thought I'd play up to the role. "Have you tried talking to him? He's your get, mayhap he'll listen to you, change his evil ways and stop trying to destroy the world."

She laughed, quite spoiling my fun. "Do you listen to your mother?"

"Good point." I sidled towards the door. "This has been very interesting, but I might as well be on my way." I gave an empty-handed shrug. "As you say, I can't beat him."

Her eyes sparkled, fever-bright. Something changed. I felt it, like a net slowly closing around me. "You're a singular creature, Breed."

"Again, I thank you."

"I don't think that I could make something like you even if I tried. You're unpredictable and yet, here you are. Whether you know it or not, your actions are guided by Fate in ways that not even I, the Eldest of the Eldest can comprehend."

"It's not my fault."

"I know, child. You're a pawn in a greater game."

"That's what I always say." I edged closer to the door.

"The problem with my children, even sweet Rowan, is that they lack imagination."

"Aye, that's a genuine pity."

"They think they can defeat Shallunsard with more powerful weapons. He, in turn, will raise an even bigger army of more vengeful demons than last time, and so it goes. She waved her hand dismissively. "You see?"

"Yes. I do." I agreed just to shut her up, but when I thought about it, I really did understand. "They do the same predictable things over and over. Bigger weapons, more powerful spells, meaner demons, sure. I get it. The Annurashi only got the upper hand last time because the Mage Lords created the warspawn who finally did for your boy."

She tried to hide her anger behind an anemic smile, but I saw it quicken, saw the blood rise in her sunken cheeks. "Ah, yes. The warspawn. An inspired creation." A flood of images boiled from her. Twisted, tortured bodies, screaming, monstrous infants, beings torn apart and remade over and over. The smell of blood and fire, the acid burn of sorcery. The brutality staggered me.

"Just out of interest, how did they make the warspawn?"

She tried to brush the question off, make it small with a weary sneer. "How is any living thing made? How were you made?"

"My mother fucked my father at least once. But I'm talking about the first warspawn. How did the Mage Lords make them?"

"The warspawn were created in a time of need, child. Things were done. Sacrifices were made. But you saw my thoughts. You already know the answer to your question." She gave a smile like a cut-throat razor.

The temperature dropped. My breath came sharp, curdled the air. "Aye, I did. I just wanted to hear you say so."

"If only they'd killed him." She sagged, her face fell into heavy folds. At that moment she looked like any other aged creature staring down the barrel of mortality, trapped in a failing body and tortured by regrets. If she wasn't a meddlesome godling, I might have pitied her. "I made a mistake," she rasped. "I thought a few centuries left alone to think about what he'd done might change him. I was wrong. My children cannot change."

"We all make mistakes."

"He is going to destroy everything. Between them, they will tear this world apart. It might take centuries, but eventually they will succeed and nothing in this world can stop them." She straightened, pointed a knotted finger at me. "Oh, you may shrug and roll your eyes, but you're immortal now, centuries will pass like that." She clicked her fingers. The serpent opened its eyes, saw nothing to hold its interest and closed them again.

"Forgive me, Dame. These are dire tidings."

"Don't be facetious."

"So, what do you want with me? If it's inevitable, why am I here? Did you just need someone to talk to? Are you lonely? What?"

She slammed her hand on the arm of her throne. "It was a whim. I'm trying to be unpredictable, but it isn't easy."

"Oh, I don't know."

"That much is evident."

The humming noise was too constant to be a mosquito but was proving to be just as irritating. "So, can I leave now?"

"Aye, child. Go." She spoke without looking at me. "Rowan will give you anything you need, clothes, a mount, food, gold." She turned her head, shot me a knowing smile. "I know you're fond of gold."

"I like the things gold can buy."

"I understand. Oh, there is something you can do for me before you go."

I smiled, made an extra effort to look amenable. I didn't trust the old snake or my ability to hide my thoughts from her. "What's that?"

"There is a gate in here somewhere that still holds power. Find it for me. I'm told you have a knack for such things."

How such a simple thing was beyond her, was beyond me. "Surely the mother of all sorcery can cast a spell and trace the gate?"

"Indulge an old woman."

I made a show of tapping a few stones and rubbing my jaw before shaking my head. "I'm sorry, I just—"

"Look again." She smiled as sweetly as Mattie the Drop would do just before she coshed her mark over the head and robbed them of everything, including their teeth. As I was keen not to fall foul of the old crow's temper I searched in earnest for the live gate while she watched from beneath her heavy brow. After an hour or so of searching, I found the damn thing. The ring hummed quietly, the stones vibrated beneath my hand. There were eight in all, carved from a greenish stone and set on a platform that was covered in sand. Like all the others in the cavernous room, they were thick with cobwebs. They also smelled faintly of salt. I was about to dramatically announce these facts when I turned to find the Eldest hovering directly behind me.

"Activate the gate, Breed." Her tone was sweet and utterly, magically compelling.

"You cunt," I said as I turned the stones.

"You have no idea." She reached out with a claw-tipped finger. The space within the ring rippled, thickened like water.

"Find a solution to our problem, Breed." Held in thrall by her will, I could do nothing as she shoved me through the gate.

Chapter Ten

I'd traveled through angle gates twice before. Once to the hived-off battlefield where the Hammer of the North had died and once across the Empire. The journey to the Hammer's tomb had been little more than a step. The trip across the Empire had been unpleasant; like being stretched on a rack while being burned alive. This was worse.

It felt like I'd been eaten alive by a swarm of ravenous fire beetles who had then crapped the remains into a volcano and that wasn't the worst of it. When the demented crone god shoved me through the gate, I was midway between drawing a breath, an act I finished when I fell into another existence. Alas, that last breath, begun in another world, where breathing was a harmless necessity, proved to be almost instantly fatal in whatever hell I'd ended up. After falling through the gate, I drew, not air into my lungs, but acidic water. I spluttered and coughed and in so doing, swallowed more of the corrosive liquid, while at the same time, I was crushed by an enormous weight of water.

It looked like I'd fetched up at the bottom of a lake or ocean, but it was hard to see exactly where I was because my eyes were burning, and I was drowning. The last thing I saw as I sank to the softly shimmering sand was a forest of kelp and the wide, shining eyes of some amphibane-like creatures peering out from between the thick, gently waving fronds. It must have been somewhat of a surprise for them, seeing a stranger appear out of nowhere, spluttering and choking and clutching their throat before dying. It might also have been a regular occurrence; a spectator sport on which bets were placed on the length of time it took to die. Perhaps unwitting competitors were awarded points for style. Either way, I was soon past caring.

***

I returned to life, in a murk-shrouded pit. Although it was probably too late, I held my breath and slapped my fins across my face in a reflexive gesture of protection which was when I realized that my hands were webbed and that I was breathing the acidic water as easily as I had previously breathed air.

I floated into a sitting position from where I could see that I had been lying amongst a pile of decomposing corpses and bones. Those that still had flesh, my previous incarnation amongst them, were being feasted upon by an army of tiny crabs and snails that were busily snipping and chewing. I realized then that the fatty taste in the water was the soapy wax of liquefying corpse flesh. I held my breath and paddled up and out of my grave, whereupon I saw the watery world with sharper eyes than those I'd possessed when I'd entered it.

I swam higher into clearer, warmer water and looked down upon the grave pit. The trench was the length of an Imperial schooner— about forty-five feet and filled with the jumbled carcasses of all manner of creatures. I wondered if the crone had sent these unfortunates here and if so, had any of them had a choice?

It took a while to master the skills required to swim effectively, to control the gases trapped within various organs that I had previously never possessed, as well as get over the fear I might drown with every breath I took. The body might be entirely different, but my instincts were still those of a thoasa, and I quickly learned the skills required to survive in this alien world. Basics of breathing and floating mastered, I flexed my fins and struck out for the surface, from where I guessed I would gain a better view of my surroundings.

I hadn't risen far before a creature emerged from the shadowed depth and darted towards me. It wasn't a fish, it was more like a brachuri crossed with an amphibane. I summoned a spell to mind. Flame bloomed in my palm and promptly extinguished itself because as all know fire and water are not boon companions. Before I had a chance to re-think the spell, the creature was floating two feet in front of me. She was unarmed and didn't look like she was about to launch an attack. She blinked a pair of huge, saucer eyes and a thin trail of air trickled from the corner of her wide mouth like a string of pearls.

"Who are you, stranger?" The creature spoke in a combination of gill flaps and throaty ululations. "You shouldn't be here. This water is unclean. Come," she said and took off towards the kelp, beckoning me over her shoulder as she sculled faster than I could swim. I took a last look at my beautiful, Annurashi corpse which was already being colonized by a host of hungry crustaceans before following her as quickly as I could.

As we sped through the water, past glittering shoals of fish and exotic sea beasts it struck me that I didn't know if I was being rescued or led to my doom. The creature I was following gave no hint as to her intentions and I lacked the wherewithal to read her body language. We had size in common, both being somewhere around eight feet tall, or long, depending on your choice of orientation and we both had rows of long, serrated fins running down our backs, arms, and legs.

"I am Layq." Her words were carried in a trail of silver bubbles that threaded through the water and burst by my ear pits.

"How appropriate. I'm Breed," I said, pushing the words forwards with some effort. I waved a webbed hand the size of a dinner plate in a bid to appear friendly. We both had long fleshy barbles that flowed from our temples, but as we passed into a shaft of bright, sunlit water, I saw that, like an amphibane, her skin was smooth. Mine was dimpled with the faint imprint of thoasan scales. We also differed in color. Where she was dark green on her back, fading to white on her underside, I was red, fading to orange. The aptly named Layq was naked save for a reed necklace, giving no clue as to her occupation if she had one, or her status. She could have been the queen of her kind or an outcast for all I knew.

I pulled up sharp, hung suspended in the water and tried to remember what the real me looked like, the fool who had lived twenty, blissfully ignorant years or so, without considering anything of import beyond the reach of my blade. *How the fuck did I end up here?* The details were hazy. I looked around. I didn't have a clue where I was, let alone what I had become.

The brachuribane stopped swimming. "Are you well?"

"No. not really. I just lost a splendid bone bag."

"What?"

"Nevermind. Yes. I'm fine. Wonderful. Couldn't be better."

"Then come, quickly."

I followed her to the swaying forest. I didn't know what I felt, truth be told. I was hale and alive, but I'd died again, and that fucking crone had thrust me unwilling from one world into another. I had lost control of my life and that vexed me greatly.

"Welcome to our home," she said as we swam into the shimmering embrace of the forest. To my eyes, 'home' was nothing more than a bed of seaweed. There were no scrapes or nests or buildings that I could discern. What I could see with remarkable clarity was the flow of sea currents as they wove through the greenery and bound the wavering branches and stems in cords of water. I could also feel the subtle pressure of oceanic waves.

Layq and I swam under bridges of coral-mantled reef and across dark fissures until we came to a silt dune in the heart of the forest. Sat upon it was an old looking cove whose wrinkly skin rippled gently in the current. Layq came to a halt. "This is Leader Trivo," she announced with a bow.

The leader didn't have a throne or crown, he wasn't guarded by a phalanx of surly bruisers, nor was he attended by a gaggle of fawning sycophants, although some curious brachuribane had come to ogle the red and orange stranger. Trivo was light green with a saggy, white gut. He was sitting cross-legged on the sand. Beside him, tethered to a spike of coral was a gelatinous sack of glittering, black eggs. "Where are you from?" he asked with a spray of bubbles. Although he appeared to be older than Layq his great, green eyes were lively and infused with a keen intelligence.

"I came through the angle gate, but I drowned, but then I got better, sort of." I didn't have the right kind of facial muscles to smile apologetically, but I did my best. "I changed into a form more suited to this world." *Not that I had any choice in the matter.*

"Did you see any people like us through the gate, or wherever it is that you came from?" He indicated himself, Layq and the others with a sweep of his fin.

"Sorry, milord, but I didn't, and I'm not sure where I came from."

"You don't know where you've come from?" The gathered brachuibanes bubbled, seemingly all keen to know.

"Not exactly. It wasn't my home. Have you heard of the Annurashi?" I hadn't expected that I'd have to give a long explanation about who I was or where I came from. It was awkward and not a little tiresome, but by the way they'd crowded around me, the brachuribane were keen to know all the details.

"No, we haven't. What is the Annurashi?"

"A bunch of pricks."

"What is—"

"Never mind. Just, if anything that calls itself an Annurashi ever comes through that gate, my best advice to you is to kill it quickly."

He clasped his hands over his massive stomach and acknowledged the murmuring of the crowd. "They might have already done so. There are legends and well, you saw the others in the pit. You're not the first to come through, although you are the first to survive." His wide mouth twitched into something like a smile. "Sort of. Are you sure you didn't see anyone who looked like us on the other side?" he asked again only more slowly.

"I'm sure. The other side is, well, it's full of air. If any of your kind went through, I don't think it would have gone well for them." They showed no sign of understanding what I was saying. "Can you breathe air?"

He blinked slowly. "What's air?"

"Never mind."

Conversation stalled after that and we floated in uncomfortable silence. I occupied myself watching streams of bubbles trickle thoughtfully from the corners of Trivo's downturned mouth as he wrestled with the significance of my presence in his domain. After some minutes he shook his head, sending swirling eddies spiraling towards me.

"How can people live in a world and not know its name?"

"You need to let that go, Trivo. Really, it's not uncommon where I come from. Why, I've met many a denizen of my hometown of Appleton, who don't know their own name, let alone the name of their town or country."

"That's very strange," he said while flicking an inquisitive shrimp off his foot. "Why did you come here?"

"I've no idea."

"Why don't you have an idea?"

"Yes, why?" Layq asked echoing the leader.

"I was sent here by an insane, old crone of a god to…" I flailed. "To save my world from an equally insane demon." Flurries of bubbles rose from the gathering. "I know, hard to believe isn't it?"

Trivo rested his chin on his palm. "And what is your world called?"

"Sweet salvation, I don't know what the world's called. I'm just a…" I was going to say Guild Blade, but that might lead to another endless string of questions. "I'm just an ordinary cove caught up in matters that don't concern me. It's not my fault. I'm a pawn of Fate."

"That's unfortunate. I was hoping you might be able to tell us why all those creatures came here to die. As I said, there are legends, but nobody knows for certain, which concerns me." He reached out and absently stroked his egg sack.

Layq piped up. "Some think it's for ritual purposes, but none of them ever live long enough to tell us."

Trivo nodded, fanned his fins, and drifted off his sandy perch to float in a midline current. "It's most disturbing."

"Ah, now they might not have known that the gate led to an underwater world. In fact, going on personal experience, I'm sure they didn't."

"*Under* water?" Trivo squinted. "Where else would it lead?" He released a rapid burst of tiny bubbles. The others joined in making the water fizz.

I looked questioningly at Layq.

"They're kreeing because it's funny," she answered.

It looked fun, so I thought I'd give it a go. I rolled water over the ridged roof of my mouth until it fizzed and tickled my tiny nose holes. It *was* funny—absurdly so. "I think they came here to steal your people, so that they could turn 'em into warspawn," I said. The kreeing stopped.

Layq swam over and floated before me. "What did you say?"

"Warspawn. They made warspawn out of them—slaves, and I'll wager not just your folk. There were these wicked coves called Mage Lords. They twisted your people, made warspawn out of them. That's what happened to those who went through the gate, or they just died. Either way, it wasn't nice." I looked around the gathering, but it was hard to tell if they were stunned, or just silently absorbing what I told them. "The Mage Lords used sorcery to warp and twist and finally breed from those they'd stolen until they'd shaped the weapons they needed to fight the demon hordes."

"You saw this?" Layq asked.

She was so close I could feel her gills flutter water against my skin. I held her gaze. "Not as such." *I lived it.* "I saw it in a vision, but trust me, it's the truth. They found beings with traits they could make use of and fucked with them."

She shook her head, released a steady stream of large, thoughtful bubbles. "Why would they do that?"

"Because they needed us to do their dirty work; fight their battles, serve their drinks that kind of thing." I looked around. There wasn't a hint of recognition on any of their faces.

"But you're one of us," Trivo declared. "A strange color perhaps, but you're one of the People." His fellows mumbled their agreement.

This was starting to give me a headache. "Fuck sake. Yes, I'm like you *now*, but I wasn't before. Inside, I'm different. I'm warspawn, mostly." Not a flicker. "It's complicated."

Trivo called Layq over and the two of them proceeded to engage in a protracted, heads-down, intense confabulation. Eventually, they came to some conclusion and I was summoned to join them.

Trivo drew himself up. I expected some lofty pronouncement but instead, he belched a cloud of mucus water in my face. "Welcome, Warspawn-on-the-inside."

Chapter Eleven

My acceptance by the People was celebrated with a feast *of sorts* because nothing says 'celebration' like seagrass and kelp sprouts. It was less strange fare than stones, but also much less tasty. During the gathering I was informed that my aquatic brethren ate for nutritional purposes, rather than pleasure. They didn't sing or dance or play any instruments either.

"So, what do you do for fun?" I asked Layq who was stripping the thick outer skin of a reed with her tiny, razor-sharp teeth.

"Fun?" She blinked. "We live. We are here together."

"Well, yes, living is a pleasure sometimes, and I've heard that spending time with one's kin is a real joy, but what *activities* do you indulge in to alleviate the daily drudge? You know, like whoring and gambling?"

She gave me a blank look. "I'm sure we don't do those things, whatever they are. We live, we breed. That is enough."

"I can see why amphibane are so valued as servants."

"What are amphibane?"

"They're warspawn. Not much use in war, but they make good..." This conversation was veering into awkward territory. "They make wonderful servants on account of being placid folk with few wants. Unlike the brachuri, who are fierce fuckers."

Her gold green eyes flashed. Her gills pumped. "Water can be placid, not the People. The sea can be fierce, the hunters are fierce, the People aren't." A flat, matter-of-fact bubble slid out of the corner of her mouth for emphasis.

I'd unintentionally insulted her. "Hey, they're not like you. It's like they took your people and somehow split them. The amphibane are easy going, they don't want much, like you lot."

"The People want to live. That is everything."

I didn't want to get into a philosophical discussion because it isn't my strong suit, and yet I'd somehow managed it. "That's true, I suppose. Lovely grass by the way, very green."

"And these brachuri, are they perhaps more strong than aggressive?"

"No, they're aggressive bastards right enough." I made a snippy snappy gesture. "Take your head off as soon as look at you."

She snorted. "Your egg sack must have leaked." The brachuribane nearest to us began to kree. I was about to ask what was so funny when a huge shadow passed overhead. Everyone scattered, leaving me alone in a cloud of swirling sand and half-chewed kelp shoots. The pressure of the water increased. I dived aside, narrowly avoiding being snapped up by a giant fish. The speed of its descent spun the water into a vortex. I was caught, turned upside down, and blinded by sediment while the fish worried hungrily and angrily at a knot of kelp.

It wasn't as big as the kraken, but it was big enough to swallow me whole and still have room for dessert. It hung perpendicular to the seabed, gray and silver, with a poorly healed gash as long as my body, running down its flank. It nosed through the murk, searching for where its meal had gone. I held my breath, not that I thought it would matter much. Sometimes I hate being right. The grey-scaled beast stopped digging and swiveled a fist-sized eye in my direction. If I'd been a thoasa I would have already been swimming as fast as

I could away from the hungry fish, but I wasn't. I was a frilly finned numbskull, floating within striking distance of a critter that was fixing to devour me. I should have tried to apport, but I didn't know how to shape a spell made for air under the water. There were specialist sorcerers who worked with the elements, but I wasn't one of them.

The fish's caudal fin flicked up. It flexed, turned, and arrowed towards me, jaws agape, eyes bright with hunger. In that moment of deathly clarity, it occurred to me that I couldn't outswim the brute, so I'd have to kill it or become its next meal. *Fuck the angles.* I brought a spell to mind and unleashed a blast of lightning.

It turns out that casting sorcerous lightning into salty, acidic water isn't the wisest thing to do if you're also in the water. The blast spread and stunned the fish and a couple of brachuribane who were hiding nearby. I did not escape the wrath of my stupidity. The backlash of energy lit up my spine and froze the breath in my lungs. The next thing I knew the fish and I were floating opposite each other, both glaring angrily and impotently, paralyzed by the power of the ill-conceived spell. This was a lesson on how not to use sorcery or it would be if I survived. Thankfully, I came to my senses before the fish, which saved me the embarrassment of being eaten because of my rash actions. While it twitched and thrashed and fought its way back to full mobility, I shoved the stunned brachuribane into the kelp. My chest felt like it was bound in hot iron and every breath I drew was as painful as if I'd been kicked. I looked around for something I could use as a weapon, but nothing suitable presented itself. The fish shook off the effects of being stunned and came at me again.

I waited until it was almost on me before diving sideways and grabbing hold of its pectoral fin as it passed. Three of my claws snapped under the strain of hanging on as it sped through the water, powerful muscles rippling beneath its scales. I threw myself on its back and straddled its dorsal fin. It bucked and tried to snap its head around, but it couldn't reach me. The bloodshot madness in its eye told me it wasn't going to give up. The fish wanted me dead and in its belly. Its gills flared, and it tore off to the surface.

We ascended rapidly through the shimmering layers of the ocean. I kreed but I didn't know why. Being eaten by a giant, carnivorous fish wasn't funny and yet there I was, hanging onto a giant, angry fish, laughing my arse off. My grip began to slip which was apparently hilarious. I grew giddy and lightheaded as we raced towards the surface. I didn't want to die again, so I dug my feet into its flanks, rammed my fists into its gills, and tore at the soft flesh inside. Blood began to flow, obscuring my vision. I closed my eyes, dug deeper, ripped, and tore at the beast as consciousness began to slip away.

The fish arched its back and thrashed violently, throwing me off. I felt like my head was about to burst. If it came at me now, I wouldn't be able to defend myself or get away. It shuddered before curling up, nose to tail. I hung around long enough to make sure it was dead before diving for the relative safety of the kelp aware that the fountain of blood would draw every predator from miles around.

By the time I reached the topmost branches of the seaweed forest the lightheadedness had passed. I looked up to see something with a crest of brightly colored spines and a faceful of tentacles dart from the vast darkness. It tore a huge chunk out of the fish, spilling its umbles and provoking a feeding frenzy amongst the dozens of smaller beasts that had gathered for the feast. Layq swam up out of the reeds. Far from hailing me as a savior of brachuribane kind, she scowled as much as her batrachian face would allow. "What have you done?" She breathed out a rapid flurry of bubbles.

"Don't worry, it's dead," I said in a bid to reassure her. "I ripped out its breathing pipes." A light drizzle of fish guts began to fall. "You can tell Trivo the critter's been snuffed."

"He knows, we saw. He just doesn't know why."

That stumped me. I wondered if perhaps I was still suffering the ill-effects of being dragged too close to the surface where these watery culls weren't made to go. "What do you mean, *why*? The fang-faced fucker was trying to eat me, that's why."

She looked shocked, as though she had been the one roughly assaulted by the ugly brute. "It was hungry, injured. It probably hadn't eaten for weeks."

"And? you could have tried to flee but you didn't, you chose to kill it." A flurry of bubbles boiled from her mouth. She was angry, and I had no idea why.

"It attacked me," I spoke slowly in case I hadn't made myself clear. "That's just cause and besides, I doubt very much that I could have got away. I'm not used to this body."

Her barbles flared. "I told you, it was sick. It couldn't help itself. You could have escaped if you'd tried."

An accusing eyeball trailing a tangle of veins and flesh drifted between us. I swatted it aside. "The prospect of escaping was not uppermost in my mind, given that the toothsome cull had the advantage over me in every way save wit."

"That's debatable."

"Well, I'm not the one being eaten by all and sundry, am I? And while we're about it, I expected something other than admonishment for defending myself, and defending the rest of you, come to that."

The angry splutter of bubbles slowed. "I appreciate your desire to live, but surely, a creature with your abilities could have withstood the indignity of reincarnating? The Yanmula is dead forever." A thin, broken trail of bubbles pearled from the corner of her mouth. "They're few and we are many. I would have gladly died in your place."

"If only you'd said so at the time, we could have swapped."

"I didn't have a chance."

"Fuck's sake, it's just a fish."

"It was."

"So, we're in accord. What's the problem?"

"We're no more deserving."

"What? No. You are." I shook my head. "I thought I was the one who'd swum too close to the sky. You're a sentient being. I came back as one of you, not a sand crab. You're a higher creature. You're more important."

She blew another torrent of angry bubbles in my face. "Who says?"

"I don't fucking know, the gods, anyone with half an ounce of sense."

"What does 'higher' mean? You say it like it's a good thing, 'higher' means death here."

"All right. You're a more *important* species. Does that suit you better?"

"How can one creature be more important than another?" She backed me into the kelp which I would have been happy to let close around me, but she swept it aside. A glob of fish drifted down and gently landed on her shoulder. She stared at me long and hard as she brushed off the offending gobbet. "Please, explain it to me."

"You just are," I retorted. Not the most reasoned or nuanced answer I'll grant, but I was a thief, not a scholar and currently out of my depth in more ways than one. "You're more important than a crab or a fish, even a big fish, so just get over it."

She fanned her fins in short, angry bursts. Another piece of tail fell into the kelp. Layq gasped. "Do you see what you've done? You've polluted our home."

"Me? Yon fish did the polluting." I pointed to the carcass that was being torn apart by a multitude of fish and squid. She ignored me. "The fucking thing could just have easily killed you, or Trivo or any number of your kin."

"Which would have been lamentable."

Her agreement threw me. I sensed a trap. "Yes, yes it would. You see my point then?"

"No." She vented an angry spray of bubbles, her gills pulsed. "Do you think that we should kill everything that threatens us?"

"Are you serious?" The hard set of her mouth told me that she was. "Yes, I am. Where I come from that's exactly what we do. If something threatens us, we kill it. If a cull has something we want then most often, we kill them and take it. Killing solves a lot of problems. We kill to protect ourselves. We kill so that others may be saved. Killing is the answer to awkward problems. Killing is what we do, and we do it well."

The look she gave me was one of bewilderment mingled with horror and worse, disappointment. "It doesn't make sense. To kill because of want, to kill to save and protect? That doesn't make sense. What could have value or meaning in such a world?"

My mind was temporarily blank. "Lots of things." A weak answer I know, but it had been a trying day.

Layq recoiled slowly. "Your world must be a terrible place. No wonder your kind come here to die."

"No place is perfect, as evidenced by our hungry friend up there, but my world has its charms. And I don't think 'my kind' as you call them knew that they were going to die here."   She didn't answer, and I had nothing more to say, so we floated in silence in rose-tinted water that tasted of blood.

***

After the carcass had been reduced to bloody bones, the brachuribane crept from their hidey-holes.

"I'm going to find Trivo," said Layq hardly glancing at me before diving into the green. I followed at a distance, aware that I'd outstayed my welcome in this place. We found Trivo on his royal dune. He was re-attaching his egg sack to a nearby shrub and arguing with a group of brachuribane youths who were all bubbling at him at once. Layq dived into the heart of the argument, spun a stream of bubbles, and definitively slashed the water with her fins. I stayed out of it. I'd dropped myself in enough arsepickle for one day. I noticed that despite the attack none of them were armed, although from what I could glean from the argument, that might be about to change.

"Why do you kree?" Layq asked me.

I hadn't realized I had been until she pointed it out. I coughed, swished the stream of bubbles away. "Sorry, Layq," I said and tried to look contrite. "It's just a nervous reaction."

She didn't look convinced. "We think you should leave."

"I thought you might."

Trivo looked up. The bags under his eyes were more pronounced. "Yes, you should go," Trivo echoed. "You've brought disharmony to our people and the shadow of death now hangs over our forest."

"With all due respect, I believe that the fish brought the disharmony and seemed bent on bringing death, but I take your point. If you could show me where the angle gate is, I'll—"

"No, don't go." One of the youngsters swam over, put her fin on my arm. "Show us how to do what you did to the Yanmula." Her friends joined her, leaving Trivo and Layq to stare with open dismay.

Excited, they all jabbered at once with the frenzied energy of those who'd survived a brush with death. They begged me to stay, repeatedly asked how I'd killed the fish and if I could show them how to do it. This wasn't anything out of the ordinary back home, but Trivo looked on like we were discussing how to make an omelet out of his eggs.

I shushed the youngsters. "I'm sorry, I have to leave."

Trivo tied off the reeds holding his egg sack and expelled a long, rolling stream of bubbles. "I agree."

"Come, I'll take you to the stones," said Layq.

Before I had a chance to say anything, she was off, leaving me just enough to time to wave goodbye to Trivo or lose her in the murk. I wasn't a sensitive cove by any measure, but even I could feel the change in the atmosphere. "It's colder," I shouted. "Has the current changed?" Layq didn't answer. I paddled harder to try to catch up, but she effortlessly outdistanced me. *Fuck this*. I stopped swimming. She noticed immediately and turned. "Come on, you must have been attacked hundreds of times," I said. She gave me a blank look. "Why is fighting to survive such a terrible thing?"

"It's not that." She swam over and stopped so close to me that I could see my reflection in her eyes. I looked good for a fish person. "Everything is changing. You are part of that change, I can feel it, I can hear it in the voices of my brothers and sisters. There is sickness here. That coldness you feel, it's been growing, spreading like blood in the water."

"What do you mean?"

"The coldness. It's you and those others from your world. You brought it." A jet of water bubbled from her flattened nostrils. Her fins flared. I thought she might attack me, but she sped away, turning water in her wake, leaving me to navigate her turbulence.

***

The gate was miles from the forest, beyond the grave pit where my previous body lay in wormy repose. Layq greeted a pair of brachuribane who were floating idly by a stand of kelp. She beckoned me over. "This is Runil and Chosh. They're the ones who found you."

"We're watchers. We saw a funny looking thing come through and die." Chosh grabbed his throat with both hands and mimed choking until his companion flicked him in the gut with his tail.

"You have to forgive him," said Runil. "He swam too high when he was a hatchling."

Chosh kreed. "Being stuck out here with you has sent me funny." He winked. He was the first decent cove I'd met since I'd been here. The kind of fellow you could have an ale with if they drank anything other than water.

"We used to live here before Trivo took the sand," Layq said as she gently drifted in the water. "But it was too close to the stones. Too cold. It's bad water." She glared at me before returning her gaze to the ring of green stones which, save for location, were the twin of those in the Annurashi's store chamber.

The stones were set on a rocky mound that rose some twenty feet above the seabed. The mound was girded with coral that spread like lace wings frozen in flight, but amid the beauty, there lurked the sinister touch of death. Old bones poked out of the web of pink, green and blue coral stems. The bones had been stained green with algae and studded with barnacles. Fish swam about the reef, picking at the carcasses of things that did not look entirely formed; fish with missing fins, or too many heads. Crabs with hands instead of pincers scrabbled over the rocks. "We just keep watchers here now in case strangers come through," Layq added.

"The other didn't last long at all." Runil shook his head.

"I noticed." I swam around the mound and looked for any indication of which stone I should move to open the gate. Nestled amongst the rocks and half buried by branching coral, I spied what looked like a human skull. It wasn't the braincase itself that caught my attention, but something bright that winked from the darkness of its vacant orbit— irresistible bait for a thief.

"What are you waiting for?" Layq appeared above the stones. She continued to talk, but I'd stopped listening. The skull and its gleaming mystery gripped my attention. I swam down to get a closer look. Disappointingly, whatever was trapped inside looked more like metal than a gemstone. I tried to wedge my claws under the skull, but my hands were designed for swimming not digging. I broke off a branch of coral and tried to lever it out, but it was tightly wedged and the coral snapped. I cursed, but I would not be thwarted. I searched for a rock.

Layq's watery yell broke my avaricious trance. I looked up to see her pointing at something behind me. "Muyamak." She pointed again, more insistent this time, a look of fear splashed across her face. I had no idea what a Muyamak might be but judging by her reaction it didn't sound like I wanted to find out. I also didn't want to leave whatever it was locked inside the skull. I kicked it as something huge surged through the water, parting the flow behind me. Fish darted into the cover of the reef as I smashed the bones and snatched the shining object before squeezing myself under a ledge. I was convinced the Muyamak must have seen me and expected at any minute to see a gaping maw open above me. Churned-up sediment rose like fog, darkening the water.

"Hey, over here!" Layq sounded like she was some distance away from where I was hiding. A wave of water washed over the mound. The sediment cleared in time for me to see a long, serpentine tail as thick as my body and covered in black and white scales whip over the mound. Minutes passed without a giant snake beast winkling me from my niche, but just in case I stayed put. While I waited, I examined my prize. The heavy medallion was encrusted with bone, plant matter, and tiny crawling things that had too many mouths. But beneath the crusty accumulation I could see the gleam of dark silver, speckled with starry inclusions. It was star steel, the rarest of metals in my world, wrought by sorcery and forged by the Mage Lords into objects of power.

I tucked it into the baggy skin pouch under my arm and cautiously inched up the mound. There was no sign of the Muyamak or the People. Beyond the mound the ocean currents threaded through the ominous, green-tinted darkness, carrying with it the faint taste of blood, hinting at their fate.

I told myself that I hardly knew Layq and her kin, but the shadow of regret fell upon me. I brushed it aside. It wasn't my fault. I didn't ask her to die for me. I turned my attention to the stones. With an eye out for hungry sea beasts, I tried to open the gate. My first effort to wake it failed. None of them would move, none of them hummed, or trembled, or vibrated. I backed away from the monument to get a better view and see if I'd missed anything obvious. Tense minutes passed, but inspiration didn't strike. I floated there, aware of how small and vulnerable I was and that voracious beasts hunted ceaselessly in the darkness.

A face appeared from behind a stand of kelp. It was Chosh. "You're lucky. We don't often see the Muyamak in this flow."

"I saw its tail."

"Ah. That's a pity, you missed a real treat." He glided over, grinning like the fool he evidently was.

"What happened to Layq and Runil?"

He blew a massive silver bubble, burst it with a claw and giggled. "They lured the Muyamak away."

"Idiots," I said but again felt the cold sting of regret.

"That's what I thought." Chosh blew and popped another bubble.

I had to get away from here. "You just make sure you destroy these stones when I'm gone."

"Why?"

The real reason was that I didn't want to get thrust back through the gate that led to this world ever again. I was prepared to suffocate and die when I got back to the Annurashi's chamber and I wasn't looking forward to it, but it would be worth it to get rid of this fish-crab body and forget this place. Sure, I'd die but I'd come back in a lovely Annurashi body and then I'd get as far away from the whole parcel of lunatics as quickly as possible while avoiding the demon hordes. *Damn, Layq, why did you do it? You didn't even know me.*

"The shit coming through the gate has brought er, evil waters to your world," I said. Chosh nodded, though it was plain to see that the brachuribane didn't have a clue what I was talking about, not that he should. "Just destroy it and you, my friend, will be a hero."

He finned thoughtfully, and his golden eyes swiveled in opposite directions. "Chosh the hero, eh? I like it. I don't know what a hero is, but it has a good sound to it, especially the way you say it. You talk funny."

"Yes, all right. Just destroy the fucking stones and you won't have to come out here and play Muyamak bait anymore."

"It was fun, but now Runil won't be around, maybe not so much. He was always good for a laugh, old Runil."

I stopped listening. I was working out the finer points of the deal I'd cut with the Eldest for the star steel, how I'd convince the old ramblebladder that it was an important artifact worth my freedom. By the time she discovered otherwise, I'd be long gone. Of course, there would only be a deal if I could get the damn gate to work before something swooped out of the deeps and ate me.

Chosh drifted past on his back. "If they're so dangerous, shouldn't we destroy the stones now?"

I didn't like that he was thinking for himself, it wasn't a trait I ever found attractive in a cull I was attempting to con.

"What? No. Not until I've gone. Trivo said I had to leave."

"So, where will you go?"

"Back to my world, I expect."

"A world full of air, eh? Strange."

"Yeah. You're better off here, trust me."

"I know. Ethuldwithan is perfect. 'Course, I've never been anywhere else."

I scanned the stones for any hint as to how I might wake them while at the same time ignoring the insidious, little voice that suggested they might not work at all and I'd be trapped here forever with Chosh and my guilt at Tobias's death. *No, not Tobias, Layq.* This place was getting to me. I felt suffocated. I had to get out, if I stayed here much longer I'd be as mad as Chosh. I stared at the stones. A web of luminous, green weed that was trapped in the current drifted past.

Now that I looked, I saw that the current turned back upon itself, nipped in tight circles, and twined around like a serpent biting its tail. "That's it." I turned the stones to match the pattern indicated by the currents' flow.

The stones woke instantly. Vibrations rippled from the individual monoliths in waves and radiated into the darkness of the ocean. Moments later they were answered by the deep bass rumble of something that made my heart shudder.

"The Muyamak," said Chosh before darting towards the nearest stand of kelp.

"Don't forget to destroy these when it's gone," I called after him before taking a last lungful of water and stepping into the slice of shimmering air that had opened before me. I knew it was unlikely, but I hoped that Layq had made it.

Chapter Twelve

I'd expected to be transported back to the Annurashi's cavern, so it came as a surprise when I stepped from a world of water into one of fire. The moment I fell through the gate, I burned. My water laden carcass and the cold star steel lump melted within seconds, leaving me just enough time to scream.

I don't know how long I lay in the dreamless sleep of death while whatever sorcery that bound my spirit created a body fit for this world. All that I know is that, minutes, hours, or years after I died, I was reborn as a being of fire in a burning world.

I took my first breath, spread my flaming wings, and leaped into the mercury sky. My consciousness reached out, spilled from me, and touched a thousand minds. They felt me, felt my otherworldliness and recoiled, afraid and unsure of the stranger in their midst. *Fuck 'em.* I encouraged their fear, reveled in it. They should shun me. I was dangerous to know. *Why did you do it, Layq?* The thought came unbidden and entirely unwanted. I flew harder, higher, faster, beheld undreamed of wonders with eyes of molten gold.

The natives lurked on the edge of my mind, a constant, distant whisper of myriad thoughts to which I wasn't privy. Physically, they stayed beyond the limits of my vision although they were kind enough to direct me to a gate and impressed on me with an undefined urgency, that I should use it before they destroyed it, that I wasn't the first, but would be the last intruder into their world. At first I was reluctant to comply. I felt at home here, I was magnificent, powerful. I was a being of grace and beauty. Alas, in the whole, brilliant, fiery world where every creature was linked to every other in a mind of world-spanning proportions, I was alone. It was profoundly depressing. I'd never felt such kinship with anyone, not Tobias or Mother Blake and I'd been content. I was a thief, an assassin, a member of the Midnight Court in good standing. I had comrades aplenty, should the need arise for companionship or someone with whom to share a mug of ale. I'd never sought or longed-for friends and certainly had never desired familial bonds of affection and until now, hadn't realized what it was that I hadn't missed, but now I knew.

I don't want to go. The thought flashed from my mind before I could pull it back. They answered with a resounding silence. I was nudged towards the gate, guided by images and their ardent desire for me to leave and never return. The gate of this world was made of thousand feet high, spinning tornados of fire. I flew around them, looped the molten sky with hesitant wing beats and trailed sorrow in my wake. I wanted what they had, would have killed to be one of them, to be one with them, which was most likely why I had to go. There was no place in this world for a monster like me, no amount of fire could burn the bloodstains from my black heart. I opened the gate, drew my wings close to my body and dived into the space between worlds.

***

"Dragon!" The cry was echoed by an entire army of bloodied and beleaguered warriors that were backing towards the edge of a cliff beside the mound on which the angle gate stood like a ring of broken teeth, jutting from the mossy ground. I gasped as the toxic air began to destroy the delicate filigree of my lungs and spewed a torrent of burning ichor over a phalanx of skeletal warriors. The gout of flame incinerated hundreds of raddled corpse soldiers that had been closing in on the retreating army.

In my death throes, I flew blindly into the ranks of undead that dominated the battlefield. None of the shamblers ran, they surged towards me, intent on tearing me apart but they melted as soon as they came within twenty feet of my molten body. Not that it mattered, I was dying anyway, but it was the air that was killing me not the undead. It fed my fire and caused me to burn with a fury beyond my body's ability to contain. Roasting in my own juices was painful. I thrashed and flailed and smashed entire regiments of animated corpses to pieces while at the same time, burning them to cinders. I just hoped that the mugs by the cliff appreciated my efforts. I stumbled and fell, but I didn't want to give up this body just yet. I wanted to fly one last time. I threw off the grasping mob of burning skeletons, planted my taloned feet beneath me and spread my wings.

It was not to be.

The wings burned up as beautifully as a dying sunset and blanketed the battlefield in a sheet of flame. I crashed onto the glassed ground and breathed this body's final, fiery breath.

***

"We shall remember this day." The youthful voice roused me from death. I opened an eye to find that I was lying face down on the back of an enormous, covered wagon, on a pile of ash and blackened bone shards— all that was left of my previous incarnation. My chest felt heavy as though a weight lay upon it. I took this feeling to be sadness at the passing of my elemental self but was more likely heartburn from breathing in my ashes.

I sat up. I looked mostly human, although I could see the faint impression of scales around my claw-toed feet and hands. A dismantled trebuchet had been shoved into the corner, no doubt to make space for my dragonish bones which would have made a magnificent trophy worthy of display in some princelings keep, just like the one hanging in the Annurashis' hall. Or perhaps they were more fiscally minded and intended to grind them to ash and sell them by the bag. Dragon bone was a popular, but expensive aphrodisiac back in Valen. Alas, neither would come to pass. The elemental's bones were as subject to the ravages of the air as its flesh had been, only the decay was slower. There wouldn't be any bragging rights or cock medicine.

"We shall never forget." the youth's voice broke as he fought to be heard over the cheering crowd. "We shall never forget that this was the day that our prayers were answered, that a savior came, and the evil tide was turned." Wild cheering rent the air. "We must not forget that we do this because we must, not because we choose to. Many of those we have destroyed were our friends, our comrades, our kin. We fought to bring peace, to them and to this land. With heart, faith, and courage we carried the day. Remember that you were here, remember that you few stood against many, and carry that memory forever in your heart."

I stood up and the world tilted on its axis. I steadied myself against the side of the wagon and fought to see through a tangle of red hair that fell past my waist. Upon closer inspection, I saw that the flesh of my shoulders was mottled orange and covered in a light sprinkling of scales. It was as though the essence of my old form was fighting to return, to push through the physical constraints of whatever I'd become this time.

I wasn't pleased that I'd died again or that I'd lost the magnificent, elemental body, but this was reasonable compensation. My senses were as bad, I imagined, as those of any human, but it was better than being a fish person. As I admired my new form the canvass cover on the wagon was thrown back and a turnip-pated fellow peered in.

"Demon!" he shouted.

Terrified, I spun on my heel half expecting to see Shallunsard grinning at me from the shadows, then I realized that he meant me. I raised my hands. "No, wait. I'm not a demon." I might as well have declared myself ruler of the heavens for all that he was prepared to listen to a word I said. He yelled in a panic and leaped from the wagon. There followed more shouting and minutes later, a half-dozen overcautious warriors dragged me unresisting into the daylight. Chaos erupted. I was bound, casually beaten, and thrown to the ground. A crowd gathered and there followed an argument between various, bellicose factions all bent on claiming the honor of slaying the demon they had found in their midst. Not one paused to ask how I came to be there or why I wasn't trying to attack them, but that's clanks for you.

While this was going on, I was kept busy dodging feet and the stamping hooves of disgruntled warhorses.

The debate raged over which of them should slay me and precisely how the deed should be done. I didn't feel in immediate danger and took the opportunity to get the measure of these culls, see if I could work out what all the undead army business was about. Confident of my ability to free myself when I so chose, I listened intently and with no small measure of amusement to the bloody merits of dismemberment by wild horses, as opposed to the tried and tested method of burning when it came to the disposal of demons. Some few held out for beheading while a shifty-eyed fellow claimed that drowning me in a barrel of pickling vinegar was the only true way to slay a hell-bound fiend and as luck would have it, he knew where he could get such a thing, for a very reasonable price.

"My friends, we shouldn't argue amongst ourselves." A sweet-voiced cull stepped forward, separated herself from the tussling mass with the sureness of one used to command, of giving rather than taking orders. "Not after what we've been through together, eh?" She indicated me with a flick of a glove that she slapped into her palm. The crowd quieted. Like all the rest, she looked like she'd just fought a battle. Her armor was bloodied, her gambeson rent, and her steel wrapped legs were dyed with mud and filth up to her thighs. Despite the battle-worn gear her gambeson was trimmed with gold braid, the steel on her hip had a jewel and gold inlaid hilt, and the mud-caked boots were made of soft, tooled leather. As a testament to her trade, she carried scars. One ran across her cheek, a pale scratch in her dark skin that enhanced rather than diminished her confident swagger. Here was a leader and a fighter, and without doubt one to watch.

Another noteworthy fellow shoved his way through the crowd not long after. In contrast to the woman, he was neither elegant nor handsome, but he was hard to ignore. He was barrel-chested, stubby armed and thick-legged. His black beard had been tarred into spikes and banded with copper rings. His piggish eyes were quick and fixed in a face that was wider at the bottom than it was at the sparsely thatched top. He'd also recently pissed himself by the look of things and not for the first time, going by the smell. Ill-favored and ill-mannered though he was, he had a dozen equally handsome coves at his back and a double-headed ax slung over his urux-broad shoulder, obviating the need for either manners or good looks.

"Fuck off, Delgaro, you poncey cunt," he growled, confirming my estimation. "I say we get some horses and tear this fucker apart, 'afore it can make any mischief."

I was still more amused than affronted, but I couldn't let that pass without comment. "Mischief? You're in error, my good man. 'Twas I who saved you." My words were met with wall-faced incredulity, as though a rock had just opined on the price of fish. "You don't know who I am, do you?" Those coves closest to me, casually edged back, leaving Pig-Eyes and Delgaro, who both looked surprised, but also intrigued by my interjection.

Pig-Eyes kicked me. "Shut up, you fucking monster," he said with a level of vehemence that was mostly composed of fear.

"Now, now, Bolin. There's no need for violence, yet. Come, have a drink with me." Delgaro held out her hand, and one of the soldiers passed her a bottle of something that smelled like brandy. She took a quick nip before offering it to the surly cull.

Taking advantage of the moment's peace, a thin-lipped, wart-nosed fellow slipped through the crowd and placed himself center stage. "Beware, brothers and sisters," he said, his voice aquiver with righteousness. He was clutching a twigish, tin stamped symbol that was pinned to his jerkin. "Look not into the demon's sulfurous eyes, do not listen to its honeyed words. Cleave to the Holy Briar and burn this fiend."

Bolin took a swig of the brandy and pointed a stubby, hammer thick finger at the cove without even bothering to look at him. "And you can fuck right off with that briar bollocks." The skinny cull curled his lip and slunk back into the crowd, but not before one last entreaty. "Do not heed the words of demons, Cleave to the Briar, brothers and—"

"Kiss my arse?" My interjection earned another kick from Bolin, but some of those within earshot laughed, easing the tension a notch. The air was thick with smoke and the stench of the charnel house drifting from the burning field. Fatigue settled on the warriors as the heat of battle began to dissipate. I'd seen enough clanks to know that next would come gratitude for being alive closely followed by grief for those who were not. In a couple of days, when the hangovers wore off, bone weariness would take over after which would come reflection and for some, regret.

I'd have to keep a wary eye out for any sudden shift in the mood of the crowd. Humans prided themselves on their individuality, but they were just like any other pack animal when it came down to it. If one jumped and decided to light a bonfire in my honor, they probably all would, and then I'd have to kill them which would be a pity after saving them. I decided to hold my water and wait and see how negotiations went between the two main players before I attempted to extricate myself.

While I contemplated my fate and the poor wager I was most likely making, my gaze wandered across the haggard faces peering down at me. Amongst their number I spotted a cull who was the spit double of Tobias, right down to the homespun robe. Our eyes met, and he tipped me the nod before disappearing into the throng. I made to stand, to get a better look at the uncanny twin of my dead friend but was warned off moving by the tip of a blade. That I could kill the whole fucking lot of them without raising a sweat made me laugh.

"What are you laughing at?" Delgaro asked.

"It's just that, I saved you and now you're debating how you're going to kill me. It's funny."

She bristled. "I wasn't debating how to kill you. I'm suggesting that my company and I should take you to the king so that he can decide how to kill you."

"Aye and snag a bag of coin for your trouble. I know you Delgaro, you mangy cuntbox," Bolin added with a suggestive sneer.

"There is nothing mangy about my cuntbox, cockshort," she fired back. "And I'm more than willing to give you your share of any reward the king might offer, given that your share would be exactly fuck all, as you've done nothing to secure this creature."

"None of you have done anything to secure me, but you carry on. This is the most fun I've had in ages." Which was true.

Delgaro frowned. "Kick it again, would you, Bolin?"

Bolin stabbed the air with a fat finger. "Don't tell me what to do, wench."

"Well said, that man. You tell her," I added.

The captain swept her scabbarded blade behind her and leaned in close to me. There was stiffness in her movement as though a wound pained her. "What the fuck kind of fool provokes those who hold their life in their hands?"

"I would say either a thoughtless fool, or a fool who has tired of life, or perhaps someone who's confident of their abilities."

"The fool might save themselves a lot of unnecessary pain if they explained themselves." She let her gaze drift to the crowd.

"They might, but where would be the fun in that?"

She stood up, thought a while, and then snorted before turning to the crowd. "It's decided then. Bolin and I will take this foul sprite to the king." She drew her sword, raised it in salute. "For the honor of the King!" Everyone cheered, except Bolin, who looked like he was having trouble keeping up.

He tapped Delgaro on the shoulder. "I didn't agree to that."

"And to Bolin the Boar!" Again, the crowd cheered with enthusiasm, drowning out any further objections. Delgaro winked at Bolin.

He threw his hands in the air. "Fuck it, why not?"

"That was nicely done," I said, but nobody was listening to me.

Chapter Thirteen

I'd never been impressed by clanks, so-called knights done up like tins of salt beef, swearing this or that oath, affecting high moral values just as long as it suited them to do so. From what I'd seen, these oath-bound coves were paragons of virtue right up to the point they wanted to rob or fuck someone, or their arses were on the line.

Although they were cut from a similar cloth to oath-sworn warriors, mercenaries were patterned after another, less hypocritical fashion. Differences in character aside, they were on the whole more pragmatic than noble, bound by the clauses of a contract, not hollow vows. As a Guild Blade, I was more than handy with the cutlery, but I wasn't the kind of cove who marched in formation or fought in the open. Having said that, I understood what motivated mercenaries. Bolin and Delgaro were of that ilk, working for the coin of King Whatever-He-Was-Called, who was fighting an evil necromancer and his bigger, more resilient army. Such I gathered as we rode along.

I say rode. They rode, I was invited to ride in a warded iron cage that was strapped on a wagon. It had apparently belonged to the necromancer's army and judging by the claw and fang marks on the bars; it had been built to contain some nightmarish, undead beast.

The sensible thing to do would have been apport out of there, find the gate, and try to return to my world, but then...

I'd seen Tobias, and not just some cove who looked like him, it was him. He wanted me to be here and I wanted to know why that was.

"Are you deaf or something? I said, get in the fucking cage." One of the mercenaries had said, as he shoved me towards the cage.

I put my hand out to stop myself falling and saw the ward rune carved into the lock and felt the spiky tingle of magic. *If I get in this, I might not get out. So? I'll die again, so what?* I'd got away from Shallunsard and the meddlesome Annurashi and I was safe here in another world. So why not stick around and have a bit of fun while I waited for Tobias to show his face again? I turned to the bemused mercenary who was winding up to kick me. "No need for violence, my good man," I said as I climbed into the cage. "I want you to know that I'm doing this purely as a demonstration of trust. I'm allowing myself to be caged like an animal to prove that I'm not a demon."

The mercenary frowned as he thought about it. "You're being caged because you *are* a demon and there are a thousand warriors in this camp, so you daren't do otherwise." He folded his arms and smiled, satisfied that he'd won the point.

"Have you ever met a demon that didn't try to rip your face off?" I countered.

His frown returned.

"It has a point, Kinsi," someone added.

Kinsi turned on his comrade. "Whose side are you on?"

"I'm just saying."

"Well don't." He snapped the lock in place. "And you can stop fucking grinning. You're going to burn."

"You've got that right."

***

"You know if you got a move on you'd catch your king on the road and save us all a journey," I shouted to the mercenary leaders, but neither deigned to answer. The cage was made for undead beasts not living coves, but it was a better way to travel than walking or riding one of the horses. I took the opportunity to get the measure of my traveling companions and earwig on their conversation and try to find out what was going on here.

After a couple of hours spent not learning much, I decided a more direct approach was required. "So, what's your king called?" I asked one of the mercenaries riding beside the wagon. He was a snot-nosed youth with freckles and the lightest dusting of hair on his spotty chin. He scowled at me.

"What's with the face? I didn't ask if your father sucked dog cock, I asked what your king was called."

"Why, you." He half drew his sword.

"Oi, fuck knuckle." One of Bolin's crew shouted at the youth. "Draw that blade and I'll shove it up your arse— sideways."

"This, *thing* just insulted my dad," the warrior protested. "Nobody insults my dad."

Delgaro was riding ahead with Bolin and cast a glance over her shoulder when she heard the raised voices. "You don't have a dad, Piet. Stop pretending and don't damage the merchandise."

Piet glared at me, while those around him laughed at his expense. He sheathed his blade.

"So, what's your fucking king called?" I pressed. "Come on, Piet, I'm not going to stop asking until you tell me."

"Malin. Now leave me the fuck alone."

"That didn't hurt did it?" I smiled, showing a hint of fang. That the cage had been warded was a minor annoyance, but I was sure if I tried I could overcome whatever petty magic had been used to fashion them. Until then I would rely on the dark art of relentless badgering to squeeze information out of my new friend Piet.

It took a few hours of whining and wheedling, threatening, flattering, and cajoling but he eventually broke and told me we were headed to the city of Galewyn, the capital of the fair land of Arduin. At least, it had been fair until a great evil had almost destroyed it.

No matter how hard I tried, I couldn't draw him on the exact nature of this 'great evil.' I knew it was a necromancer of some kind, but the very mention of the word drew stiff rebukes and threats of violence from those within earshot. I let it drop and listened instead to the general flow of their comradely banter. Out of their various discussions I learned who had slotted the most restless dead, who'd had the closest escape, which one of them had the biggest cock, and which one had the smallest tits, the usual salty warrior raillery.

Their idle chatter didn't include anything useful, like their captain's plans for me, but I did learn what was the most efficacious treatment for foot fungus and the best way to eat fermented pigs' trotters.

I also discovered that the battle I'd interrupted had happened two days ago. Which meant that, thus far this had been the longest it had taken me to reincarnate. I wondered if it took longer to come back the more often I died, if I was using up the magic with every death. Alas, my knowledge of the metaphysics that governed my gift and my curse was limited to guesswork.

"What's that, then?" Piet pointed at my hand which I'd been absentmindedly scratching while mulling over my situation. It was too late to hide the mark in my palm, not that he would recognize either Shallunsard or Rowan's sigil for what they were. What I hadn't expected was that I wouldn't recognize the marks either. "The fucking star steel."

"Eh?" Piet enquired.

"Nothing. It's an oath. 'Holy, fucking star steel, aren't you the nosy one?' Like that." I turned my back on the snot and examined my hand without an audience. Entwined in my newly minted palm was a mix of both Rowan's and Shallunsard's sigils. The last time I'd paid them any heed, one had been black and the other silver. That was no longer the case. Now they were joined in a continuous line of silvery gray. I gazed at my hand and saw the tiny star-like grains flowing through the metal, much like blood flowing through a vein. I'd found the star steel in the water world, a place where I hadn't seen any other metal, in a human skull. It had melted with me in the fire world but rather than being destroyed, it had become part of me.

"That's a demon mark, innit?" I turned to see a smug grin spread across Piet's, pimply face.

"And just what would you know about demon marks, bumfluff?"

"I know enough. Thems who serve demons, get demon marked."

"A few hours ago, I was a demon. Now I've been demoted to one who serves demons. Should I be flattered?"

He shrugged. "I ain't never heard a demon speak is all. Those I've seen just sort of growl or groan or snarl." He mimed monstrous lumbering and pulled a twisted expression. "That kind of thing."

"Gods' sake, boy, you'll be inviting it to your ma's for Bride's Day feast next," said a gruff old cull with a mean-as-fuck mien. Her gaze switched from the boy to the captain. "Del, are we hauling over here for the night?"

The lone sun had shone for only a few hours before it began to dive for the horizon, ahead the road forked offering a forest on the right that was studded with faint, jewel drops of lamplight. On the left the road cut through farmland that lay cold and bare, gilded silver under the slanted plow of dusk as it dragged the light to the edge of the world.

While the captains of both crews had a swift confabulation, the old warrior pulled up alongside the wagon and slowed the horses. "We should take a watch here if it's got an inn."

Delgaro's gaze turned briefly to me. "Aye. Send someone ahead and find out, please Skurden. And warn the innkeep about our guest. Drop them a little extra coin if you have to, but don't let them take the piss."

Skurden leaned on her saddle. "Never have."

Delgaro reached into her belt and took out a coin purse, which she tossed to the older woman. She then turned to Bolin and held out her hand. For a second he feigned ignorance but when the hand wasn't withdrawn he conceding with an ill-tempered grunt and fished a coin purse out of his breeches. He took out some coins and handed them to Delgaro with a leering grin. "Kept 'em nice and warm for you."

She raised an eyebrow. "So long as they spend I don't care."

"Yes, indeed, stopping is a wonderful idea." I beamed. "See to it that there's a hot bath and a chilled bottle of wine waiting for me, would you? And tell them to plump the mattress, I do so hate a hard pallet." I scattered my comments around the group, but my gaze came to settle on Delgaro as she seemed to be the one most likely to appreciate my dazzling wit.

She smiled. "I'm sure we'll find you suitable accommodation."

***

My accommodation was the cage on the wagon, which was left outside. The horses got a stable and some hay, the mercenaries got the inn, a warm fire, and some ale and I got rained on, poked with sticks, and lightly abused by children and their lackwit parents. I say lackwit out of spite. For all I knew they might very well have had a full complement of wits. It was more that, in their minds I didn't deserve the same respect as one of them because I was different or as some would have it, a monster. I'd experienced that kind of prejudice all my life. In a funny sort of way it was comforting to be so reminded of the past when life was simple.

"Is it a demon, ma?" one of the snotlings asked as he poked a piece of straw through the bars of the cage. I obliged his childish efforts to provoke me by bearing my fangs. The imp squealed as much in delight as fear and leaped into the protective embrace of a woman I took to be his mother. She scolded the bratling, but rather than curse me, she took off her shawl and threw it into the cage.

"Why thank you, ma'am, it is a touch inclement this eve," I said as I wrapped the shawl around my shoulders.

"Tis a sin in the eyes of the Crone to leave you sitting there, all naked like, even if you are a demon."

"The Bride wouldn't mind, though. She likes a bit of nudity," someone said from the shadows of the stables. For a second I thought the speaker was wearing a priestly robe, but when he stepped into the light. I saw that he was wearing a shirt and breeches and a patched overcoat. He walked with a limp, probably from leaning on the fork he was carrying rather than using it. "And it ain't no demon. I saw too many of the bastards at Ice Break Pass to ever forget what they look like, or what they smell like. This ain't one of 'em."

"Thank you." I could hardly believe that I'd judged these culls wrong.

"This is another kind of hellspawn."

"You had to spoil it." I sighed and tied the shawl around my hips. "There, is that better?"

The woman tugged the earflaps of her cap down a little lower to hide the redness of her embarrassed lobes. "Not really, you've uncovered as much as you've hidden."

I grinned. "In that case, ma'am, you should have given me a bigger shawl." I stretched out as much as the cage would allow and had a good scratch around my nethers. Ears aside, she couldn't do much to hide the flush in her cheeks, which spoke volumes about the depth of her piety. She hurried on her way, dragging the kinchin cove behind her.

This world reminded me of home, but at the same time it was markedly different. There was only one sun for a start and the vegetation was stunted because of it, but despite this it bore a strong resemblance particularly the part of the Empire where I came from. There weren't any magnificent, pre-schism ruins towering over sorcery tainted wastelands, at least not that I'd seen on the short ride between the battlefield and here. There were abandoned, burned out homesteads, but they were crude, poorly constructed and on a modest, provincial scale. There was also an abundance of horses— rare and expensive animals in my world. Now that I thought about it I realized that I hadn't seen an urux — the most common beast of burden back home. In fact, most critters I'd seen here were furred and feathered rather than smooth or scaled.

"Passing strange indeed."

"What was that, demon?" Bolin asked as he relieved himself on a pile of horse shit and straw which continued to steam despite the rain. "I said, what was that, demon?" The mercenary spoke more slowly and louder as he stuffed his piss pipe back in his breeks.

"I said I'm surprised you bothered to pull it out given that you've obviously pissed your pants rigid."

"That's a bit harsh. I only asked what you said. And I'll have you know that I got a kick from a horse what done for my bladder when I was a lad."

"Oh." I was taken aback by his unabashed honesty.

"Aye. Take it from me, it's a miserable condition. The fucking thing almost killed me though, so I suppose I'm lucky."

"I didn't know."

"I don't shout it from the rooftops. It's embarrassing."

"Sorry." More peculiar than my apology was that I felt a genuine touch of regret. It wasn't much, just a sly nip, but unexpected all the same. "And stop calling me demon. I am not a fucking demon. How many times must I tell you people?"

He toyed with the tarred spikes of his beard. "You look like a demon and you appeared out of nowhere after a battle with Unhallowed corpses. If it looks like a fish and swims like a fish, more often than not it's a fucking fish."

"Unless it's a brachuri."

"A what?"

"Never mind." The door behind him opened, offering the briefest glimpse of the common room of the inn. The smell of tallow, ale, and meat rode over the stink of horse shit and carried with it the sound of laughter and the strains of some stringed instrument being cruelly tortured by someone with no discernable talent for music.

"If you weren't such an ass, you could have that, Breed," Tobias said. My dead, former comrade was standing by the wagon. This was no winding sheet specter, no pale shade materialized from the netherworld. He was as real as I was. I saw rain fall on him, watched it gather and flow in spidery rivulets to the edge of his cowl where they grew fat before pearling, bright as falling stars. I moved closer, felt his breath on my cheek. His watery, blue eyes shone with amusement and like always, his thin-lipped smile was warm and smugly condescending.

I might have made a fool of myself and embraced him if the cage hadn't come between us. I instead gripped the bars for want of something to do with my shaking hands. "I don't mean to be an ass. It's just that people wind me up." I blinked, and Tobias vanished. In his place was the mercenary. He was staring at me with a mix of curiosity and skepticism written across his face.

"I never said you were an ass." He tugged absently on his beard spikes. "Although it must be said, whenever you open your mouth, most folks want to punch you, demon or not." While talking candidly to my dead friend it seemed that I had inadvertently made a not-entirely-unfavorable impression on the rogue who was now standing dangerously close to the cage.

It was tempting to make him pay for his error. The warded lock only stopped the use of unnatural force, not me grabbing him and smashing his brains out against the bars. I could have done that, bust out, and then as a lesson to all not to mess with sorcerers, leveled the inn and the entire fucking village. This was one of those knife blade moments when choices that were made mattered. Choices I made in the past were most often dictated by a strong, nay *overwhelming* sense of self-preservation. But not today. Today I had seen my dead friend and on the strength of that undoubtedly illusory visitation, I decided that I was not going to kill Bolin... today. I dismissed the possibility of escaping with a wave, oddly proud of myself for eschewing the use of violence to save my skin, a first for me. The warrior must have misconstrued the gesture as an acknowledgment of the truth of his claim because he offered a begrudging nod and almost smiled before heading back into the warmth of the inn.

***

After another two hours of getting soaked I began to regret my forbearance. The moral high ground wasn't mine for the taking. I was about as wet as it was possible to be without actually being submerged because I'd tried to play a part to which my character wasn't suited. Fuck these culls and fuck their king and his cause. The only thing I got from trying to be reasonable was ill-treatment. *Fuck that*. "And you, Tobias, fuck you too," I said to the rain-shredded air. I took hold of the lock and prepared to apport to the battlefield when the inn door creaked open and a couple of mercenaries came out carrying a tarpaulin and a heavy cloak. Without a word, they threw the tarp over the cage and stuffed the cloak through the bars before retreating to the inn.

I didn't pass comment on their unexpected act of kindness, and neither did they. "Everyone has their story, Breed," Tobias whispered in my ear.

"Do fuck off. There's a good fellow." I wrapped the cloak around me and fell into a restless, demon-haunted sleep.

The morning brought with it more rain and some food. I'd expected the one, but not the other and yet a hatchet-faced cull wearing Delgaro's colors and a sour expression thrust a loaf of bread and a lump of cooked meat through the bars. She mumbled something as she left, but I couldn't hear over the sound of my furious chewing, I'd never been this hungry. While I ate, the mercenaries drifted out of the inn. There was a lazy discipline about the way they went about their business, something between backstreet bravo and soldier. They swaggered, told filthy jokes at the same time as cleaning their war gear and making sure their kit was stowed tidily. I didn't see any of them drill and few were called by rank or title, but things got done.

Delgaro and Bolin were last to appear. Despite earlier appearances, they were obviously tight. Now I understood why they'd posed as enemies at the battlefield. Their loud masquerade had been enough to distract any other rivals for whatever reward money they thought the king might offer for me. I hoped they wouldn't be too disappointed, but I had no intention of being sold. When and if I was taken to the king, I was going to give him the chance to free me, or I'd have to do it myself. Either way, I wasn't sure they'd get paid for bringing such a dangerous cove as myself within blade's reach of their liege lord.

Kings aside, I wasn't happy that I'd gone soft on Bolin the night before and half convinced myself that it was because I'd been distracted by the hallucination of Tobias. It was a rare moment of hesitation on my behalf, one that would not be repeated. I ate the bread which, being stale, was as dry as a desert and sucked all the moisture from my mouth. I tipped the edge of the canvas and directed a thin trickle of water towards my lips. It tasted of ash.

"Thirsty, demon?" Piet sniggered. Piet who was too close to the cage.

Without thinking about it, I grabbed the neck of his breastplate and pulled him towards me. His head rang off the bars. While he floundered, I lifted his dagger, spun him around, and held the blade against the pulsing heart vein in his neck. It felt good to act on the spur like that, fluidly and without overthinking things. It felt like the old me.

The shout of alarm went up too late. Swords were drawn, and arrows were nocked. I pulled my new friend closer. "Listen up, boy," I spoke calmly, but not quietly. I wanted them all to hear. "I have had the misfortune to be tortured by demons, but, despite my kind and forgiving nature, you and your fellow, fucking rejectables' insistence on calling me one has finally pushed me beyond the limit of my tolerance." I felt movement behind me. I tipped the blade to a more acute, cutting angle and held it shave close against the throbbing artery bobbing raggedly under his pimply skin. "If the motherless cunt at my back shivs me, I will open this little shitlark like a bottle of claret." The movement stopped. The air was charged, drawn as tight as the bowstring that I could hear being held under tension somewhere behind and to the right.

I ignored the itching, crawling feeling of being aimed upon and fixed the whole of my attention on the quivering pukejelly I had by the scruff. "Now boy, I am many things, many of them unpleasant, but I am not a fucking demon. Got it?"

He nodded, mute with terror. I slid his knife back into his belt and let him go. Although I heard both Bolin and Delgaro shout at their crews to stand down, a hot, sharp stab of pain bloomed in the meat of my shoulder before the command to hold had died on their lips. I slumped against the bars and reached over my shoulder for the shaft while watching Piet stumble away from the wagon like it was about to explode.

The pain didn't hit immediately. It took its time burning its way into my back unsure as a virgin on nuptial night. If I acted quickly, I might save myself more pain and show these sellswords how a Guild Blade dealt with the minor inconvenience of being arrow stuck in the back. I reached over my shoulder, snapped the shaft, gritted my teeth, and locked eyes with the little scrote who'd provoked my anger before throwing myself back, against the floor of the cage. I hoped I'd hit at the right angle to drive the shaft up and out below the bow of my clavicle, above the thickest part of the muscle, and away from ligaments and joints that were clustered in the vicinity. If I got it wrong, it could break and kill me slowly by infection, or it could skid off the bone, puncture something vital and likewise sign my death warrant. But fuck it, I'd get better.

I hit the floor square on, punching the shaft through my shoulder like a nail through a board. The narrow bodkin head passed easily through muscle and flesh, although it must be said, not without hurting like a bastard. "I'd have used a broadhead, or something barbed, bloody amateurs." My right arm was numb, so I grabbed the arrow with my left hand and pulled it out. Blood welled from the hole and spread a warm wet blanket over me. I had nothing to wad the wound, but other than that I'd done a neat job. The world began to fray at the edges. "Here I go again," I said and waited for my next death.

"No one's dying unless I say so." The cage door was thrown open and Delgaro jumped in. Cursing, she pressed her hands to my shoulder. "Fetch Muraid."

Chapter Fourteen

What happened next remains vague. I recall that I was unconcerned that I was bleeding out and that I wasn't in any pain. I was carried into the inn and remember hearing the muttered concerns that my blood might be poisonous, which made me laugh.

Whoever commented, I think it might have been Piet, was still complaining about the possible, ill-effects of contamination as I was rolled onto a table. I drifted on the edge of consciousness as a typically taciturn saw-bones stuffed and sewed my leaky skin sack. I wanted to tell him not to trouble himself because I'd be reborn, but I couldn't find the words amid the tumble of thoughts in my confused and fading mind. I settled for dying quietly while he worked, my wavering gaze fixed on the robed and hooded figure standing in the shadows, watching with the cold detachment of a dead man.

***

I opened my eyes and saw the rough edge of a cracked and fissured roof beam. I was laying under a low, sloping ceiling that was plastered with lime and mud daub. A cool breeze played against my cheek. *I didn't die.* I was sore as all hell, but I was alive and in the same body. Attentive to the dull register of aches and the throbbing heat of the wound in my shoulder, I lay still. It had been such a long time since I'd survived a fight, I'd almost forgotten what it felt like. Sharpened by pain, consciousness returned quickly. The room smelled of hops, fresh straw, and tallow. I craned my neck to follow the whip of breeze that fishtailed past my face.

"Back in the land of the living, eh?" Delgaro was sitting across from the bed with her back to the wall and her foot resting on her knee. A single candle stood vigil against the night which was trying to squeeze between the ill-matched shutters. She was holding the broken arrow.

"How long?" I asked. I was wearing a nightshirt. My shoulder had been bandaged and packed with wadded wool and pungent herbs. I tentatively stretched and felt stitches pull, swiftly followed by a pulse of pain deep inside the muscle of my shoulder.

"Yesterday. It happened yesterday." She brushed the question aside, leaned forward and pointed the arrow at me, as though I hadn't seen enough of that particular point. "You said you were tortured by demons, but there's hardly a mark on you, not a single scar older than a few days. That's odd for anyone, let alone someone who says they've been tortured."

"Yes, I am feeling better, thank you for asking." I tried to sit up, but my arm was leaden, and my back felt like it had been danced on by a drunken wedding party. "My compliments to your sawbones." I rolled on my side. The pallet was an unyielding biscuit of straw which was probably old when my grandsire's grandsire was young.

Delgaro snorted. "I'll pass your thanks on to Muraid. The bill for the extra night's lodge I'll pass to the king."

I raised an eyebrow. "I doubt your king will pay for damages that you caused to his prize."

"Prize?" She chuckled. "You think highly of yourself. And if you hadn't tried to be a smart arse, there wouldn't have been any damage." She stood up, paced the length of the narrow, slope-roofed garret, and dropped her gaze on me like a slap. "Does that mark in your palm have anything to do with the demon you spoke of?" Her tone and determined posture told me that this two-handed wench was not going to let the conversation die until she had answers that satisfied.

In my experience, those born into privilege often held the unshakeable belief that what fell from their lips should be attended to like the sacred tears of angels. Delgaro seemed to be of that ilk.

"It does, but don't worry. The demon in question is busy destroying another world. This," I waved my hand. "Is also the mark of an angel, if you believe in such things."

"I don't."

"And yet you believe in demons?"

"I've seen demons. I haven't seen an angel."

"Must you see a thing to believe in it? Where's your faith, Delgaro?"

She gave a wry smile. "Same place as that dragon. It's dead, it died on a battlefield." She sat down, put her elbows on her knees, and absently twirled the broken shaft.

I turned to face her. The simple maneuver hurt, but I didn't mind the pain. I was enjoying the novelty of being alive, of surviving. "What do you think dragons are?"

"I'm not here to answer your questions."

"But you expect me to answer yours?"

She patted her sword hilt. "She who holds the blade asks the questions. I'll give you this though, you're not like any demon I've seen. But you're not a dragon either. Or if you are, you're toying with us."

I smiled. "Trust me. I am the dragon. I flew through the gate and cooked those undead."

The wry smile appeared again. "I just don't believe you. I can almost believe that you're not from here, that you're not entirely human, but I don't believe you're the dragon. I mean look at you."

"I'm disappointed."

"You don't know what it's been like. If you did, you wouldn't joke. Can you imagine the dead climbing out of their graves, your friends, your family, coming for you?"

I raised my hand. "Let me stop you there. Yes, I can. It's more common than you know. In fact it's a bit of a cliché, but then in my experience, evil fuckers lack imagination." I shrugged.

She looked at me from beneath the arch of her brow. "I'm glad you can laugh, that you can dismiss what has devastated this land and its people— that you are not haunted by horrors beyond imagining." She tilted her chin, sighted me down her nose like it was the groove of a crossbow. "Whoever, whatever you are, you're a lucky cove."

"You think so, eh?" *If only she knew.*

She hurled the arrow at the wall. It was a solid throw. The head bit into the crumbling plaster and stuck. "Instead of lying there with that smug grin on your face, why don't you prove what you are?"

"Careful what you wish for, Captain. There isn't a lot of room in here."

"Fuck you. We were all out, back there. We had nothing left and nowhere to go. That was it, the end. Malin got down on his knees and prayed. *Prayed*, do you hear me? We all fucking prayed." She gasped for breath, fought emotions that tore through her composure.

Someone pounded up the stairs, no doubt drawn by the shouting. "You all right, Del?"

"Yes. Stay out." Her voice was stiff with fury. The footsteps retreated, but not far. "That was all we had. No hope, no chance, just a fucking prayer. And the dragon came and saved our asses. And you, you think it's something to joke about, to lie about?"

"I—"

"Shut up."

I shut up. This was impressive. This was real passion, and highly entertaining.

"This isn't a joke to us. This is our life. I just hope that you're insane." She pointed to the window. "Those Unhallowed, those walking corpses? They were our comrades, our friends, do you understand? If you are what you say you are, prove it, do something. Help us finish this, but don't just sit there, taunting me."

"You finished now?" I asked. She stood there, tight-lipped and glaring, charging the air with her anger. "Given as you're not merely a fucking sellsword but also an expert on arcane lore, what do you think I should do? Should I turn into a dragon and kill this Blight cove just so you can carry on, happily burning anyone who doesn't look like you?"

"Do I look like any of these coves?" She shot back indignantly.

"Yes, you fucking do. You all look alike. Lumpen, angry, and stupid. Give me one good reason why I, an outsider from another world, should help you? Why I should help a bunch of nasty cunts who abuse and promise to kill someone they know nothing about, someone who has done them no harm?" I stabbed an accusing finger at her. "Typical ignorant, fucking humans, blinded by your own importance. You all nearly died? So fucking what? Your friends were killed? Well, I've got news for you, we all lose friends. It doesn't matter. It never did, because everyone dies in the end."

"If it doesn't matter, why are you crying?"

I put my hand to my face. It was wet, hot with tears. "I'm, not crying." *Fuck, why am I crying?*

"Yes, you are."

"Get out, Delgaro. Just get out, or this will go badly." She thought about it, I'll give her that, but sense prevailed and she left. I heard voices outside followed by footsteps retreating downstairs.

I pulled the blanket over my face.

"That went well. A real charm offensive," Tobias said.

I pulled the blanket down. Like a magic trick, he'd appeared in the room and was standing where the angle of the roof and the crook of the eaves cut a shadowy diamond from the candlelight's glow. His cowl was up, and his hands were tucked into the sleeves of his robe. "You look more enigmatic dead than you ever did alive."

He inclined his head. "Thank you."

"Don't. You're still a twat."

He drew back his hood and rubbed his stubbly head with his stump. It was a small gesture yet so familiar, so painfully like him. "I'm a twat? You're the one who fell on an arrow."

I couldn't believe he was here. If I'd had a heart it might have broken. I surreptitiously wiped my face. "Why are you here?"

"I got bored of the afterlife."

"Being dead hasn't improved your sense of humor."

"It's that whole violent murder thing. It quite takes the shine off the hereafter." He paused. Guilt and anger rushed into the silence that fell between us but could not fill that aching chasm. "You could help them, you know that, don't you?"

"Did you miss the part where they put an arrow in my back? Or that they're fixing to sell me to a king who will most likely want to burn me, which in of itself is an irony since it was my burning that saved them."

"Now be fair, most folk who meet you want to kill you. You have that effect on people."

"Apparently so, and like most people he'll fail, but that's not the point. I'm done trying to save folk who don't give a shit about me. I'm particularly tired of being Fate's pawn. I played along with them until I got the chance to speak to you and find out why you're haunting me."

"Who said I was haunting you? Maybe it's the other way around. Maybe it's your guilty conscience that won't let me go."

"We both know I don't have a conscience, guilty or otherwise."

He smiled. "What are you going to do now? Go back to the Annurashi?"

"Am I fuck. I told you, I'm tired of being used."

"Nothing much left then is there?" He leaned against the wall and folded his arms. "I mean, your home's been destroyed, you don't want to save your world, and you don't like this one."

"There are other worlds."

"So you're just going to run?"

"I was thinking of apporting rather than running, but yes, in essence, that's the plan." An expression part disappointment, part sadness, scored his face. "Don't give me that look, priest. I tried. I gave this lot the chance to prove that they were different, and they attacked me. I played along, and they abused me."

"You provoked them. You were difficult, ornery. You could have given them something, thrown them a bone." He pointed his stump at me. "You're like a kicked dog who's learned to snarl first, to bare your fangs to keep the world at bay."

I hated it when he was right. "You're dead wrong. I just don't care. I don't belong here. And anyway, it's the same old shit. A kingdom in peril, evil necromancers, noble young king. I've heard it all before and I know how this story ends." I threw the blanket aside, swung my legs off the bed and stood up. My arm dropped painfully against my side, I yelled and cradled my injured limb.

"Then change the ending. Stop being a pawn and do something with all that power you've got."

"What are you talking about, priest?"

"What if you played the heroic, dragon sorcerer that you've pretended to be, indeed that you *were,* albeit briefly. What then?" He wandered over to the window and flicked the shutters open with his stump and stared into the night.

"That would be a lie. Don't you disapprove of lies?"

"What I disapprove of is irrelevant. You could make a difference here, for the good."

"You forgot to add 'for a change'." He was pushing me to make a decision that I didn't want to make. "Still, it would be a fine jest, would it not? Can you imagine me playing such a role?"

"A hero, saving people for no other reason than you can, for no reward, no gold?" He shook his head. "No. I can't. But that doesn't mean it isn't possible. What else do you have to do?"

"Lots of things." *Nothing, nothing at all.* I sat down, punched the lumps out of my pillow in lieu of his face. "The last hero I saw had his head stuck on a pike. Not much of an incentive, is it?" He didn't answer. I looked up. "Tobias?" The wind snaked through the open window, blew out the candle leaving me in darkness and alone. "Arsehole."

My arm throbbed, but it was nothing compared to the ache his absence caused. "No good ever comes of me trying to help anyone, you fucking know that. I

wasn't made to help, I was made to steal, lie, kill..."
The wind knifed the shadows, chilled my bones. My
words fell on empty air. "All right. We'll play it your
way, but like I told you, I know how this story ends."

***

"Where do you think you're going?" The guard at the
bottom of the attic staircase put his hand on his sword
hilt and the other on my chest, which he quickly
withdrew. "Crone's paps, you're burning up."

"And so will you if you don't get out of my way."

He thought about it, weighed the cost of his life
against the coin he was being paid and stepped aside. I
headed to the nearest door watched by curious but
wisely circumspect guests. *Be the hero, Breed. Hero,
got that?* I looked for the memory of flight, saw
tornadoes of flame burning beneath a ruby sky, and
felt heat quicken within me.

Wool doesn't burn on account of it being the oily
hair of a sweaty, odd-eyed creature called a 'sheep'. It
burns slowly, like a festering wound, it eats away at
itself with a waxen, lackluster flame. When I walked
into the bar, my nightshirt was slowly falling off me in
blackened clumps, leaving me garbed in a web of
scorched seams.

"Be the hero? I'll fucking show him," I said to
myself as I barged through the packed room. The
bubble of conversation died in waves as all eyes turned

to me. Steel slid from scabbards. "You can all put your prickers away, they will avail you naught, save as a means to a swift end."

Delgaro stood up from her seat next to Skurden, took a thoughtful suck on her pipe. "Pray, what do you think you're doing?"

"I'm giving you a chance." I scanned the crowd and let my gaze linger on any who would meet it so that they might see the sincerity I was doing my best to feign. "Now, you don't deserve a chance. You have treated me abominably and I should immolate the lot of you, but then, you are only human." It felt good to see both anger and confusion take root on their ale-reddened faces. I had the moral high ground which was a profound rarity. "Given your species natural inclination to be..." *Don't call them cunts.* "Skeptical, I've decided to show you the truth of what I've told you, throw you a bone so to speak." Chairs scraped, but other than the sound of a dog sloppily cleaned its nethers silence descended upon the room. I gave it a moment for my words to sink in before heading to the door. A gaunt mercenary hovered before it and cast a questioning look to Delgaro.

"Leave it, Janni," said the captain once again proving she was as smart as she looked.

A blast of cold air greeted me as I stepped outside and blew a scurf of firefly sparks from the shreds of my nightgown. Pale moonlight pierced the ragged shroud of silver-limned clouds and painted the rain-inlaid wheel ruts as bright as steel. I crossed the tracks and made for a field where dead stems of an unharvested crop stood black against the night like broken spears. The mercenaries piled out of the inn behind me.

"All right, that's enough. Stay where you are." Delgaro's voice rose above the low-level mutterings.

"Or what?" I said without turning as I made my way to the middle of the field. "Are you going to shoot me in the back?" No answer, no arrow either which was all to the good.

Excited chatter spiced the night with nervous speculation and drunken nonsense, as mercenaries and locals jostled for a better view while maintaining what the loudest amongst them deemed a safe distance.

"You wanted proof, remember?" I called over my shoulder as I squelched across the muddy field. She didn't answer but blades were drawn. When I reached the point which I deemed to be far enough away to keep the nosy culls safe, I shrugged the knots out of my neck, cleared my head of useless thoughts, and fixed my gaze on the horizon. The edge of the world was hidden behind the teeth of a nameless mountain range that curved like a scimitar towards the pink-tinged threat of dawn. I took a moment to savor the view given that it might be the last thing I saw in this or any world. It wasn't the possibility of death that concerned me, it was the thought that I might break the Paradox of Power and turn myself into a living puddle of slime. The Paradox stopped sorcerers destroying the world by overreaching themselves and I'd got around mine by not giving a shit about anything or anyone. I stayed within those bounds, kept myself safe from the backlash of magic that way, but I wasn't sure that was still the case. Didn't I care about Tobias? Didn't I want to do something for, dare I say it, the greater good? If that was the case then perhaps I should settle for casting an illusion, rather than attempting to actually transform. The bigger the spell, the bigger the backlash. "Where are you now, you one-handed cock knuckle?" The wind blew, dead stems rustled. "Fuck it."

I screwed up my courage, tightened my ring piece, and kissed my arse goodbye as I dived into my memories and hunted for the shape of the fire elemental I had been. The flesh might fail but my mind, my essence remembered. It took a while wading through the dross to force my racing mind to focus, but eventually I found it. Slumbering within me was the dream of the dragon. *Time to wake up.* Flames outlined scales, fire lit within the rounds of its molten eyes. Ruin was written in the curve of its saber fangs and despair carried on its burning breath. *Yes, that's it.* I summoned a spell of fire, wove it into the air, and spun a blazing tornado on the fallow ground with me at its heart. I reached for the shape of a spell of transformation and drove the intent within. *I will change. I will.* I felt it form, first a flicker then a roar as the sorcery woke in my flesh like a serpent uncoiling. It screamed from the pit of my stomach, lit up my spine like ungrounded lighting. I threw my arms wide, as the poles of the world tried to tear me in half. My heart thundered with the strain, but I didn't die, not this time. This time, I was reborn.

Flesh became scales, hair turned to horns, fingers to talons. I staggered, stumbled, and crawled before rearing on massive haunches. I thrust my chest to the sky, lifted a ribcage the size of a dray wagon, roared with bellows as powerful as the raging sea. Standing head and shoulders above the roof of the inn I spread my mighty wings, tilted my beautiful, bone-crested head to the beckoning sky, and breathed.

Liquid fire bubbled in my chest, gathered in my throat. I exhaled. Air ignited the spray and turned the black night to gold.

I lashed the field with a tail as long as a good yarn. Thumbprint faces stared at me, wide eyes burnished by my reflected glory. Flames shone in leaded windows, light flashed on naked blades and gilded the warriors' harness. I picked Delgaro out of the crowd, arrowed my frightful gaze upon her. "Now do you believe me?"

Chapter Fifteen

"You've honestly never heard of the Blight?" Delgaro laughed, but there was an edge to it, a measure of nervousness and uncertainty which was entirely understandable after I'd so dramatically revealed my 'true' nature.

I plumped the mound of soft pillows piled in the back of the cart, which along with quilts and wine had been provided for my comfort and convenience as there was no way that I was going near a horse unless I was going to eat it. "I told you, I didn't get the chance to chat before slaying the army of undead and nobody wanted to talk to me much after that."

"Because you looked like a demon and talked like a mad person."

"Lucky for you that I'm not, eh?"

She smiled but didn't answer.

I flicked a strand of scarlet hair away from my face. After proving that I was a dragon, I'd changed shape into something more practical than a forty-foot fire-breathing beast. This body wasn't an exact copy of the half-thoasa, half-human I'd been born, but it bore a close enough resemblance for comfort, with a few added characteristics reminiscent of the Annurashi thrown into the mix. 'Be the hero', he'd said. In which case I decided that I'd better look the part. Rather than garb my new, heroic human-ish body in castoffs, I created an outfit as befitted a dragon sorcerer. I fashioned it after the Shen-style, incorporating layers of flame-colored silks, bound at the waist by a golden obi. I kept the long red hair, which was all well and good until the wind blew and it wrapped around my head like cobwebs.

Delgaro was riding beside the cart, reins held loosely in one hand, the other resting on her thigh, completely at ease on the surly brute. Like her battle-hardened crew, she was accustomed to fighting demons and undead and all manner of unnatural horror, so it hadn't taken her long to adjust to the change in circumstances. Of course, the night before they'd all been scared shitless when I'd stomped over to the inn and demanded an apology. But we were all friends now.

"Tell me more about this evil cull."

"Where to start?"

"I pray you explain in brief. My mind is apt to wander from boring details. Stick to the notable events because life is short, even for dragons."

She rolled her eyes and sketched a mocking bow. "As you wish, but you must understand that I wasn't here when this sorry tale began. I was in the Yarrow of Vishan, suppressing a popular uprising—"

I yawned.

"Really?" She sucked her teeth. Her brow shot up, describing her displeasure. "When Blight first showed up, he claimed to be a visitor from another world, much like yourself." The emphasis wasn't lost on me, but she blunted the barb with a tight smile. "He said he was a mage and was going to transform Arduin into the envy of the world, that's how the story goes. Anyway, from what I've been told, it all turned to shit when it was discovered that he was a necromancer, ill-using Arduin's dead. There was a confrontation, during which he killed the old king and queen and Malin's older sister and declared war on Arduin, or Malin declared war on him, either way, the call went out." Her smile fell away. An expression of unease flitted across her face.

"Arduin didn't have enough troops to fight without the need to hire sellswords?"

"They didn't maintain a standing army and not everyone in the Witnergan— that's the king's council of nobles, are keen to commit forces, especially those furthest from the fighting. Luckily the Free Companies came to the rescue."

"For a price."

She inclined her head. "A very reasonable price."

"Have I seen Blight? Was he there at the cliffs when I turned his army into charcoal?" I asked the question although I knew it was too much to hope that I'd already done for the cove.

"No, but you did a fine job of mopping up what was left of his horde."

"'Mopping up'? I think I did slightly more than that.'"

A hint of a smile tweaked the corner of her mouth. "You didn't see the half of it, no offense, but by the time you showed up, we'd whittled him down to a fraction of the size of his army at full-strength. We lost a lot, threw everything we had at him, but the bastard wouldn't quit. You saw the tail end." She spread her hands. "Of course, it's not finished yet. He can always raise more troops."

"Anyone consider speaking to him and suing for peace?"

She looked horrified at the suggestion. "What? No. He's a necromancer."

I shrugged. "If he's slotting folk to make an army of mindless slaves, that is indeed, disagreeable, but if he's just using the existing dead..." The growing expression of horror on her face told me that in this land, necromancy wasn't just another type of sorcery. "That is a terrible, terrible thing and he should be stopped and made to pay for his crimes."

She narrowed her eyes but let my comments pass. For the first time since we'd met, the mercenary let her guard drop, let her fatigue show through the world-weary facade. "This land has been ravaged, torn apart. On top of that, crops have failed, half the population's starving, and the other half is dispossessed."

I tucked my feet under the hem of my hakama. "This King Malin, is he a lackwit, or is he wise and considered?"

She gave a dismissive wave. "He's fourteen and has been thrust into a role he wasn't born to."

"Shit." The fangs I'd given myself were just a little longer than I'd been used to, and I bit the inside of my mouth. Delgaro mistakenly took my exclamation of pain for one of concerned curiosity and nodded her agreement.

"I know. He's a child dealing with the loss of his family, a blow for anyone, and on top of that, he's the king. Not sure how much longer that will last though."

"Rivals?"

She snorted. "It's a damn shame. The boy's a surprisingly good leader, he listens, takes advice. He's smart but not arrogant, brave but not reckless." She leaned in, lowered her voice. "And let me tell you, those are rare gifts among those born into privilege. I've served many a prince who wasn't bright enough to wipe their own arse, or wise enough to thank those who did." I must have given her a look she didn't like because she bristled. "I wouldn't fight for a fool." As soon as it rose she killed her ire with a laugh. "Not for what he's paying."

"I'll take your word for it." I huddled into the blankets, ironically grateful for the warmth. Changing into a dragon had been exhausting, changing back less so, but combined, both had stretched me to the limit of my strength and abilities. I was drained, threadbare. I wanted nothing more right now than to roll over and fall asleep for a year.

"I shall rename the inn 'The Red Dragon' in your honor," the innkeeper who had provided the blankets had gushed effusively. In payment for charring his field I'd given him a loose scale not that he'd dared to ask for anything. It was interesting to see the change in character forty feet of muscle, fangs, and talons had wrought.

"I'm tired." I yawned.

"Hey, I kept it brief."

"Yes, you did thank you. I shouldn't have stayed up last night."

"Do dragon sorcerers need their beauty sleep?"

"Something like that." After I'd changed out of my dragon form and into my lovely new body, I was invited into the inn, and plied with the best food and drink they had to offer. It was piss-poor fare but as there was a war on and I was starving, I forgave them. With hindsight, I should have eaten more, drunk less, and slept later, but I enjoyed the attention and the fact I'd managed to cast a more potent spell than any I'd ever cast before. *Mother would be proud.*

I yawned and smiled at Piet as he rode past on some errand or other. He didn't say anything, he just looked sheepish and put his head down. I watched him ride along the column which was when I realized that Bolin's crew weren't with us. "Where's Bolin's crew?" I asked Delgaro.

"They've gone ahead to Galewyn, to inform the king that you're with us and what to expect."

"Any idea how that might go down?"

She wiped her mouth with the back of her hand and peered into the distance where the road snaked between fields separated by patches of woodland. "Hard to say." She shrugged. "The Witnergan are a bunch of backstabbing, scheming cunts."

"Nothing I haven't seen before."

"No, me either," she answered absently as her attention was drawn to something up ahead. She stood in her stirrups. "What now?" A tree had fallen across the road. As there was a ditch on one side and a stream on the other they'd have to move it or back-track. "Marvelous. We'll have to get some saws up here and a hoist. Unless you want to…?"

"Do I look like a farm laborer?"

"It was worth a shot." She kicked her horse on and began shouting orders.

The column slowed to a halt and those who hadn't been assigned to clearing the road took their ease. Pipes were lit, flasks passed, and the hedgerows watered. I could have moved the tree, but I was bone weary, so I lay back and watched the mercenaries work around me. Whatever ills had befallen this land, no matter how brutal the fighting, the mercenaries had done well for themselves. More than one sported a gold earring or jeweled cloak pin. Their weapons and armor were sound and their garb, although bloodstained and patched here and there was cut from fine linen, luxurious velvet, and damask. Their mounts were likewise well accoutered, plump and, healthy looking specimens. My stomach rumbled at the thought of just how plump some of them looked, which surprised me. I'd never beheld any vittles and desired them, I'd eaten when I was hungry which was usually every couple of days, but unlike humans, I'd never treated the necessity as a pleasure. Now here I was, craving lightly roasted horse. While I pondered my newfound lust for barbecued quadruped, the road was cleared and the column moved off. The cart rocked gently, I was warm, comfortable, and soon asleep.

***

Regarded by many as an escape from the trials and tribulations of the waking world, sleep is oft described as a balm, a gift bestowed equally upon beggar and king alike, but not today— not for me at least. No halcyon fields or sweet flower meadows and frolics awaited me when I drifted off. I was cast into a vivid nightmare where I was back in the fire realm, only this time I was in my thoasan body, trying to reach the towering angle gate as my flesh shriveled and burned. I walked on the blackened stumps of my feet until my bones split apart and leaked bubbling marrow and then I crawled, dragging my hands from the fiery ground, leaving imprints of flesh behind, but I didn't die, I kept crawling towards the gates.

After enduring what felt like hours of torment, I decided that this dream could just fuck off and I willed myself away to a place less fraught with horror. I found myself somewhere dank and dark. Before me was a doorway, sitting atop the lintel was a cobwebbed skull in which a mouse had made its nest. *This was more like it.* I'd taken myself home to the Mouse's Nest Inn that was hidden in the sewers under Appleton. A gentle breeze sighed through the tunnels accompanied by the constant chiming drips of water. I pushed open the door and the cool dark yielded to bright light and smoky heat, the heady smell of pel, and the hot babble of conversation.

The first person I laid eyes on had not, to my knowledge, ever frequented the establishment which was run and owned by my dear Mother and was the headquarters of her guild. For one, he would never have come down here, being averse to hardship and squalor. Second, had he ventured into the sewer, he would have been mugged before he set foot inside this dubious establishment that I liked to think of as home, despite his tremendous, sorcerous powers. And yet here he was, a flagon of ale cradled in the crook of his handless arm.

"What are you doing here, priest?" I kept my tone neutral. Causing a scene in the 'Nest was amateurish and apt to draw unwanted attention.

Tobias snapped his fingers before my face. "Never mind me. You need to wake up."

"I don't want to. I want to stay here, drink ale, and gab with my fellow Blades. I want to catch up and remember the good times."

"There weren't any good times. Now wake up— there's something you have to do."

I folded my arms. "No. Get lost, shade."

He raised an eyebrow, sighed dramatically. "Have it your way then."

I was skeptical of his capitulation because he was a stubborn little bastard once he got an idea in his head. He took hold of the tankard nestled in his arm and put it to his lips. A wicked gleam lit in his watery eyes.

"Don't you dare," I said as he threw the ale in my face.

***

I woke with a start, spluttering imaginary ale. I was in the cart, but the landscape had changed so entirely from what it was like before I fell asleep that for a second, I didn't think I'd woken up at all, but had instead slipped from one dream into another. The air was gritty and laden with smoke. The bare fields and woodland had been replaced by a fecund and lugubrious forest on the right of the road, and on the left by scorched heathland.

Teams of men and women, swathed against the choking smoke were burning and hacking at the skirts of the twisted forest. Every hundred feet or so they planted signs by the road that proclaimed something in a language that I couldn't read, although the red skull daubed beneath the words conveyed with sufficient eloquence that death and danger lurked in the undergrowth. Smoke billowed, birds flew out of the gnarled treetops and spiraled away from the fire which was hungrily devouring the edge of the wood. Somewhere in the distance screams rose on the wind before being stolen away as flames began to tear through the foliage.

"Where the hell are we? Did you hear that scream?" I looked around, but no one met my gaze or seemed inclined to answer. The mercenaries rode on in silence, their horses' hoof beats muffled by the thick layer of ash that caked the road. We passed the forest burners with barely an acknowledgment. They kept their heads down and scarves over their mouths, which must have been scant proof against the smoke that was billowing from the necrotic forest. I stood up. "I said, what is this place?"

Delgaro rode over to the cart and pulled down the scarf she was wearing over her nose and mouth. "This is cursed land, poisoned. It's as close as Blight's forces came to Galewyn before we stopped them. It used to be a nice place, rich farmland, thriving villages, prosperous towns."

We came upon the outskirts of a deserted village. An inn sign was swinging from a single chain outside of a dead-eyed building. The faint image of a dancing bear was just about visible beneath the sickly yellow moss and purple fungus spreading across it. The buildings themselves had been claimed by rampant thorns and choking vines which bore fat, white berries that were bursting in the heat of the flames, splattering everything close in bile bright juice that blackened what it touched.

The burners moved along the eaves of the woods and torched some of the buildings nearest the road, loosing a storm of burning thatch into the sky. Along the length of forest, I could see about fifty men and women working the line. They were a scrawny, dead-eyed crew, but they were well equipped for the job. Each soot-greased gang of four had a handcart stacked with barrels of tar, water, scythes, billhooks, and torches. They were wearing thick leather aprons and water-soaked hides to shield them from the heat.

"Conscripts?" I asked Delgaro.

"Volunteers. Mostly those who used to live in these parts." She squinted against the drifting haze. "They think they can get it back." The air was acidic and made my skin tingle like it was being pricked by a thousand tiny needles.

"I don't fancy their chances."

"Nor do I. The blight that has taken root in these places is hard to kill." Not far ahead an altercation was taking place by the side of the road. A bearded cull with a swaddled infant in his arms was trying to shove past a woman who was standing between him and the burning village. She was screaming at him, begging, and threatening by turns. He was holding her off with one hand as she tried to snatch the babe. If he'd been facing away from the fire the scene might not have been so sinister. As a sideshow to the main performance, a couple of grey-haired culls nearby were remonstrating with a crew of weary, smoke-streaked burners. Even though they were shouting it was impossible to hear what they were saying over the roar of the fire that devoured their words before they reached us.

The man holding the bundle was doing his best to avoid looking at the woman, as though she might turn him to stone should their eyes meet. Every time he pushed her away she came back at him, wild, raging, but despite her ferocity, she was outmatched in size and strength. As we drew closer I could hear the child shrieking fitfully.

"He's fixing to burn that maggot," I observed as the man backhanded the woman and sent her sprawling in the mud. He froze when a tiny hand squirmed from the swaddling and grabbed reflexively at his beard.

"Morgu, please. For the love of mercy!" The woman's voice was raw, torn from shouting and shrill with emotion. Blood flowed from her nose and mouth, but she paid it no heed. He saw her then, saw the work of his fists and froze. His cast-iron expression melted. Tears coursed down his cheeks. Then he looked at the babe and saw something that hardened his resolve.

The woman saw it too and screamed as he turned again towards the burning village. Fury lent her strength and she threw herself at him, wrapped her arms around his legs. He tried to push her away, but she had latched on and refused to let go. He hit her without enthusiasm, tried to scrape her off, but she dug in and hung on. The babe voiced its protest and gave vent to its shrill desire not to die in the flames.

We continued, the road curved away from the burning village and the warring couple making it easier for those soft-hearted souls who didn't want to pass too close to the unfolding tragedy. Having said that, none of the mercenaries looked like they were desperate to interfere, most refused even to glance at the commotion, which surprised me. I'd thought humans to be at least curious, if not compassionate culls. I looked at Delgaro, but her gaze was fixed on some point in the distance. "Aren't you going to do anything?" I shouted to her.

Her face was lit by flames that snarled and recoiled and snapped at the village like rabid dogs. "I told you, this place is cursed," was all she said before she spurred her mount and rode off without a backward glance. I would have questioned the mercenary's lack of sympathy, but I was distracted by the man with the bundle who finally plucked up the stones to kick the woman. Winded, she gasped and fell clutching her gut. He strode towards the village, which was quickly being engulfed by fire. The way the wind was blowing he wouldn't make it out before the flames cut across the path and trapped him within the inferno. He wasn't just fixing to kill the child, he was after killing himself along with it. The old couple ran to the woman's side and stopped her crawling after him. She screamed, railed against them like a wounded animal, but they held on to her, determined, but not ungentle.

The cart's tail turned framing the bewildered group of burners shuffling awkwardly by the roadside, the old couple grappling with the woman, the woman screaming at the man, and the man carrying the babe into the inferno.

Chapter Sixteen

"It's raining," one of the mercenaries mentioned in passing, as though I might have missed it. I jumped off the cart and plodded towards the cull with the babe, taking the rain with me. As I drew closer I strengthened the spell and turned the light drizzle I'd created into a lashing downpour. By the time I reached the miserable tableau of startled burners, screaming woman, and tearful elders, I was soaked to the skin and smoke was rising twenty feet in all directions where the flames had been extinguished by the deluge.

"Don't even think of relighting those fucking torches," I said to the burners as I passed. They wisely took note of the warning in my tone, because as one they cast the smoking, tar-dipped brands away. "Look at me, being the bleeding hero," I muttered to myself as I hitched up my silks and tiptoed through the mud.

The would-be immolationist didn't hear me coming. He was squatting in what looked like the village square, weeping over the squirming, yelling bundle. When he felt the rain, he looked up and cursed. Buildings began to smolder and hiss as the fire was extinguished. Confused and overwrought the daft cull looked around, his tears lost in the blur of rain. "What a fucker, eh? Can't even burn yourself to death," I said.

"What?" He rubbed his eyes.

"The rain." I gestured to the sky. "It's as though the gods themselves don't want you to fry yourself or the kid." I made a space in the storm so that I didn't drown those I'd come to rescue.

"Why do you care?" He narrowed his gaze as he saw me clearly for the first time. "What are you? Did Blight send you to torment me further? I'm going to kill us, isn't death enough for you bastards?" Spit flew from his trembling lips. Despite his fury and his avowed intention, I noticed that he held the child protectively to his chest and half turned away from me, as though I was the frothing, murderous lunatic fixing to slay the brat.

"In truth, I don't much care, but I have a friend who does, so it's your lucky day." He didn't show any sign that he understood, his mind was spinning like a flywheel unable to grasp the simplest logic. "Listen, if it was up to me, I'd let you kill yourself and the brat, but then I'd get it in the ear, so, you know, I can't let you burn to death, sorry."

"You don't understand." He shook his head.

I laughed. "No, my friend, you're not listening. I don't care." He stared at me, face as blank as a paving slab. "I tell you what, you seem like a fellow who's reached his majority and as I'm not a monster, if you're fixed on self-immolation I won't stop you. Just hand over the babe."

He clutched the child tighter. "I can't. He's cursed. The Holy Briar says we cannot suffer the unclean to live." Snot and tears dripped from his nose. "Those cursed by the Blight must die."

"And just how is yon kinchin cove cursed? Has it joined the ranks of the restless dead?"

He gaped at me. "Sweet Bride's life, no. It's my fault, my pride…"

I sensed a long story brewing.

"We left when the evil came, but I wanted to save the farm, so we came back, but it was too soon." He buried his head in the child's blankets, a few wracking sobs escaped before he composed himself and continued. "Me and Jenna wanted to be at home when the babe came, not in a tent in the middle of nowhere. But we shouldn't have come back." He drew a shuddering breath. "He bears the mark of the Blight. He's cursed."

I had an idea of what he was talking about. "Show me." I offered the man a hand up. He stared at my claws. "You're a demon, aren't you? You've come to take my boy."

"No, I'm not a fucking demon. I'm a dragon sorcerer, I've come here to save your babe and you if you're inclined. If I were a demon I wouldn't bother talking nice would I? I'd just cackle, tell you what horrible things I was going to do to you for eternity, and get on with doing it." I offered my hand again. "I promise, I'm not a demon and I don't bite." The cull took my hand. I hauled him up and waited for him to show me the child. After some hesitation he peeled back the blankets. And then I understood.

"You prick." I chuckled.

"What?" The man looked rightfully confused.

"Not you. Tobias, a friend of mine, allegedly." He gave me a blank look. "Never mind." The babe was a chubby little thing with wisps of pale hair and gray eyes. It looked as robust and well put together as any infant should save for one thing. Instead of a left hand to match the right, the child had a splendid fleshy pincer. I reached out, and like any other kinchin cove of a similar age, he grasped my finger with his claw.

"You're the sire?" I asked as I eased the child out of the man's arms. A slew of emotions crossed his face, but he didn't fight me. He nodded. "And you were going to kill yourself and your babe because of this little touch?" It wasn't hard to believe. I'd seen the tiny bundles floating down the river and heard the cries on lonely mountainsides swiftly silenced by wolves, or at best, a freezing night. It didn't matter if the unwanted offspring was whole and hearty, let alone schism touched, many a cove disposed of their unwanted spawn like yesterday's garbage. It was the human way.

"It's the mark of the Blight. The chaplains say it's evil." He wiped his nose on his sleeve. "Even the priestess of the Mother says it is a curse on us."

"They're talking shit. It's just magic. Powerful, dirty magic." He blessed me with another blank stare. "You don't do much magic here, do you?" He shook his head. "And I suppose you don't know what a warspawn is, or 'schism touched'?" More vehement head shaking. Delgaro's words came back to me, about the Blight being from 'somewhere else'. This was the result of Schism magic, powerful enough to raise the dead, warp the unborn, and poison the land. "You'd do well not to move back here for, I don't know, a few hundred years, maybe longer."

He looked stunned. "This is our home."

"Was." I turned to leave with the child when some suicidal impulse overcame the fellow and he grabbed my elbow. I slowly turned my gaze upon him. He let go.

"Where are you taking my son?"

"He's your son now, is he? I thought he was a monster, cursed by evil." I kept walking as there was little sport to be had or satisfaction to be gained from arguing with a superstitious bumpkin.

"He's still mine. He has my blood. He belongs to me." He called after me, resolve dissipating in the rain.

The infant squirmed, restless and hungry he quested towards my chest, mouth agape. I shuffled it into a different position. "Nothing for you there, sprout. As for you." I fixed the fellow with my best, withering gaze. "You gave up any claim on this child when you tried to kill him."

"Then leave him with Jenna. Please, I beg you, leave him with his mother."

"I'm a stranger, not stupid."

"What do you mean?" He shuffled nervously, refused to meet my gaze. He knew well enough what I meant.

"Do you seriously think I'd leave this little snot here so that when I'm gone you can get a bunch of your pitchfork-wielding relatives together and finish what you started? Do I look that stupid?" I gave him the dagger eye. "Be very careful how you answer that."

He backed away. Fresh tears stained his face.

"Morgu, you bastard, what have you done? Where's Sceafa?" The woman flew at the unfortunate Morgu, grabbed him by the hair and shook him like a dog shaking a rat. She was so focused on trying to scramble his brains by vigorous agitation that she didn't notice that I had her brat until it mewled. Like some predatory animal her head snapped round, and she fixed me with a venomous look. Her eyes were wild, although her face was swollen and bloody her fury was undiminished. She bared her teeth, snarled. She looked so ferocious that I took an involuntary step back.

"Give me my baby." She dropped Morgu and advanced towards me. I made the rain fall a little harder on the off chance it might dampen her rage. It didn't. "I said, give me my baby." She rushed me, hands clawed like she was going to tear my head off. I could only assume that Morgu had taken the babe when she wasn't looking.

I raised my hand, palm towards her, held her at bay with a sharp blast of air. "Hold on there, fustilugs." The sudden gust startled her, she gasped and fell into the arms of her mate who she shrugged off like he was a snake made of shit. "If I hand him over, what could you do to protect him from this thick fuck and his Briar friends? Where would you go to get away from them, you can't stay here. I take it you have a coin purse stuffed with gold to pay for guards, a carriage, provisions?" I wished I knew a soothing spell because my words were doing nothing to appease her rage.

"It's got nothing to do with you. He's my baby, give him back to me." Her voice was full of anguish, for his part the kinchin cove was happily sucking his pincer, oblivious to the storm centered upon him.

"No," I said. She screamed and came at me again. The babe wailed, I hit her with a stronger blast of air which put her on her arse. "Now listen, Jenna is it? Damn, I know more about you culls than I do my own kin. I was sent here to save the child, not pander to some she-bear's maternal instincts."

"I'll kill anyone who tries to hurt my son. Even you if I have to."

I had to smile at that. "Somewhat optimistic, but I admire your spirit. Tell me, where in this land can you take your son so he'll be safe from fuckheads like him?" I chinned at her man.

She opened her mouth but then caught herself, sagged under the weight of realization. The rain beat down, turned the blood on her face to tears. She sank to her knees, clawed at the muddy ground. "Crone help me." She sobbed as she squeezed the fouled earth between whitened fingers. Her words trailed off into an incoherent litany of sorrow, the same impotent and oft-recited prayer spoken by all those helpless coves whose lives have been destroyed by war and oppression. Morgu reached out, tried to comfort her, but was again violently repulsed. Beyond the bounds of my storm, the fires were still gnawing at everything that had grown or been built here. Faint shadows that I took to be the burners moved through the glowing haze.

Within my wet sphere of influence, the flames had been entirely vanquished. Ghostly coils of smoke reached through blackened branches and strove for the sky. It was time to leave the happy couple before Delgaro and her crew came looking for me, or worse, left me in this gods' forsaken shithole.

"Wait," the woman half begged, half demanded.

I waited. "What?"

"You're a sorcerer?"

"*Dragon* sorcerer, yes. What of it? Come on, hurry to the point. I've a mind to get out of this rain."

"Heal my son. Undo what's been done to him." Her infant grew bored of sucking his claw and latched onto one of my knuckles that had come within range of his questing maw.

"I can't," I said, distracted by the hungry child.

"No, listen." She raised a trembling hand. "You can change the weather, make that wind. Surely, you can give my boy a hand? Surely you can do that?" Her desperation was so palpable I could almost taste it.

I looked down at the little maggot nestled in my arms. I'm no seer, but even I could work out that Tobias wanted me to save it. But how much did I have to do for it to be deemed 'saved'? Would it be enough to dump it in an orphanage far from these superstitious and murderous culls and the cults they followed? Or did he intend for me to keep it and raise it as my own? "Gods, no. That's too much."

"Why too much?" The woman demanded, misconstruing my words.

"I wasn't talking to you." Just then the child grunted and turned scarlet. I thought it might be choking, but it was worse than that. Tiny eruptions drummed against my arm through the swaddling blanket in advance of the stink. In that moment of pungent insight I realized that I didn't want to go anywhere near the shit-caked nethers of a human infant, or an infant anything come to that.

"A hand you say?" The smell emanating from the bundle was impressively malodorous for such a small parcel. "As it happens, I've recently learned a bit about transformation, but I'm not sure." It farted again. "I'll give it a go." I fixed the woman with my best straight face. "Are you certain this is what you want?"

"Give it a go?" Morgu repeated, seemingly horrified at the prospect. "What if you fail? What if you hurt him, or make it worse?"

"You're fickle and no mistake. You've gone from murderous to paternal within a half hour. I'm surprised your seed had the wherewithal to set, let alone take root and sprout." I gave the woman a questioning look. "Is he the father?"

"Yes! Now please," she implored. "If you can make it rain when prayers to the Bride, the Mother, and the Crone couldn't squeeze a tear from the heavens, you can fix my boy."

"He's not broken," I snapped. "But then, I suppose we judge these things differently."

Her fury broke. Whether from the onslaught of my reason, which was doubtful or because the weight of the world had finally got the better of her. Whatever it was, she sagged, came over, and gently tucked the blanket around the smelly little impling's fat chin. "He's hungry. At least let me feed him before you take him." She scrubbed tears away with mud-slicked fingers "He has no chance here, not like this. I know that. If they don't kill him, he'll be an outcast."

The look she gave me might have softened Mother's flinty heart. "Look at me, wench. I've been an outcast all my life. No one cares overmuch. Idle hate passes like flatulence. The bovine slobs he'll mix with will throw stones, poke him with sticks, knock him down, if he lets them." I shrugged. "He'll either toughen up or be beaten every time he raises his head, no matter where he ends up. Or he might get killed, same as any cull, in any rough world." I pointed at the blanket to where his little pincer must lay. "This just gives those with evil minds an easy excuse, but two-handed or one-handed, or no-fucking-handed at all, it doesn't matter. Those who are inclined to evil would pluck the scales from an angel's wings if they thought they could get away with it. Sick creatures will always find an excuse to indulge their turpitude. You want my advice? Encourage him to be tougher and meaner than any fucker who might cross his path, like—" Realization struck me like a stone. "Like my mother did me. Or let your mate get on with what he intended."

She grabbed my arm. "You fix him, you bastard. You fix my boy." I stopped listening as I contemplated the possibility that Mother might have given a shit about me after all, that she might have been fucking horrible because she'd cared.

"It's funny, isn't it?" I smiled at the babe who was gurgling and making faces. "Those silly things that sneak into your head when you should be thinking about more pressing matters." The woman let go and backed away, confused. Morgu shuffled nervously, unsure of where he could stand that wouldn't provoke his woman to attack him again. "I remember being in the market in Appleton. I'd just lifted a nice, silk pocket square when a gang of bumpkins set upon me. Not because of the theft, they hadn't seen that, but because I was different. It wasn't personal, not really. They were out to hurt someone. If it hadn't been me it would have been some other cove." I laughed as the memory turned red and the echo of their pitiful cries reached across the years to delight my ears once again.

"Funny, eh?" I turned to Jenna. "Do you still want Morgu?"

"What do you mean?" She turned to her man and shrieked when she saw what I'd been watching lurch towards him while the old memories had played themselves out in my mind's eye. "Unhallowed!" Jenna yelled, directing Morgu's attention with her terror-stricken gaze to what was behind him. The dopy cull tried to run and look behind at the same time, knotting his gangly legs like old rope. He stumbled and fell, presenting an easy target for the charred undead that were staggering out of the flames. Jenna screamed.

"I'll take that as a yes, then."

There were four and a half Unhallowed creatures. The half being what was left of a woman who had already lost her legs to some catastrophe. The fire was busily working on the rest of her, but she continued to crawl towards Morgu, driven by an insatiable desire to feast on his flesh. I didn't fancy her chances of reaching him before she was cremated, but one had to admire the mindless tenacity.

"Did you know any of these culls?" I asked the woman, but she just continued to yell and point. I looked to Morgu for an answer, but he was attempting to row back on his arse as the most robust of the walking corpses staggered towards him. Its arms were on fire, but that didn't slow it down. In my experience, the restless dead felt nothing other than the agony of knowing that they were dead. "Right then, Sceafa," I addressed my comments to the babe as he was the only one who wasn't yelling. "This is how we cast a spell of lightning, or sky fire as some call it. First off, you have to make sure the angles are right."

I brought the spell to mind and focused on the foremost undead. Judging by what was left of his garb I guessed he'd been a farmer in life. His back was bent from long years of toil and although they were rapidly withering in the flames, I could see he had hands like shovels. I imagined the fellow alive, standing on the edge of the fields that his family had tilled for generations, chewing the pipe which had worn a cleft in his teeth. Year in, year out, he would have done the same thing. In fact, being one of the Unhallowed was probably the most exciting thing that had ever happened to the old scrote.

Jenna grabbed my arm again. "Don't just stand there, pointing. Do something," she demanded.

"This isn't easy you know. One slip and your man gets fried along with them. Oi, Morgu, keep your head down." I shoved her aside and squinted along my line of sight to the restless dead. "Now, Sceafa, the angles are just about perfect, I think." I drew a breath, inhaled smoke, touched the spark of magic nestled in the infinite space somewhere between gut and mind and cast the spell. A coruscating whip of white fire hit the lead corpse in the chest. The deadling looked confused for a sliver of a second before it exploded, casting its limbs to all points of the compass.

I focused on the next shambler. This unfortunate was clad in shreds of mail and listlessly waved a broken sword that had fused to the flesh of its melted hand. The lighting hit it in the face and wreathed its helm in a halo of fire thorns. There was a hissing noise as what was left of the soft matter within its braincase heated up extremely quickly. The skull burst like a rotten egg. The lightning forked from the now headless corpse and struck the third and fourth of the benighted crew. Already well ablaze, both were instantly reduced to ash. Finally, the lightning earthed itself in the fifth's back. In seconds it was over. "And that's how you cast a blast of lightning at more than one target. A friend showed me how to do it. Oh." The babe had fallen asleep. "Well, there you go. I hope you're happy," I said to Tobias.

Chapter Seventeen

The smell of lightning was replaced by the stench of burned, putrid flesh. Unlike fresh meat, long dead bodies do not smell like a succulent roast. Reasonably fleshy, but rotted corpses burn sickly sweet and coppery if they're still full of claret.

I sniffed my robes. They smelled of burned hair and boiled spinal fluid. "I'll never get the smell out." Jenna gave me a questioning look before returning her worried gaze to the sleeping child. "He's well," I reassured her. Her man climbed unsteadily to his feet. What little color he'd had before the attack had completely drained from his face, leaving him paler than death.

"You saved us," Morgu conceded, but didn't look me in the eye.

"Yes, I did. Now, I suggest we trot out of here in case the fire flushes more of them toward us." I didn't wait for their reply. I'd had enough of wailing women, suicidal men, and the restless dead for one day. "I must say," I said to the babe. "I'm surprised that Delgaro and her crew haven't come looking for me. 'Bet they haven't even notice that I've gone." The infant stirred and snuggled into his blankets.

"They noticed," Delgaro called from the smoldering edge of the forest beside the burners and her company. "They just weren't going into Blighted land to get you."

"I can't say as I blame you." I smiled. "Some nasty things in there, and the odd idiot." I glanced at the shamefaced Morgu who was shuffling along behind Jenna and then at the babe. "That's right isn't it, little one? Your sire's a fuckwit, isn't he?"

"You appear to have a baby. Are congratulations in order?" Delgaro pointed her drawn sword at the child. For all that she said she wasn't going to come find me, she and her crew had accoutered themselves for an expedition into the fire even going so far as to soak their cloaks in water.

"I do, and no, they aren't." No sooner had the words left my mouth than Jenna sparked up.

"He's mine. I want him back."

"Why do you want him? I haven't *fixed* him."

She ignored me and turned her pleas to Delgaro. She was wasting her time if she thought she'd find sympathy from the mercenary, but who was I to spoil her day? Delgaro was watching the proceedings with an air of amused detachment when Jenna approached her, hands clasped like a supplicant. "Lady, I beg you, tell this, whatever it is, to give me back my son. I don't care about his hand. He's my baby and I love him. Please, lady, make it give him back to me."

Some of the younger sellswords, those who hadn't yet bled out the full measure of their compassion on the battlefield, were moved by the woman's self-inflicted plight. I didn't want to hurt any of them, but I was going to placate the ghost of Tobias and save the fucking child, even if it killed them. I dropped my cold gaze on the woman. "Are you addled, wench? You just saw what I did. Do you want these coves to die?"

She left off pleading and unflinching, squared up to me. "I want my son." Again, I marveled that Morgu had managed to take the infant from her in the first place.

"We've discussed this. Fuckface over there." I nodded at her man. "Will try to kill him again if I leave him with you."

"I won't, I swear," Morgu said and threw himself at the woman's feet. "Jenna, please, believe me, I would have died with him. We'll go away, far from anyone who'd hurt him." She made to move away, but he grabbed her hand. "Please, Jen. I mean it. I'll kill anyone who tries to harm our boy."

Tears pearled in her eyes. "To the Pit with killing, I've seen enough of death. Will you live for him and love him just as he is?"

Morgu looked to the baggage slumbering in the crook of my arm. I could see the conflict in his eyes, see the battle raging within him between his conscience, his fear, his love for his child, and his duty to his elders. It wasn't a position I'd ever found myself in, but then I wasn't stupid. Battle won, relief spread across his face as the weight of indecision lifted. "Yes. I swear by the Bride. I'll love him. I do love him, and I will live for him, protect him with my last... with everything. And you, love. My Jenna, my lovely Jenna. I've been a fool, worse. Please forgive me." He buried his head in her skirts and sobbed.

"This is all very moving," Delgaro side-mouthed to me. "But what's wrong with the babe? How's it cursed?"

"Touched. We say, 'touched' where I come from, not 'cursed'."

"Your pardon. How is it 'touched'?" She made to peek beneath the blankets, but I twisted away and gave her a scolding look.

"Put it this way, he'll have to be careful how he picks his nose, but he'll have a mean left hook."

"He has a hook hand?"

"It's more of a claw."

"Oh." Delgaro looked disappointed.

"Jenna," the old fellow shouted. In all the excitement I'd forgotten about the old couple. He barged through the bemused mercenaries with his woman trailing wearily behind him. He saw me and my little burden and a look of disgust spread across his gaunt face. "Like calls to like. Let the demon take it," he exclaimed.

"A demon you say? You people are obsessed." I laughed off the slight, it was either that or kill him and I didn't want to wake the babe. His proclamation roused some of the friskier mercenaries who gave me the fish eye. Despite everything they'd seen, some of them still distrusted me.

Morgu found his spine somewhere and faced off against the codger. "No, father. He's coming home with us. I should never have listened to you in the first place."

The old man's face softened, his voice cracked with emotion. "You've always been a good boy, Morgu, obedient. The child is cursed, son. You heard the chaplain. Leave it with its own kind." He shot me a knifish look. I smiled, inclined my head. He straightened, clutched a pendant tied around his neck that looked like a twig. "Come, Morgu. Bring your wife and let us leave this place."

Jenna's mouth firmed to a hard line and she stared resolutely at her man. She was giving him the chance to redeem himself. I almost felt sorry for him, for whichever way he turned he was going to mortally offend someone. I only hoped that for his sake it wasn't me.

Delgaro made a disgusted face and stepped away from me. "Sweet Trinity, that child needs its arse cleaning."

"Are you offering?"

She threw back her head and laughed. "Not in this lifetime."

"It was worth a try."

The old man took hold of Morgu's arm. "The chaplains won't accept the child, son."

Morgu snorted. "To the Pit with the chaplains. They've done nothing for us. Nothing except tell us that the coming of Blight is our fault." He gestured to the burning village. "I'm tired of being blamed for those things we haven't done."

"Enough." The old man shook with indignant fury. "The chaplains are the bearers of the Word and the guardians of the Holy Briar."

Jenna pushed between the two of them. "We'll leave the country. We'll not trouble the Briar or its servants."

"No, you won't." It was the old woman, steel-haired and steel-eyed. She looked a bit like Skurden, had the same aura of someone who not only knew where the bodies were buried but had buried them herself after dispatching them. "This madness has gone on long enough. Crone's sake, we should be celebrating, not destroying our family. We survived. How many others are dead, or worse?" She turned to the old man, "You should rejoice. Your son is alive. Your grandson is alive."

"That thing is not—"

She slapped him across the face, drawing a collective wince from those gathered. "If you want to go live with the other old fools in a tent by the river, you keep talking, Renold." Renold's cheeks reddened, but he wisely kept his mouth shut. I would have laughed had she not then marched over to me. I sighed inwardly. I was tired and lightheaded with hunger. I just wanted to throw myself in the back of the cart and sleep for a month.

"You. What are you?" She demanded.

"I'm a dragon, ma'am." I bowed. "And a powerful sorcerer. I saved the young king's army. What the fuck are you?"

I'll give the old cull her due, she blanched but held her ground. "Whatever you are, you have no claim on my grandson."

"I saved his life. In any world that would give me a claim. Your son was fixing to kill the boy."

"My son is a weak-minded fool who'll have to work damn hard to prove otherwise." She licked her dry lips. "This madness grew out of fear. It ends today. I knew the moment I laid eyes on that child that he was as good as any babe ever born, but I let them wear me down. I let the chaplains get the better of me because I'm old and tired."

"What's changed in the last few hours?"

"You. It's taken a, whatever you are—"

I rolled my eyes. "I just told you—"

"*A stranger*, to show me that I, that *we* have been the worst kind of fools. If it takes the rest of my life to make amends to my grandson then so be it. Please, I beg you. Give him back to us."

The little maggot farted again. I don't know whether it was the stench or the fact that I hadn't recovered from the exertions of the day before, but my head began to swim. "Oi, Fustilugs," I called out Jenna. "Take him." I held the little stink blossom at arm's length. She rushed over and took him from me. "If anyone hurts him." I scanned their faces to lock my coldly earnest expression of sincerity into their memories. "If anyone hurts him, I will know, and I'll come back, and I tell you this; if I do, I'll make the Blight seem like a benevolent, fucking angel of mercy. Do I make myself clear?"

They nodded mutely, either out of relief or, I hoped, a healthy dose of fear because I meant what I said. Their heartfelt pleas hadn't moved me to relent; my gut had told me it was the right thing to do. It had also told me that I had suddenly become unwell. I was lightheaded, weak, and sweat was dripping down my back. It took all my resolve to stay upright and not pitch over into the mud. *So much for being a 'powerful dragon sorcerer'. You've caught a chill, you idiot.*

The family crowded around the babe. My head ached, my palm itched. I looked down at my hand. The silvery, star steel sheen had faded to pearl gray. The world grew dim and distant, frayed at the edges. "I feel odd."

The sound of shouting roused me somewhat from my stupor. I looked up. Jenna was hugging the child, Morgu and the old couple were hugging each other. Some of the more curious mercenaries, Piet and Delgaro amongst them were also crowding around the happy family and their stinky offspring. I stumbled over to the sanctuary of the cart.

"Wait," Jenna called after me. "You, dragon, whoever you are, hold up."

Swaying like a sapling in a gale, I waited. "Gods' sake, wench. I gave you the brat, what now?"

Tears shone in her eyes as she rushed over. "You were testing me all along."

"I was?" I had no idea what she was talking about until I saw what lay within the blankets. Young Sceafa had changed. Instead of a pincer he had a human hand, in shape at least. The new appendage had the requisite number of fingers but unlike its opposite, it shone with a distinctive, star steel glow. Then it dawned on me why I felt so ill. The Paradox of Power. *Oh shit.* I waved the woman away. "Look after him. The boy has a future beyond this shit pit." I staggered drunkenly towards the cart, my head pounding like a tilt hammer.

"Where are you going?" Delgaro shouted from what seemed like a great distance.

"For a nap," I mumbled. Back in Appleton, I'd seen what was left of a sorcerer who'd overreached himself and been turned into a puddle of living slime for breaking the Paradox of Power. I made it back to the road, threw myself into the cart and burrowed into the blankets, wracked by painful spasms, thirst, and hunger. "Please don't let me turn into a puddle of living slime," I begged the unfathomable unknowable on the off chance some benevolent power might be listening.

As I slid towards the cliff-edge of sleep, I saw the company pass the cap round for the family, to give them a grubstake to start a new life somewhere less grim and murderous. Delgaro and the others rattled on excitedly, like something miraculous had happened and they'd been part of it. I heard boastful pronouncements about legends and heroes and other such bollocks as I lay there, praying that my guts didn't turn inside out as the sky darkened to the vibrant purple of a fresh bruise.

***

After promises were made and oaths were sworn, we set off at a brisk clip. I drifted in and out of consciousness, listening to snatches of the mercenaries' conversation and the repetitive creak of the cart's wheels.

"How far to Galewyn?"

"Eight miles, ish."

"Is it fuck. It's more like six."

"Bollocks is it six miles. I can see the lights now."

"That's not Galewyn, pig-eyes. Them's torches."

"It's riders."

"I'm telling you, them's the Duke of Anchal's colors."

"The Keeper of the Faith?" Tension crept into Delgaro's elegant drawl. "What the fuck is he doing here?"

"Maybe he heard about the demon and sent his troops to investigate?" Skurden offered. "Perhaps he's caught a whiff of coin."

"Maybe," Delgaro's words were accompanied by the unmistakable sound of a blade being drawn.

Chapter Eighteen

I didn't wake up in the back of an arthritic cart, but on a soft feather bed, in a curiously familiar room. It was a warm summer day and the suns' light bled through gauzy curtains, stirred to lazy rippling by a city-scented breeze.

"Did you really say, 'the angles are right'?" Tobias folded his arms and leaned against his desk, the epitome of smug amusement.

We were in Appleton, in his room at the monastery of the Scienticians of Saint Bartholomew and I was in my old body. "It was a joke. You wouldn't understand, lacking as you do a sense of humor." I sat up. My gaze yearned towards the window. I knew this was a dream, but as was the way with dreams, I accepted the impossible without a second thought. I flexed my claws. It felt good to be me again. I wanted to climb out of the window, swing onto the roof, and run back into my old, uncomplicated life as a Guild Blade.

Tobias brushed a speck of lint from his robes. "I think our interpretation of 'joke' differs somewhat."

"Why am I here? I did what you wanted. Why don't you just fuck off to whatever dull-as-dog shit heaven you saintly culls go to?"

He smiled. "I didn't ask you to do anything." He gestured to himself with a silver-veined left hand.

"See? You set me up with that kinchin cove."

"I didn't make you heal the boy. *You* undid the damage wrought by dark sorcery." Just to rub it in, he picked up a book with his silver hand and began to flick through the pages.

"It was an accident. I just make it up as I go along. Stabbing people that's my forte, not sorcery."

He peered at me from under the ridge of his brow, disapproval written across his soppy face. "That's nothing to be proud of."

I gave a thin-lipped smile. "Depends on where you live, doesn't it?"

"You've broken the rules of the Paradox of Power, you cared. Although, I think it was worth it."

"That makes me feel so much better."

"It does?"

"No, of course not." I went over to the window and breathed in the city. Rooftops and chimneys stretched out before me, indistinct in the haze; a rough sketch painted in light and shadow. He was right. I'd broken the rules that protected me from the backlash of sorcery. "It was just a baby. A tiny, mewling, shitting scrap of life. How can changing its claw for a hand break me more than turning a troop of clanking knights into a pile of molten slag? You can wipe that smug grin off your face. Do you know? No, you don't, so shut up."

Tobias's grin broadened. "It doesn't matter what I know. I'm dead, remember?"

I sighed. The smug twat was right. "I let myself care which, by the way, is your fault. I didn't plan on healing that brat."

"When have you ever planned anything? You're a creature of impulse and a slippery cove to boot. Not even death can hold you for long." He put the book down.

"I'm sure one day I'll be very proud of me if I don't die a horrible, permanent death before then. Shit, shit, shit." I paced. "Stop grinning, this is serious. Did I ever tell you about that sorcerer who was working for the Grundvelt Separatists? The one who tried to assassinate some noble's whore? Long story short, he screwed it up, broke the Paradox and turned himself into a puddle of living slime. The Empirifex kept him in a jar for years, as an example to others. Can you imagine that?"

"I was killed by a demon, so yes, I think I have a good idea."

"You always have to make it about you, don't you?" I picked up one of the books, which he immediately plucked from my hand. "I wasn't going to eat it."

"I thought you might use it to wipe your arse."

"Nah. Books on theology are always written on priest-soft vellum. That stuff's too slippery to get to grips with the nitty-gritty if you catch my drift?"

"Yes, unfortunately."

"Give me a cheap novel of the fantastical variety that has been written on coarse pulp any day." He grimaced which made me smile. "My preference for arse-wipe aside, it's your fault the child was healed. I just wanted to appease you so that you'd stop haunting me."

"You keep telling yourself that if it makes you feel better."

"If you weren't already dead. I'd fucking do you, I swear." There was a shift in the breeze and the sweet summer air took on the bitter edge of ash and smoke. "Can you smell burning?"

Tobias's face became waxen, devoid of emotion. "You can't escape the Paradox, Breed, but you can survive it."

"Would it kill you to speak plainly?"

He sighed. "Very funny."

"You know what I mean." The room was growing hotter by the second and a small incense burner set before the plaster icon of Saint Bartholomew was throwing out a surprising amount of smoke for such a small object. "Something isn't right here." Tobias stared at me for a moment before melting like a wax doll.

**

I woke with a start to find that I was coughing and choking, blinded by cloying smoke.   Every muscle ached. My eyes were streaming, and it felt like my blood was on fire. Not only did I feel like hammered shit, but I was also chained to a tree. A group of jeering clanks I didn't recognize were thrusting torches into wood that had been piled around me. "Oh. Bollocks."

Beyond the baying ranks, I could see that the mercenaries had been herded together and disarmed. It looked like some of them had taken a beating which was comforting to know. I'd hate to think they'd handed me over for roasting without putting up a fight. A gust of wind woke a few lazy flames within the tangle of kindling but given that the wood was wet and green I'd probably be smoked to death before I burned.

"You didn't plan this very well did you?" I said between fits of coughing.

"The demon speaks," one of the soldiers yelled. "Do not heed its wicked words, brothers and sisters."

"Don't look in its eyes. It'll steal your spirit." another expert demonologist offered.

A prissy looking cull rode through the smoke prodding Delgaro in the back with a lance. The mercenary's hands were bound, and her face was bloody, but neither humiliation had diminished the murderous gleam in her eyes.

"Your demon is awake, bitch. Any last words before we send it back to the Pit?" The over-loud ponce said with amused contempt, clearly impressed by his wit.

"Listen, you idiot. You're making a mistake. Breed isn't a demon," said Delgaro.

"Breed, eh? Is that its name?" Delgaro didn't answer. "How fitting." The cull on the horse raised his visor and narrow-eyed me through the smoke. "What manner of demon are you?"

"Come here, dung-swiver, let me whisper it in your ear."

The fellow stiffened. "Do you know who I am?"

"I know what you are."

"I am Staver Stalmun, First Chaplain of the Holy Briar." He pointed the lance at me. It was fashioned to look like a branch, garlanded with thorns at the tip. A bit literal for my tastes but religious types love overt symbolism. "You have no power over me, fiend. We shall destroy you as we destroyed the Unhallowed, as we destroyed Blight's army."

"Hold on there. *I* destroyed Blight's army."

Delgaro turned to glare at Stalmun. "You have no jurisdiction here. Breed must go before the Witnergan and the king."

Stalmun feigned shock. "The gall of the woman. Despite our woes, the day has not yet come when a tar-dipped, outland, sellsword can tell a son or daughter of Arduin that they do not have the jurisdiction to smite demons in their own land." His well-rehearsed screed was greeted with gruff cheers from his troops. Playing to the gallery, Stalmun stood in his stirrups. "I was there when Bolin the Boar demanded, *demanded* if you please, an audience with His Majesty. These foreigners were going to bring this malignancy into the presence of the king."

A hearty cheer rang around the troops. "Briar bless the Duke of Anchal," one of them shouted.

"Aye, bless him." Stalmun shook his fist with righteous anger. "He saw the danger, thank the Holy Briar." His words were answered with more cheering.

I hated to break up a good rabble-rousing, but this fellow was starting to piss me off. "That might not be as lucky a happenstance as you think, old love." I gave a toothsome grimace. "Now, why don't you save us all a lot of unnecessary bother and release me?" The smoke thinned as the fire began to take hold. Flames burst through the kindling, chewed on logs, and crawled towards my feet, questing with flickering tongues, as though trying to fathom which part of me to devour first.

"You're making a mistake, Stalmun," Delgaro snarled, earning herself a kick in the back that knocked her off her feet. "Breed isn't a demon, you fucking idiot."

"It's true. I'm not." The pyre woofed into glorious, crimson life. Firelight swam in my eyes. I breathed in ropes of smoke, breathed out heat, stoked the flames with my breath. Clarity descended. I stopped shaking. Saving my skin didn't break the Paradox of Power.

"Look at it." Stalmun jabbed the lance in my direction. "Look at the malevolence burning in its eyes. What creature other than a demon could burn and yet still bandy insults?"

Flames were indeed coiling around my ankles and ferreting after the hem of my hakama.

"Oh, I know this one," I said. "Is it perhaps a dragon?"

Stalmun's horse sensed the danger before its rider and tried to flee. Delgaro scrambled out of the way as Stalmun fought to master the terrified animal. When he managed to bring the beast under control, he drew his arm back to cast his lance at me.

Too late. I wasn't trying to 'do the right thing' now, I wasn't playing the hero and going against my nature, I was saving my arse, preparing to unleash a great deal of harm on the chaplain. "Come here, chaplain and give us a kiss." Stupefied by fear, Stalmun barely had time to scream before I surrounded both of us and his unfortunate mount in flames.

A few of his warriors put their shields up and braved the edge of the conflagration but they were driven back by the white heat. As I'm not a monster, I stopped the horse's thundering heart with a touch of lightning before the poor beast burned to death. As he was so fond of pyres, I let Stalmun burn.

***

"Round those fuckers up," Delgaro ordered when the flames died down. After seeing their glorious leader reduced to ashes, the fight quite went out of Stalmun's Briars. "Hey, Breed, aren't you cold?" Del grinned, looked me up and down.

"No, I'm fine, nice and toasty." It took a moment before I noticed some of the mercenaries were leering at my nakedness. "You humans are a grubby lot." They sniggered, some performed suggestive mimes that would not have been possible even if they'd had twice the amount of hands and much longer necks.

I conjured another outfit, much like the last one. It was a simple spell, but I was as weak as a kitten and the effort almost dropped me. Not that I was complaining, if I hadn't dreamed of Tobias, I would have roasted instead of Staver Stalmun.

The mercenaries formed up with their prisoners. I licked the bitter taste of chaplain off my lips and dragged my weary bones to my chariot. Delgaro came over as I crawled under the blankets. She seemed no worse for wear other than a purple swelling under her eye. "The Duke of Anchal had Bolin arrested." Her jaw tightened. "We need to get moving."

"We do? I mean, yes, we do. Where are they holding him?"

"Galewyn."

"I take it this Holy Briar crew have the whip hand in Arduin?"

She shrugged. "It seems that way. From what I know they were just another cult before the war, fucking doomsayers, they played on people's fears." She spat. "They preach repentance, atoning for sins, all that shit. They claim piety will counter the decadence that caused the Blight to come and punish the people for—"

I raised my hand. "No need to go on, I know this story. What I can never understand is why the 'Free Ale, Drugs, and Fucks for all' cults never become the dominant ideology."

She laughed, she looked tired and stiff. "I suppose people— *humans*." She smiled. "Like to be told what to do, and how to do it. Oh, we pretend we want free will and to do as we please, but I'm not so sure. Although, I've never come across a cult that offers free ale, sex, and drugs. You come from a fascinating place."

"You don't know the half of it."

"You'll have to enlighten me one day."

"I will, but first we should spring your blade brother from those righteous fuckholes."

She narrowed her eyes, a look I was growing accustomed to, if not overly fond. "You know, you talk more like a street tough than a dragon sorcerer."

"And how many dragon sorcerers have you met?"

"Fair point."

Chapter Nineteen

"Right, you. Tell the nice dragon mage what you told me." Delgaro shoved the terrified cull towards me.

I was lounging in the back of my cart having just finished a delicious meal of charred warhorse. Sated and ready for a kip, I wasn't best pleased by the intrusion. I wiped my greasy fingers on the straw rather than my new robes and settled my gaze on the unfortunate trembling before me. "Are you about to confess undying love for me? Only, I'm not in the market right now."

Delgaro rolled her eyes.

The acolyte of the Holy Briar blanched. "What? No."

"Probably for the best." I fixed her with an impassive stare. "I eat my mates."

We were laid up in an abandoned farmstead which I was informed was a few hours' ride from the capital. The plan was to lie-low here until Delgaro's scouts returned from the city. Though they tried to hide it under a thin veneer of boredom, the mood in the camp was gloomy and tense. For the most part, the chaplain's remaining troops were smart enough to keep their heads down, particularly after a few blowhards got a basting for taunting the mercenaries.

Delgaro prodded the mawkish looking creature before me. "Go on, talk. You were happy to flap your lips before your comrade got his arse handed to him, weren't you? You should have heard her, Breed, promising all manner of retribution until Arthan beat the living shit out of the big man over there." Del chinned in the direction of a fellow who was lying on the ground cuddling his wotnots. Arthan was standing nearby wiping blood off his knuckles and grinning like death. The woman stared resolutely at the ground.

I picked a shred of horse from between my fangs. "Are you sure I shouldn't just, you know...?"

She shot me a terrified glance. "Please, don't eat me. I've told them all I know."

I peered down at her from my rustic cathedra. "In that case, wouldn't now be the perfect time to eat you?"

"No, wait." She raised her hands as though to ward off an imminent attack. "I overheard the chaplain talking with the duke before we left Galewyn."

Delgaro prodded her again. The woman cast a furtive glance over her shoulder before whispering. "They were talking about the duke. He said something about making himself the head of the Witnergan."

"Shut your mouth, Braska," said the fellow who was cradling his balls.

"Piet, Holbor, bring him," Delgaro ordered. The mouthy, shave-pated brute was encouraged to his feet by a crossbowman. He had a brawler's build and a long scar ran the length of his bloodied and swollen face.

"What's your name, soldier?" Delgaro asked him. He didn't answer. She sighed. "Why are you people so intractable?"

"Fuck you."

"Not in this lifetime." She gave him the once-over. "You don't look like you've got it in you anymore."

"Untie me, bitch and I'll show you." They squared up against each other. Neither prepared to concede so much as a blink.

Delgaro snorted. "Haven't you been beaten enough for one day?"

I like a good fight as much as the next cove, but there's a time and a place. I conjured a crackling ball of light in the palm of my hand. "What's your duke planning?"

He set his jaw.

"Suit yourself." I sent the ball slowly floating towards him. "First it'll burn your eyes out and then it'll eat its way through whatever passes for your brain. It will not do this quickly, and it will hurt a great deal." It was an entirely harmless conjuration, but he wasn't to know that. Despite being a simple spell, casting it made my brain ache.

Thankfully the cull only toughed it out for a few more seconds before yielding. "All right, stop. Damn you." He squinted at the light. I let it hover a hand's span from his face. "We just overheard Stalmun and the Duke talking."

I belched. "Pardon me, that warhorse is repeating. Do go on." I folded my arms.

Shave-Pate grimaced. "It was after the mercenaries were arrested. The duke said that they would have to wait until the king had been dealt with before executing anyone, or something like that. That's all, I swear by the Holy Briar."

I didn't say anything, neither did Delgaro. Beads of sweat pearled on the fellow's lip. I sucked another shred of horse meat from my teeth, let the light drift a little closer to his face. He tried to shy away but the mercenaries held him fast. "Braska," he said. "Tell them it's the truth."

Braska shot him a venomous glare. "It's true," she said. "That's what we heard. The Staver said something about accusing the mercenaries of demon-worship when they went to trial. The duke said they wouldn't need a trial after the king was 'out of the way'. I don't remember exactly." Her gaze slid away. She remembered well enough.

I looked at Delgaro. "What do you think we should do with these sorry culls?"

"I'm tempted to give them a taste of their own medicine and throw them on a pyre."

"We don't need a pyre to burn them, you just say the word and I'll roast the lot of them." With that happy thought seeded in their minds, Delgaro had them dragged back to await their fate with the others. I dispelled the ball of light. My stomach rumbled. "I can't believe I'm hungry again. We should probably slot this lot and head to Galewyn before they kill your friend," I suggested.

"I'm more concerned that we reach the capital before they kill the king. And we won't 'slot this lot'. I'll leave a squad to guard them."

"That's surprisingly unmercenary of you."

"No. it isn't." She grinned. "Malin owes me money. Bolin hasn't got a pot to piss in and I don't want lynching by a mob for slaying this sack of pricks."

"Fair enough. What's your plan?"

She looked surprised. "You're deferring to me?"

I laughed. "No, don't be silly. I just want to know what your plan is before I ignore it." I flashed her a smile. "What do you think of the robes by the way?"

"They're lovely. Can we get back to planning a rescue?"

"Yes, sorry." I lay back, nestled into the blankets. "I know my eyes are closed, but I am listening."

***

I woke up when the scouts returned. They told a worried Delgaro that Bolin and his crew had been arrested on trumped-up charges, but that thus far none of them had been made to dance the hempen jig. The king had apparently summoned the Witnergan at the request of the Duke of Anchal. Between me, Delgaro, and Skurden it was decided that, despite my offer to slot the lot of them, a handful of mercenaries would be left to guard the Briar Thorns, as the contemptible lackwits called themselves. The rest of us would disguise ourselves and slip quietly into the capital in small, unobtrusive groups. When they were in the city, they would take up positions and wait for my signal to either defend the king or rescue their fellow mercenaries, depending on which was more pressing at the time. But first things first.

"You better do it over there, downwind of the horses." Delgaro pointed to a patch of open ground, upwind of the camp.

"Horses are stupid creatures," I said as I made my way across the farmyard and headed to the overgrown fields "What's the point of riding into battle on something that's scared of its own shadow? Now an urux wouldn't be scared. An urux would just stand there if it saw a dragon."

Delgaro chuckled. "Bring some with you next time."

"There won't be a next time. When I leave here I'm not coming back, trust me." I spoke in jest, but as the words left my mouth the cold touch of certainty tapped me on the shoulder and told me in a manner I couldn't fathom that it was true.

"Right then, here goes." I cracked my knuckles. The coral blush of a languid evening was sweetened by birdsong and gentled by a silken breeze. I looked within myself for the place of fire, for the dragon. This time it came easily, like slipping on a well-worn glove.

I hadn't time to notice before how different the world looked through my dragon eyes. Vivid shades of purple, blue and orange leaped from the landscape transforming the mundane into a kaleidoscope of clashing vibrancy. I dragged my gaze away from the glowing fields and radiant bowers when I happened to see a passing insect that was flying from flower to flower. It was entirely unimpressed by my magnificence in its single-minded hunt for nectar. A beast like me didn't even register, whereas every detail of its remarkable form was a marvel to me. I held my breath as I watched the iridescent plates of its body flex as it breathed and heard the flittering beat of its wings as they played a symphony upon the beads of the air. I was so enchanted with this new perspective on the world that I didn't notice Delgaro until I almost stepped on her.

"Hey, watch out," she cried snapping me from my trance.

"Sorry." I carefully repositioned my forelimbs.

"Are you all right? You looked a little odd for a moment there. Sort of distant."

"I'm perfectly well, thank you." I could hear the steady rhythm of her heart beating, feel the heat of her blood pumping through her veins, filling her cheeks with light and life. I shook my head and tried to focus on the general, rather than the particular. How could something so big see, smell, and hear the least noticeable details of existence? It was a question I could have spent a lifetime pondering and perhaps would one day, but not today.

"You know what to do, right?" she asked again.

"No. Why don't you tell me for the tenth time?" I raised my forepaw to stop her when she opened her mouth to do just that. "It was a joke. I know what to do."

"So, what are you waiting for?"

"The respect I'm due, but that seems to be in short supply."

She laughed and backed up. "Just get on with it, your greatness."

"That's something, I suppose." I dropped my weight on my haunches, felt muscles contract, heard the creak of sinew and tendons drawn tense, ready to spring. I lifted my chin, pulled my wings close to my body, and leaped at the sky like it was my worst enemy. My hindquarters thrust me twenty feet into the air in a bound, my tail kept me balanced, doing whatever it is tails do to earn their place in draconian physiology. My wings worked the hardest, or rather the muscles they were attached to kept me aloft and powering into the sky. I watched the world shrink beneath me, awed by the majesty of this body and what it could do. I didn't just look like a dragon, I *was* a dragon and I liked it.

Flying wasn't effortless but thought swiftly translated into action and I soon grasped the basics. I learned that I could trim my flight by dipping a wing, and that angling the long finger bones slackened or tightened the leathery membranes between them, enabling me to execute a bank. A sharp flick of my tail spun me into a roll. When I looked down at the distant earth, the plight of kings and princes suddenly seemed inconsequential. The thought occurred that I could just keep going and leave them to it. But no.

Be the hero, Breed. Be the fucking hero.

I followed the plan and flew close enough to Galewyn for the inhabitants to see me before heading north along the course of a river. The further I flew, the blacker the river ran, poisoned by the runoff from dozens of mines that dotted the plains, interspersed with quarries and iron works in what had to be the industrial heartland of the country.

After executing this part of the plan, I climbed higher to where the bite of ice turned my breath to glass. Breath from my nostrils that was— breath from my mouth didn't dip below the temperature of a warm breeze. Invigorated by the cold, I flew higher still, sailing untrammeled winds to where I could see the rind of the sky curve around the orb below. On the horizon, the light of a single sun erupted from the pale band which separated the void from the earth.

I hung there a while in the frigid air and beheld the beauty of this strange world. Ice rimed my spines. My wings shed diamonds with every beat. I breathed out a spray of liquid fire just to see what it looked like out here on the edge of the heavens. The liquid smoldered and burst into sporadic, guttering flames before sputtering out, leaving the remaining droplets of oil to tumble like rubies. When they reached warmer air, the frozen droplets flared into life and streaked across the night-skinned sky like a shower of meteors. When the last mote of fire died, I drew my wings close to my body and stooped to a dive.

Chapter Twenty

A city at night is a joy to behold and that's every city, shitholes included. Night casts a seductive glamor over even the most squalid burgh. It hides the ugly and makes intriguing the uninspiring. Night's grace and torchlight gold hide the beggar's scabs and soften the doxy's wrinkles.

It was evening when I entered Galewyn's west gate, guised as an unremarkable traveler. This was the rump of night, the fat hours where the denizens of the day handed over to those who pulled the night shift and sly interlopers passed unnoticed. In the full bloom of evening, Galewyn threw off the shabby robe of day to reveal a glittering thing made of velvet shadows, stitched with gold and rubies. Beautiful and dangerous, cities at night drew out gaunts and bravos as fresh blood draws wolves. I was waved inside by a jittery guard, who like his comrades, had his eyes fixed on the yawning darkness for any sign of the dragon.

Just inside the gate, a ballista was set in the middle of the street, attended by a bored looking crew. The weapon would be of little use against me, but they weren't to know that, just like the barrels of water on every street corner, their precautions were more hopeful than useful.

I set off for the palace, but I didn't get very far before having to dodge into an alley to avoid a roaming patrol of Briars who were stopping people and turning them back the way they'd come. I watched a while and tried another road, but the cordon had been thrown around all routes leading to the palace. I could have apported, but my knowledge of the layout was based on a quick look as I overflew the city. Not to mention, appearing out of thin air in a camp full of knights on high alert was guaranteed to start a fight.

"Looks like I'll have to do this the old-fashioned way," I said to the air before throwing off the human disguise and clambering on a roof. Gaelwyn was not what I'd imagined the capital city would look like. I'd expected neglect due to the war, but I hadn't expected it to be so rustic and more like a sprawling, country village than the seat of power. Despite this, I was overjoyed to be back on familiar territory, up amongst the chimney pots.

I set off at a run. The bright splashes of torchlight blurred beneath me. For a brief, beautiful moment, as I traversed roof ridges, ran lightly up crow-stepped gables, and swung across alleyways from brace to jetty

spur, I could almost pretend that I was the old me, out
on some darkling errand in the poor quarter of
Appleton. I pulled up near the palace, watched a
knightly patrol pass beneath, oblivious to my bladed
gaze upon them. The hard truth struck me then. I
wasn't even in the same world as Appleton. I didn't
know anything about this place, or why I was allowing
myself to be embroiled in another benighted conflict.
Hadn't I had my fill? What was the point of running
from my troubles just to get involved in someone
else's war? Vertigo threatened to tumble me to the
ground. I slipped and had to hold onto the gable end
until the world righted itself. It wasn't my balance that
had failed. It was the realization of just how far I'd
come and how little I'd achieved or changed that made
my head spin.

I sat on the end of a beam like a gargoyle, feeling
angry and foolish as the wind drifted cool fingers
through my spun sugar hair. It occurred to me that I
could dive headfirst into the alley below and break my
neck and maybe this time I'd stay dead, putting an end
to the chaos. The thought had some appeal. *But what if
Tobias is waiting for you on the other side? Can you
imagine, being lectured for all time...?* Resolved that
there were worse fates than living, I leaped across the
alley instead of into it and climbed the wall of a bell
tower that overlooked the palace complex.

A pair of gulls eyed me dubiously as I slipped over
the low parapet onto the roof of the tower. From here
I'd have an excellent view of the palace compound. I

liked high places, probably why I loved flying around as a dragon. Everything looked neat and small, like toys that I could move around where I wanted. The palace grounds were thronged with the retinues of the nobles of the Witnergan. From what I could gather from the bluster and posturing there wasn't much love lost between the various factions.

When I was a kinchin cove, I believed what I read in the histories of the Empire. When the land was threatened, an army of patriots, drawn from all corners of the country would rally to the call to defend their homes, united in a single, noble purpose. After listening to Mother discourse on politics with older members of the Midnight Court, I soon learned not to believe everything that I read, and that history was mostly bollocks. I learned that every tome ever written on the subject was crafted to write over the folly of the past and obscure the truth with gallons of ink. Now here I was, watching 'history' play out in a strangely familiar land where humans were getting on with doing what humans did best which was fucking each other over.

The grizzled warriors garbed in the king's colors looked more like brigands than a noble retinue. They were lean, mean-eyed, and scruffy looking, possessed of sharp tongues and gleaming weapons. They regarded the comings and goings of their fellow countrymen and women with ill-concealed contempt. I didn't blame them, some of the primped-up dollies parading around, swilling the king's ale, and scoffing his vittles didn't look like they'd seen any combat rougher than a pillow fight in a whore house.

Enjoyable though it would have been to watch the brawl that was undoubtedly brewing between the veterans and the unbloodied, I had work to do. The layout of the compound was easy enough to commit to memory. I made a note of guard stations, times, and positions of patrols, points of entry and the where I suspected I would find my target. Satisfied that this job wouldn't tax my skills, I prepared to...

Idiot.

I pulled up just before I vaulted over the parapet. I didn't have to sneak past dozens of soldiers. I wasn't a Guild Blade out on the dub. I was a sorcerer, a dragon. I was here to save a king and his bumprugging, undead-infested country without breaking the Paradox of Power *again* and turning myself into living slime. "Easy, eh?" I said to the gulls. They didn't answer. "Well, fuck you too." I picked a spot behind what looked like a chapel situated in a quiet garden in the least busy corner of the compound and apported.

The only light in the quiet corner was from the cast-off glow of votive candles that spilled through the chapel's stained-glass windows. The muted sounds of feasting and drinking drifted across the compound from what had to be the great hall, but it was quiet over here, peaceful, save for the sounds of someone being choked to death inside the chapel.

As I'm of a curious disposition, I peered through the window to see a young human pinned against a tomb by a fellow in a monkish robe. Another cove dressed in the same gray garb was staggering around, waving a dagger in one hand, and cupping his wotnots in the other. From where I stood, I could see the lower half of a body lying in a spreading pool of claret. I made to leave to find the king. And then it occurred to me who was being throttled. "Shit."

I apported into the chapel near the fellow cuddling his jewels, whereupon I plucked his dagger from his flailing hand and cut his throat. He gurgled and doubled over. I rolled across his back and stabbed the strangler in the kidney. The tip of the blade snagged on mail, but where there's a will, there's a way. The tip snapped as I rammed it in, but the links split and the blade slid home. I hastened the killer's exsanguination with a twist. The boy dragged himself back from death's threshold with a ragged gasp. His dark hair fell across his thin, currently purple face, and his brown eyes shone with tears. "You saved my life," he eventually managed to say between gasps.

"Aye. For the second time as it happens." I made sure that both bravos were dead, or well on their way to being so.

The boy wasn't listening. He rushed over to the third body, that of an old fellow with short, grey stubble on chin and pate and a mean cast to his dead face. He was wearing armor and the king's colors; his sword was undrawn. Trembling like a newborn calf, the boy sought signs of life. Given the pool of blood I doubted he'd succeed. "The cowards stabbed you in the back because they knew they wouldn't have a chance trying to take you in a fair fight," the boy said to the corpse.

I'd take the odds of two young bulls getting the better of an aged warrior front or back, but I kept my opinion to myself. On the other side of the chapel I spied another, seemingly unconnected splash of claret. I went over and found two more bodies had been unceremoniously dumped behind the altar. Silent in death their corpses nevertheless told the tale of how they'd died. They'd been stripped to their breechcloths gagged and bound and then crudely knifed in the back like the old warrior. They'd died messy deaths in their underwear, killed for their clothes, and because they were in the wrong place at the wrong time.

"I'm so sorry, old friend." The boy closed the warrior's eyes and bowed his head in prayer. He was a skinny thing and looked younger than fourteen, but I knew he was the king because I recognized the voice from the battlefield speechifying. "They've killed a good man in my family shrine. May they rot in the Pit for both offenses," he said at last and carefully stepped around the bodies that were bleeding out all over the floor. "I trusted him." He cast a loathing glance at his attacker.

"Who was he?"

"My uncle's man. He used to take me hawking when I was a boy." He spat on the corpse. "I will never speak his name again." He stumbled. I caught him, felt the wiry strength in his skinny arms.

"You'd best sit a moment." I tried to guide him to a pew, but he pulled away.

"Wait. Who are you?"

"I'm the dragon and a sorcerer." I flipped the knife. It had a real heft. "You may call me Flameheart."

He sniggered. "Wait, what?"

What the fuck are you thinking? Why not just call yourself 'Dickhead' and have done with it? I cleared my throat. "Breed. Call me Breed. I take it you're Malin?"

"Yes, did you say, Flameheart?"

"No, I said Breed. All the blood is er, rushing to your ears, very common after almost being strangled."

"You're an expert in such things?" He sounded defensive, which was a bit late in my opinion.

"I told you. I'm the dragon."

He coughed. "Look, I don't mean to sound ungrateful, but that's a little hard to swallow."

I laughed. "That's very funny."

"It wasn't intentional."

"Well, it was still funny."

"Who the fuck are you, *really*?" He folded his arms.

"All right, if you must know I'm a self-centered, ex-thief, ex-assassin, who was blessed by the gods and cursed by a demon. I'm also a sorcerer who really can turn into a dragon and I am without doubt the most dangerous cove you'll ever meet. I'm also here to help you, not because I'm soft-hearted or a hero or any of that nonsense, but because I told a friend I would." I folded my arms. "There, are we done now, are you satisfied?"

"No, not really. My bodyguard is butchered by men I've known for as long as I can remember who also try to kill me. You, the strangest stranger I've ever laid eyes on appear out of nowhere, save my life and then tell me you're a dragon. No, I'm not satisfied. I'm confused, I'm upset, and I'm angry."

"Strangest stranger? Are you sure, I mean, surely the Unhallowed are stranger than me?"

"Living, then. The strangest living person I've ever seen. I presume with all that huffing and sighing you're a living being?"

It wasn't supposed to go like this. I was going to sweep in, introduce myself, at which point he would be in awe. I was then going to tell him we'd come to save him, and he would happily agree to go along with our hastily concocted plan. I resisted the urge to slap him and instead took a deep breath. "You're right, majesty. This is confusing, and deeply upsetting for you, I'm sure, but we don't have time to get into the details." I went to the door and stole a look outside. It was quiet save for the distant sound of feasting coming from the hall. "How long before you're expected back?"

The boy didn't answer. His gaze turned to the dead bodyguard. A torn piece of surcoat was clutched in his lifeless hand bearing the badge of Bolin's crew.

"How long?"

"An hour, perhaps longer. Why?"

"We, that is Delgaro and I have a plan to save you from your murderous uncle and free the mercenaries that have been arrested."

"Which mercenaries? I haven't ordered anyone arrested."

"Bolin the Boar and his crew have been arrested by your uncle."

He leaned on the altar and gazed up at the gilded triptych of the Maid, the Bride, and the Crone. "I didn't know. How is it that I didn't know?"

"Your uncle didn't want to spoil the surprise." I tossed him the bloody piece of surcoat.

He spotted the bodies behind the altar. "Holy Maid of Heaven. They killed the priests too."

"Your uncle is making his play for power."

"My uncle is a holy man." He shook his head, no doubt at his inability to reconcile the image of his uncle, the pious guardian of the Holy Briar, with that of power-hungry usurper. "I don't understand. Why now when we have Blight on the run?"

"To lose a king during a war would be demoralizing. Now, however, when the danger is less..." I shrugged. It seemed obvious to me, but Malin was young and probably still had faith in his fellows.

"He's my uncle, my blood kin. I looked up to him."

"Not everyone believes in the sanctity of blood." My mind turned to the farmer fixing to slay his child, my mother who sent bounty hunters after me, and Tobias's brother Marius who almost had him dead on several occasions. "Hardly anyone in my experience."

The boy trembled, his face full of pain and sorrow. "I thought when the dragon came my prayers had been answered." He laughed mirthlessly. "I thought the people of Arduin would unite. When it flew over the city I thought it was a sign that we would defeat Blight. I came here to give thanks and to tell my parents that we had been saved." He swallowed, took a moment to master the emotions that were bleeding into his voice. "You must think me a fool."

"Did you miss the part where I said I'd been a thief and an assassin? I forgot to add fool to that ignoble list, but the past is as dead as these poor bastards. Let it go. And you were right. The dragon is a sign. I am going to help you win back your land from Blight and as a bonus, I'll help you sort your miserable, fucking uncle. But you have to trust me."

"You just told me you were a thief, a fool, and a killer."

"Reformed. I also told you I was a sorcerer and a dragon."

"How much innocent blood have you spilled?"

"Far less than any of those noble lordlings stuffing their faces in your hall I'll wager, only when I kill it isn't with taxes or hunger. It's up close, face-to-face, blade against blade."

"I don't know." He flailed. "It's hard to take in."

"The dead walk, your uncle is trying to kill you, and I just saved your life and made you an offer of help."

"I didn't mean in that way. There's more to it."

"No, there really isn't. That's the problem with you humans you make things more complicated than they are."

He gave a heavy sigh. "I don't know." Minutes passed in silence. The smell of death mingled with the smell of incense. I couldn't say what thoughts ran through his mind then, what arguments raged or what instinct tipped the scale in favor of trusting me. But something did. He stood up, dusted his doublet, straightened his shirt collar, and looked at me with an honesty few could forge. "All sense says I should be wary of you and I am, but you saved my life and I'll trust you until you prove that I should not."

"Thank fuck for that." I rubbed my hands together. "Now, first things first. We're going to have to kill you."

Chapter Twenty-One

"Tall, wearing your colors, long face, bit of a stoop. He looks like a horse, greasy hair."

"Blonde?"

"Aye."

"That's Greyholt. Is he alone?" Malin said from where he was sprawled on the altar.

"Yes. Now lie down, he's almost here."

Malin lay back and tucked a dagger between his arm and chest and we waited. I'd hidden the bodies behind the altar and his parents' tombs and snuffed all but one of the candles. Anything more than a cursory glance would reveal that a fight had taken place here, but by then it would be too late for Greyholt, the captain of the king's guard. His footsteps grew louder, and I hid in the shadows behind the door. There was a tentative knock. Neither Malin nor I made a sound. A second knock followed the first and the door slowly creaked open.

"Sire, I'm so— dear gods." Greyholt saw the king, lying on the altar with what looked from that angle to be a knife in his chest. The knight drew his sword and entered. I stepped behind him and put a blade to his throat.

"Don't move, pukepail or you'll be as dead as your king."

"You bastard." I felt him stiffen, knife at his throat or not, he was going to fight.

"Oi, Malin." I hissed. The king sat up and waved. Greyholt jumped so suddenly I almost cut his throat by accident.

"My king, I thought you were dead."

"Not quite. Forgive the ruse, Rishar. I just needed to know you weren't in on it."

I released Greyholt and kicked the door closed. The man was spitting-nails, furious at being tested but unable to vent his ire on his king. He turned on me, the blade live and twitching in his hand. "What the fuck are you?"

"I'll let the king explain."

He didn't budge. "I don't take kindly to having a knife at my throat."

"I'm sure you'll get over it."

"Just who the fuck—"

"Put your cock away Rish and come here." Fuming, the warrior obeyed his king. "Sit down and listen well. We don't have much time."

"What are you doing here by the way? I told you I didn't want to be disturbed which, with hindsight, was perhaps not the wisest order I've ever given." Malin jumped down off the altar.

"Anchal sent me to find you. I told him that you'd said you didn't want to be disturbed, but he insisted." Greyholt looked as angry and confused as a scolded dog. "Majesty, who is this person, what's going on. Is that blood?"

"Yes. My beloved uncle arranged for me to be murdered. Breed is a dragon and a sorcerer and my savior."

"A what?"

"Dragon and sorcerer," I said.

"Er. Right. Hmm. Where's Eth?"

"Dead. You've been sent to make the grim discovery of our murder; a vile act carried out by mercenaries. At least that was the plan."

Greyholt surged to his feet. "I'll call out the guard."

"Not yet. If we accuse my uncle of trying to kill me, it's his word against mine."

"But you're the king."

"With a slender grasp on power. I'm fourteen, Rish. He's had piles longer than I've been alive and he has the respect of the Witnergan. If I arrest him his followers will riot, and his damn Briars are all over the palace just waiting to seize control. The game is unequal. We must bring more pieces into play."

"I suppose now I can tell you how much I loathe those fucking Briars with their stupid twigs and self-righteous preachifying." Greyholt mimed clutching a pendant and mouthing a prayer. I revised my earlier opinion, he looked more like a bloodhound than a horse with his sad eyes and soft jowls.

Malin nodded. "I'm no theologian but I was never convinced that one line in the Golden Book of the Trinity could be drawn out to a whole religion."

"You never mentioned it, Majesty."

The boy shrugged. "I needed an army. I would have gone along with just about anything."

"You did. Remember the Yelland Marchers?"

The king winced. "Aye, that was a mistake. Still, no lasting harm done. Although, I will never get the image of the Blue Knight and his 'squires' out of my mind."

I cleared my throat to remind the king to push on. He gave an imperceptible nod. "I need you to speak to Mortlan, Rish, quickly and quietly."

"But the Witnergan, your uncle?"

"The Witnergan are still drinking and eating me out of house and home, and then they've got to empty their bladders and stagger back to the great hall for a nap. By my reckoning that gives us an hour and a quarter or thereabouts. My uncle will have you and this place watched. He thinks he knows what you'll find here so he won't be concerned. When you leave, look like you've found your king dead."

The captain bristled. "I was planning on using stealth to leave unseen."

I sniggered. "Because nothing says 'stealthy' like plate armor."

"I'll have you know I can tumble like a dancer in my plate. It's like a second skin."

"Made of tin."

"Enough, both of you. I'm supposed to be the child here."

"Your sorcerer is in danger of impugning my honor, sire."

I raised my hands in a gesture of peace. "I don't give two shits about your honor, honestly. Do what you want with it, give it a fish and a pat on the head, but right now we need to get on with exposing the culprits behind the plot and deal with them."

Malin guided Greyholt to the door. "Just go and find Mortlan, there's a good fellow. Tell him to seek out Captain Delgaro in the Hag's Head and give her this." He gestured for me to hand over the ring Del had given me as a vouchsafe token. "Tell Mort to do as she commands." Greyholt nodded and took the ring although he still looked unconvinced. "We'll let the Witnergan get settled in the hall before you break the terrible news of my demise." Are you listening, Rish?"

Greyholt was staring at me. I smiled. "Aye, sire. But…"

Malin rolled his eyes. "What is it, man? Out with it."

"I'm struggling to put my faith and your safety in the hands of someone who just appeared out of nowhere and has made outrageous and thus far unproven claims."

"I'll prove my claims anon, don't you worry, old fruit. You just play your part."

"Oh. I will just make sure you do."

I mimicked his somber tone. "Oh. I will."

The boy king clapped him on the shoulder. "Good then, we're all agreed now get going, Rish."

***

An hour later, wrapped in a sorcery wrought cloak of obfuscation I made my way to what the king optimistically referred to as the 'Great Hall'. It was more of a barn than the centerpiece of a palace and was distinguished only by its great size rather than its architectural merit. By now news of the king's death had begun to spread throughout the palace, and the booze-soaked voices of the nobles and their retinues troubled the darkness with nervous chatter.

I slipped into the kitchens which adjoined the hall on the north side. After the feast, the cooking fires had been left to burn low, and the cooks had adjourned elsewhere for a meal of leftovers. The fire watch was being kept by a sleepy pot-boy and a pair of snoring sighthounds that sniffed but otherwise didn't stir as I passed. I found a spy hatch in the wall where servants could watch from the kitchen to check on the progress of banquets without disturbing their betters.

In contrast to the quiet kitchens that were bathed in shadow, the great hall was noisy and brightly lit. A raised dais ran the length of the south wall and halfway along the east and west. The king's throne was in the center of the dais and notably vacant. Sitting a few, *worth-killing-for*, feet away was a tall, robed fellow with salt and pepper hair and beard. He had to be Malin's murderous uncle. He looked just past his prime, but age hadn't dimmed the fierce intelligence burning in his eyes. What struck me, other than the fact he stank, was how closely he resembled Malin. He had the same, hard to ignore stare, the same angular jaw, and pensive-yet-thoughtful set to his mouth. The difference lay in his age and garb. Whereas Malin was dressed no better or worse than a country lordling in plain grey breeches and doublet, the Duke of Anchal was clad in richly embroidered robes and decked out in gold and jewels, the ensemble completed by a gold Briar pendant.

The would-be king was feigning a casual conversation with a couple of knightly looking thugs who, in contrast to the Duke, were as tightly wound as cotton reels. With them was a middle-aged woman as plump as Anchal was slender. She laughed too loud, betraying her nervousness. A silver, briar twig pendant hung around her fleshy neck. Although more relaxed than his companions, Anchal couldn't hide the flush in his cheeks or the occasional smirk that no doubt appeared when he thought about his impending victory. Or perhaps he had wind, it was hard to tell from this distance.

The other members of the Witnergan had gathered into factions and cliques. Their conversation made the air hum as they spun wild speculation faster than the arrachids of Shen could spin silk. One thread above all knotted the whole into a tapestry of panic-laden excitement. *"The King is dead, the King is dead, the King is…"* The rumor flowed like wine. A few of the cooler heads in the Witnergan sat apart from their fellows and waited quietly for the drama to unfold, taking note but not taking part.

I deepened the shadows around me and waited for the final act in this comic-tragedy to begin. As time passed the duke's composure started to slip. He grew agitated, less genial with those around him. The smirk became a sneer. As I scanned the faces in the crowd, I scratched my palm and compiled a mental list, placing each in order of who I judged to be harmless, who was worthy of note, and who was a threat. Naturally Anchal was at the top of the list. He was trying to usurp the throne and kill his kin and his doctrine left ample room for his followers to kill anyone they didn't like the look of. But there was more to it than that; something I could feel in my gut but couldn't put words to. Perhaps it was the stench that offended me more than his courtly scheming. Anchal reeked and yet no one aside from me seemed to notice. True, the place had open sewers, and dead people walked abroad with more vigor than many of the living but even so. The background funk of this primitive society was nothing compared to the steaming ripeness of His Holiness, the Duke.

A door creaked behind me. I turned to see a familiar figure ushering the sleepy kinchin cove and his mutts towards the door. The price of a no-questions-asked departure was a shiny penny that winked in the slatted light as it passed from Delgaro to the child. Yawning, the kid vanished the coin before ambling out with the hounds at his heels. The mercenary slid the bolt behind the boy.

"Del. Over here," I whispered. She froze a moment, peered into the darkness before approaching.

"Blessed Trinity." She flashed her hand. The gold signet ring winked. "Thanks for getting this back to me."

"Don't mention it. Thanks for coming."

"I couldn't miss this now, could I? Who would have thought old iron breeches would make this play? I mean, doing away with some mercenaries and the odd dragon is one thing." She grinned. "Nothing I wouldn't expect from the Vidun Bloodbacks at home, but regicide? That's a surprise. I always read him as a bit of a stuffy, old fucker." Her breath smelled of brandy, which told the tale of the hours she'd spent waiting in the grimy stew on the outskirts of town.

"What did you do with Mortlan?"

"Sent him back to his captain. And before you ask, when you give the signal and the king makes his move, Skurden and our lads will spring Bolin and we'll sort out the Briars."

"I wasn't going to question you." I tried to sound like I meant it, but she saw through the ruse and gave a lopsided grin. "Of course, you weren't. But no need to worry, this isn't my first royal housecleaning job."

"That's good to know. If you need me, I'll be in the wine cellar."

"What a cunt."

"Bit harsh."

"Not you. I meant Anchal for trying to kill his sister's son, and after everything we've been through with the Blight. May I see?" She gestured to the hatch. I let her take my place. "Greyholt's just walked in. He's a humorless prick, but a good man in a pinch. He's going over to Anchal."

"Does he look sad, pissed off? Is he crying? What's he doing?" I resisted the urge to shove her out of the way.

"He looks weighed down by grief, all right. Sweet Trinity. He's gone to his knees before Anchal. His head is bowed and he's even shaking with emotion. He'll make a good actor should the time for blades ever pass in this land."

"What about Anchal? Is he buying it?"

"Oh yes. Bastard's trying not to smile." She snorted. "Now he's patting Rish on the shoulder."

"I should have told Greyholt to gut him while he was up close." A wave of nausea swept over me, flipped my stomach. "Can't you smell that?"

"What? Anchal's getting to his feet. His leg doesn't seem to be bothering him today. Rish's getting up, bowing again, no gutting, unfortunately. Anchal's embracing him like a long-lost son." She glanced at me. "Are you all right?"

I wasn't, I felt sick to the pit of my gut. I put my back to the wall for support. Sweat ran down the crease of my back. It had taken a while but now I knew what the smell was and why my palm was itching. "I'm fine. Are you sure you can't smell that?"

"Bride's sake, smell *what?* What are you talking about?"

"Demon."

Emotion drained from her face. "Are you sure?" She hid it well, but her voice trembled as her blood rose, preparing her for imminent conflict. I'd seen it often, felt it myself, but now I just wanted to puke. I managed to nod. "Shit." She breathed blood into the word. "Where?"

"The Duke, it's Anchal." I stood up, my legs were leaden, my back rigid. I wasn't scared *as such*. I was nauseous because of the vile stench and lacked any desire whatsoever to face a creature like those that had tormented me, but I wasn't afraid.

"Where are you going?" Delgaro hissed.

Without realizing, I'd set off towards the kitchen door, driven by a self-preservative compulsion that overruled conscious thought and my avowed intent to be a hero. "Er, I'm just nipping outside for a thing."

Del made a face. "That's a poor excuse, even by your standards."

"Brothers and sisters, fellow members of the Witnergan, my friends." A voice rang out in the hall, silencing all conversation. "My heart is broken." It had to be the Duke. The voice carried enough weight and authority to hush the lords and ladies gathered within. Added to which, whoever spoke also cast a spell of compulsion to underscore the request.

It would have been easy to leg it then while Delgaro was listening to the demon. I could have apported to the gate and left this grim world and its demons behind. *But can you leave your ghosts behind?* The nagging doubt thwarted my desire to flee.

Some of the servants must have heard enough of the demonic hierarch's words to be drawn from their hearth. A handful wandered through the kitchen, and into a small anteroom adjoining the hall, paying no attention to Delgaro and me. All eyes were on the Duke who was standing on the raised dais, arms spread in mockery of supplication.

Despite the stench, I slipped into the anteroom with the servants to get a better look.

"The king is dead," Anchal intoned. The announcement was met with exclamations of grief and disbelief, some of which sounded genuine. The Duke's benevolent gaze fell on Greyholt, who was standing to one side of the empty throne, head bowed in feigned sorrow. "Captain Greyholt found our beloved king, murdered in his parent's mortuary chapel." More gasps were accompanied by the sound of steel being drawn. "Slain by mercenaries at the behest of demonic forces." He waved the patch of bloodstained tabard.

Playing his part to the hilt, Greyholt made to interject because our version of Malin's untimely end, the one I'd primed Greyholt to tell Anchal, made no mention of demons, just that the poor mite had been strangled by mercenaries as evidenced by the bloody rag found in the bodyguard's hand. As expected, nay, *as was required* for the noose to be settled like a champion's garland around his lordship's neck, Anchal was rewriting the script. He silenced Greyholt with a raised hand and a frosty glare. "The king was slain by demons, my son, but be not afraid for we shall avenge him and destroy the agents of evil, once and for all." Anchal's baritone hammered through the hall. "But first, brothers and sisters, join with me in prayer for the spirit of our beloved king." He choked up.

"Speaking of whom," Delgaro whispered in my ear. "When is Malin going to put an end to this travesty?"

"Soon enough, Captain. I'm to give the signal when Anchal's hung himself good and proper."

The Duke dabbed at his eyes, wiped away imaginary tears, and clutched his holy symbol. It was a fair performance, worthy of applause. As the Witnergan bowed their heads in respect for the dead, an old cove unfurled her knotty limbs and climbed to her feet with deliberate poise. "As a priestess of the Trinity, I admire the sentiment, Lord Anchal." She gave him a tight-lipped smile. "But where is the king's body, and how was he found? Greyholt must provide us with the full details of this tragedy so we may grieve and act accordingly as a united Witnergan." She coughed, giving Anchal the chance to roll over her misgivings.

"And I shall see that he does, but now is not the time to discuss the vulgar details, now is the time to pray." The demonic fraud spiced his words with another spell of compulsion, drawing them all imperceptibly under his power. Only I could feel the filaments of magic threading through the room, binding the humans to the demon's will. It struck me then that the inhabitants of this kingdom, possibly the entire world, had no defense against sorcery. I could destroy this demon and rule them like a god, bend them all to my will. The thought made me smile. *Maybe later.*

Anchal raised his hands. "May the Holy Briar bless our king, delivered too soon into the bosom of his family, into the Heart of Thorns."

With strength of purpose, Delgaro was able to throw off the suggestive power of the spell. "I can't listen to much more of this bilge," she said and drew an inch of blade. The flash of steel caught the eye of a plump wench who was standing nearby. I smiled, grabbed her elbow, and drew her into the shadows before she could bolt. I would have used a spell of compulsion on her and ordered her to be silent, but I didn't want to risk alerting the demon to my presence by using magic. I resorted instead to threats and intimidation to keep her quiet. "If you so much as breathe too loud," I growled in her ear, "I'll chew your fucking face off." She whimpered, sagged in my arms. She smelled good, like fresh bread.

"What are you waiting for?" Del asked. The woman yelped.

"She doesn't mean you," I hastily reassured her.

"Please, don't hurt me," she begged.

"I can't make any promises, fustilugs. Now hush."

The members of the Witnergan bowed their heads. The Duke began to chant a litany. Mid-verse a soft glow bloomed before the throne. The little woman in the Duke's company screamed and pointed as the light resolved into a ghostly image of Malin.

Chapter Twenty-Two

The illusion was a simple trick, but these coves had little experience of sorcery and weren't to know that. Even Delgaro shot me a questioning look. I shook my head, mouthed the word 'illusion'.

"What?" She asked.

The servant whimpered into my sleeve. "It's an illusion," I whispered. "A simple spell. Oi, do you mind?" I asked the wench who was wetting my sleeve with her sniffle.

She wiped her nose, again, on my sleeve. "I can't help it you're scaring me."

"This isn't scary, trust me."

"The king's spirit!" one of Anchal's thugs declared as he pointed at the apparition. Someone else yelled in alarm and shouts of dismay rang round the hall.

"Uncle, you must save our people." The shimmering phantasm moaned. It wasn't even a particularly good illusion, more like something you'd see an apprentice mage conjure in the marketplace to earn some extra coin. Here it was being used to terrify the rulers of a kingdom.

"The Holy Briar must save the land. I beg you, Uncle, lead the people from the darkness of ignorance."

"I think that's enough rope." I put my fingers to my lips and gave a sharp whistle.

Del looked at me questioningly. "That's your signal?"

"What did you expect, fireworks?"

She muttered something that was anatomically impossible even for a dragon and unsheathed her sword. The servants scattered, the ghost of Malin wavered, and the sound of fighting and battle cries echoed outside the hall.

I released the wench who immediately made to run into the hall where there was a good chance that a vicious fight was about to break out. Touched by a pang of guilt, I grabbed her apron strings and swung her about as the door in the south wall burst open. Two of Anchal's Briars stumbled in before being taken down by Malin's guards who stormed into the hall after them. Greyholt drew a knife and shivved the nearest one of Anchal's henchmen before he had a chance to react. The king pulled up sharply when he saw his ghostly image hovering by the throne.

"It's just an illusion, Malin. It's harmless," I shouted over the din.

The architect of this travesty didn't so much as twitch as his plans began to unravel before his eyes. Those of the Witnergan who weren't either drunk or in their dotage were on their feet by this point. Some shouted orders, others drew weapons, while some hid behind their retainers, and the more fleet of foot ran for the doors. Amidst the chaos Anchal remained an island of stillness. He was the eye of the storm, silent and seemingly unmoved as his Briars were disarmed or dispatched around him.

Malin cautiously approached the illusion, jabbed his sword at it. The blade passed straight through and the boy jumped back as the image faltered. "I don't look like that do I?" He asked Greyholt, who was wiping his knife on the body of Anchal's man. The warrior looked at the illusion as he helped himself to the dead man's shield while the other thug was surrounded by the king's guards. "A little, sire, aye."

Malin glared at Anchal. "This is a fine trick, Uncle. You'll have to explain how you managed it before you're executed." He next addressed the Witnergan. "As you all can see, I am very much alive. No thanks to my treacherous uncle." He turned to the man in question, fury burning in his eyes. "I am disappointed that you didn't flatter me more with your illusion. You could have made me taller, more handsome perhaps. It would have been some small recompense for murdering me. Leave the court ladies with a pretty image to remember me by, wouldn't you say?" The boy advanced on his uncle, sword in hand, ready to dispense summary justice.

I opened my mouth to warn him away from the fiend when someone stabbed me in the arse. I spun ready to smite the attacker only to see the serving wench standing there with a twin-pronged carving fork in her hand. I snatched it from her. "I've a mind to stick you with this, see how you like it," I said. She squealed, tripped on her skirt, and fell on her arse. "Why the fuck did you do that?" I demanded.

"D... demon."

"Yes. Him. Over there." I jabbed the fork in the direction of Anchal who still hadn't reacted to what was happening. The wench's face crumpled, and she began to wail adding her voice to the growing cacophony. Malin's soldiers closed in on Anchal who put his back to the fire pit and faced them seemingly unconcerned that he was almost certainly about to be hacked to pieces for his crime.

"I trusted you, Uncle." For a moment, Malin looked to be on the verge of tears, but only for a moment. His resolve quickly hardened, and the tears vanished. "You betrayed me, you tried to kill me, and for that there's only one punishment."

The woman who was part of Anchal's crew threw herself at the boy's feet. "Malin, please. Please, show mercy. He's not himself, he's been sick..." Her words trailed into incoherence.

"He's going to get a lot fucking sicker." I limped into the room, bleeding from my injured rump.

Anchal dropped his gaze on the woman. His eyes were shining, fever-bright. "Thank you, my dear, but it is too late for that." He hacked, his voice bubbled from his chest. He grabbed her and dragged her towards him. "Far too late." The nobleman's eyes rolled back in his skull and a glistening, black worm wiggled between his bloodless lips and began to push its way out. Another joined it, then another, stretching his mouth wider and wider.

The woman was splattered with ichorous blood as his flesh tore. She screamed and clawed at her face as the blood began to burn. Anchal's face twisted beyond recognition as a pair of spidery hands ripped his face in half. His eyes burst from their sockets and there was a loud *crack* as his skull shattered, spilling brains across the floor. Black blood fountained, the body jerked and spasmed as the demon within tore its way out. Desperate to escape, the injured woman fought free of the monster's grasp.

"Fuck's sake, don't just stand there," I shouted, having just stood there like everyone else, frozen by the sight of the demon's birth. My shout broke the spell, people ran for the exits and Malin's guards formed up between the beast and the king. What remained of the Duke fell to the floor like a wet sack, revealing the monster in all its infernal glory. Bathed in the firelight, it stood, steaming, its night black body glazed in blood. Four, slender horns wormed from its elongated skull. A second pair of arms burst through its torso below the first. A forked tongue flicked from its fanged mouth and tasted the air. It hissed and stalked towards the warriors and the boy king. People began to gag. Now they could smell this delinquent from the charnel house.

"Oh, Malin." The demon sighed, venom dripping from its lips. "This would have been so much easier if you'd just died." The petulance of the voice didn't match the death dealer's demonic form. "Anchal could have taken over and we would have had peace. Now all these lovely people are going to be slaughtered because of your, frankly, selfish behavior. Are you happy now? Hmm?" It spoke like the kindly uncle it had purported to be, gently chastising his scampish nephew for some minor transgression, rather than a demon who was ruing the fact that the boy had survived an assassination attempt, leaving it no choice but to kill everyone in the room.

Before Malin could answer, it lunged at him with its razor claws. The warriors locked shields. One brave soul circled and tried to blindside the monster. Without bothering to look, the demon rammed its blade-slender hand through her neck as she charged in. Shock froze her features. Her blade dropped from lifeless fingers, black veins of corruption spread across her skin as she choked and died. The demon let the body slide from its fingers.

"Well that was silly, wasn't it?" it said, before trying again to force its way through the cordon of guards. Seeing the danger, the warriors loyal to the king left off fighting the Briars and surrounded Malin with a thicket of blades.

I'd seen enough demons to last several lifetimes and would have left the clanks to it had the fallen warrior not begun to spasm and twitch as a parody of life returned to her mangled corpse. A sickening inevitability dawned on me as I watched the new-minted Unhallowed climb to her feet and leap on the nearest of her ex-comrades, much to his short-lived surprise as she bit a chunk out of his throat. I would have to get involved or watch them fall, one after the other to the virulent, demonic infection. As I weighed up the options, the woman who had begged for Anchal's life collapsed in a dead heap of smoking flesh.

"Oh, no you don't." I grabbed a poker from the hearth, raced around the ring of warriors, and thrust it through her chest, pinning her to the floor like an oversized bug. "Sorry," I said as her eyes which were now as pale as pearls flickered open. She groped ineffectually at the poker, seemingly perplexed by its presence in her ribcage. The good thing about this breed of Unhallowed was that they weren't very bright. Alas, the same could not be said of the demon.

To give the terrified warriors a fighting chance, I raised a wall of earth between them and the fiend and cast a blast of lightning at its back. With preternatural speed, it spun, raised a taloned hand, and caught the bolt.

"That's new," I mused. I'd never seen a spell 'caught' before, let alone had it happen to me. I didn't know what to do as the chain of fire arced and spat and burned the air between us. The demon gave a leering grin and coiled the lightning around its fist.

"What's this?" it said. "A fellow sorcerer, arrived in my domain unannounced? Come now, speak up. Who are you, stranger? You must be the one who broke my army at the cliffs. That was you, wasn't it?" It entwined a spell of compulsion with an olfactory illusion of the smell of ivy, decomposing leaf mold, and granite. It didn't feel like an attack, more an introduction with a sorcerous flourish.

"It's none of your fucking business who I am," I said as I didn't know how to answer in kind and therefore defaulted to the gutter-born bravado I knew best. "But don't you worry, pukepail. Even guised as a demon, I know who you are, *Blight* and you my son, are fucked."

It didn't have any eyebrows to arch, but it gave a look that implied skeptical disbelief. "I don't think so, dear." It twirled the lightning around its spindly fingers. "You know, I should have guessed that another mage would turn up sooner or later. Let me do all the hard work of finding a nice plump cache and go to the bother of mining and refining it while you sat here, all nice and comfy, just waiting for your chance to steal it from me. Well, that's not going to happen. This place is mine. I've laid claim to this realm and everything in it."

I didn't have a clue what it was talking about, but I did see the attack coming a second before the lightning was hurled back at me. I dived into the antechamber between the hall and the kitchen. The wall took the brunt of the blast and was reduced to a pile of burning timbers leaving a gaping hole between hall and kitchen. I crawled out of the rubble with my ears ringing and bright lights dancing before my eyes. A strong smell of burning hair added to the malodor which, upon inspection, I realized was mine.

While I waited for the room to stop spinning, a handful of warriors charged the demon. Nearer to me, another of the Unhallowed rose and attacked an elderly nobleman who mercifully seemed to faint before the corpse tore his throat out. Black veins formed instantly and began to spread across his face.

The same thing was beginning to happen all around the chamber. If this fiendish plague wasn't checked sharpish, the dead would soon outnumber the living.

While I gathered my wits, the demon collapsed the wall of earth and messily dispatched most of the warriors. In an act of insane bravery and desperation, Greyholt charged the fiend, yelling an incoherent battle cry he swung at the demon. It swayed aside, slapped his blade away with contemptuous ease, throwing him off balance. I expected it to strike his head from his shoulders, but he managed to raise his shield as he fought to regain his balance. The demon scored deep gouges in the wood and struck sparks from the iron boss.

"Hey, Breed," Greyholt shouted. "It's time to prove yourself." He ducked another vicious blow and thrust his sword into the demon's gut, surprising all three of us. The infernal stared at the steel before taking hold of the naked blade and pulling itself towards the stunned warrior. It took him a moment to realize what it was doing before he had the sense to let go of the blade.

Fighting had broken out everywhere by now. People were running and screaming and being gnawed upon. It was pandemonium etched in blood and fire and it was only going to get worse as the dead continued to infect the living with the demonic plague.

There was only one thing for it.

I drew a deep breath and woke the elemental within me. A rush of blood spun the world. I stumbled, fell on the rubble. A group of velvet-clad lordlings lit upon the idea of escaping the carnage through the lightening fashioned hole and ran towards me in a panic. I pushed myself up on all fours. "Get back, *now*," I growled as my hands burst into flames. They immediately backed up, avoiding instant death as the transformation took hold.

Rafters cracked as the spines on my back pierced the roof. The kitchen wall collapsed entirely. I crouched, tried to make myself small, acutely aware that the king and his followers were a stumble away from being crushed by me. The demon didn't appear to be fazed by the sudden appearance of a dragon. It snarled at its Unhallowed minions who all stopped attacking the humans and came at me.

I laughed. "What do you think they're going to do to me?" I didn't have to wait long to find out as one of the recently departed sank its teeth into the tip of my tail. The tiny bite burned. I flicked my tail and smashed the undead wretch into the floor. Another staggered towards me, teeth snapping, its fingers hooked like claws. A well-timed backhand hurled it across the room. The pain in my tail began to throb and black veins spidered from the wound.

The demon chuckled. "I'm sorry, I shouldn't laugh, terribly rude. But perhaps you should have chosen a less conspicuous form? Don't mistake me; a dragon is impressive— vulgar, but impressive if you like that kind of thing, but a terrible waste of power, no?"

"Perhaps I like wasting power."

The demon tilted its head. "What? That doesn't make sense."

A burst of pain reminded me of the bite. I slashed at my tail, severing it above the spreading infection. "Yeah? Well, you don't make sense and you stink."

The demon leaped at me, trailing its intestines behind it. I didn't try anything fancy, I plucked it from the air, pinned its arms to its sides, and squeezed until its bones shattered and its stinking flesh burst.

"I may be vulgar, but size has its advantages." I threw the lolling carcass on the fire. "I fucking hate demons."

More warriors charged into the hall, Delgaro and Bolin's crews amongst them. While they finished off the Unhallowed, I picked up the amputated end of my tail and tossed it into the fire. "Throw the bodies on the fire." I gave a low, rumbling growl and brought my muzzle so close to Greyholt's face that my breath ruffled his hair. "Is this proof enough for you?" He stared long and hard at my fangs before nodding. "Good."

One of Bolin's crew toed the remains of the Duke of Anchal. "What shall we do with that?" I deferred to Malin.

He looked to me. I nodded.

"Burn it," he said, and his uncle's remains were unceremoniously shoveled on to the fire. "How could someone like Anchal fall to such evil? Someone who had been so strong, so loyal?"

"He either made a deal with the Blight, in which case he was fleeced, or he was an innocent victim."

"My uncle was never what you'd call 'innocent'. He was a shrewd politician, although I would like to think that the more noisome aspects of Briar doctrine were because of the influence of that bastard in the north rather than my uncle. That's what I'd like to believe."

My tail throbbed, distracting me from Malin's heartfelt prattle. "I'm sorry," I said to cover for my lack of attention.

"It's not your fault." He clasped his hands behind his back. "It wasn't his. The more I think about it, the more I'm convinced that he was most cruelly tricked. Anchal would never make a pact with a demon. At heart, he was a good man. Not a nice man by any means, but a good man."

It would have been churlish to gainsay the boy as he grieved for another dead family member, but I'd met Anchal's kind before. He was an ambitious man, bred to be ruthless and shrewd. At best his arrogance had opened the door to the evil that had consumed him. At worst, he'd invited it in, heedless of the cost in his single-minded pursuit of power. The sigils branded into my palm reminded me that, depending on the circumstances, any cove; be they beggar, prince, or god could make a bad decision. I looked at the marks in my paw and noticed that the silver was now a faint, sparkling vein.

Chapter Twenty-Three

After the fight, I transformed into my more human guise and promptly passed out. The swoon was probably due to the less than ideal combination of changing into the dragon and being poisoned by a demonic minion. Whatever the cause, I was sick and as weak as a day-old calf. I hid it as best as I could and asked for a room where I might, 'meditate upon what the demon had said,' or some similar bullshit. 'Truth was, I just needed to sleep.

A chamber was made available, and food was provided along with about a gallon of piss-poor wine. I gave strict orders on-pain-of-fiery-death that I wasn't to be disturbed and after stuffing my face and drinking my fill, promptly fell into a sleep as deep as death. I was so exhausted that I slept through the whole of the next day and night and woke on the morning of the second day after the demon's attack. I might have slept longer, but I was roused by a timid esquire who informed me that the king wanted to see me in his chambers before the meeting of the Witnergan. I keenly wanted to tell him to fuck off or I'd eat him, but then I remembered I was *being a hero*. I sent the lad to fetch more wine while I gathered my sleep-muddled wits and tried to fathom why the silver in my palm had faded so much. "I don't understand."

"It's really very simple," said Tobias. "Now that you don't have the Hammer's hammer you're using up the power of the star steel you stole from the water world."

I leaped to my feet, expecting to see the priest lurking in the corner but I was alone. "Tobias?" I looked under the bed, found nothing but dust, mouse droppings, and a sock. "And now I'm going mad. Wonderful." I created some robes in somber black and ashen grey to match my mood.

The king's servant led me through a warren of dingy passageways and cramped chambers that were thick with cobwebs and the whispers of a thousand intrigues and schemes. To keep out the cold and the speculation of prying eyes, the windows were small and narrow. The taste of tallow greased the air but couldn't mask the stink of open sewers and festering gong pots. *And this is the palace*. I'd either arrived in this world just in time to help these culls or too late to do anything but watch their demise.

The king hadn't claimed his parents' apartments which were situated in the heart of the palace. I was told in hurried whispers by the esquire, who was a lad called Ferdus, that they'd been sealed and left as they had been found the night the royal couple had been slain in their beds. Malin's modest chambers were in the east wing of the palace where vigilant guards greeted me with a mix of awe and suspicion but let me enter without hindrance.

The first chamber eloquently described in artifacts the worlds that the boy had been forced to straddle after the murder of his family. An army of toy soldiers had been pressed into service and now stood on a map, representing not a game of strategy, but the real and bloody war. A desk, scarred by youthful vulgarities was stacked with ledgers and documents of state that were signed in a deliberate hand and sealed with wax as red as the banners which were hanging from the rafters.

What books of idle fancy he'd enjoyed in peaceful times now gathered dust in the corner. They'd been piled beside wooden wasters that had also been discarded in favor of a real blade that lay against his burnished and battle-scarred harness. I didn't pity him, he'd had more of a childhood than most, but credit where credit was due. I couldn't command myself, let alone a nation for all that I was six years older than Malin.

Raised voices drew me to the bedchamber. I peered inside, happy to find that this time no one was trying to strangle him although he was arguing with a retainer so aged and withered that I almost mistook him for one of the Unhallowed.

"I don't give a damn, Mallory. I won't wear it." The boy cast a scarlet velvet tunic on the floor. The hoary servant grumbled as he retrieved the garment, dusted it off, and laid it on the bed beside a pair of matching breeches, a jeweled dagger and belt, and a crown studded with rough-cut gems.

"Have I come at a bad time?"

"It's always a bad time." The boy smiled. "Although I'm pleased to see you. I thought you might have died, but I was informed you snore like a dragon. Have you really slept for two days?"

"Certainly not. I've been meditating." I spied a table laid with cold cuts, cheese, bread, and pickles which reminded me that I hadn't eaten for days. "Do you mind?"

Malin gave a dismissive wave. "Help yourself."

I snagged a butter pastry pie that was stuffed with meat and berries. It was delicious and gone in two bites. I took another two and went over to the fire and warmed my stiff limbs. All the shape changing and demon killing had taken its toll on me. Everything ached. The canopied bed that dominated the chamber beckoned invitingly. I suppressed a yawn. "What's wrong with the garb, red not your color?" I waved a pie in the direction of the clothes and jewels.

The retainer muttered, earning a reproving glance from the boy. "How can I stand before the Witnergan and beg for their aid while I'm dressed like a…"

"King?"

He frowned. "If I wore that it would look like I have coffers full of gold, which I don't."

I ate another pie. "These are very good. You want money? Sell these. You'll make a fortune."

He laughed. "I'll think about it. Thank you by the way. You saved us, again."

"I did. Damn sneaky of Blight, wrapping his proxy in your uncle's skin."

"Indeed." The boy picked up an apple, took a bite, tossed it aside. *No wonder he's skinny.* "We owe you a debt of gratitude."

"I know. Will you take some advice against that boon?"

"I'll listen, but that's as much as I'll promise."

I ate another pie. "My compliments to your cook. These are tasty."

"You should tell her yourself." He smirked.

"What's so funny?"

"It was the pastry cook who stabbed you in the arse."

My behind twinged at the memory of the grievous assault. "A wench of many talents it seems."

"You'll have to find that out for yourself." More youthful smirking. "What's your advice?"

"It's the butter." The retainer offered without anything as useful as an explanation to accompany the statement. "The Melcham cows graze by the coast. The grass is salty which makes Melcham butter the best butter in five kingdoms. Why I remember—"

"Another time, perhaps." Malin turned to me. "What advice do you have for me?"

"Put on the noble motley, play the part."

He shook his head. "It wouldn't be right."

"It would. I don't mean to be rude, but you're not the most impressive specimen of humankind, are you?"

The boy looked momentarily stung but swallowed his ire, and even allowed himself a wry smile. "You're right. I'm short for my age, I'm not particularly strong, but I am stronger than I look. 'Wiry' they say when they think I'm out of hearing. I'd like to think I was brighter than most, although I fear that I'm just bright enough to know that I'm not that bright. No. As you say, I am unremarkable. Doubly so in the presence of a being such as yourself. You have strengthened my resolve, thank you. Perhaps you'd like the crown?

Take over from such a pathetic being." He sketched a mocking bow.

"Sweet salvation. I don't have tender feelings like you humans, so if I've hurt yours forgive me, it wasn't my intention. I meant to say that you are, what you are. And you seem like a bright lad, as humans go."

He picked up a pie, sniffed it before taking a bite. "You're too kind."

"You're welcome. But wit aside, bright or dull, weak or strong, you're more than a boy. You embody the hopes of your people. Don't roll your eyes like that. You might only be king because of bad luck and a quirk of birth or because your ancestors were smarter or indeed more vicious than those of your pot boy. I understand that. I'm the child of the Queen of the Midnight Court, through no skill of mine. But there it is. We cannot choose our parents. You can choose to accept your birthright, or if it displeases you, change the system, put a horse in charge if you want. But not now. You must lead until the war is won, play the part destiny has set for you and be seen to do so. Garb yourself in velvet and jewels like the king you are. It's your uniform, blind the people to their woes with the gleam of gold and the sparkle of gems." I steered him to where his clothes were laid out like a glittering body waiting to be inhabited. "This is your armor; your cause is to inspire. That's what all the crown and scepter bollocks is about. They're trappings, they imbue you with more than human authority. Give the people someone to look up to, someone who is more than they are."

"I'm not 'though. Well, I'm better than *some*, like the fellow at the carnival who hammers nails into his head and eats horse shit. I think the kingdom is safer in my hands than his."

"Just do your best, eh? That's all any of us can do."

"I don't mean to be rude, but that's easy for a dragon to say."

I grinned. "Aye, it is. But even if I were a half-breed, sewer-born, bravo I'd make sure that I was the meanest fucking bravo that ever prowled the darkness. I'd look the part, talk it, walk it."

"All right. All right, you've convinced me. I'll play the part." He scoffed his pie and then clapped his hands. "Come on Mallory, help this noble jester into his motley."

***

The boy entered the study where I'd waited while his ancient retainer had stuffed him into his dandy rags. He'd scrubbed up well, his black curls had been tamed and oiled and the crown set upon his frowning brow. He buckled a jeweled dagger sheath to his belt. "Apparently I now look more like a king than a stable boy." He smiled at Mallory. The old gruff bowed. "He thinks you look strange and otherworldly."

"I am." I tossed my shockingly bright hair over my shoulder. "If you prefer I can change my appearance to something that won't offend the sensibilities of your court." I had no intention of changing. I was testing him, as I was sure he was testing me. There was a thoughtful pause where we sized each other up before he shook his head.

"To the Pit with them. Be who and what you are, even if I cannot." He smiled and so did I.   While he and his man fussed with garters and aglets, my gaze wandered to a pair of poorly executed portraits that were hanging over the fireplace. The boy looked like the woman, dark and lean, sharp-eyed, much like his uncle had looked before the demon had discarded his bone bag like an old glove. I assumed that the man was his father, although there was little resemblance. The fellow in the painting was broad featured, blonde haired, and had a prominent, broken nose and pale eyes. "These must be your parents." *At least, the woman's his mother.*

"Aye. It's a poor likeness of my mother." He walked over to the cold hearth, looked up at the paintings. He turned away, feigned interest in his belt to hide his expression, but the tremor in his voice betrayed his feelings. "She laughed a lot. Found humor in most things. The painter hasn't captured the liveliness of her eyes." He gestured dismissively at the portrait of the man. "That looks like my father."

I never understood the seeming depth of affection humans had for their families, but I tried to appear sympathetic. "I'm sorry for your loss. You must miss them a great deal."

He paused a moment before turning his searching gaze upon me. "I miss my mother and I miss my sister. My father was a bastard. I cannot say I miss him overmuch."

His candor was disarming and deserved acknowledgment in kind. "I never knew my father, but my mother was likewise a proper bastard. She's dead too." It struck me then that I missed her like one misses a disease when it passes. I'd grown used to her unpleasantness.

He poured two mugs of ale, handed one to me. "A toast then, to terrible parents, long may they rest in peace."

I raised my mug. Not to the restful dead, but to Malin and the birth of our enduring friendship, not that I realized it at the time.

***

We talked briefly about family, each careful to avoid questions that might cause discomfort to the other. I'd always been a cagey cove, but as everyone that I knew was dead and my world was lost to a demon horde, I didn't think talking about myself would matter. We also discussed the Witnergan. Malin explained that in principle the council was a good idea, but in practice was a lumbering bureaucracy, rife with corruption and self-serving nobles. According to the boy king, they were content to sit back and watch other parts of the kingdom burn while they protected their own fiefs and interests.

"The Blight will get around to them all eventually. Surely, they know that? Power hungry bastards are never satisfied," I said and wondered if Shallunsard had completed his conquest of my world.

"They know that, by the Trinity, they've been told often enough but..." The creaking elderling draped Malin in a gold chain of office. "It's like a disease. They know what will happen, but they choose to ignore the truth in favor of believing the fantasy that Blight will leave them in peace, that they can weather this storm."

"Then they're fucking idiots."

He laughed. "And therein lies my problem. How do you deal with idiots?"

"Well..."

"Other than killing them."

"That's me stumped then. Are you sure you want me at the meeting?" I knew I didn't want me at the meeting, which was guaranteed to be drearier than the previous one unless there was another demon lurking amongst the Elders.

"I can't compel a dragon, so I shall ask you to come with me." The king spoke out of earshot of his servant who was waiting with a half a dozen clanks all garbed in their best tin.

I yawned. "What do you reckon your chances are of getting troops out of your nobles?"

"Better now that Blight's influence over my uncle has been unmasked. He was the instigator of a great deal of dissent. Are you still tired?"

"What, me? No. I'm just relaxed." I was so relaxed I could have fallen asleep where I stood. "Do you want me to persuade them, I could do that you know?"

"No. But thank you for the offer. This is my battle."

I nodded my agreement and resolved to enhance his speechifying with what skill I had at sorcerous persuasion, which is to say, not much. I also resolved to mark out any of the remaining Witnergan who had a hang gallows look so that I could settle their accounts when all this had blown over.

On the way to the hall, I noticed that the king was greeted with unfeigned warmth and affection by his household and retinues. The boy was agreeable which was a useful trait in a leader and would make my self-appointed task of saving his kingdom easier. Nobody held him in awe, but he was greeted with heartfelt smiles by most of those we encountered. It gave me confidence that I'd made the right choice to support the lad. *You could have been a god. Hell, he even offered you the crown.* It was a seductive thought that lurked in the old, unheroic corner of my brain. I was a born thief and a killer; I didn't have the kind of head that fit a crown or the arse that could sit on a throne. I had claws, a knack for violence and that was enough.

Horns blared when the royal procession reached the hall. Unfortunately, the hall was a wreck which undermined the pomp and spectacle somewhat. If I'd known that Anchal was a demon I'd have done for him before he forced me to break things. "I promise, when this is over, I'll build you a palace that'll be the envy of the world," I said to Malin.

"Have you seen much of our world? I'm told there is a palace in the north of Gutamar that is made anew every year out of ice."

"All right. How about when the war is over, I'll build you a palace that will be far grander than that which was here before."

"I like this palace. And who'll pay for this grand affair?" Malin sidestepped a puddle.

"You like this? The walls are plastered with dung. And I'll pay for it."

He looked up. Rain splashed his face. "I'd settle for a roof that doesn't leak."

Malin took his place on the throne that his uncle had died trying to possess. I settled myself in the

corner. I didn't darken the shadows around me because
I didn't have the strength. I huddled into my robes as
the Witnergan paid obeisance to the king and made a
point of staring down those who dared to look at me.
Some nodded respectfully, others, particularly those
Malin had said were close to Anchal, were less
friendly. I made a mental note of their names and
faces.

I'd like to give a detailed account of what was
discussed. I'd love to describe in exacting detail the
cut and thrust of courtly politicking, mudslinging, and
partisan campaigning, but I can't, because I fell asleep.
I remember the doors closing and the king standing up
to speak, and that was the last I knew until I was
prodded awake by Mallory, who offered me a cup of
strong spirits. The Witnergan had dispersed, the king's
household now occupied the hall, and a pair of hounds
snuffled around the empty seats. I recognized the
gilded silhouettes of Malin, Greyholt, Delgaro, and
Bolin standing by the fire. I got up and joined them.
"As you're smiling, I take it that you got what you
wanted?"

Malin had divested himself of the crown and chains
of office and unlaced his doublet. He was rosy-
cheeked from ale and heat and looked as close to
happy as I'd seen him. "Less than I wanted, but more
than I expected. Four thousand cavalry will ride north
with you and Captain Delgaro, who for some reason
has decided to stay."

Delgaro gestured to the hall, mug in hand, eyes shining beer bright. "How could I leave all this, sire?" This wasn't the first round of drinks. Their relief and optimism were palpable, understandable. I didn't share it, I wasn't feeling up to fighting a sorcerer, but I liked them enough not to tell them and spoil their celebration.

"Breed?" said the king. "Are you well?"

"Yes, of course."

"I was just saying, that I should go with you to face Blight."

Eyes rolled, laughter died. Mallory gestured for a servant to refill the mugs.

"With respect, but no, sire," said Delgaro. "I could flatter you and say that you're needed here, which you are, but the truth is, even with Breed we don't know what we'll face up there. Imagine what would happen if you died and rose from the dead like others have, what then?"

"I'm not planning on dying, Captain, Delgaro." He smiled.

"Of course not, sire. But after everything we've been through, to lose you now when victory is in sight. It would be a disaster."

The king stared into the flames. "I count losing my mother, father, and sister a disaster. The destruction of this kingdom, the horror visited upon the people for the past four years. We live in disaster. It is the air we breathe, the food we eat. All I know is disaster. My death or yours, could not add to the misery that Blight has visited upon this land and its people. I would gladly die a hundred deaths and consign all of you to die with me to put an end to Blight."

It was well said and the resolve of some of those gathered begin to falter which wouldn't do at all. "Fuck's sake. Please, I beg you. Stay here, Majesty, so that we might fight freely, knowing that you're safe."

Delgaro gave me a sharp look. "You should mind your manners, sorcerer."

"I thought I was."

Swaying, Malin raised his hand. "It's all right, Del. While I have you all here, I want all of you to promise that we will never dissemble for fear of offending, irrespective of rank." He drained his mug and belched.

"Fine by me," I said. "I have no rank, Delgaro's a mercenary, your man Mallory is on his last legs, and nobody respects Greyholt anyway."

"Hey, what?" Greyholt polled those gathered with a questioning look. "I'm respected, aren't I?" Some of his men who were loitering nearby offered drunken reassurances that he was highly respected. What was more impressive was that some of them did it with a straight face.

An amused gleam lit in Delgaro's eye. "Breed's right. It's just you, Majesty."

"All right, it's just me then. None of *you* stand on ceremony with *me*, but you know, don't…" He waved his hand as though trying to conjure words from the air. "Don't…"

"Take the piss?" I offered.

The king slapped his thigh. "Exactly. Be honest and be yourselves, but don't take the piss, or you know, I'll have you executed."

Chapter Twenty-Four

Three days after the Witnergan met and before the sun had even blistered the horizon, I was torn from a bout of rantum scantum, by a loud rap on my chamber door.

I gasped as Ellia, the stabby serving wench with the lovely paps and a way with pastry, finished me off. We collapsed in a tangle of hair and sweaty limbs and would have stayed that way but for Delgaro's punctilious observance of the tradition of riding off to war at the crack of fucking dawn. I got dressed and exchanged lies and fragile promises with my comrade in carnality while she loitered on the edge of a post-fuck snooze.

I opened the door to find Skurden acting as Delgaro's knocking proxy. "Mercy's sake, it's still darkmans," I said. "Why do we have to set so early? It's not like Blight's going to start the battle without us. Or does Captain Bright Lark think he might do a runner once he knows we're on our way?"

All I got instead of an apology was a shrug. "She wants to get a jump on the day in case the levies try to do a runner. Now get a move on, would you?"

***

Delgaro was waiting in the courtyard astride her horse, garbed for war, and beaming like a hangman on court day. As I was made for shadows, this woman was made for war. She fair glowed in anticipation of the fight. Forget 'sacrifice and courage', for the most part those who made their living by the sword lived for the fight. "Good morning, sorcerer. So glad you could join us."

"You said dawn. 'Be ready to leave at dawn'." Those were your exact words. This is the middle of the fucking night."

"I said that we are *leaving* at dawn, which it will be when we depart." She nudged her mount, turned it to the gate. "I'm sure your cook will keep it warm until you return."

"Is Bolin keeping it warm for you?" I lifted the hem of my hakama clear of the sucking mud. Another thing I swore I'd do after we'd slotted Blight was to introduce the good people of Arduin to paving slabs.

"Bolin can do as he pleases with whomever, so long as he can keep that shower of shit militia sharp while we're away."

"Bolin the Blusterer? I'm sure he'll do a bang-up job of barking orders. I don't know what you see in him. He stinks worse than the demon."

"Not when he's with me he doesn't. And he hasn't tried to stab me lately. Imagine taking up with someone who stuck you the first time they'd laid eyes on you?" She smirked at Skurden.

"It was a misunderstanding," I said. "She's a sweet-natured girl when you get to know her."

"With an outstanding pair of dumplings," Skurden weighted a pair of imaginary breasts, much to Delgaro's amusement.

"But it's your face that I see when I'm fucking her, Skur." I winked at the old warrior who returned fire with a filthy glare. Delgaro laughed so hard that she almost rode into an inn sign.

***

Knowing the army was on the move, the city came out to bid us farewell and lamps burned in every window casting the illusion of warmth in the chill, predawn darkness. Bolin and his crew were standing honor guard for the king. As we passed them at the gate he and Del exchanged a look full of meaning and silent promises. I'd never shared a close bond with a lover, not that I yearned for it, it wasn't in my nature to love as humans loved. Given how it seemed to torment those afflicted while imparting no particular benefit coin couldn't buy, I thanked the Mage Lords for their consideration when they made my kind.

It began to drizzle while we waited for the king to arrive. Malin didn't look best pleased when he rode out to see us off, no doubt he was still smarting over being left behind. He made a speech, during which his voice broke randomly, but nobody laughed. No one had the stomach for mirth after he reiterated that if Blight wasn't destroyed, he'd come back and finish the job he'd started. The horns blared, standards were raised against the grey morning, and we rode off with the fate of a kingdom resting on our shoulders.

Delgaro insisted I ride at the head of the army. I say, 'army,' but each faction remained distinct and separate from the other, bound only by their princes' commitment for them to be there. As much as I didn't like horses, they were also not enamored of me, probably because I stank of death and dragon. The most docile nag offered to me started stomping and snorting, flattening its ears, and rolling its eyes when I took the reins. A compromise was found by commandeering a supply wagon. Those captains who hadn't met me before were affronted by the repurposed baggage cart trundling at the head of their force, but Delgaro dismissed their objections out of hand.

"You're the reason we're here," she said while messengers and heralds rode through the ranks relaying her orders to captains who until now, had mostly ignored her. "When they see what you can do they'll change their attitude."

"Until then they'll bitch and whine and drag their heels. You need them on your side." I said from my seat on a pile of turnip sacks.

"I'm an outsider, a mercenary. You're the one they'll rally behind when they see the dragon."

"So, what about us?" I heard Piet whisper to Skurden.

"What, 'What about us'?" she said. "We're mercenaries and proud of it. That's enough."

"Aye, it is. But it'd be good to get some recognition now and then, wouldn't it? 'Oh, look there go Piet Maudney and Skurden Chase, heroes of the battle of Rygor Plains, or something like that. That would be nice, wouldn't it?"

Skurden chuckled. "That battle has yet to be fought and I'd rather have a bag of gold crowns than be hailed a hero. My youngest is getting married this year. I need the money for the dowry. Most heroes I've heard of are dead."

"Married, eh? I can't marry until I've killed my first Nuntka." He snorted. "And that ain't going to happen while I'm in this iceless land."

"No ice?" Skurden groaned. "What do you think the white stuff is on the mountains?"

"Oh, yes. I've never thought about that. Do you think there are Nuntkas up there?"

"Idiot." Skurden playfully cuffed him, provoking laughter where until now tense silence had prevailed. I liked these coves and was tempted to suggest that we forget all about fighting Blight and just keep going, see where the road took us. One look at Delgaro told me that suggestion would fall on deaf ears. For all her talk of being a mercenary, it was plain that she'd come to believe in Malin's cause and took pride in his trust in her to lead his army. I liked the boy too, but I had no intention of staying longer than was necessary to ensure Blight was gone.

***

Mid-morning of the fourth day after leaving Galewyn, we reached the Plains of Rygor. The single sun was shining, and white-bellied crows wheeled away from eagles that were hunting high in the cloudless blue. The land had flattened the further north we'd traveled until it rose to a long, pie crust ridge beyond which lay the plains. Beyond the plains was Blight's keep.

Delgaro was in a vile temper after spending the entire journey arguing with the captains of the other contingents over every order she gave them. Putting her in charge was either an oversight, or a clever ploy on Malin's behalf. He knew she had the steel to handle the militia and levied troops and perhaps thought that while they were engaged in internecine bickering, they weren't scaring themselves witless thinking about the battle that would end the war one way or the other.

Aside from egotistical posturing, nothing of note had occurred on the journey. There hadn't been any demonic ambushes, no wandering hordes of marauding Unhallowed, but signs of war were never far.

I was enjoying a post snooze nap when the column came to a halt. I opened my eyes to see Delgaro and her captains gathered on the ridge. There was something down there, on the other side, something that made my hackles rise. The horses sensed it too and danced skittishly.

"Captain says you should come." Piet's voice was thinned by fear. I got up, brushed the wrinkles from my haori, tightened my obi, and put the pleats back in my hakama before following the mercenary. If I was going to get basted by a Mage Lord, I was going to look good, like an arch nib on their way to meet Old Lord Rope for a spot of dancing. I drew a deep breath, warmed it with the fire lurking in my lungs.

"There better be a good reason to wake me in the middle of a particularly pleasant kip." My words hung unanswered in the air. Delgaro turned. The color had drained from her face, turning her features grey as granite. "What is it?" I asked. If the battle-hardened warrior was scared, it occurred to me that I should probably leg it. *No. No running for you, hero.* I held my ground, armored myself with the lie that I was everything they wanted me to be. "Come Delgaro, tell me…" She pointed to the plains.

Two hundred yards along the road, a lone figure sat upon a nightmare steed. Its flesh was withered, fallen away, and flyblown. Sitting atop the long-deceased warhorse was an equally, well dead warrior.

She had lost her helm, probably when the dozen or so daggers had been driven into her skull from which her long black hair had started to peel away. Enough remained of her maggot-ravaged face to show that she bore a strong resemblance to Malin. Her battered, bloodstained armor was a testament to a fierce, final fight. The steel was dented, scratched, and pierced in a dozen places. The plates of the left leg were, along with the flesh, missing. Her ribs showed through where the lower half of the breastplate had been ripped away by a savage blow. Ragged shreds of a red velvet cloak whipped in the warm breeze.

"Every queen needs a crown, no?" The corpse reached up with a fleshless hand and gingerly touched one of the bloody blades protruding from her skull. "She was still just about alive when we did this." The voice that came from the corpse was the same nasal whine that had spoken through the Anchal demon. Behind me, I could hear cursing and groans of disgust and dismay. The Unhallowed warrior heeled the steed in its ribs. It plodded towards us, shedding skin with every step.

"Do you know who this was?" I side-mouthed to Delgaro.

"Althera. Malin's older sister."

"Ah. Right. Did she join up willingly or?" I made a throat cut gesture. Del glared at me. If I didn't know better, I'd say tears had brimmed in her eyes and were only kept in check by the strength of her anger.

"No."

"I, that is my master," the corpse intoned. "Would meet with you, sorcerer. A parley, between equals." A smile of sorts twisted her ravaged lips.

"That sounds like a marvelous idea. Or perhaps I should just assassinate myself here and save you the effort? And while we're about it, who said that we're equals?"

The corpse laughed, whether at her own or Blight's volition was unclear.

"Tell your master he can rot in the Pit," Delgaro shouted. Her cohorts cheered haltingly. Judging by the reaction, this gaunt had been loved in life and mourned in death. It turned its milky gaze on Delgaro.

"Be silent whore, lest I fill your cunt with maggots born of the flies birthed on the bloated corpse of your grandsire."

That was a good hit by any canting cur's standard. Like the rest of those within earshot, I looked to Delgaro to see what she made of it. She bared her teeth in a snarl which, to my surprise broadened into a grin. "My grandsire was a Blood Sworn, Inhamalak of Khandrisha. His flesh was too poisoned even for flies to gorge upon, but I get what you're aiming at, fucker."

Skurden raised a fist and cheered the riposte with gusto, breaking the spell of misery that the gaunt had laid upon the company. She was joined by what sounded like the entire army, but the sight of the fallen hero, mocked and used as a puppet by Blight had sapped their enthusiasm. The Unhallowed queen was a tangible example of what lay in store for them should they fail.

"I would meet with you," Althera mouthed. "You have my word as a Mage Lord. No harm will come to you."

"Like under a flag of truce?"

The corpse shrugged. "I promise that I won't cast any spells at you or set any of my minions upon you." Something fell off the corpse. "Do we have a deal? Can we meet and try to sort this mess out without further bloodshed?" Althera fixed me with her unblinking stare. A fly landed on the milky lens of her eye, but she didn't notice. I looked at Delgaro, but her gaze was locked on the corpse. I turned to Skurden who shrugged. *Up to me then.*

"Very well. Upon your word as a Mage Lord, I accept your invitation."

Chapter Twenty-Five

"What do you mean, you think it's a bad idea?" I asked Delgaro while trying to remember how to cast wards against just about everything.

"What do you mean, 'what do you mean'?" She looked at me like I was deranged. "I think it's a bad idea because it is obvious to any fool with half a brain that it's a bad idea to meet with Blight, in Blight's keep, alone. You saw what he did to… you saw it."

"Yes, I saw." Now was not the time to tell her I'd seen and indeed, had experienced worse because I didn't want to sound like I was bragging. Neither did I comment on the fact that all Blight had done was make an example of the ex-queen to demoralize the living. Most of her injuries were no worse than those sustained by any warrior killed in battle. That she was still walking around was the hook that tore their guts out. It reminded them that war was shit, and they had everything, including their dignity, to lose if they went against him.

As well as the morale of the army being well and truly flattened, after the conversation with the Unhallowed proxy there was also a minor rebellion. A contingent of piss-poor cavalry from some backwater left immediately, citing bad omens and religious beliefs as the cause of their flight. Delgaro let them go without a fight. It wasn't like her, even if they were useless but seeing Althera had shaken the mercenary. The grim encounter had also obliterated any idle fantasy that this would be a glorious battle that the bards would sing of for years to come. Any voices raised after this would be in lament, no matter the outcome.

"Well?" Delgaro demanded.

"You think it's a bad idea, yes. I heard you. Sweet Salvation, I'm trying to prepare here." I fashioned a ward against ice, fire, thorns, and creeping tentacles of ichor just in case. It was late afternoon, and the entire army had watched in silence, as Althera rode back to Blight's imposing fortress. After she'd vanished in a blinding cloud of dust that swept across the plain, Del ordered us to make camp on the ridge. The higher ground gave no advantage save for a false sense of security. No one we'd be fighting was going to get tired running uphill, but at least we'd see them coming.

"How does this look by the way? Does it say, 'wise and powerful' or that I'm a dirty saddle tramp? Should I create a new outfit?" Most of the mercenaries looked at me as though I'd asked if I should conjure myself a second arse.

"I think the black looks serious," Piet offered. "Like you're not to be trifled with. It's not something I'd wear, it's more suited to old folk." He ducked as he glanced at Skurden, but she cuffed him anyway.

Delgaro was less effusive. "You're about to walk into Blight's fortress alone and all you're worried about are your fucking clothes?"

"I was hoping you'd accompany me at least part of the way and no, clothes aren't all that I'm worried about."

She shook her head. "I don't know why you're doing this. You can't bargain with monsters."

I thought I'd seen her angry before. I hadn't. I'd seen her mildly perturbed. *This* was angry.

"We'll see," I said.

Del followed me. She looked like she wanted to punch me. "We'll see? We didn't come here to talk."

"I know." I rounded on her. "You came here to fight for coin and king or die heroically and probably end up like what's-her-face. I'm sorry for your loss, I'm sorry for your pain. *I just don't share it.* "All I'm suggesting is that there may be a better way out of this than fighting to the death, so just trust me a little longer." Her jaw tightened but she held her tongue. I pressed on. "You have somewhere near three thousand warriors at your back, not many by any general's standard and you know many of them are little more than farmers with swords. They are ill-fitted to fighting mortal foes, let alone Blight and his Unhallowed. Give me a chance to end this, so that your army can go home alive." I knew she heard me, but warriors weren't the kind of people to bow before good sense. They had one answer for whatever ailed, and it was sharp and pointy.

"We can't afford to lose you," she said.

"I'm not important," I lied. "With or without me, you'll do what you must. But this is a chance I can't let pass. Now, be honest, how do I look?"

***

At the appointed hour I headed off with Piet and Skurden who'd volunteered to accompany me as far as the fortress. Officially, they were going as an honor guard, but their real task was to scout ahead just in case my plan didn't work. Delgaro wished me a stiff-necked farewell. She was still sore that I was going and that there was fuck-all she could do to stop me.

The mercenaries were mounted, but as I was in no great hurry to reach Blight's stronghold I set out on foot. The road cut directly across the plains, tributaries led to abandoned mines, quarries, and watermills on either side. All work had ceased, all human endeavor ended. The only activity was the business of rowdy carrion birds, fighting over the best perches on the piles of bleaching bones that littered the landscape.

"I saw this place before he went evil and killed everyone," Piet said as we plodded across the plains harried by swirling dust devils and the sun's hard glare. "You should have seen it. The mills and mines worked day and night. Wagon trains ran the length of the plains, nose to arse, coming and going. People came from all corners to work here."

"There was even talk of moving the capital here, so I heard," Skurden added in a rare attack of loquacity.

"That explains why the keep's so big."

The old warrior snorted. "More like his overblown ego. You know how they are." She crooked her little finger.

"No, not really, dragons' have two." I smiled. "Of everything."

Blight's fortress had been hewn from a mountain, an architectural style often favored by evil arseholes. The main entrance was two hundred feet above the plains, flanked by twin statues of a grim-visaged cove in flowing robes. A winding, switchback that was wide enough for an army of humans to march on twenty abreast led to the intricately sculptured façade, the whole of which was cut into the rose-hued sandstone mountain. "It's not what I expected," I said as we approached.

"What do you mean?" Piet asked, his gaze shifting nervously.

"Here we go." Skurden worked a crick from her neck.

"I was expecting something with more skulls and bones, you know? More undead horror, spikes, and black iron gates, that kind of thing."

The old warrior's gaze tracked up the causeway. "I think they heard you." The gate chains rattled, and the doors swung open to reveal a detachment of Unhallowed warriors. Althera was at the head of the legion on her mangy horse. They marched out carrying black standards girded with fear spells and adorned with skulls, just in case the walking dead themselves weren't frightful enough. The mercenaries' horses snorted as the Unhallowed approached, chaperoned by a flock of carrion birds, their bones knocking within their mail.

Skurden and Piet calmed their mounts, but it was time for them to leave. They knew it too, but they held their ground, grim-eyed and determined. "You two better fuck off now," I said relieving them of their duty.

Piet gave a grateful smile, saluted and turned his mount.

Skurden waited. "You sure you want to do this?"

"No, but I'm here now."

"I think you're mad, but it's up to you. Good luck, sorcerer."

"Thanks."

"Don't thank me. If he kills you, I'll have your bones mounted on my wall and take the name 'Dragonslayer'."

"Technically, you'll be 'Undead Dragonslayer' if you got that lucky."

She reined her mount about. "Never let details or truth get in the way of a good story, you should know that, *dragon*." The warrior waved, and she and Piet kicked their mounts into a canter and thundered down the road.

I watched them go while keeping an eye on the advancing undead, who like me didn't seem to be in any hurry to meet up. They didn't look like they were about to attack, but I brought a spell to mind just in case. Piet and Skurden's horses churned up a cloud of dust and turned the air around them to gold as they rode towards the army massed on the ridge.

"Welcome to my humble abode," the Unhallowed queen inclined her head. The undead stood in silent ranks, their garb troubled to movement by the wind alone. Not a muscle twitched, not an eye blinked. Ghastly though they were, it was good to see that the soldiers of this army were long dead. It looked like Blight was running out of raw material, something I hoped Skurden and Piet had noted because Delgaro's crew could use whatever good news was to be had.

"Thanks for the invitation and the welcome."

"A pleasure, although I am surprised you came."

"I said I would, didn't I?"

"Yes. You must forgive me. Honoring commitments is a rare trait in this perfidious nation. Please, after you." She gestured for me to walk ahead of the infernal company, her crown of blades haloed by flies. This was all for show. Blight knew full well that I could have apported to the gate. He was either trying to impress or intimidate me. It didn't matter which. Despite what Delgaro might think, I hadn't come here to make a deal. I'd come here to kill him.

The closer we got to the gates the stronger the stench of death became. "You lot are lucky you can't smell this," I said to my escort. Althera didn't answer, she stared ahead, seemingly oblivious to the crow perched on her shoulder pecking at what flesh still clung to her slender neck.

The causeway had been scoured clean by wind and rain, but the expansive promontory above was another matter. Here the debris of violent death was banked twenty feet high against the walls of the keep, swept into nooks and piled into the angles of the walls. I lifted the hem of my hakama clear of the mess. It occurred to me that Skurden might be right. Hadn't one visit to hell been enough? The sensible thing would have been to apport now. *Oh, that's right, I don't do the sensible thing, I'm a hero, and everyone knows heroes are fucking idiots.*

I didn't have long to chastise myself or wrangle with my morals. Sconces fashioned to look like skeletal hands set into the walls of the gatehouse flared into life. The flames were an unnatural, icy blue and bathed the promontory in an eerie light, at odds with the rose glow of the sunset bleeding out on the far horizon.

Within the gatehouse, a shadowy, black-robed figure loomed out of a cloud of boiling darkness. "How wonderful to meet you," the figure said. It was the same voice that had spoken through the demon and Althea. "Do come in. You'll have to excuse the mess. I'm terribly busy, you know how it is." He beckoned me with a wave. I made sure my wards were in place and entered the keep. The Unhallowed followed and the gates closed behind them.

The darkness surrounding Blight dissipated to reveal a fellow standing on a mounting block who was about a handspan above five feet tall. The wind blasted through the gatehouse and hit me with the fetid stench of rot. My stomach heaved. Not for the first time I wished that I still possessed my thoasan constitution.

Blight either didn't notice that the courtyard looked like a corner of hell brought to the mortal realm or didn't care. But it wasn't the Unhallowed or the piles of rotting corpses that caused me to recoil, that rare honor was taken by the *things* that grazed amongst the necrotic middens. Repulsed, yet at the same time mesmerized, I watched a headless torso with six, mismatched legs crudely stitched to its flanks blunder into a three-headed monstrosity. By the power of necromantic sorcery, the three human heads had been grafted onto a pair of broken arms. None of the heads had eyes, but all three mouths snapped savagely at the torso spider as it stumbled away. Other, equally horrible, and improbable things crawling through the feculence, but they didn't come near us.

"You've been busy," I said to Blight. He threw back his hood, gave me the fish eye. "What do you mean?" A bundle of arms cartwheeled between us and comprehension dawned on his weak-featured face. "Ah, yes." He blushed. "It's just a hobby really." I wondered how so much evil could be contained in such a small package. Blight was a small fellow and wore the tired, wilting expression of a man for whom the glass wasn't just half empty, but also cracked and full of piss. His mouth was wide, his lips unappealingly fleshy. He had quick brown eyes which were lit by a calculating intelligence. "Have you eaten yet?" he asked as he led the way across the courtyard.

"Yes thanks, I'm stuffed. I had some lovely wild boar. Very filling." I sidestepped a bundle of hands that looked like a sea urchin made of fingers. It had managed to catch a rat and was busily tearing the hapless beast apart to no purpose, as it had no mouth with which to eat it.

"I'm not much for game. It plays havoc with my digestion. Although, I insist you join me for a drink." He gave a shy smile. "I have a bottle of rather splendid wine that I've been saving for a special occasion." We entered the keep. My first impression was that nothing so massive could have been built in a decade, let alone four years even with an army of builders. The basic structure alone would have taken years, nevermind the towering statues that flanked doorways and supported grandiose porticos. Althea followed us silently like a faithful, rotting hound. I kept a wary eye on her, which Blight noticed. He smiled but didn't comment.

I'd expected to be taken to an ostentatious, gore-splattered throne room and was therefore surprised when he showed me into a cozy study, wall to wall with bookshelves. The room was hexagonal and had a window overlooking what seemed to be a narrow, inner courtyard. Faded carpets covered the polished stone floor and a couple of overstuffed armchairs flanked a button back sofa that was strewn with colorful cushions.

Althera shuffled into a niche by the door where she collapsed upon her gilded throne like an unstrung

puppet. Blight lit some incense and took off his black
over robes. "That's better. It gets cold here at night.
Not that you'll feel the cold, I'll wager, eh?" He
picked up a dusty wine bottle which had been set
beside two, delicate crystal goblets. "I've never been
able to abide the cold. I found one world that had all
the star steel a body could wish for, but it was freezing
even in summer." He shuddered, offered me a glass.
Though the style was archaic, there was something
familiar about the cut of his doublet and breeches. He
noticed me scrutinizing his duds. "I had them made
before the *misunderstanding*. Do you like them?"

"Yes. Very nice."

"Your attire reminds me of the style favored by
Argathial of the Many Mirrors." He searched my face
for a reaction, as though we were playing a guessing
game. I didn't rise to it, mostly because I didn't know
who the fuck he was talking about. I tried the wine.
"It's good." It was.

A smug grin spread across his face. "I told you.
And now, a toast." He raised his glass. "To Valen!"

Chapter Twenty-Six

"To Valen," I echoed. I was so stunned that he mentioned the capital of the Empire that I almost missed my mouth.

Blight saw the stumble and grinned. "I knew it. I knew I recognized a fellow Imperial Mage Lord when I saw one."

"I don't like to brag." I went over to the window, to give myself a moment away from his scrutiny while I attempted to recover my composure.

"So, what brought you to my, ahem, that is, *this* world where I happen to have made my home?" As I'd already noted the window looked out onto a narrow inner court faced with other, similar windows where strange things slid and crawled through the whispering dark, hidden from plain sight. Far below, pale flames winked in the well of shadows. "But I'm being rude." He laughed like we were old friends instead of deadly adversaries. "We should introduce ourselves, don't you think?"

As befitted a Mage Lord, I felt a title was in order. "Breed of the Fiery Heart." I regretted it as soon as I'd said it. *Dickhead.*

He didn't laugh as he offered his hand, so I guessed I got away with the cringeworthy appellative. "Ozbert, the Unruly, as was. Ozbert will suffice." He gave me another questioning look. "You haven't heard of me?"

"The Schism War was a long time ago."

He frowned. "How long?"

"Put it this way, you look good for your age."

His face darkened. "How long?" Given what he'd done to the people of this land I enjoyed watching him squirm.

"About seven hundred years, give or take a decade."

He slumped down in one of his battered armchairs, visibly shaken. "We were forced to use obscure, unstable gates, you see." He drained his glass. "We didn't have a choice because that old witch was destroying them at such a rate. I must have chosen an unusually wild one to be cast so far from home. Or perhaps it happened after that when I used gates further from the source." He ran his child-like hands across his scalp. "It's not an exact magic as you know. And I've wandered far since leaving Edolis. Very far."

Edolis. So, my world had a name. Layq and Trivo would be pleased. I relaxed. I could handle this fool. He might have been a legendary sorcerer, but now he was just a psychotic necromancer and I was still a damn good Guild Blade. I drained my glass, took a turn around the study pretending to peruse his many books. It could have been the den of any scholar had it not been for the mangled corpse slumped in the corner.

Blight must have seen me looking at Althea. Like an over-protective lover, he drew close to her as though jealous of my gaze upon his grim trophy. "She was very beautiful. Very strong and brave." He plucked a strand of hair from her cheek. "I was going to marry her. That was my plan. Marry the future queen, become king, and drag these rustics into an age of enlightenment."

"What went wrong? May I?" I gestured to the bottle on the table. He nodded. I refilled my glass. "I've only heard one side of the story. I'd like to hear your version." A blast of white light and heat woofed past the window. "What's that?" I was sure that I could taste star steel.

"That's my heating system and ventilation for the er, lower levels. Now, where was I? Ah, yes." He paced the room, hands clasped behind his back. "I'd had to cast so many divination spells to make sure that

I didn't travel through a gate to somewhere that couldn't sustain life, that by the time I got here I was weak. But the gods smiled upon me and I discovered a rich source of Stellaris Metallium." He licked his lips, as though like me, he could taste it. "I could have mined it out and left these mud-grubbing peasants to wallow in their ignorance for the next few thousand years." He took a slurp of wine and stabbed a finger in my direction to emphasize his case. "But I didn't, because I'm a Mage Lord, a devoted bloody servant of humanity wherever I find it and whatever backward state I find it in. I tried to help them, to educate them, but it isn't easy when one has to deal with such ungrateful miscreants."

"That's very decent of you. If only they were more understanding and accepting of your Restless Dead."

He looked aggrieved. "The Restless Dead are demonic in origin. I am not an infernalist. I am a Mage Lord who specializes in the animation of flesh."

I didn't know or care where the difference lay. As far as I, or anyone else I'd met was concerned, screwing with the dead was grim fuckery, whichever way you sliced it. "Forgive me, a slip of the tongue. Although that thing you sent guised as Lord Anchal looked very much like a demon."

He looked away perhaps to hide his embarrassment at being caught in a lie, or perhaps to hide a sly grin. Either way, he was a twitchy cove, genial and in high spirits one minute, sulky and petulant the next. "It was a hybrid," he said over his shoulder. "Anchal came to me, you know? I did not seek him out. He wanted to make a deal. Came begging at my door. Let that be known, eh?"

"I will. But why animate the dead when you know how humans hate and fear such things?

"Humans?"

Fuck. "Mortals, I meant mortals. You must forgive the dragon in me sometimes speaks."

He paused a moment and eyed me thoughtfully before continuing. "Quite. I didn't use Unhallowed in the beginning. I tried to create warspawn, like in the old days." He waved dismissively. "Damn useful creatures, warspawn, once you get them breeding. Alas, the material I found through the gates of this world was either entirely useless or like the creature I hid inside Anchal—"

"Demonic?"

"Possessed of an inimical nature and hard to control. They were more..."

"Demonic?"

"I'm sorry, who are you again?" he put his fists on his hips in a most un-Mage Lord fashion. "What kind of a name is 'Breed of the Fiery Heart'? Are you sure you're not one of the Annurashi?"

I feigned indignation. "I'm positive and I'll have you know that Breed is a perfectly ordinary name when I come from."

"And do humans look like the Annurashi *when* you come from also?"

"I look like everyone else from my time." I beamed what I hoped was a charming smile. "I'm a Mage Lord from the future of Edolis, but enough of me. You were telling me how these ingrates spurned your munificence."

My slip was instantly erased by flattery. "That's right, I was. And they did, the swines. I needed a workforce, but I couldn't create viable warspawn with such inferior raw material and my summoned hybrids only want to feast on human flesh." He rolled his eyes. "So, I did the best I could with the resources available to me." He paused and looked at me for approval. I smiled like you do when forced to humor a maniac. "You know how it is. Unhallowed are plentiful, obedient, cheap. I was trying to help these yokels. I freed them from the grind of mining and quarrying. I would have freed them from all manual labor if they'd given me a chance and if they'd got over their primitive prejudices," he jabbered excitedly. "Think of it; the entire populace at liberty to study science, art, philosophy, and literature, such as it is. Everything would have been so much better under my tutelage and with my guidance. But that *bitch* jumped to conclusions and wouldn't let me explain." He glowered at the Unhallowed. His smile twisted into a snarl, his fists clenched as though he was about to attack her. I wondered how often this scene had played out since he'd killed her, how many hours he had spent driving himself even more insane by arguing with a corpse.

"Do go on, Ozbert."

"When she found out about my workforce she ran to her mother and father, like a dirty little tittle-tattle. You didn't tell them I was building them a palace more magnificent than anything they had ever dreamed of, did you? Or that the ore I was mining would make them rich beyond their wildest dreams." Being as she was dead, she didn't answer. "You turned everyone against me. No nuance, no subtlety that was always your problem, Althea. To you everything is either black or white, right or wrong, good or evil. You're so provincial. To think I was going to marry such a simple creature." He spun to face me. Spit flecked his lips. "She raised an army against me. Me! I was forced to flee like a common criminal. After everything I'd done for them."

"And the star steel. Let's not forget that."

He didn't like that. *Well, fuck him, he'll be dead soon.* "Yes, that too." He sounded peeved. "But everything else was for the benefit of those thankless wretches. He put his hand on the corpse's shoulder. "Oh, Althera. You could have been my warrior queen.

We could have conquered the whole world, you and I." She gazed straight ahead, eyes as white as a fish belly. I felt like I was intruding on a private moment.

He half turned to me. "I know why you came. Didn't it occur to you that someone might have already staked a claim to this world?"

"No. Sorry. We thought you were all dead. And I didn't mean to come here. It was an accident."

He calmly refilled his glass. "Who was your master?"

"Mother Blake."

He scowled. "You said you came here by accident, but surely your master taught you about the gates?"

"No, she didn't. She was a mean old fuck who only taught me those things that would be of benefit to her." Like lead under the gilt of a counterfeit coin, it was always the little truths that added weight to lies. "Why did you leave Edolis after the war? Why did you go and why did the Annurashi destroy the gates to try to stop you?"

He smiled ruefully, picked at the filth beneath his blood-stained nails. "They really didn't tell you anything about it?"

I shrugged apologetically. "You know the Annurashi. They're pricks." Again, I could say this with complete honesty.

"True enough. We beat that monster Shallunsard, which was no mean feat let me tell you. And do you know what those meddlesome demi-gods did by way of thanks for saving the world?" I shook my head. "They demanded that we stop using the skills they'd taught us. They said sorcery was poisonous to the land and the people. We helped them put down that demon and they treated us like..." He grappled with the air as he struggled to find a suitable revilement.

"Warspawn?"

"Exactly. They tried to use us like tools that they could cast aside when we'd served our purpose." The little bastard looked as angry as I felt.

"What a bastard."

"Quite. 'Don't use sorcery, don't use the gates. Don't hunt for star steel'. In their arrogance they tried to cripple us, and they didn't even kill Shallunsard. After everything he'd done and everything we'd sacrificed to bring him down. They just imprisoned him."

"I had no idea." I put on the face I saved for special occasions, like when I was pretending that I didn't know anything about the demon I'd loosed on the world.

"No, of course not. How could you? You're just a child." He laughed bitterly. "Seven hundred years. It feels like yesterday."

"I can imagine. You obviously didn't obey their command."

The light in his eyes quickened at the memory. He smiled. "The spineless ones capitulated. Oh, a few, like Halda the Red vowed vengeance, but their threats were empty. Some of us made a pact to throw off the yoke of Annurashi oppression and become masters of our own destiny. Do you know they even said that warspawn should be given their freedom after fighting Shallunsard? Fucking animals given the same rights as humans. It was too much. We waited until they were distracted and then we escaped through the gates before they could destroy them and us."

"And you ended up here."

He inclined his head. "And so did you and for the same reason I'll wager." He nudged me like we were fellow conspirators. "Star steel draws us, doesn't it?" I might have been born in a sewer, but my flesh crawled at his touch. "I confess, I was a little miffed when you came through the gate and destroyed my army." He smiled without conviction. "But after I'd had time to calm down and think about it, I realized it was just unfortunate timing. You couldn't possibly know that I was about to destroy that little bug Malin once and for all. You were just following your nose to the Stellaris."

"I can see there's no fooling you, not that I was trying to. There would be no point." *Stop talking now.*

He put his arm around my shoulder and gave a friendly squeeze. "Don't worry. I forgive you. I'm sure one day we'll look back on this and laugh." He smelled of wine, and corpse but sounded like he meant what he said and so far hadn't tried to beguile me or cast a spell of any kind. His unexpected forbearance made me wonder if I might be able to deal with him even though he was a disgusting little prick. Given the right combination of flattery and cajolement, might it be possible to persuade him to leave this world, to do what I'd told Delgaro I was going to do and end the war without further bloodshed? She would be disappointed I'm sure, but it would please Tobias and show him that I could do the right thing, for the greater good and all that bollocks.

"That's very decent of you."

"Isn't it?" The pestiferous little puke chuckled and poured another glass of wine all the while standing unpleasantly close. "Don't mistake me, at the time I wanted to peel your scaly hide and leave your flayed carcass for the crows to devour. I wanted to…" He licked his lips. A mad gleam ignited in his eye. "Suffice it to say, I was perturbed. But I'm a man of reason. When I realized your actions were unintentional blundering, I decided that I would make you leave, but now that I've met you, I've changed my mind again."

"Oh, aye?" Something told me his mind was apt to change more often than the wind.

He nodded. "I'd like to make a deal."

"A deal, you say?" *Now, where have I heard that before?*

"I'm willing to share the star steel and the country with you, for there are none to oppose us." He wiped a drop of wine from his lips. "Join me, and together we shall remake this world in our image and rule it like gods."

"That's a very tempting offer. It really is." It really wasn't. Sharing air with this repellent corpsemonger was more than I could bear. "What do you want from me?"

His smile broadened. "Glad you asked." He leaned in close. "I'd like you to turn into that magnificent dragon and help me teach these peasants a lesson. Together, we'll harvest the imbecilic people of Arduin like ripe corn and from these dregs of humanity, create the mightiest army this world has ever seen, and then we will conquer everything." He made a sweeping gesture as though to show me the ranks of Unhallowed that were marching through his sick imagination.

I drained my glass because the wine was too good to waste. It had been a short-lived fantasy, but now I saw that was all it had been. There was no dealing with a monster like Blight. "You know that wine was exquisite."

An expression of regret garnished his unrefined features. "That's a no, isn't it?"

I summoned a spell to mind. "I'm—" Was all I managed before he shivved me. This was the second time that some, finger-wiggling twat had got the drop on me. I looked down. Tiny stars shone in the metal of the blade that was sticking out of my gut.

"Beautiful, isn't it?" He drove the blade deeper, and slowly twisted it. "All my own work." I tried to think of a spell to repulse him to smash him, blow him to pieces but nothing came to my pain-blinded mind. I tried to change shape. Again, nothing. Upon seeing my confusion, he smiled. "Yes. You're wondering why you can't cast a spell, aren't you? Why whatever pathetic wards you've woven aren't working. It's because I warded the room against sorcery, all sorcery, even mine." I tried to push him away, but my strength failed me. I stumbled into the table. The bottle of wine fell on the floor and smashed. He tutted. "That's going to stain. I must say, this has been ever so exciting. Being here with you, knowing that all I had to rely on was my wit and speed, hoping that you like everyone else would underestimate me. Don't be embarrassed, you're not the first. I imagine you took one look at me and thought, "What a pathetic, little twit, and that voice! He's ridiculous." You of all people should know not to judge a book by its cover."

"You fu—" He ripped the blade up. Pain stole my words and obliterated thought.

"I'm going to raise you in your dragon form and send you back to your friends. Won't that be fun? I haven't as yet worked out how, but I do so enjoy experimenting." There was a soft, sucking noise as he withdrew the blade. Warmth spread across my stomach. I wrapped my arms around my guts to try and hold myself together. He stepped back and wiped the blade on his breeches. "I would have kept my word, probably. Such a shame that you lacked vision and courage, but then, as Rubin the bard often sang, 'Fools dance upon... something, something.' You know what I mean." He sheathed the knife up his sleeve. "If you'll excuse me, I'm just nipping out to destroy that risible 'army' waiting on the plains, and then we'll school Malin for the last time."

The room began to fade as my senses unraveled. I'd been here before and would have just given up and died when it struck me that if I expired in a room that was warded against magic, I might not be able to resurrect at all. Spurred on by my desire to come back and revenge myself on the miserable little fuck, I pushed away from the table. Ozbert yelped, drew the blade, and backed away towards the door. *Fuck, fuck, fuck*. I wouldn't live long enough to fight my way past him, even if I had the strength. A blast of heat whooshed up the shaft. *Yes.* I threw myself out of the window. The world spun, and pale flames rushed up to greet me. *This is going to hurt.*

Chapter Twenty-Seven

My fall was broken by the chimney of a smelting furnace. I crashed through the pipe and landed in a tangled heap of flesh and metal. The furnace I'd smashed into belched smoke from its broken vent. In its belly blue-green flames danced above a sloshing pool of molten star steel.

Corpse-powered conveyors, hammers, and rock grinders continued to pound and smash the steel bearing stone despite my unexpected arrival. Noxious smoke billowed from the broken pipes troubling none but me. Of course, I'd be dead long before I choked to death. Rather than let me expire in peace, Ozbert appeared a few feet away. He stumbled and almost fell. I would have laughed and told him how shit he was at apportation, but there was no air left in my bellows with which to make words, so I gasped instead.

"I've never enjoyed apportation. Bad ears, you know." He took a kerchief from his robes and held it over his nose and mouth. His blade winked in the baleful light as if to say, 'Did you hear the one about the Guild Blade who got shivved by a bacon-faced mage?' "Your masters the Annurashi sent you, didn't they? There's no point lying."

"Not... lying... dying." I coughed.

He knelt beside me, a shadow now, his voice faint. "Yes, you are. You know, now I think about it, I don't need an Unhallowed dragon. Why waste power animating you, when I can play the part myself? You can stay here, a slave forever, close in death to that which you craved in life and then whe—"

Not a moment too soon my old friend Death came calling and I fell into welcome oblivion.

Or not.

***

I opened my eyes to find that I was lying where I had fallen. I was in the cavern beneath Blight's keep, but the wheels weren't turning, the fires were cold, and the Unhallowed were absent. But I was not alone.

"Not you again." I stood up, shrugged my shoulders, found that I was hale and whole. No broken bones, no stab wounds. Tobias was sitting on the conveyor, toying with a fist-sized lump of ore.

"You've done it this time."

"Which particular 'it' are you referring to?"

"A spark of life must remain for a corpse to be animated. Just the part which remembers how to move, hear, see."

"I didn't know you were an expert on necromancy. Or have you learned this post-mortem, in Scholar Heaven?" The cavern was huge, supported by the same massive piles that underpinned the keep above. A dozen or more tunnels wormed into the darkness where carts stood abandoned in this ghostly parody of the real world. Tobias tossed the rock on the conveyor, wiped his hand on his homespun robe. He looked well for a ghost; pink-cheeked, bright-eyed, and with a stupid, know-it-all smirk tugging the corner of his mealy mouth. "What are you trying to tell me? What have I done?"

"Your corpse has been animated."

"So?" I didn't see what he was getting at. He looked at me like I was an idiot. "What?"

"You're not entirely dead."

I still didn't get it. "And?"

He jumped off the conveyor, came over, and thrust his hand through my spectral body. "If you're not entirely dead, you can't reincarnate. If you don't reincarnate, you can't stop Ozbert. He'll destroy

Arduin, the whole of this world, beyond perhaps." Tobias smelled of peaches and just a hint of fish. It made me smile.

"While we're on the subject of worlds. Don't you think it odd that there don't seem to be any native sorcerers here and yet there are gates and star steel? Why do you think that is?"

"Why do you think?"

"I asked you first."

His smile faltered. "I don't know. But this world has a native sorcerer, thanks to you. Of course, he probably won't live to grow into his powers, which again, is thanks to you."

"Come again?"

"The child, remember?" He waved his stump.

"Oh. Him. His inbred kin have probably snuffed him already."

"They haven't, but if you don't pull your finger out, Blight will snuff this world."

I wanted to bang someone's head against the wall, his or mine, I wasn't fussy right now. "It's over, priest. Don't you understand? I did my best. I tried. It's not my fault that the Annurashi made a cunt like Ozbert to fight their battles and it's not my fault that the Mage Lords made the warspawn to fight *their* battles. I've done all I can."

"Very well. Stay here in limbo, sulking like a child." He turned away and put up his hood before heading for one of the tunnels.

"Where are you going?"

He stopped, half turned. "You don't expect me to stay here with you, do you?"

"Well, yes. I thought we might catch up, talk about old times."

"Because they were such a delight?"

"Some of it was all right. Wasn't it?"

He fixed me with a hard stare. "No, it wasn't."

"Bullshit," I shouted. He kept walking, but I wasn't going to let him go like that, not without saying my piece. "I remember you laughing, you miserable prick and so do you if you're honest. We had good times, you, me, Clary, and Tosspot, the whole crew. It wasn't all bad and you know it. It just…" I remembered Shallunsard showing me their heads stuck on pikes. "It just didn't end well for you and the others." No answer. "Typical fucking human. You lot expect every moment to be filled with joy and happiness, and then you piss and whine when it isn't, like you're owed something just because you exist. Well you're not, you arrogant cocksnot." Darkness swallowed him. "Wait. Tobias, come back. I don't know how to come back from this."

"It doesn't matter, does it?" His petulant voice echoed from the tunnel.

My heart quickened. "No. I mean, yes. It matters."

Footsteps. Tobias emerged from the darkness and looked at me expectantly.

"It matters, all right? I want to help Malin and the others, but..." I felt uncomfortable under his scrutiny and stared at the ground. It sparkled with star steel dust.

"But what?"

I couldn't answer. I didn't want to admit what I knew to be true.

"But what?" He pressed.

"It always turns to shit, all right? Is that what you want to hear? Everything I do to help turns to shit. So, what's the point? And don't look at me like that, you sanctimonious..."

He smirked. "What's the matter, run out of insults?"

If this hadn't been a dream, I'd have basted the smug fucker. "Stop looking at me like that you sanctimonious, one-handed, toss-weasel."

He tutted. "You're losing your touch, Breed. Your act is getting old. And I'm not looking at you like anything. I'm just looking at you."

"Bollocks. I know pitiful condescension when I see it."

"It's mostly just condescension. You've caused too much hurt for me to pity you."

He had me there. "Just tell me what I need to do to reincarnate."

"Why are you asking me?"

"Is that a trick question? Are we playing riddle-me-ree? I'm asking you because you told me why I hadn't reincarnated."

"Don't you ever think for yourself? You need to free the part of you that's trapped in your body."

"How the— Hey." He headed back into the tunnel. "Wait, how the hell am I supposed to do that?"

He was gone. I ran into the tunnel and darkness engulfed me.

***

I sat up. I was lying where Blight had left me. My limbs were heavy. My brain foggy and I could hardly see or hear. I was Unhallowed. I wanted to say, "This isn't good." But what came out of my sticky pipes was a breathless rattle followed by a slimy glob of blood and mucus that had clotted in my throat.

I didn't know why, but I had an overwhelming urge to go over to one of the wheels that worked a pulley lifting buckets of ore into the furnace, take hold of the crank, and start to turn it, so I did. Some minutes passed before I remembered that I wasn't supposed to be doing that. I let go. And then I started to turn the crank again. *No. Stop.* I stopped, and then I started again. *Fuck's sake. Get a grip.* I ripped the crank out of the wheel. *That should do it.* That was what I wanted to say but all I managed was a groan. Not that any of my co-workers were listening. From somewhere above I heard a thunderous roar. The cavern shook. Dust trickled from the roof. I knew it was a bad sign, but my dying brain couldn't remember why.

Crank in hand, I looked around for a way to destroy this body and release that vital part of me that was stopping me from reincarnating. My thinking was muddled and slow, but I eventually decided against lying under the giant hammer that was flattening lumps of metal. The rock crusher looked more promising, but I couldn't work out the best way to climb in. Beside the furnace a pile of ingots glowed with an eldritch light that my living eyes hadn't seen.

Still clutching my crank, I loaded the ingots into the buckets. It took a while, I was clumsy as well as slow, but I got there eventually. I stuck the crank handle back into the wheel and did what Unhallowed me had been created to do. I cranked. The buckets rose on their chains and dropped the star steel back into the furnace. I couldn't feel the heat, but as I approached the furnace, my robes began to smoke.

A desiccated Unhallowed was raking slag off the molten metal that was pooling in the fiery belly of the furnace. His skin was blackened and so dried out from the intense heat that he creaked like an old gate when he moved. I shoved him aside and opened the door. The wash of heat instantly set my robes alight. My hair began to smolder, my hand stuck to the handle. Had I had more than the smallest portion of wits about me, it would have been a test of courage to step into the blazing inferno. But I didn't, being dead numbed me to fear and pain. I climbed into the fiery bath. Before my eyes melted, I caught a glimpse of my palm, and the sigils of Shallunsard and Rowan burning there with a fierce, silver light.

***

I woke with a start in the furnace. It was dead cold and licked clean of all trace of metal. I was human-ish but looked nothing like the skimmer. I had an abundance of thick, tightly-curled, red hair. My skin was mottled with the faint echo of scales. Between the scales my human skin was dark, which told me that at least one of the mercenaries was nearby and alive. I scrambled out of the iron womb and looked for the quickest way out of the cavern. There was the shaft down which I'd fallen, a flight of stairs, and the tunnels leading into the mine. I decided to apport to the place where I knew at least one of those led and appeared outside of Ozbert's cozy study.

I snatched a metal sconce from the wall to use as a weapon should he still be in residence and kicked in the door. It was empty save for the corpse in the corner. I snatched a robe off the back of the door and put it on. It was much too small in every way, but it would do. I ran out and apported to the courtyard where I was greeted by fresh devastation. The skull mounds and Unhallowed horrors had been ripped apart, crushed, burned, and most disturbingly, melted. Given Ozbert's repugnant predilections, it came as no surprise that he'd taken time to practice his newly acquired destructive abilities on his malformed creations. That they were finally, entirely dead was an accidental kindness.

Unlike me, Ozbert had never experienced what it was like to be a real elemental. However, it seemed that this fake, necromantically inclined parody was doing a fair imitation. The flagstones had been smashed and gouged by claws as big as plow shears and the gates had been torn from their hinges. Judging by the damage, it looked like Ozbert's dragon vomited a noxious, acidic black ichor instead of fire.

Beyond the keep, framed by the rubble of the gatehouse, a pall of smoke rose in the distance, signaling ruin. I climbed over the mounds of bones, my heart pounding as the star steel coursed through my veins. To save confusion, I changed shape to that of the Annurashi-human the mercenaries knew, although, when I looked across to where the army had been camped, it seemed like a pointless precaution.

The ridge was outlined in smoke and flames and blackened banner staves pointed accusingly at the lowering sky. Dreading what I'd find, I apported across the plains.

I couldn't see Delgaro, Skurden or Piet amongst the embattled mercenaries still fighting for their lives and I didn't look for them amongst the Unhallowed who were threatening to overwhelm them. I raised my arms to the hard face of heaven and calculated the angles.

Hell had never looked as beautiful as the moment I brought it to Rygor Plains. Faster than sin, I chained the rampaging dead with lightning and turned them to ash, banishing the darkness with coruscating, sorcerous fire. When the smoke cleared, an injured living warrior staggered towards me, relief written across his bloody face.

"It was a dragon. Another fucking dragon." He gasped. "Never seen a one in my life before a month ago, now I seen two." It sounded like an accusation.

"What did it—" I was going to ask what it had done, but that was a stupid question, one that he answered nonetheless.

"It flew over us, and then…" He was shaking from the shock of the encounter. I helped him over to where most of the stunned survivors had gathered. "Then it turned into Blight and fell out of the sky. We thought he was dead, but the bastard got up and changed into that dragon again. I wouldn't have believed it if I hadn't seen it."

Knowing that he'd fucked up made me happy. "The little piss-weasel should stick to playing with corpses."

"Eh? What do you mean?" The soldier looked confused. "Why are you smiling?"

I cleared my throat and composed myself. "I'm not. I'm grimacing at the horror. Now go on with your tale, lad."

"It was fierce strange. The dragon kept... I don't know, changing. It was like it was made from wet clay or something, but then it seemed to get a grip of itself and attacked us. It, it." He shuddered at the memory. "Youlia." He grabbed my arm. Tears fell from his bloodshot eyes. "It melted her, burned her to nothing. The dead that were left got up and came at us." He screwed his eyes shut, tried to banish the vision of horror burned into his mind.

"Did it fly off, or just vanish?"

"It flew away, sort of. Only it kept crashing like it didn't know how to fly proper."

I squeezed his shoulder. "Your sacrifice will not be forgotten," I said because warriors like to hear all that nonsense about sacrifice and heroics, it's all bullshit. Death is death and in the end it makes fools of us all. The sobbing cove nodded and gave me a comradely hug before stumbling away to join the others. I went in search of Delgaro.

"Breed?" Piet called from somewhere within a milling group of warriors. I pushed my way through to find the boy cradling Delgaro. She was pale, her skin ashen, bloodless. "Thank the Crone you came. She's dying," he said. *Of course, she's dying. She knows me. Death makes fools of us all, eh? You're not laughing now, are you?*

"Skurden?" I asked the sobbing youth. An icy lump of sorrow began to burn in my gut.

He bit his lip, fought to compose himself. "Dead."

Delgaro's eye flickered open. Her leg was poking out from under the cloak that covered her. What I could see was burned to the bone. The smell of cooked meat hung in the air.   She tried to sit up. "You took your time." Blood rattled in her throat. She fell back against Piet.

"Please. Save her. Please." Piet's voice trembled. The survivors closed in around us. The weight of their desperation pressed in on me.

"I can't. I'm sorry." I backed away. I didn't want to see her die, but my retreat was halted by a wall of flesh and steel.

"You healed that kid's hand. Heal her." He begged. Others voiced their agreement. I had to get away from here, but I resisted the urge to apport. I wasn't being cowardly, *as such.* I just didn't want to see another friend die. "It's your fucking fault she's dying," Piet insisted, grief fueling his anger. "We wanted to go home, but she stayed because of you."

I'd heard and seen enough and fought my way through the grim-faced mercenaries who were glaring at me as though I'd done for their captain. "Don't look at me like that. I didn't ask her to stay, did I?" I addressed my comments to all of them, for all the good it did. My words were met with scorn. "Hey, I didn't ask and even if I did, it was up to her. This isn't my doing. This isn't my fault." Thunder rolled across the sky, echoing my mood. "I didn't put a knife to anyone's throat to make them come here." I pulled up short when I came face to face with Tobias. I shoved him back and turned away. I couldn't face him either, not now. My gaze fell on Piet and Delgaro. I sought for the spell of apportation, but my mind was blank.

"Listen, all of you. I can either destroy Blight or try to save your captain and I mean *try,* because I don't have a fucking clue how to heal what he's done to her." My words were greeted with disbelief, curses, and not a few threats— much like the first time I'd met these coves. Like then, the air was hot with the same seething anger, distrust, hate. Steel sang from scabbards. "Sweet salvation. Hold up, you fucking idiots. Hear me out before this turns all unnecessary." Lightning arced across the sky. It was a coincidence, but save for the odd murmur of disgruntlement, the mercenaries took the hint and paused on the edge of their violent extinction. "I'm not trying to dissemble. I'm not trying to gull you. But saving isn't what I do. I break things. I blow them up, I pound them, stab them, and burn them. Killing. That's what I'm good at, that's all I'm good at." I scanned their battle-ravaged faces, grateful that I could no longer see Tobias amongst them. "Do you want me to slay Blight and end this war, or try to save just one person? And mark me, I *like* Delgaro, which is a rare occurrence." Few met my gaze. "That's what I thought." I pushed my way through the near-silent crowd and bumped into Skurden. Sweat sheened her craggy face. She had a sword in one hand and an ax in the other. Her helm was dented, her armor battered.

"Save her," she said, like I could just click my fingers and Delgaro would leap to her feet as good as new. "Fuck Blight. You save our friend."

"Not you too." I rubbed my face. My hands were cold and the palm of my left hand was glowing where molten star steel flowed through the sigils. I looked the old warrior in the eye, felt the inevitability of Fate's hammer poised above me ready to deliver the killer blow. "I don't know how to save her, Skur. Fuck's sake, look at her." I pointed behind me, but I couldn't bear to turn and look.

Skurden snarled through bloodied teeth. "I've seen her. When Blight's dragon came on she led the charge. I saw her stick her lance in his face. I saw it burn her." She jabbed a finger at me. "I've seen her. Now you fucking save her. You do for her what she did for you."

I looked to the sky for inspiration and then, with a jolt, I remembered what Piet had said. "Wait a minute." I looked around, but she was gone. "You're dead." A soft breeze kissed the gooseflesh rising on my cheek. "Fuck's sake." I went over to Delgaro and knelt beside her. After all his whining, Piet was reluctant to let her go now that I was here. "Fuck off out of the way, eh? Give me some room to work," I said, not unkindly, for I am not a monster. "All of you, get back." After a moment's pause Piet got up and moved everyone back. The space around Del and I opened like a blood-soaked iris. She winced and opened her eyes as I wrapped my arms around her and drew a deep breath. "Right then, milady, let's see what we can do." I gathered her into my arms and willed her to live, willed her body to heal.

Nothing happened.

Delgaro's eyes flickered open. "What are you...?"

"Shh. I'm trying to save you." She either laughed or groaned. I wasn't sure which because I'd closed my eyes. I didn't want to see the warriors' skeptical faces reflecting my own doubts back at me, and neither did I want to see my ghosts standing there, waiting for me to fail. I didn't even want to look at Delgaro whose life I could feel ebbing away. I looked inside and tried again to summon the power to heal her. Again, nothing happened. The power of the star steel burned within me, wild, eager to be unleashed. I reached for it, felt it leap to my touch, ready to destroy, to blast— *No. Fucking no, not that.* I couldn't do it, not like this. I was bursting with a power greater than I'd ever possessed, but I didn't know how to use it. I was pathetic. I was dying of thirst in an ocean of tears. I thought about the child with the silver hand. I'd healed him, but I'd broken the Paradox of Power and that had hurt, a lot. *That's why you can't save her. You're afraid.*

It was true. I got around the Paradox of Power by not giving any shits about any cove save for myself, but I liked Delgaro. If I demonstrated my affection and saved her life, that would break the Paradox, *again* and I'd pay for that.

"Fuck it." I let go of my fear.

Cold, blinding light bled through my skin and warped the unfathomable, formless stuff of the air around us. I'd died many deaths and had been reborn. This was different. I heard myself scream as immortality was ripped from me. The curse which had both damned and saved me was sundered in an instant by the immeasurable power that balanced the scales of all existence. The light around us died. I looked down. Delgaro's hair was rimed with frost and ice glittered on her flawless skin.

She opened her eyes. "What a ride."

Chapter Twenty-Eight

"The answer's no."

"You're telling me no, why?" Delgaro demanded. Despite being too weak to do much more than point, she was still trying to order me and everyone else around from the litter her crew had rigged for her.

"You've recently been as close to Death as it's possible to come without shaking the bastard's hand. You need time to recover, and more importantly, you'll slow me down and get in the way." I'd been trying to leave for close to an hour, acutely aware that Blight was probably laying waste to Galewyn while we wasted time arguing. The world swam briefly out of focus. I waited until it swam back before continuing to dress in clothes more appropriate for the journey. I was dizzy, my mouth was dry, and I had a skull-crushing headache. It felt like the worst hangover I'd ever had, without the pleasure of earning it.

"You'll need us. We're bloodied veterans."

"You're bloody something," I muttered.

"What was that?"

"Nothing." I smiled. She didn't look convinced. "I'm no expert on matters military, but you've got about four horses between you. I'm sure they're a requisite for cavalry."

"We've got legs too, you know?"

"Yours aren't working too well right now, though if talking was fighting you'd have the battle won already. Now, please, keep your people back." I headed out of camp, far enough away from the mercenaries so that I wouldn't accidentally crush any of them when I changed into the dragon. I summoned a spell to mind took hold of the power within and brought about the transformation.

Or not.

I tried again. The world flipped, I felt intensely nauseous, swallowed bile, and completely and utterly failed to transform. Piet jogged over.

"Captain says, 'Are you all right?'"

"Yes. Thank you. Tell her I'm fine."

He jogged back and relayed my message before returning. 'Captain says—'

"I'm fine." I puked. "Just dandy." I wiped my mouth and saw that the marks in my palm were almost black. Cloud shadows raced across the plain, anointed me with their sorrow. I'd thought losing the curse of immortality had been payment enough for saving Delgaro. It seems I was mistaken. "Why doesn't anyone tell you the rules?" I said to no one. "They're not written down anywhere. There's no wise mentor to explain what you can and can't do." I threw up again. Blood flecked the bile. "All I have are whining ghosts."

Piet was starting to sweat from running back and forth. "Captain says, 'what did you say?'"

I gulped a mouthful of lumpy air before answering. "I said, find me a couple of sharps. None of those big, head-chopping cleavers you clanks favor. I want some fine needles, crafted for precision work."

Piet went off and returned in short order with a couple of decent blades. They weren't a pair, but they were sleek and well balanced. I took one from him and drew it across my right palm. Blood spoke and cast its iron scent into the air. The meager essence of star steel passed from me into the metal and imbued the blade with an edge that I hoped would be keen enough to pierce a warded hide. I drew the other sword across my left palm. The shock knocked me off my feet, and the blade flew from my hand narrowly missing Piet.

I'd never considered that the sigils themselves held power. With my ears ringing, I got to my feet and pretended that nothing at all was the matter. I tore a strip from Ozbert's robe and bound the stinging cuts while Piet retrieved the sword.

"Are you sure you're all right?" Piet asked.

I shot him a warning look which seemed to suffice for an answer. He shuffled back. "Follow me to Galewyn as quickly as you're able. Or not. Up to you." I told him.

"How come you ain't the dragon?" He made a clawing gesture, just in case I didn't get what he meant.

I smiled, perhaps a little too enthusiastically, but given that I was in a murderous ill-temper, it was either that or punch him. "Ah, but I am. I just don't look like it."

He nodded his acceptance of my bullshit answer, and then his brain caught up with his ears. "But if—"

"Sorry, Piet, no time to explain. I've got a necromantic pukepail to inhume." I apported before he could ask any more awkward questions. I didn't have time to discuss my plans, not least because I didn't have any beyond killing Ozbert.

***

Two piss-poor apportations later, I blundered into the city and promptly threw up again. Nobody was screaming, which was the best thing I hadn't heard in ages because it told me that by a wild stroke of luck I'd beaten Blight back to Galewyn. Spurred on by this unexpected piece of luck I legged it to the palace. The city blurred around me. When my way was blocked I took to the rooftops, hopped fences, or vaulted walls and in no time at all reached the compound.

In my absence a crop of stakes had sprouted outside of the gate. Angled menacingly at face height and sharpened to wicked points, they were ready for the army of Unhallowed that wasn't on its way. My apporting into the bailey surprised those within and had archers and arbalest crews scrambling to draw on me. I ignored their challenges and headed straight to the hall where Malin was holding a council of war. My arrival ended all discussion. Malin opened his mouth, primed with a weight of questions that I had neither time nor inclination to answer.

I raised my hand. "Blight's on his way. The army's fucked." I saw Bolin's worried face amongst the generals and mouthed, "Del's alive." He nodded his thanks. My grim announcement got the attention of everyone. Silence blanketed the hall. "Blight's taken the form of a dragon. It's a terrible impersonation, but he'll still tear us a new one." I went over to Malin. "Give me your sword." He looked unsure, but drew his blade, flipped it, and offered it to me hilt first. It was a sweet bit of steel, light and well-crafted with excellent weight and balance. Unlike the jeweled toothpicks favored by many lordlings, it had seen a fair amount of wear. The notches had been filed, but the flat was patinated with battle scars.

I unwrapped the strip from my right hand, gripped the blade and drew it across my palm. The bite of the new cut was bright and intense. "There has to be a better way to do this." The cut bled like fuck, staining the steel with crimson and silver. I handed it back and rewrapped my hand. "You can hurt him now, which he'll sniff out, so watch yourself." The world tilted. I saved myself from stumbling by gripping Malin's bony shoulders. "He's an egotistical bore, so will most likely prattle a bit before killing you. Let him."

"Let him kill me?"

"Prattle. Let him prattle." The world righted itself. I released the boy and addressed the room. "Light fires around the city, lots of smoky fires, hide the sky." I shook Malin's hand. "Good luck," I said and headed for the door.

"Wait, where are you going?"

"Elsewhere."

"Where's Delgaro?" Greyholt demanded. "And what happened to the army. What exactly do you mean by 'fucked'?"

I ignored him. "Just remember to strike at the right time, Malin." I called over my shoulder, wrapped

myself in a cloak of shadows, and left with shouts of
'coward' ringing in my ears.

Chapter Twenty-Nine

*K*ing Malin boldly stood upon the battlements, surrounded by his bravest knights, and waited for the black dragon, Blight. The people cowered in their homes and prayed to the Bride, the Mother, and the Crone for deliverance. Warriors set their lances against the gathering gloom as an evil darkness swept over the city. King Malin prayed to the Trinity and a pure golden light shone upon him. "To me!" he cried. "Come, brave warriors of Arduin. Stand in the light and be not afraid, for this day evil shall be vanquished and good shall triumph!"

"You fool," the dragon intoned. "Your pathetic gods cannot save you. I am Doom, I am Darkness, I am Despair." Blight roared its fearful roar. Like a nightmare it flew over the city, destroying all in its path with its pestilential breath, stopping hearts with the touch of its shadow. Fear flowed in its wake, the sky rained bitter ashes that scorched the ground, but

*King Malin and his brave knights stood firm in the
blessed light of the Trinity.*

*"Behold, King Malin, death has come for you,
black in tooth and claw." The dragon spread its wings
and roared a challenge. Warriors cowered, horses
reared in terror.*

*"I do not fear you, Blight," King Malin replied, his
voice strong and unwavering. The gods protect me.
The Bride, the Mother, and the Crone are my shield
against your heathen evil." The king raised his
sword..."*

This is but a sample of the official account of what
happened that day. As I'm a kindly cove, I'll spare you
the full version for it is a dreary work as these things
often are. The prose is halting, overblown, and florid.
There's a lack of detail where one would expect it, and
too much where it isn't required. I'm no expert, but in
my humble opinion, it's bollocks. This is what really
happened.

Malin marshaled his remaining troops and fires
were lit across the city. Those inhabitants who hadn't
already fled cowered in their homes beneath the
spreading pall of smoke. I climbed to the roof of
Malin's parents' funerary chapel and hunkered down
behind the parapet. The tower overlooked the palace
and the city, but out of a misguided sense of respect
for the dead, there weren't any catapults or archers up
here. Stupid I know, but that's humans for you.

Before I saw it, I felt it. There was a sudden shift in the wind. It rushed to the north and then a moment later, came roaring back like a tide. And so it continued. Out, in, out, in... I knew this tune, had played it myself.

Before I saw it, I heard it. A shriek split the sky then rolled into a menacing, guttural snarl which tailed into a sibilant, mocking laugh. Huge wings creaked and snapped, and Blight finally emerged from the haze with ghost serpents of smoke coiling around his ragged, shadow wings.

From snout to tail his scales were black. An unfeasibly large crown of spikes adorned his narrow, bony head and his eyes were as red as a demon's arse piece. I stayed low and watched him land outside the palace, crushing those buildings nearest to the gate without a thought. There were muffled screams but otherwise nobody moved, no catapults were fired, no arrows loosed. Everyone was spellbound by his vile majesty and the fear spell he'd woven into the fabric of his being.

"Malinnnn…" The word was drawn out and sieved to a hiss by vicious fangs. It gave a toothsome grin before vomiting acidic ichor over the defenders on the gate, melting them into a slurry before they had the chance to scream. "Come out, boy." This voice was a sorcerous projection, for the dragon's nightmare maw was fit only for rending. He sneezed, somewhat diminishing his menace and rubbed his eyes with a massive forepaw. "This smoke is bloody awful. I would have been here sooner, but I took a wrong turn at Epperton, you know, where the valley forks?" He stamped on a dying warrior who was trying to crawl away from the puddle of her melted legs. "It was an easy mistake to make because I've never seen Galewyn from the air. It's much smaller than I remembered." He chuckled, shook the warrior's remains off his foot.

If nothing else I'd kill him just to shut him up. That whining voice of his, now amplified by sorcery, set my teeth on edge. I coughed. Blood spotted the parapet. Of course, desire was one thing, ability quite another.

The gate opened. "Ah. There you are." Blight sat on his haunches as Malin pushed his way through a wall of warriors who were reluctant to let their king stand before the beast.

"You utter prick," Malin shouted with the insolence of youth. His warriors cheered.

The dragon looked as shocked as it was possible for a dragon to look. "Is that any way to talk to your old tutor?"

"You killed my family, my friends, my people."

"They didn't give me a choice." The beast placed a paw upon his breast. "They attacked me, remember? I was just defending myself." Blight took a step towards the king. Warriors swarmed like ants, locked shields, and tried to herd Malin into the compound.

"No, you idiots," I said under my breath. "I need him outside." I used a spell of compulsion. Just a little push to encourage Malin to go around the shield wall and out amid the sharpened stakes. It wasn't hard. I didn't have to overcome his will because Malin didn't need any encouragement to confront the killer of his kin. The warriors made to follow him, but the dragon snarled and sprayed a fine mist of ichor at them which pitted their shields.

"Stay back." Malin's voice rose unevenly, but they did as he commanded.

The dragon turned to face the king.

"Good lad. Now just keep him talking," I said and climbed down the tower.

"I don't want to kill you, Malin," Blight cooed, again the annoying voice was completely at odds with his terrifying appearance. "You just have to accept that we'll be doing things my way from now on. Don't pull a face. If you serve me well, you'll do well. The whole of Arduin will do well. I can't say fairer than that, can I?" The dragon swung his head around to glare at the warriors. I just caught a flash of his blood red eye and dropped, hoping that the newly risen moon hadn't in that moment smiled upon me. "You will all serve me, one way or another," said Blight. "You might as well do it willingly and live. Yes, I'll give you that, I'll indulge your desire to breathe, for I am not the monster you take me for. My advice is that you accept my offer, because I assure you, you will not like the alternative."

Malin drew his sword. "I'll never serve you. No citizen of Arduin will ever serve you."

I crawled along the wall. The dragon raised his paw. My heart sank. For a second I thought I'd read Blight wrong and he was going to rub the boy out without further debate and before I was in position. I held my breath but kept moving. He didn't. He crooked a single claw and pointed at the blade in Malin's hand. I smiled. *Got you.*

"Where did you get that?" The dragon asked.

Malin turned the blade, admiringly. "Do you like it? I got it from... it doesn't matter. It's your doom, Ozbert."

Blight howled with laughter and smashed his tail through a row of buildings like an over-excited puppy. "My doom? Did you really just say that? Not only is it trite, but it is also wildly inaccurate, I taught you better than that, boy. Now, I ask again, where did you get it?"

Blight's spell of compulsion hit the boy so hard he gasped. His jaw tightened, he tried to make a seal of his lips, tried to hold back the words. It was a brave, if futile attempt. "Breed!" the word exploded from him.

"That scoundrel?" Blight chuckled, but his tail thrashed angrily through the rubble of the buildings he'd just destroyed. Fire was spreading rapidly through the city now, and scarlet flames flashed through the billowing smoke. "Your friend is dead, and that weapon won't help you. Now, put it down before you hurt yourself."

A whole city of smoke cannot hide a dragon. Dragons are mighty, powerful, and majestic. I knew their arrogance, understood it because I'd experienced it. Ozbert thought he was invincible in this form, unassailable, which was precisely what I wanted him to think.

"For Arduin!" Malin's battle cry ran from a high-pitched squeak to manly growl in two words. Pre-pubescent hilarity aside, the boy had some stones, because the next thing he did was charge the dragon. It was a heroically futile gesture because dragons are hard bastards to kill. Short of dismembering or beheading them, you have to destroy all three of their hearts to slay them. Easy, eh?

I exhaled. Focus sharpened, aches fell away, and time slowed. Before me, embodied in the black dragon were all the hells I'd ever lived through. Behind me was the angle gate and freedom. I rolled to my feet, drew my blades, and prepared to jump either towards danger or away from it.

Like it was ever in question.

I leaped at the dragon. The wind ruffled my hair, dragged tears from my eyes, and sucked the breath from my lips. This was what I did. The world receded, all that remained was the target and the cold certainty that one of us was going to die. I landed on his back and thrust between his bony spine and giant scapula, angling the swords, and driving them in until I found my mark. The shuddering death of the organ trembled the blades. Blight roared in agony.

One.

I put my foot against his back and pulled the steels free. Even with the enchantment upon them his acidic blood was already eating into the metal. Emboldened by the dragon's distress, the king's guards bellowed their war cries and charged, shields up, spears leveled. I rode down the nodes of Blight's spine and thrust both blades between the third and fourth ribs. The dragon's reptilian scream splintered the air. Black blood splashed my arm and raised blisters as big as hen's eggs. I bit back the pain.

Two.

The dragon stumbled and made a gift of his throat to the king. "Malin, Now!" I screamed. His head swung around. I leaped from his arching back. His teeth clashed on air as I rolled into the angle between his massive belly and knee and dived out the other side. Blight tried to keep track of me, but he was slow, clumsy with pain, and unused to how his immense body worked. I ducked beneath the scything blade of his wing and scrambled beyond his reach.

Blight glared at me with pain-maddened eyes and his lips drew back in a venomous snarl. "You little—" was all he managed before Malin stepped forward and with a two-handed stroke, opened his scaled throat. Greyholt tackled the king aside as Blight staggered and his viscous blood gushed from the wound and burned the ground where the king had been but a moment earlier. Blight clawed at his neck and staggered back on his haunches. I saw an opening between the third and fourth rib on the left side of his heaving chest. I ran at him, jumped on his knee, and plunged my blade into the space over his remaining, beating heart where three scales met. The dragon gasped. I roared and drove the sword deeper, felt the heart spasm in the shocking moment of its destruction.

Three.

I twisted the blade, not to make sure because I knew he was dying. I just wanted to return the compliment he'd paid me and hurt him. I might not be a monster, but I do have a vengeful streak. He shuddered and lifted his head to the sky as though seeking salvation in the soot-streaked clouds. None came. I dived aside and dragged my sword from the wound as the monster crashed to the ground.

"Is it over?" Malin asked, his voice thick with tears.

"Yes, it's over." I spat on the quivering corpse. Tears ran down the boy's cheeks. After years of marshaling his resolve, of being the king he wasn't born to be, he could finally let go of the sorrow and anger that had sustained him. He didn't cry alone. Seeing their tormentor finally dead, battle-hardened warriors wept unashamedly. Others laughed and hugged each other, some hacked at the body and cursed.

Humans are such silly fuckers. They felt so much, all the time; anger, hate, love, joy, sorrow, and the rest. They always had to be feeling something. Like gluttons, they stuffed themselves beyond the point of reason with this or that 'feeling'. It must have been exhausting. I wrapped my least painful arm around the boy's shoulders and pulled him to me, let him weep against my chest.

It started to rain. My blistered arms and hands burned. I looked at Ozbert's carcass and wondered if somewhere not too far from here he was reincarnating as a human. No. He wasn't like me. *I* was no longer like me.

While I stood there in the rain, hugging the boy, and contemplating my doubtful future as a mere mortal, the terrified citizens began to emerge from their hiding places and gather around the king and the dragon. Some dared to touch it, some ran screaming, but they all had to see its body even if it was the quickest glance, just to be sure that the dreaded Blight was truly dead.

"You've got a big fucking mess to clean up, Malin my boy."

The boy drew a shuddering breath, wiped his tears. "My sword." He broke away from me and began looking for the weapon. I was about to tell him not to bother because it would have been turned into a puddle of melted slag by the dragon's blood when he pulled it intact from under its head.

"That's interesting," I said. "Let me see?" Malin handed me the sword. My blood and the star steel patterned the blade which was otherwise unscathed despite having been bathed in Blight's ichor. "That's a rum tol." I gave it a heft.

"It's a what now?"

"A good sword."

"Ah." His eyes glazed again but this time he held the tears in check. "It was my sister's."

I handed it back hilt first. "Does it have a name?" He shook his head. "A sword like this needs a name." Greyholt climbed over the dragon's back, saw me, and made to retreat. "All right there, Greyholt," I called, stopping him in his tracks. "What was it you shouted earlier, as I was leaving the great hall?"

"Er, nothing. Just, you know, goodbye and good luck." He slid down the dragon's flank and out of sight.

"That's what I thought."

"How about 'Sting'?" Malin wiped the blade on his cloak. "As a name for the sword?"

"What? No. It deserves a better name than *sting* for gods' sake. It's a powerful weapon."

The boy rolled his eyes and swung the sword. "I know. It's supposed to be ironic."

"It's not ironic, it's shit. Think of something else." The boy pondered the question while Greyholt and Bolin set about organizing cleanup squads and fire crews. "How about something like Shadowmaker, or Blooddrinker. Oh, no, wait. What about Bloodstorm?" I expected him to be thrilled by my suggestions.

Malin pulled a face that told me he wasn't. "Why don't I call it Dragonbane and have done?"

"I'm not keen on that one. People might get ideas. Anyway, just think about it while I'm gone." I prepared to apport.

"Wait, where are you going?"

"Don't worry, Majesty. I'll return forthwith."

He wiped the blade on his cloak. A finger of moonlight raced along its edge. "I think I'm going to call it, 'Leech'."

And so, the legend of Malin Demonbane and his sword Leech was born. Although I still prefer Blooddrinker.

***

I found Blight's keep much as I'd left it, save that Death had finally claimed its due. By the looks of it the Unhallowed had fallen the moment their master and the magic that made them had died. Even the 'things' had ceased roaming, although some few grisly oddments still twitched as what passed for life drained from them.

Now that it had been freed from sorcerous bondage, I could taste the hot metal tang of star steel in the air and feel it sting my face like a thousand, tiny needles. Over time the poisonous residue would soak into the ground, corrupting all that came near. Sick at the thought, I apported to Blight's study.

Althera was slumped on her throne where Blight had left her. Before attending to the corpse, I made a note of just how he'd worked the ward upon the room, unpicking what fragments I could discern from that which remained. Satisfied that it was something I might accomplish myself with a little practice, I turned to the corpse.

"Right, your majesty, time to go."

It took a while, but by sunrise the pyre I'd built in the bailey from the remains of the keep gates was worthy of a queen. If she didn't like it, she didn't say. I placed her corpse atop the bonfire and covered it with a banner I'd taken from the battlefield. I could burn her now and mark this place on a map with a skull so that all would know to avoid it. Eventually, the stories of three headed children being drowned or exposed by their not-so-doting parents would reach me, and I would add their shades to my lengthening tally of ghosts, for if I did not own those lost in this land to the sickness of sorcery, who did? "Well fuck that. I'm not having it, do you hear? It's not going to be my fault," I shouted at the sky, at gods that either didn't listen, didn't care, or didn't exist. I shouted at Tobias, the Annurashi, anyone who might be paying attention. "Not this time, you bastards. I will not play the role that Fate has decreed."

I drew the magical essence of star steel into me. All the errant strands, each and every tiny, poisonous grain. And I changed it. In me, in the alembic of my unnatural, cursed, and blessed body. I changed it to fire and transformed myself into the dragon.

Chapter Thirty

"The dragon rose on blazing wings and breathed upon the pyre, destroying it, and wiping the memory of Blight and his demon-haunted keep from the face of the land. They say that flames from the conflagration could be seen in Galewyn, where it is now celebrated as the Day of the Second Sun." The scribe took a sip of water and looked at me expectantly. "Well?"

"Well, what?" I shrugged. "It's more or less correct. The explosion was heard in Galewyn— beyond in fact, but I'm not sure they could see the fire."

"I have numerous accounts that it could be seen."

"Oh, well if you have *accounts*, I suppose they must be right. I mean, I was only the one there doing it." I walked away from the scribe lest the urge to slap her get the better of me.

"And exactly when was that? The date if you can remember."

I'll give her this, for such a slight creature she had some stones. "Forty years, give or take." I clasped my hands behind my back and idly scanned the city from the landing platform of my eyrie. The irritating scratch of quill on parchment paused. I looked around to see the scribe squinting at my silhouette. Her pale face was lit by the dying rays of a rudely beautiful sunset. Didn't it know that today was not a day for warm gold and rose, but for ice and darkness?

"Give or take?"

"You heard me."

She continued to stare and to tap the quill on her writing slope. The thought occurred that I could just transform, kill her, and eat her. No one would ever know and no one would suspect the wise leader of the Citadel of Sorcery of such a heinous murder. *Powers for good, Breed. Use your powers for good.* "It was a long time ago, I've slept since then."

My answer didn't please her. She pursed her lips but held back whatever cutting remark she might have made to someone who wasn't a dragon sorcerer. She dipped her pen and angrily scribbled something, splashing ink on the pink and silver marble floor. I bitterly regretted agreeing to recount the tale of Blight's end, what with Malin…

They'd asked me when I was distracted, damn them. I knew that in their own way they wanted to feel like they were accomplishing something in the face of the looming tragedy. But why did they have to annoy me in their quest to fill the aching void forming in the heart of our world? I wished I'd never created the bloody Citadel or taught anyone how to use magic. I should have known they'd turn into bothersome, supercilious arseholes. "They don't know me. That's all it is. We come from different worlds."

"Pardon?"

"Nothing." Delgaro and Bolin's faces loomed out of the well of fading memories. They understood me, but they were both dead and soon so would... *I'll soon be alone here*. The world spun, the scratching of the quill went through me like a blade. "That's enough. Get out." I thought I'd pushed enough steel into my voice for her to get the message. I was wrong.

"With all due respect, but Thaumaturge Emest was keen that we finish the Chronicles before..." She let the last part go unsaid. I knew what she meant. Everyone knew what was about to happen, but no one wanted to talk about it, least of all me, that much I'd made plain with the injudicious use of a lightning bolt several days earlier.

I drew a slow breath, counted to three and breathed out hoping to find a measure of calm. "We killed Blight, destroyed his monsters, and cleansed Arduin of

all evil influence." My words were a spell that
summoned vivid memories, some sweet, some painful,
none welcome. "We built the finest city in the world,
created the Citadel of Sorcery to harness the power of
magic for good. We have a mighty fleet, a powerful
army, and you can't move for culls what can read and
write just as good as I does." I smiled. She didn't get
the joke and kept on scribbling. "In short, life is good.
We live in a land of plenty, a golden age. The end. Oh,
and while we're about it. I don't like 'chronicles'. It's
too common. 'The chronicles of this', 'the chronicles
of that'. It's just tacky, so change it. All right, you can
fuck off now."

She took off her spectacles. "But there are still—"

I growled, not quite as loud as a dragon because I
was in my human form, but the implications of what
would happen if she didn't take the hint and leave
were clear enough. She packed her inkwell, pens, and
writing slope, this time without argument, and scurried
to the door leaving a spattered trail of ink behind her. I
felt a touch of guilt for scaring the girl. She was only
doing what that old fart Emest had commanded, but I
couldn't be bothered with the Citadel or their
emissaries, not today. *Touch of guilt? When did I start
feeling guilty about things*? "Tell Emest he's done
well," I called after the scribe. She paused, clutched
her book to her chest like a shield. "Tell him... Just
tell him that." She ventured a nervous smile of
gratitude as though my words had brightened her day.
It had never ceased to surprise me that to these people,

I wasn't just a common thief of small renown. I was the advisor to the king, the preeminent sorcerer in the whole, bloody world. Fuck, *I was a dragon*. They'd raised statues of me, written stories and songs about Malin and me, most of which were shockingly bad, but it was the thought that counted. The door opened, startling the scribe on her way out.

"Breed." Sceafa of the Silver Hand touched his fist to his chest. Warrior wary, hand on sword hilt, he had manners enough to acknowledge the girl with a curt nod before marching in.

"You can fuck off too." I looked down at the scuffed edge of the platform at the scarring on the marble caused by decades of use. A trail of cloud momentarily obscured the sprawling city of New Galewyn. When it passed, the beauty of what Malin and I had built was revealed in all its glory. Although I'd seen it a thousand times, the view still took my breath away. "We've done well here." Malin and I had plucked this city from our dreams, healed our hurts as we designed its intricacies over long hours ensconced in his chambers. We'd created a place of rare beauty in this world or any other. A particular, secret wish of mine had been realized when thieves moved into the sewers. Of course, I didn't tell Malin that I'd designed them with such a possibility in mind, there were things that a king didn't need to know.

Malin.

A wave of nausea swept over me. I felt faint, and my chest hurt like my heart was about to burst and yet here I was, calmly watching birds fly to their roosts instead of raging and cursing as storm clouds gathered on every horizon.

Sceafa approached but he didn't speak. Like me he knew that the air couldn't be trusted to support brittle words forged of sorrow, words that at any moment might shatter and turn to tears. Like me, he stared intently at the birds as they stitched silver into the clouds, as though some comfort might be divined in the graceful sweep of their wings. Long minutes passed like this, but eventually the brooding silence outweighed the discomfort of talking.

"There's grey in your hair," I observed. I hadn't noticed it before or that the hard lines of the warrior mage's body had begun to soften as age worked its dark magic upon him. That was another curse. I might not be immortal, but I hadn't aged. I just had the pleasure of watching those I loved wither and die. *Ah, Ellia. Best damn pastry cook in Arduin. I was never very good to you, was I?* She at least had the decency not to haunt me.

Sceafa grunted. "I'm getting old. Unlike some."

"You're going deaf too. I said get out and close the door behind you."

"Actually, you said 'fuck off'. I might be getting old, but I can still hear." The captain of the Dragon

Guard gave a wry smile. A shimmering light lit briefly along the edge of his silver hand, kissed the fluting of his breastplate before sparking away into nothing as he mastered his temper. "I didn't come here to fight."

"I know."

"He's asking for you."

"I know." I would have left it at that, as would Sceafa had he not been here at the behest of others. Sorcerers either walk away from conflict with each other or go at it like wolves and neither of us wanted that. The slap of running feet on marble broke the stubborn silence. I groaned as the king's eldest daughter burst in. Althera was named in honor of her aunt and had proven more than worthy of the name. I'd known her all her life. I'd taught her how to drink, how to pick locks, where to stab someone so they couldn't cry out, all the useful things a child should learn. I glanced at the girl through the scarlet veil of my hair. "I can't do it, Alti."

Tears glazed her cheeks. Her hair was tangled and her hunter's garb disheveled. "You have to. He says…" She gulped. Tears fell. "He says he won't go until he's seen you and he's in such pain, Breed. He won't take anything for it. He says he wants to die awake."

It hurt to hear that he was in pain. "He's such a fucking idiot. Someone should make him. Your mother?"

Althera shook her head. "You know what he's like. He says it dulls his mind. But the…" Her words became an incoherent jumble lost in wracking sobs. I couldn't bear it.

"Fuck's sake." I leaped off the platform, turned into the dragon, rolled, and dived down to the king's chambers which were below my own. Even though the sky was dark and threatening, Hurgarunya, the White Palace shone like a pearl.

***

By royal decree, the dragon-sized windows of Malin's chamber were always open. I landed, furled my wings, and stalked into the candlelit gloom setting torches aflutter and scattering black clad courtiers like crows driven from a corpse. *And isn't that what they are?* The bed and its occupant looked like toys in the vast chamber that had been constructed more to suit my size than his.

Accustomed as she was to seeing the dragon, Astilin spared me only the slightest glance before returning her gaze to her husband's pallid face, as though he might die if she didn't keep a constant watch. The heat of my body caused petals to fall from the garlands of moon moth blossom that had been hung over the bed. The pungent smell of the white flowers was said to repel evil spirits that came to steal the essence of the dying. Despite the muttered prayers and hand-crossing, it was a myth, one of many that rose like miasma around the particulars of death. 'Don't let the candles by the deathbed burn out'. 'Don't let a bird fly into the chamber unless it's a red wrath'. 'Don't wear green', 'wear purple', 'eat meat after midday if you want your loved one to go to heaven'. Death and hope conspired in folklore to make fools of those who floundered in grief.

Malin's eldest son was standing behind his mother. His face was a mask of stoicism marked with the sure knowledge that very soon he would be in charge of everything and that he wasn't fit for the task. Despite this, he loved his father and his eyes were shining like broken mirrors. Courtiers and members of the Citadel of Sorcerers stared at their feet, some whispered, some were silent while they politely waited for this game to finish before the new one could commence. A few, like old General Greyholt, actually gave a shit about the man, not the office. Sorrow being contagious, old friends and loyal retainers avoided making eye contact with each other and so remained locked in solitary misery. Malin's youngest children, Timmal and Garenth slept soundly at the foot of their father's bed. Having barely grasped the knack of living they had yet to understand the cruelty of death and so were immune to grief. I drew closer. The sound of my claws scraping on the floor rang around the chamber. Malin opened his eyes and smiled triumphantly.

"I've seen Unhallowed that looked healthier," I growled. The walls shook.

"I knew you'd come." His face was almost unrecognizable, all sharp angles beneath thin, parchment skin. His eyes were sunken pits and his breath rattled in his hollow chest. "All of you, go." He breathed the sweet scent of death into the air. Astilin kissed him, whispered the word, 'forever' as they shared a lovers' look. The sleeping children were picked up and carried out, they stirred but didn't wake. Reluctant to miss the bragging rights born of witnessing the king's last moments, scowling courtiers trailed out after the family. Greyholt swept his cloak behind him, drew his blade in a single, fluid motion, and knelt before his liege. It was a noble gesture, somewhat undone when the old fool got stuck and had to be helped to his feet by his squire.

When we were alone, I put my head close to Malin's and whispered. "Let me try." Dragons are incapable of whispering, so the voice I used was a magical projection.

He shook his head.

"In the name of all the fucking angels, why not? They still need you." *I need you.*

He shook his head again.

"Why?"

"Ozbert." He propped himself up on his pillows. I hated to see how weak he'd become. I'd seen him grow from boy to man. This disease born decrepitude was too cruel. "Keeping me alive with sorcery leads down the same path."

"No, it doesn't. You'd have to be dead first. Do you want me to kill you? I can do that."

"Oh, yes, please. Would you? That would be great." Fire woke in his eyes. "Do you have any black, spiky armor too? Only, if I'm going to be an Unhallowed king, I'd like to look the part."

"I think you should take this seriously."

"I think you should shut the fuck up about using sorcery to keep me alive beyond my time."

He coughed. The fire in his eyes died. His breathing grew labored once again. In times past, we would have argued back and forth for hours. We would debate sorcery, law, morals, or in my case, the lack thereof. Astilin would sit by the fire and when the argument grew too heated, or just too loud, she would tell us to shut up. If I was in my dragon form, the children would clamber over me, slide down my tail until they were exhausted, and then they would fall asleep in the folds of my wings, and I'd get cramp. And that was how it was supposed to be, forever. No ghosts, no Unhallowed. And no fucking dying.

"You stopped coming to see me?" He posed the fact as a question.

I flicked a strand of hair from his face with the tip of a claw. "I can't stand watching you turn into a skeleton."

"You've turned into worse."

I laughed. "Do you remember that time I masqueraded as the Mayor of Broughton on Bride's Feast night?" He nodded. "He was such a strangely put together fucker. Do you remember?" I mimicked the mayor's shrill voice. "Free cheese for all!"

Malin laughed until a cough got the better of him. "My arse hurts." He managed to say when the coughing fit subsided. His pale lips were speckled with blood.

"I can help you with that, without compromising your moral code." Before he had a chance to object, I created a cushion of air beneath him, just enough to ease the pain of the sores that he wouldn't let me heal. He closed his eyes. The lines of tension in his face softened. His head rolled to the side. "Mal?... Malin?" Nothing, not a flicker. I was seized by panic. "Mal!" I roared. Guards charged into the room.

He opened his eyes. "Got you."

I was so angry, I could have slapped him. "You prick. You know what I think?"

"It would be hard not to. Your mouth and your thoughts are as one," he said, still grinning from his cruel jest.

"I think you enjoy suffering."

"Oh, you do, do you?" A bout of coughing stole what else he had to say. The blade of his chest rose, his ribs winged as he fought to drag the merest sliver of air into his tired lungs. I could taste his pain. His breathing slowed. Quiet fell over the room. The guards retreated.

A peel of thunder cut through the silence, and it started to rain. Lightning flashed and burned the shadows away. A cold wind rushed in and would have troubled his bed, so I stopped it, a few feet away. Rain threw diamonds against the warding shield which scattered like stars against the wall of hardened air.

"Show off," Malin wheezed.

I couldn't stand it. "Please, Mal, let me try."

He found a little strength from somewhere, reached out, touched my snout. "Shh."

"You, shh." I was grateful for the magical voice. It wasn't subject to the embarrassing punctuation of tears. Not that I was subject to all that human-ish, weepy nonsense. I was half thoasa, warspawn, I...

"I love you." His voice was distant, as though it was being drawn out, a slender line holding life to death. "Always have."

"I know," I said. "D'you fancy one last flight?"

He smiled his assent. I picked him up, swaddled him in blankets. He was as light as silk, but I could feel his heart fighting like a bird caught in a net, striving for every beat. I ran to the window, leaped into the storm, and carried him above the clouds where we watched the lighting stitch the sky with fire.

"I'd forgotten how beautiful," he whispered.

I waited for the next rattling breath, but it never came. Just like that, he was gone. All I held was an empty bone bag, bereft of his wit, his sarcasm, his kindness, all the things I'd grown to... it was a cruel trick, one that hit harder than a hammer blow and cut deeper than any blade.

I should have taken him back then. His family, the court, everyone would want to see the dead king, to marvel at his lifeless husk, the loss of grace. They'd want to anoint his withered limbs, paint his face in mockery of life, and dress him in gaudy robes that would make him look like an overstuffed, deceased peacock. Prelates would drone on for days, pray for his soul to gods that he didn't much care for and then, finally, when he was as ripe as a bucket of week-old fish, they'd seal him up in a magnificent tomb. There he would lay, shut in the darkness to rot in royal seclusion, safe from worms and carrion. In the distant future, when the offspring of his offspring had gone to dust, a cove like me would happen along with a hammer and a chisel and an avaricious heart. They'd slip into the sacred vault, smash his casket, and strip him quicker than you could say 'thieving bastard,' leaving his scattered bones for the rats to gnaw on. *Fuck that.* My friend deserved better. Asti would understand. Or not. I didn't care.

"We're going to make one last legend, you and I." He didn't answer. He lay in my arms in a cruel semblance of sleep, the lines in his face caused by pain now softened by death. I saw the boy again, the young man. Like thoasa, dragons cannot cry, a boon for which at that moment I was most grateful.

I flew to a place I'd hardly visited in forty-two years. It hadn't changed much. The sea still boiled beyond the cliff and broke luminous and raging against the black rocks which lay beneath the cairn where I'd buried the angle gate. I'd built the chamber over the stones years ago and concealed it with spells and wards in case any of the new crop of sorcerer apprentices came nosing around and fancied exploring other worlds. Standing there, I knew why I hadn't destroyed them years ago. Somehow I think I'd always known that I'd come back here, that the life I'd lived disguised as a different, better person would come to an end.

"Forty years and for what? It doesn't seem worth it, no offense. Tobias, are you here?" I don't know why I thought he might be. I hadn't seen that whey-faced specter for a long time. "I've been the fucking hero, I've done all the right things, and my friends still die. First Del, then Bolin, and now Malin. How is that fair?" There was no answer save the howl of the wind and the song of the sea, their roaring voices raised in plashing mockery of my self-pitying lament.

I shed my dragon body and became the half-thoasa, half human me as I carried Mal inside the cairn. Glow stones flared into life as I made my way through the narrow passage. When I reached the central chamber I collapsed the shaft behind us and placed a ward on the cairn so powerful that time itself would forget this place had ever existed.

The stones were as I'd left them, preserved on the mound where grass still grew despite the lack of sun or rain. I bundled Malin up in the blankets. I didn't want to see his exhausted, pain-aged face again. I wanted to see the one that lived in my memories, remember the Malin who laughed and smiled and called me a cunt when he mistakenly thought I deserved it.

I was about to turn the stone and wake the gate when a thought occurred. "I'm losing my touch." I dug into the blankets and eased the gold and ruby signet ring off his finger and put it on. "Well, it's a shame to waste a nice bit of sparkle on a dead man, innit?" I turned the stone. The air contracted, the emptiness of the void opened before me, as welcoming as a lover's arms. I held Malin close and stepped through.

Breed's epic quest continues in Something Wicked.

Type the following link into your internet browser to get your copy of *Something Wicked* now. http://kdavies.net/asw

Free Books

If you haven't already read them; I would love to offer you two free *Chronicles of Breed* prequel novellas!

I love telling the stories of Breed's exploits; *The Best Laid Plans* and *A Fistful Of Rubies* are available for free if you just type the link below into your web browser.

http://kdavies.net/nltac

Author's Note

You've read *Tooth and Claw*! As it's the second book in the series you have probably read the first, but either way I'm glad you chose my book(s). I hope you enjoyed Breed's further adventures and will want to check out *Something Wicked* to see what happens next.

I would like to ask that you consider leaving a me review because they really help. Obviously it would be awesome if you tell everyone how much you liked it, but even if you didn't it's always great to get feedback from my readers. Typing this link into your internet browser will make it really easy for you: http://kdavies.net/rtac

It would be great if you could.

Thanks

K.T.

About The Author

When I'm not writing books, I work the day job, wrangle my kids, four dogs, and a grouchy, old cat. I play computer games, ride horses, practice medieval martial arts, grow vegetables, throw axes, and read, not at the same time, that could get messy.

I have a website here http://kdavies.net

And a Facebook page here:
https://www.facebook.com/KTScribbles where we can hang out, have a couple of brewskis, and talk about the good old days.

You can also find me on Twitter @KTScribbles.

Once again, thank you so much for going on a ride with me and Breed. I hope I see you again soon.

All the best,

K.T.

Made in the USA
Middletown, DE
15 January 2019